NO PISTOL TASTES THE SAME

A PTSD NOVEL

Jacob Paul Patchen

NO PISTOL TASTES THE SAME
A PTSD NOVEL

by Jacob Paul Patchen

Published Independently

Jacobpaulpatchen.com

Cover by 100covers

Edited by Christina Consolino

ISBN: 978-0-578-28927-4

Printed in USA

First Edition

For more information, you can follow Jacob Paul Patchen on Facebook (author.jacobpaulpatchen), Instagram (@jacobpaulpatchen), TikTok (author.jacobpaulpatchen), and Twitter (@jacobpaulpatchn)

For those who suffer.

For those who have suffered.

And for those who ended their suffering.

Introduction with Note from the Author

PTSD or Post-Traumatic Stress Disorder is a mental health condition that may occur after a traumatic event, such as war, sexual assault, a serious injury, or other forms of trauma. Some symptoms may include: flashbacks or nightmares, distress, avoiding situations, people, places, or thoughts of the trauma, irritation/anger, unable to concentrate or focus, easily startled, panic attacks, increased blood pressure, headaches, tension, interrupted sleep patterns, feelings of guilt, blame, shame, and fear.

People who experience this disorder may feel alone, unable to cope, or hopeless. PTSD can be hard to understand for both those who suffer from it and those whose loved ones suffer from it. This book is intended to bring awareness, hope, and understanding to the stigma that affects over **11 million** people each year in the United States alone.

The Earth's magnetic field protects the planet from solar wind and radiation that would damage or kill modern technology and electronics. The magnetic field has lost over 10% of its protection in the last 200 years. But that loss is said to be speeding up. In fact, some experts warn that Earth's magnetic field is now losing about 5% of strength per decade. This is accompanied by the shifting and moving magnetic North and South Poles, which may cause a magnetic reversal of the Poles (North would be South and vice versa). Some experts believe the magnetic poles could shift within the 100 years or so. This current shift is believed to be a factor in why the earth is losing its protective shield.

The sun is entering its 25th solar cycle (the 11-year cycle of increased sunspot activity) with the peak coming around 2025. Some experts believe this could be one of the strongest cycles on record. With the increase in **sunspots** (magnetic areas on the sun that can erupt) comes the increase in **solar flares** (intense bursts of radiation) and **Coronal Mass Ejections** (plasma and magnetically charged particles) that can explode toward and causing radio and magnetic disturbances. It's this radiation, plasma, and charged particles that wreak havoc on our electrical grid, communications, navigation, and other satellites.

In other words, the earth's protection from the sun is weakening as the sun's eruptive state is currently increasing. It is just a matter of time before the sun releases an eruption that fries all electronics on Earth.

Introduction with Note from the Author

The following are a few personal stories and thoughts about PTSD from real people who have experienced it—including the author.

"PTSD is a bitch. That's what one of my marine buddies said when I asked for his thoughts on the subject—and I agree with him. Truthfully, after the war, it took me a long time to find myself again. I wish I could remember my 20s better than I do. But they're a distant mist hiding what was really wrong with me. Instead, I tried to drown the man I had turned into with booze, bad decisions, and good times.

What I remember the most is the constant feeling of needing to be prepared for anything, for *everything.* I remember the stress, the anxiety, the planning, the overthinking, the struggle to make simple decisions without first trying to outthink every threat or defuse every danger. If I couldn't conquer it, I avoided it. I remember being worn out, exhausted, and in need of constant entertainment. Boredom brought trouble. The loud noises, diesel exhaust, trash, and wires along the road made my body react without me having any control over it. At night, I searched the backyard with a flashlight and a loaded gun. I don't know what I was looking for, but finding nothing helped me sleep. I kept a hollow-point bullet in the chamber of the pistol on my nightstand. I adjusted it each night to make sure I could grab it if I woke up to danger. Under my pillow or mattress, I hid a blade, just in case I couldn't get to my gun in time.

I was angry. Good lord, was I an angry man. At what? I don't know. But everything seemed against me. No matter how hard I fought back, I'd lose. I hit walls, windows, my pride, and dignity. I bloodied my hands to take my mind off of the wounds inside of me. I wanted love. I needed love. But couldn't love myself. There were times I'd walk home from the bar because I was mad, I felt insecure, or that I didn't belong. I relived my fears and regrets in my dreams. Damn those dreams. I still vividly remember one dream where I felt the blood drain from a shrapnel wound in my neck. I felt the life leaving me, the warmth of the blood rolling down my skin. I felt myself dying. And I lived my final thoughts in that dream…that I should have been better. I shouldn't have let them get me. I should have killed them first.

You see, PTSD is a slow poison that erodes the security, the happiness, and the freedom you once knew. It turns them into a dark alley dagger, a drowning last breath, or an unexpected fall. It steals the life from you.

I'd like to thank all the service men and women who have put their life on the line for me, our country, and our freedom. Sometimes it's not the battle that kills us, it's the war we fight long after. I think of you. I pray for you. And I wrote this book for you."

-Jacob Graham (Jacob Paul Patchen)
Marines, Rifleman, Iraq 2005, Cambridge, Ohio

Introduction with Note from the Author

"I was ready for war. Like a tourist, I soaked in the sights, sounds, and smells. At first it was fresh and exciting; every explosion or sound of gunfire was a new shot of life into my veins. Then, like an addict, it began to wear off. You need more to feel the rush. You become numb to the experience, to the daily threat. We were told before returning that we had changed and life wouldn't be the same. I didn't believe them. For years I thought it was everyone else who changed, but I've come to realize that I was wrong. It was me all along. But life is all about perspective. I wouldn't change my experiences for the world because I don't believe anyone truly knows joy unless they first know true pain. Luke 7:47"

-Daniel J. Geisel, Marine Sgt. and bestselling author of the novel, King's Blood.

"First and most importantly, always know that as a person living with PTSD, you are not alone! When you seem to be stuck in that dark place, inside your head and consumed with negative thoughts, you are not alone. Reach out to anyone, other Veterans, family members, or the Veterans Crisis Line 1-800-273-8255. As soldiers, we were expected to be tough without showing weakness. Reaching out for help is not a sign of weakness, it is the toughest thing you can do when you are down. It is ingrained in us to put the mission first and ourselves last. You have to prioritize yourself now. That is the mission."

-Josh Birch, SPC, U.S Army, Iraq 2003-3004, Cambridge, Ohio
(Dedicated to Heather, Dade & Cole)

"My 11-year-old son hasn't spent time with his dad since the last big holiday, when his dad shoved him, almost knocking him down. He's completely off the deep end, PTSD and alcoholism and I also think a TBI. He wanders around the country in his bare feet, all hours of the night, because the wolves are out there, and he is the sheepdog. I am completely devastated at the thought that it's only going to get worse and my son is not going to have meaningful interactions with his dad, and maybe not at all. He drinks from the time he wakes up. He lost his business. My son has nightmares/dreams about his dad nearly every night. There are no answers."

-Anonymous, Ohio

Introduction with Note from the Author

"I'm Travis, and I was with Kilo 3/25 in Iraq. Shout-out to my man, Jake! Even though we were in different platoons and didn't really talk much over there, which means we had different experiences, we still saw the same shit. I've been battling PTSD since we came home in 2005. My big thing is loud, unexpected noises or bangs. I even jump if my wife sneezes loud. When we first came back, I went out, came home late, and thought someone was shooting at me. I went pounding on the door at my parents' house and told my dad I was being shot at. It was just a damn car backfiring up the road. So, yeah, PTSD is real, and those are just a few of my stories about it. Thank you, Jake!"

-Travis M., Rifleman, Marines, Iraq 2005, P.A.

"For me, living with PTSD is physically and mentally draining. I'm always in flight or fight mode, and my mind never rests. I dread nighttime when my mind constantly overthinks. When I finally fall asleep, the nightmares wake me up to a dark, silent room, where I, once again, have nothing to keep my mind occupied. Others dress for fashion or comfort, but my first thought is to dress to fight or escape quickly. I wear things that could be used as a weapon if needed. I constantly look over my shoulder and sit with my back against the wall. I know where the exits are, who's in the room, and what could be used to defend myself. I can't trust others and would rather be alone than have to read a room or wonder what others are thinking.

Most days, I cannot answer the door out of anxiety. Friends and family know to tell me they're coming over or I won't answer the door. It took a long time for me to be able to go anywhere alone and I still have a hard time focusing on anything. I miss life before this and get angry a lot that this happened. But I'm finally getting some peace back into my life and look forward to the better days."

-Megan, W.V.

<u>Prologue</u>

Real news headlines.

"ISIS is Using the COVID Distraction to Rearm and Regroup"
(-USA Today)

"Suicide Rate Among Veterans Up Again Slightly, Despite Focus on Prevention Efforts"
(-Military Times)

"Veteran suicides are 'public health and national security crisis'"
(-Dayton Daily News)

"'Reach out. It's OK to not be OK': How Michigan veteran helps others like him cope with PTSD"
(-Click On Detroit, Local 4 News)

"Solar Storms Are Back, Threatening Power Grids and Satellites"
(-Bloomberg)

"Earth's Magnetic Field is Mysteriously Weakening, Causing Satellites and Spacecraft to Malfunction"
(-The Independent)

"Earth's magnetic field flipping linked to extinctions 42,000 years ago"
(-NewScientist)

"Solar Storm Destroys 40 New SpaceX Satellites in Orbit"
(-The New York Times)

"'Cannibal CME' sun storm marks rise of new solar cycle in space weather"
(-Space)

"A Tech-Destroying Solar Flare Could Hit Earth Within 100 Years"
(-New Scientist)

Chapter One

To Feel Alive

No pistol tastes the same.
Mine
is a bourbon-muzzled truth maker;
as bitter
as those night terrors
of a columned world around me
    exploding;
as real as self-inflicted regret;
so familiar in my hand,
    and cold on my tongue;
It burns
    on the way down.

No pistol tastes the same…and mine…is a bourbon-muzzled truth maker.

His grandfather's Vietnam era M1911 trembled in his crusty hand, and both heavy across his muddy lap. JP's forest eyes, encrusted with dirt and dried blood, fixated on the gun—a charcoal chunk of steel with dark brown and checkered grips. Two pounds of metal and shame was a sharp boulder pinning him to the V-shaped trunk of that tree.

Beads of rusty sweat rolled down his bristled face. His dirty blond hair waved with the breeze as he sat, defeated, in his farm clothes under the old oak shading his grandparents' gleaming headstones. A faded American flag, stabbed into the grass between them, fluttered and whipped in the wind. The calloused bark scraped at his sticky back on a steaming spring day. But what he felt most was repentance…and that cold, loaded shackle chaining him to his past.

No, mine is bittersweet and savory.

His grandmother's strawberry rhubarb pie, fresh from the oven and steaming on the stovetop, flashed into thought. *How fitting.* His chest shook as he exhaled, glaring at her shiny gravestone at the far reaches of the shadow cast by the tree his grandfather swore he planted at the top of that ridge the day after he got home from the war in '69. The same ridge and one same tall oak that JP would ask his grandmother to picnic under on those hot summer days. Even then, her sweet smile and playful hesitation would spark the begging and pleading of a small boy and an old man until she gave in with a chuckle and announced, "I guess I'll have to make some sandwiches."

The crest of the ridge stood just a few hundred yards from the farmhouse. It proved to be an adventurous climb. One best traveled on his grandfather's lap in the buggy or giggling and bucking in the back of the dump-bed Grandpa used for hauling. But on the days they walked, JP took a stick—his walking stick, ninja stick, bazooka, rifle, magic wand—because, without it, he might not have reached the top. When they did, the reward was great: a cool breeze and a view ripe with rolling hills and sagging power lines that cut paths through green woods and waving fields.

The hill on his grandfather's sixty-acre farm was the perfect place for a boy with a wild imagination to explore. A place to play army on his belly, peering through his camouflaged binoculars at his grandfather tinkering in the barn or his grandmother sweeping the porch. A place to wait on her famous strawberry rhubarb pies as they baked in the oven, while he *bang-banged* at crows in the corn with orange-tipped toy guns and tree limb missile launchers.

As a kid, he snuck through the rows of corn with his stick tucked under his arm as a rifle, sweeping the muzzle back and forth as he crouched along the narrow pathways and gunned down the bad guys from row to row. Back then, his grandfather would bellow from the barn to stay out of the corn. But with his cornball hair, muddy war paint, and a missing-tooth grin, he'd be swaying the stocks again sometime later. Because some kids have imaginations too big for rules.

On extra brave days, after one of grandpa's war stories or one of the X-Men movies, he tip-toed and belly crawled into the cow field and ambushed the small herd until they ran to the far corner of the barbed wire fence. His grandfather hollered about that, too. And JP, in full retreat, bounded back to the hilltop to snipe the distant army marching through the tall, golden grass and over the belly of the land his grandfather called 'Paradise.'

It *was* a paradise for an only child left orphaned by a holy war and taken in by his gracious grandparents. And that spot under the bushy arms of the towering oak on top of that little knoll was *his* paradise. That chosen place his grandfather planted the tree so many years ago was more than just his favorite place to play or picnic. It was special: a shared spot, "their spot," that belonged sweetly to his grandparents before he made it his own. For Grandma, it was a magical peak in her very own fairytale, with a green castle, backlit by blue skies, whose leaves flashed in the breeze. A place where, long ago, her noble knight reached deep into the pocket of his greasy jeans, pulled out his folded knife, and carved out those still prominent and beautiful, jagged letters: CLG LOVES BRG.

But now, with his bruised back against the sharp bark and a heavy pistol in his tired hand, JP knew this enchanted place would never feel that magic again. A gust of wind ruffled the leaves as a glare sparkled across his grandmother's name: Barbara Rose Grimm. His gaze sank to the handwritten letters and pictures of home still clenched in his left hand. Sent by mail to Iraq and brought home in the bottom of his seabag, they now fluttered and flapped with the rising gusts, reminding him of what he came to do. He slugged a long gulp from his bottle of Jim Beam, then tucked the letters and pictures under the bottle to hold them still. The corner of a colorful photograph caught his attention, and he pulled it from the middle of the stack. His heart bounced at the sight of the last picture his family took together before he left for war.

They all stood under the shade of the oak tree. Lisa, his lovely wife, stood next to him in her favorite yellow sundress. Her blonde hair pulled up into a messy bun and her blue eyes gazing at his high-and-tight haircut with a smile. His gaze was upon his seven-year-old son, Adin, who was leaning against his marine desert cammies. Adin looked at the camera with his hazel eyes and a big grin upon his face, proudly wearing dirt stains on his brand-new jeans. JP's grandparents, Charley and Barbara, stood next to him, both fresh from church.

The day the picture was taken, they splurged on hugs, kisses, laughter, and tears. They told stories about "the good old days" and ate Grandma's fried chicken and noodles until they had to loosen their belts. Adin ran wild with his cousins, playing army in the barn and in the mud—rendering the comment "he's definitely *your* child" from his grinning grandmother. But the mud stuck to them all. While wiping his boots clean in the grass, JP had contemplated whether he should bag up a pinch of it and take it with him. He wished the same for his wife's and son's kisses that lingered down the road as his hand waved out the window.

Looking back, the sorrow in their proud smiles had dug into him the most. A sadness he saw again and again—a sadness of which *he* was always the cause. And with that anguished thought, the life slowly faded from him as he stared into his son's fuzzy eyes. Another tear tickled down his nose and splashed on the steel slide of his Grandpa's M1911.

His grip tightened on the .45. *I don't deserve them. I don't deserve any of them.* He bit down until his jaw trembled. Hate and rage flowed through his veins—hate for himself and for his decisions, hate for the Corps, for the war, and for all of those who took away his happiness, one disfiguring explosion at a time. That hate brought a self-harming kind of satisfaction—the kind of pleasure one gets from feeling *something,* even if it's the dragging pain of a rusty blade across the skin. But he needed that kind of pain. In his numbness, he needed to feel *anything.* He glanced at the happy life he held in his left hand, crushed it with his balled-up fist, and tossed the photo at his grandmother's headstone.

"I'm the worst thing to ever happen to this family." The words stung and clung to his tongue like a canker sore. He took a powerful swig of bourbon to wash them out.

As the wind came again, it agitated the paper and envelopes piled on the ground. They buzzed until the top letter slid and lifted into the air. With a crinkled tumble, it disappeared over the edge of the ridge. But he didn't bother to move. Instead, he just sat there holding his bottle and gun, tormented. His eyes twitched as another piece of him soared away into the clouding sky. He let the bottle slip from his hand back onto the letters without bothering to twist the cap back on.

His vision and thoughts blurred, mixing with the past and the present, with the bourbon and the pain, blending with the hum of the interstate off in the distance. *Or was it a helo, or maybe air support?* He scoffed at the thought as anger gripped his throat. He knew what he was there to do, and with the storm building in the westward sky, there was no reason to wait any longer.

The pistol grip was warm and sticky in his grasp. The edges glistened like the worn-out rifles issued to his reserve unit. *But things that flash bring death.* He thought of the snipers who painted their rifles a sandy brown to blend in with the Death Land. His death land became cozy and kind, hugging his backside like a deathbed. The cold steel shivered when he jerked it to his temple.

No pistol tastes the same.

He snapped it from his head and jammed the muzzle into his mouth with both hands. His tongue pressed against the cool, smooth barrel. He tasted the iron in the steel, the blood on his lips and teeth.

Good, he thought. *Bleed, you little bitch. Bleed.*

The tree creaked and groaned. The leaves sounded like water raining down to wash away his sins. A crow cawed and took flight from the wood line to his right. His determined stare at the metal in his mouth broke at the swift movement and ruckus of the black bird laughing at him. He watched it flap and glide away into the murky wooded horizon.

Not even the birds give a shit about you.

His dirty fingernail punched through the trigger guard. The curved and familiar feel of death in his grasp was a comfort he did not expect. But there it was, the answer to all his torment, the cure for his illness, the drug to put him down.

A faint rumble came from beyond the hills and flickering canopy of the horizon. The air—a warm stew of sorrow and blunder—hung onto him like a sweat suit in the summer. Above him, the leaves and branches waved, distracting him from his mission. To the west, the sky boiled, bringing in another pop-up storm to soften the hard humidity. But it was too late to soften a thing. Only the pricks of memories and regrets were there to coddle him.

A gust blew up the hill in waves through the tall grass, and JP wobbled as dust and debris peppered his face. The sting in his eyes was gritty and sharp, but a welcomed pain. Louder and louder, the leaves shook. They felt bigger than they were, hovering over his head like the palms along the Euphrates. Those palm trees, with their sharp, jagged tips—like the dagger on his flak jacket—were such a conflicting contrast to their comforting tropical feel. His squad would take shelter from the sun under their pointy tips, and he'd drift off in thought to the last beach vacation with his parents—back before the planes took down those towers, and their business trip ended in flames and rubble.

He pinched his eyes tight, and the sound of the leaves took him back to that desert sand and tropical paradise by the river in a place of death and destruction. He saw the palms waving in the shadows of his warm eyes. He saw the young, dirty faces of his squad smiling and scarfing down Slim Jims sent with love from home. He felt them there beside him, joking and snickering, making fun of the gun in his mouth.

"What is that, a paperweight?"

"Is that from the civil war?"

"It looks like you're trying to swallow your boyfriend's cock."

"You just gonna sit there all day and cry about it or what?"

"Do it, ya pussy."

Thunder grumbled from his left and rattled his thoughts. The earth beneath him shook and shuttered his spirit. Like a great quake through the crust, he wobbled and wondered if his world was splitting open. Or was it rockets launched from the back of a black Nissan truck?

Incoming?!

His anxious eyes popped open, but the desert wasn't there. His marine brothers were not with him. No bombs or explosions fell from the sky.

Jesus! Get it together, man!

A small branch cracked behind him and flipped across the ground. An eerily familiar sound, like a rifle round snapping by him.

A sniper?

His breath came faint and quick. His chest, tight and flexed. He ripped the pistol from his lips and scanned the hill behind him.

No. No, just a branch.

It tumbled and rolled until it met the edge of the hill and disappeared. The damp muzzle, splattered with blood and spit, fell back into his lap.

The clouds grew in the sky like dirty bubbles in bathwater, dulling the scenery. Flashes of light flickered toward him. He blinked at the sparks in the power lines on the next hill over.

What the hell?

Thunder roared up the valley. Lightning seared in the darkened sky. Bright bolts slashed the faded horizon. He shielded his eyes with the back of his hand and forearm. Both began to shake. His will began to falter. A streak of jagged lightning sparked down to the ground just past the next wooded hill, immense and brilliant, bigger and brighter than JP could ever remember. It was a storm like no other. The buzz and fizz in the air was electric. The lightning zapped across the sky and stabbed at the fluttering hilltops. The deep growl in the sky lingered like that of a snarling dog at the end of a thick, tight chain. Reds and greens flared in the black, bubbling mist flooding out the sunlight above him. Strange hums and horns echoed through the valley. It was clear to JP and all witnesses soaking in its wrath—this was no ordinary storm—this was the sky tearing open to the ashy depths of the Hellish void above them. This was the apocalypse. This was the end.

His teeth clenched until they hurt. "Good! Go on! Go on and end it all while it's all ending, anyway!"

A tree snapped and crashed to the ground, and a faint black trail of smoke lingered in its place. Then, like a smack on the face, a large raindrop popped him in the forehead. It startled him, pulled him from his daze. He gazed down at the pistol with contempt, lifting it from his lap to examine it like it was broken.

Come oooon! Do it! Pull the trigger! Pull the goddamned trigger!

His finger twitched and rubbed across the curved trigger. Raising the firearm to his mouth again, he wrapped his lips around the muzzle.

A tremendous boom roared across the sky, a noise so loud his teeth rattled. An explosion that shook him from the ground into his chest and deep into his shaded memories. It threw him to the grass, where he squirmed and thrashed, tearing at the ground as he tried to crawl for cover underneath the soil. Another monstrous boom and blinding flicker curled him into a fetal position, where he covered his head and neck with desperate hands.

Oh, God! Here they come! They're walking the mortars in on us!

"Take cover!" He yelled, clawing his way deeper into the earth.

The storm was upon him. Leaves and dirt, twigs and pebbles pelted his skin. Limbs cracked and snapped. A flash to his left, and the Iraqi rooftop ledge appeared. AK-47 and RPK automatic fire blasted the surrounding concrete. Chunks and dust splattered his face. An RPG swooshed by the building and exploded into the next house behind his squad. Fragmentation rounds from his team leader's grenade launcher thumped and exploded into the windows ahead of him. Another RPG ripped from the rooftop diagonally to his right. It shook the two-story house they took cover in. Black smoke billowed up from the hole in the wall. His ears rang; his body was numb. He looked around in the chaos as his squad returned fire. Brass casings pinged onto the concrete.

Thump! Thump! Thump! The mortars came in threes, exploding closer and closer and closer. He shut his eyes as the rocks and pebbles rained down.

CRACK!

A thick branch above him split and fell mere inches from his face. The leaves slapped him on the nose, snapping him back to reality. Stunned by the fog of it all, he sat up and pressed himself into the trunk of that mighty oak.

A thin mist sprayed his face while the letters of his family and friends danced around him. They swirled with the leaves, tumbling in the breeze. Those not secured by the weight of water, mud, or the bottle of Jim Beam fluttered away in a blur. He sobbed and shook in defeat. Then he lifted his head and watched the arms above him whip back and forth, like hands frantically trying to get his attention. Crimson streaks rode the rain down his face. He slapped himself on the cheek.

Stop it!

Again, but harder.

Stop it, right now! You know where you are! You know what you came to do! It's just a fucking storm!

He squinted up and hollered at the sky. "You're just a storm! You ain't nothin'! I'm not afraid of you!" His pistol stabbed at the air as he shouted. His chest puffed and rocked with a deep, shaky breath.

The rolling black clouds churned above him. He looked beyond the branches at the different swirls of gray, black, and blue. He felt connected, like the sky was a mirror, and he was staring at himself.

"I can't live like this! God? Do you hear me?"

The thunder rolled across the farm, dampening his cries above. *Or was it a reply?*

"I can't fucking live like this," he confessed, defeated, to the damp tombstones.

The pistol slowly shook back toward his temple. He pressed it hard into his skull.

"You feel that, *don't ya?*" He pressed until his neck slanted to the left, until the muzzle dug into his skin. Its pressure biting down above his jaw, throbbing and ricocheting through his head.

"Good. Cause it's the last pain you're ever gonna feel!"

The click of the safety sounded exactly like his M4. His gut turned as he blew rain from his lips. His finger trembled with the thunder on his trigger. He closed his eyes one last time to think of anything worth living for, anything he hadn't already lost or damaged or *hurt*—anything he hadn't pushed to the edge of hating him.

Then, in the buzz of the wind, something wet and flat slapped against his face, sticking there. He flinched, growled at the interruption, and snatched it— one of the pictures from the letters scattered around the tree. The photo felt heavy and awkward, like an unfulfilled promise.

He smeared the water drops from its color and shook it before bringing it closer to his face. He gasped at the image of the hill and oak outlined by a sunny sky. He remembered the picture well. Flipping it over, he read what his boy had written in orange marker on the back.

Don't forget about me and your favorite spot! Come home soon, Daddy!

Love,

your best buddy Adin

Chapter Two

Rockets like You

How strange a sound
ripping through
this "love songs to think about me"

mixed-tape cd,
that you scribbled half-shaded hearts
and I love you's upon,
before you sent it out to this desert death land;

a sound roaring to life from afar   and dreamy,
dragging jumping Marines
from their lover's arms
to this concrete floor
of filth and care packages.

Their presence is shaking.
And I have to watch the freeing grit
rush out like South Carolina waves
through the sunrays
gushing in from the sandbagged windows
just to know that I am still alive.

Just as alive as I was with you
while pretending to be a shark
grabbing at your ankles
in the salty tidal pools
of a past summer's vacation.

Now, the air-raid siren sounds,
blasting validity through the barracks
of sober faces.

It should have been a warning well received,
about the woman that you would become;

of how you would make that rumble
in the yard become the roar inside of me;

how your uncertainty and unfaithfulness,
your fire and your shrapnel
left me charred and dying

in a world of new beginnings.

One Year Earlier

"Hello?"

"Hey, baby." JP turned his back to the long line of marines stretching outside the concrete room of the call center at Forward Operating Base Hit, Iraq. They all looked the same: perpetually dirty in their sun-faded, salt-crusted desert cammies and tan faces with sweat streaks from their temples to their necks. Their black rifles were slung against their backs and across their chests, slapping against their backside when they walked.

Young faces, chiseled and hardened by the hacks of war, filled the line. Yesterday, the two-days-late resupply finally brought down three landline phones from Al-Asad—only slightly better than the few SAT phones they had to share and recharge. Now, twenty Lance Corporals waited to make their third or fourth phone call home to their cheating girlfriends and sleepless mothers.

This war was different. Technology had become a weapon of the enemy. No personal cell phones or computers were authorized. Instead, they had to do it the old-fashioned way—three wall phones for the whole company to use. *Brilliant.* Good intentions, but poor execution. And Sgt. JP Grimm learned quickly that only two of them actually worked when he had picked up the receiver, and the line was dead. Yet another *FAIL!* by the higher-ups. Something they were used to by now. *What a shitshow.*

The line of marines extended out the open door, curving between the concrete wall and earth-filled Hesco barriers. The peppered Forward Operating Base was not much more than three two-story concrete buildings forming an 'L' in the desert sand a thousand meters from the Euphrates. The base had been captured by ISIS after the second war, and his company had to retake the FOB, the city, and everything else in their Area of Operations. But just like everything else, ISIS destroyed it all before they were destroyed themselves. The marines had to rebuild it, rewire it, reinforce it, and yet it was still so far from satisfactory. FOB Hit was an easy target for rockets and mortars due to its proximity to the main highway running Northwest through Baghdad and because the pockets of defilade bumped and swallowed the surrounding desert.

JP's head hung low while he leaned beside one of the orange operations security informational posters plastered around the room, dubbed The Emotional Clinic, or EC, by some annoying marine who thought he was witty.

He pushed the receiver to his ear, plugging his other with a scratchy finger. The chatter behind him—marines trying to talk over top of other marines—made it difficult to hear.

"JP! Oh my God! Is it really you?" Lisa's high-pitched squeal cracked through the static line. She almost didn't answer the unknown number. Another robocall, she thought. But her pleasant surprise didn't lack any emotion or volume.

Sergeant Grimm's body warmed while he tried to hide the huge smile tugging at his crimson cheeks. It had been over a month since he last heard her voice, and only now did he allow himself to miss it, to miss her. Her contagious laugh, slender waist, and sunshine hair kept eyes glued to her halo and made young men's hearts thunder, especially his. What he loved most was her youthfulness, her playful, free-spirit, and pure, overflowing heart. Finally, he allowed his mind to drift back home, back to Lisa, to their bedroom, where they would spend lazy Sundays wrapped in each other's arms. He dipped his toes into those warm waters of his memories, but covered his beaming face by turning away from the nagging eyes and teasing banter of his brothers behind him.

"It's me, babe. I promise," he said over the crackling connection.

"Ahh, I'm so excited! And surprised! When did you…how did you…? It doesn't even matter! Oh my God, I've missed your voice! I love you, baby. I love you so much! I got your letters! I read them every night to Adin. Well, *most* of them, anyway. Of course, I leave out the *good stuff* or the *bad stuff*—however you wanna look at it. Basically, I'm just trying to say that we miss you and can't wait to see and hold you again." Finally, she took a breath long enough for him to speak.

Laughing, he pressed the phone closer to his mouth. "You gonna let me say anything or what?"

"Shut up!" He could hear the red-cheeked smile in her voice.

And his was impossible to hide any longer. "God, I love you so much," he said softly to the concrete wall.

"Wait. What? I couldn't hear you. There was static."

"I said, I love you so much."

"Huh? What? Could you repeat that?" Her reply had a playful tone.

He stood up a little taller, still facing the wall, while getting lost in her playful antics.

"I love you." It was quicker, but louder.

"You…*glooove* me?"

"Yes."

"*With your glove?*"

"What? No. Lisa!"

"I'm sorry," her playful tone melted his heart, "you're just going to have to say it a little louder."

He grunted in defeat. "Damn it, Lisa! I LOVE YOU!"

A few snickers sounded close behind him, and overtop those jeers came a deep voice, slick with a hint of the streets of New York. "Ohhh, Liiisaaa! I miiiss youuuu! You're so priiiitty. I wanna make *LOOVE* to you…all…night…looong!"

The entire line of marines erupted.

"See, that wasn't so bad," she teased, hearing the jeers in the background.

"Yeah, okay. Hold on a sec." Sgt. Grimm snapped his head around, covering the phone with his hand. His tall, rounded shoulders and thick chest puffed out with authority. He wasn't one to yell or to play the game that marine staff NCOs wanted him to play: to be loud and fierce, to scream and shout, to force his men to do what they were told—instantly. He wasn't one of *those* marines. He was a lead-by-example, a respect-me-and-I'll-respect-you kind of marine. A true leader—one who did more than just direct others to accomplish a goal. Sgt. Grimm was a free thinker, a visionary, an artist in his craft. He saw his men as *men*, not as pawns on a chess board. JP knew their lives outside of the Corps, often talking to them about their families, their dreams, and what they wanted out of life. He was a philosophical man, a poet with a rifle in his hand. Sgt. Grimm was a leader of men, not just a robot for the big green machine to program and alter. But sometimes—.

"Shut up! Shut the fuck up! All of ya!"

The room simmered down to just a few marines' escaping snickers.

Tightening his jaw, JP glared at the two goofy-looking Lance Corporals who could always make a joke of anything. But this time, they weren't the ones who dared to dish it out to Sgt. Grimm. No, this time it was Corporal Treadwell, aka Joey—a short stocky marine from the Bronx with a New York accent that turned incoherent when he got angry. JP and Joey had bonded during the predeployment training when Joey's fiancé ended their relationship only a month after their unit was activated. JP was one of the few he could talk to and keep him focused.

Joey's proud smirk popped out from behind a red-faced Private First Class, and Sgt. Grimm's scorn started to unwind.

"Ahh, you son-of-a-bitch. I hope you catch shrapnel in your annoying New York ass," he said, grinning and shaking his head. The room stirred with amusement.

"Listen, do y'all wanna talk to your boyfriends or not? Leave me alone, or I'll just stay on this phone all damn day. Got it?" He pointed the phone at Cpl. Treadwell. "Especially you, Joey. Shut the fuck up." JP's smirk matched Joey's.

Turning back toward the wall, he glared over his shoulder before he pushed the phone to his ear again.

"Are you happy now?" JP asked.

"Very," Lisa said, gleaming.

"Good. But, anyway. You know I love you. I love you and Adin more than anything." His voice was sincere before he paused. "But I only have five more minutes."

"Well, then talk to me. I just want to hear your voice. Tell me anything. Anything at all." It came across more heartbroken than she intended.

He felt it, and his heart ached, too. How much he missed her soft body pressed up against his…her delicate blonde hair that always smelled like lavender when he would brush it aside and kiss her neck. How much he longed for her body on his was almost enough to drive him insane—crazy enough for him to throw down that phone, run out into the courtyard, steal a Humvee, flip his CO the bird, drive to Al-Asad, and jump on the first plane heading Stateside. Sometimes, he questioned whether it was a good idea to call home at all, swallowing the tingle creeping up in his throat.

"How's everything at home? Adin? Grandma and Grandpa? The farm? Did you get my last letter about the chickens down by the river? They even had a windmill like the one on the farm, just not as tall." He paused. "Talk about a punch in the gut when you're out there trying to stay focused. All I could think about was you, Adin, the old folks, and those stupid cows."

"Wow, that's crazy. They have chickens there? In the desert?"

He laughed and imagined how cute she looked during her little *ditsy moments.* Lisa didn't lack intelligence—she even owned her own marketing business—but that couldn't stop the inevitable from happening. Sometimes, she was just a bit quirky. It melted him each time, reveling in the opportunity to pick on his wife.

"Sweetheart, yes, they have chickens. It's not like the kind of desert where all they have are camels and sand. There're even palm trees down by the river."

"Palm trees?" She giggled at her lack of knowledge about Iraq. "Oh. Well, who knew?"

They chatted like the old days. Back when Lisa's dad didn't know about her sneaking out the window to meet JP down the road in his rusted Chevy truck. Back when they'd drive the dusty back roads for hours, talking like they had known each other in a past life. She wanted to be a veterinarian. He wanted to do something that mattered. She was into love songs and poetry. He was into football and hunting. Sometimes they would drive out to Seneca Lake and park down by the shore. Their young hearts were full and wild as they stretched out a blanket by the fire and listened to the ripples of the waves trickling in. They would talk and joke until the first glimpse of light turned the waves silver. Then he'd rush her home blasting, hollering, and giggling to "Ain't Going Down Til the Sun Comes up" by Garth Brooks.

Joey cleared his throat. "Hurrryy uuup, Ser-geant Grriiiimm!" he growled in his drill instructor voice.

"Are you kiddin' me! Hold on!" JP spun around with his arms outstretched as if to say *seriously?!* Then he pulled the pen from his breast pocket and slung it at Joey, hitting him squarely in the chest. Satisfied, JP turned back to the phone.

"Sorry, Joey's being an ass. Go ahead," he said, holding the phone to his ear with his elbow resting on his arm across his chest.

"Well, anyway," she said with sunshine in her voice. "Everyone is doing fine. We're just missing you, ya know? Your grandfather is as stubborn as ever. He still thinks he can run the farm by himself. He has his good days and bad days. You know? Like the other day, he was stressed out over the cows being all weird or something. He said they wouldn't go to the north field like they usually do in the afternoons. He was going on and on about how strange they've been acting lately, running around in different directions like they were lost. I don't know. You know how he is."

"Oh, definitely." He laughed through his nose.

"Yeah, I see exactly where *you* get it from. You should've seen him out there chasing them around with a big stick, all out of breath, yelling and cursing. When I offered to help, he just mumbled on about how north isn't north anymore, or his compass is broken, or *something* like that. I don't know. He was probably drinking."

"Hm. Interesting. You know, sometimes I think he might be losing it. But actually, Command had to update our GPS's when we first got in country. So, I don't know, maybe he's not as crazy as we think." JP chuckled. "And Adin?"

"You'd be so proud of him. He started a group at school for all the kids who have someone deployed. You should see all those little first graders sitting at the kitchen table drawing, coloring, and picking out snacks to go in their care packages. It's so adorable."

"Wow. Adin did that? Are you sure we're talking about the same kid here?"

"Yeah, I know, right? You should see him, though. He's so cute looking over the other kids' pictures and giving them compliments. You know, maybe we're actually doing something right. Maybe we got this whole parenting thing on lockdown, no matter how much we fake it. And maybe he won't grow up to be like his father and never compliment his wife."

"Ohhh! *Okay*. Here we go!" They laughed together as if six thousand miles and a war didn't stand between them.

"I miss you," she said, "more than you could possibly imagine."

"I don't know. I mean, I could imagine some pretty crazy shit."

"JP, I'm serious." His glow faded as he sucked in a deep breath of hot, sweaty air, and eased it out to hold back the emotion that suddenly shook him.

"I miss you too. Just as much, if not more, than you do. I swear it. You're everything to me, Lisa."

"I know. I know how much you love me and how much we mean to you. *Allegedly,*" she poked. "I just…I just wish you didn't have to go fight. I mean, I understand why. We all do. But we need you here with us. We…we'd fall apart if…."

"No, stop. Don't. Don't think like that." He pressed his head against the concrete. "Everything will be fine. I promise."

"Okaaay. Okay, I believe you." She sniffed and dashed away a tear with the back of her hand.

"Is Adin awake? Can I say *hi* real quick?"

"Mmhmm. Hold on." Over the line, Lisa told Adin to come say hi to Daddy quickly because he didn't have much time.

"Hey, Daddy!" Adin burst onto the phone.

"Heyyy, Little Buddy. How's it going? Are you being a good boy for your mom and Grandma and Grandpa?"

"Yeahhh, I'm always good," he replied without hesitation.

JP chuckled. "I know you are, Bud. I know. But, hey, listen…I just wanted to tell you that I love you and I miss you, okay?"

"I love you too, Daddy. When you coming home?"

"Well, not for a while, Buddy. But it'll be here before you know it. Just keep being good for Mommy, okay?"

"Okay, I will."

"And take care of her for me, too. Okay?"

"I promise."

"Good. I love ya, Bud. Now hand the phone back to Mom. Be good."

The other end knocked and thudded until he heard her voice again.

"Hello. Sorry, he dropped the phone on the table and ran to his room. He really misses you."

"I know. I'll be home, eventually. And then we can all hang out so much that you'll get sick of me."

"Mmm, that sounds so good. I'm not sure if I could ever get sick of you, though."

"Uh-huh. Sure." He paused, and she could feel the mood change on the other end of the line before he spoke again. "Babe. Uh, hey…hey, you're not gonna hear from me for a while. Okay? But I don't want you to worry. All right?"

"What do you mean? What's happening?"

"Nothing. Nothing to worry about. I just want you to know that I might not be able to send any letters for a few weeks. Don't get scared if you don't get one for a while. Okay?"

"Tell me what's going on!" she pleaded.

"Sweetheart, I can't." He looked up at the OPSEC sign and back down at his sweat-ringed boots. "Just know that I love you."

She started to cry. "I love you too!"

Just then, the air-raid siren blared through FOB Hit, sending a flurry of bodies running for cover.

"Gotta go! Love you!"

The line went dead as, one by one, the explosions rocked the courtyard. The phone dangled and swung from its cord.

~

An angry couple of weeks passed since rockets knocked out the two working phones installed at FOB Hit, just one more jolting turn and dizzying loop on the emotional rollercoaster that had become daily life for the young marines of Kilo Company. As for Sgt. Grimm, his resistance to the *typical deployment bullshit* teetered. A rancid tumor of irritation swelled in the cluttered corners of his mind. It talked to him like a friend, but he knew better, at least at first. And a man can only take so much turbulence before his screws rattle loose. He knew it. He felt it. He hated it. But the more he tried to hush that voice, the stronger it became.

But JP didn't have time to think about that, although it jabbed at the back of his mind like a child with a pointed stick. He had to stay focused, alert, and do his job. With his rifle slung across his chest and his dry, cracked hand in control of the black pistol grip of his M4, he trod forward, searching the alleyways, rooftops, and windows of the mud-brick, Iraqi village they patrolled. He commanded his squad's staggered column from the center of the hardball road, as the line of marines to either side of him bounded across the allies, scoped the rooftops, and kept their eyes peeled for any insurgent activity. Only his radioman, Corporal Richardson—an athletic, former division one football recruit—kept pace with Sgt. Grimm's erratic kicking of trash piles, probing of disturbed dirt, and searching of parked vehicles.

The village was just another tan, heat-waved smear along the Euphrates river, an outcropping of concrete and stone just a half a mile from the river's palms and marked by the little puffs of smoke from the outside kiln cooking pita bread and scraps of butchered goat. Not much more than a small clumping of a hundred square houses or so, made of concrete block or sandy brick and stone. Some sort of makeshift wall, whether plaster, brick, or block, surrounded most, while all the buildings had a varied degree of structural integrity. Some structures were crumbling or had fallen over, others had at least one wall piled in a heap of rubble at its foundation. Some homes used tarps, tin, or burlap blankets for doors, walls, or roofs. It was a poor village, one that had not found its way out of the previous few wars, which permanently marked the walls in shrapnel scars, graffiti, and bullet holes. Most of the flat-roofed houses—hard and sharp but not bomb-resistant—blended into their dusty surroundings.

Often on these patrols for weapon caches and high-valued targets hiding in plain sight, Sgt. Grimm's men would enjoy a warm chunk of bread from a grateful or fearful native. At times, his marines would offer money, candy, or a pocketful of Slim Jims in return. Little did they know the consequences for their actions: immediate conviction by ISIS fighters and execution for helping the infidels. *The price of humanity.* It was everything that these warriors were fighting for.

"Sgt. Grimm, possible spotter. Roof top. Eleven o'clock. He has a cell phone." Third squad's point man radioed over the headset. They called him Hound Dog for his incredible ability to sniff out danger (and maybe perhaps more because of his big ears and stocky build). But he ate it up like a can of wet dog food.

The raised hand signal to *halt* passed down the two lines of battle-ready marines, and they all crouched to a knee. Some raised their scopes, eyeing the roofs and alleys in their sectors of fire; others searched the dirt and trash for wires of death. They all planned their next move, whether it be destruction, death, or diving out of the way as they leaned into the cover of crumbled walls.

Giggles from a group of boys booting an under-inflated soccer ball pulled JP's gaze to his left. The tallest child, no more than nine or ten years old, underfed and lanky, kicked the ball too hard across the dirt yard. It rolled down the embankment and dribbled across the street toward Sgt. Grimm. The three young siblings, all filthy and full of giggles, followed in chase.

A small slip in his concentration and he was back playing ball in the yard with his own son. Adin had begged for a soccer ball on his sixth birthday. His face illuminated with glee when he unwrapped the last gift—his "favorite present"—and immediately asked his dad to go play with him. JP's linebacker skills didn't help when it came to kicking a soccer ball. But he tried his best, awkwardly missing a time or two, much to his son's enjoyment.

And now, as the three playful children ran toward his squad, their youthful spirit embraced him. He warmed at the thought of a child's innocence and happiness.

"Stop! Stay back!" Lance Corporal Kerns raised his rifle at the children. They stopped in their tracks, the two youngest cowering behind the eldest.

"Whoa! Whoa! Whoa! Kerns, lower your rifle!" Sgt. Grimm thundered.

Stunned, Kerns lowered his rifle. "But Sergeant, what about SOPs?"

"Kerns, they're just playing. Look, they're scared shitless. You think they're running around kicking a soccer ball with a bomb strapped to their chest?"

The ball twirled in a dying circle a few feet in front of JP. He pointed to the kids, to the ball, and back to the kids. One boy, who looked to be about six, took two steps forward, half-smiling but keeping shifting eyes on the hard-postured marine with the swift rifle, now pointed at the dirt.

This time, JP wasn't going to whiff. He took two steps forward and booted the ball back up the hill. The children laughed and chased after it as if nothing had happened.

JP grinned. "C'mon, Kerns. Stop trying to kill the kids," he said, motioning with his head.

Back to business, Sgt. Grimm focused up the road and pressed his radio. "Hound Dog, is the guy on the roof a threat or not?" he said, squinting through his scope and following his point man's muzzle toward the rooftops a few hundred yards ahead.

"Well, he's definitely got that *resting-threat face*," Hound Dog retorted.

"All right. Keep eyes on. I'll push up to your position." Sgt. Grimm motioned for his men to hold their positions.

An elderly woman in the traditional black robe with a jagged scar from her left eye to her chin popped out of the doorway and smacked the dust from a rug with a wooden paddle. The noise, resembling a gunshot, startled JP's radioman. He spun to his left, raising his rifle on her chest. She looked up, scolded him in Arabic like a disobedient child, and continued beating the rug.

"A little jumpy, are we?" Sgt. Grimm poked.

Cpl. Richardson lowered his rifle and shook his head, half laughing and half relieved.

"Did she just yell at me?"

"I'm pretty sure that you're grounded for the weekend," JP joked.

"Aw, hell. I was finally gonna go all the way with your sister too."

"Well now, I guess you'll just have to stay home and listen to your mom scream my name all night," JP coolly shot back. "C'mon. Let's go." And they were off, trotting up the street, back to the mission at hand.

That mission, as their need-to-know-only Platoon Commander put it, was to disrupt the flow of weapons up and down the river. In reality, that meant scouring the desert in a three-week foot patrol, speaking with the locals, rummaging through their belongings for contraband, and hand digging the freshly disturbed earth they came upon. The Battalion-sized mission, codenamed Operation Blood Hound—was nearly a week underway. But the marines had already discovered the value of their E-tool shovel, bayonet, and the C4 the engineers brought along to blast the caches of mortars, rockets, landmines, and RPGs found roughly covered beneath the loose soil. By now, a few months into their deployment, third squad had painfully learned that an innocent military-aged male on a rooftop could easily be a lookout or forward observer. And it was very likely that a mortar or rocket team was hastily set up off in the desert, waiting for a phone call to help guide their bombs down onto the marines, the village, and unfortunately, all that happened to be nearby.

Puffing from their jog up the road in full gear, Sgt. Grimm and Cpl. Richardson took a knee beside Hound Dog. He leaned across the hood of a blue Nissan truck, watching the bearded man on the roof. And then he wasn't; the man had disappeared.

"Where'd he go?" Sgt. Grimm asked, leaning against the front fender, poking his rifle over the edge and looking through the tactical scope on his M4.

"Ducked behind the ledge when he saw you slow-pokes comin'."

"Well shit, that can't be good." Sgt. Grimm reached for the *talk* button on his radio. "Stay alert, gents. They might be throwing us a welcome party," he relayed to his squad.

"Uhhh. Where did everyone go?" Cpl. Richardson asked, looking around at the eerily quiet village.

That brief moment of silence, while their tactical minds told them trouble was coming, when they all felt that jolt of warm electricity firing through their blood and bones—in that small pause of stillness and wonder—three distant thumps resonated down the empty street and pounded directly onto the waiting eardrums of Sgt. Grimm.

Staring into Cpl. Richardson's confused face, JP's eyes widened with realization.

"INCOMING!"

He grabbed Hound Dog by the back of his flak jacket, pulled him to the ground, and dove on top of him. Each mortar shook the ground, falling closer and closer. The thumping in their chests, like a shotgun kick to the heart, resonated in their bones. Debris rained down like hail stones, clicking and thudding off their ballistic helmets.

With the taste of gunpowder stinging his tongue, Sgt. Grimm raised his head and brushed away the dust in his lashes. As he blinked away the blur, evaluating his existence, scanning the damage, it hit him. One of the mortars demolished the house his new soccer buddies had disappeared into. Now, heavy, black smoke billowed from the crumbled blocks. Nothing moved. No cries for help, no screams or whimpers. He listened intently, ready to sprint to their aide if needed. But only a deathly silence came from the rubble. They didn't stand a chance.

He swallowed down the image of crushed and mangled children that was pinned to his mind. A boiling rage rushed up from his tender heart and squeezed his teeth until they hurt. He gripped his rifle, pulling it into his shoulder as he kneeled behind the truck. His sights swept the rooftops looking for flesh to down. Desperately, he wished for someone with a rifle to pop into the dusty sky, letting him seek vengeance and justice. None did. Nothing but rage and smoke smoldered toward the cloudy Heavens.

Sgt. Grimm turned his attention to his marines behind him. They were black needle points sticking out behind the corners, blocks, and rocky berms. All waiting for the fire, waiting for the ambush.

"We good?" His gaze darted from one side of the street to the other, squatting beside Hound Dog and Cpl. Richardson as they aimed in on the rooftops and windows. "Team leaders! Are we good?"

"First team, up," a deep voice cracked over the line. "Did anyone see where that came from?"

"They'll be gone before we can get air on station, anyway. Keep your eyes peeled for an ambush and stay covered. Two?"

"Roger that. Second team's good," a calm, twangy voice replied.

Without waiting, JP pressed the talk button again. "Third team? Are we good?"

"Uhh, all accounted for, Sergeant. But Johnson busted his elbow taking cover."

"How bad?" Sgt. Grimm stretched his neck, catching a glimpse of the Corpsman tending to Lcpl. Johnson beside a pile of tan bricks a hundred yards back. He turned to Hound Dog and Cpl. Richardson.

"How 'bout you? Hound Dog? Richardson?"

They both nodded.

"Uhh, Sergeant, you're bleeding." Hound Dog pointed to JP's left hand, which had a streak of blood dripping from his fingertips and dotting the leg of his tan, digital trousers.

Sgt. Grimm turned his hand over to see his palm was gashed. A deep growl rumbled from his gut, and flung the blood from his hand, wiping it on his trousers. Then, with a demented grin and wink at Richardson, he smeared the blood in streaks down his face. "War paint," he grunted.

Richardson snickered and shook his head. "You look stupid. Have Doc take a look."

"I'm fine." He pressed his radio. "How's Johnson?"

There was a short pause, "Ah, he'll be okay. Doc fixed 'em up with a Mickey Mouse Band-Aid and a little kissy-kiss. He'll be fine."

"I thought he was more of a Paw Patrol kinda guy," Grimm quipped. "Good. Stay alert. We're pushing up to the two-story building at our eleven o'clock. Gonna see if we can't catch us a Chatty Cathy. Got it?" He pointed at Cpl. Richardson with his bloody hand. "Send the COC a SITREP and let 'em know we're pushing ahead." In his best hillbilly accent, he radioed his squad, "All right, now, let's see if we can't jump this rabbit…boys, it's huntin' time."

Chapter Three

Iraq, April 26, 2005

Tears swell and drip like open wounds.
They fall wet, but dry before sandy streets
can taste their pain, when wind as warm
as Satan's breath carries each drop off into
the burning sun.

How many tears did it take to fill the Euphrates?
How much deeper must it go?

Shhh! The thunder of Death comes.
Blow by blow, rain from a cloudless sky explodes.

And again, gardens of fouled flesh bloom.

Or, up from the quaking ground, the Devil grabs
at our limbs, pulling us back into this earth.

"I never met his mother, but in my dreams
she wore my mother's face. Alone, bent
over needle and thread, rocking and sobbing,
sewing Joey and tears into the flag. Then,
we stand before her under an unforgiving sun,
lined in perfect ranks, saluting with perfection.
One by one she stitches what it means to be American
across our breast."

"I've never understood what it means, but I wake
up every time with a pain in my chest."

Again, the thunder of Death comes….

There's no Jesus left in this fucking land!
Allah walks freely in streets lined with wired death!
One shot killers blend in a nation of covered faces.
Mercy—has fled—with the innocent!

On my cot, prayers are sent by mail, kisses on pictures.

I put home back under my rack. There's no room for
weakness in my blood today. I print JOEY onto brass
and let him ride the bolt into my chamber.

Today he patrols with us again. Today he is my trigger.
Today he will rest in peace.

"Listen up, gents," Major Taylor demanded of the room packed wall-to-wall with
notepad-wielding officers and NCOs. He stood before a cluttered board of
maps, platoon count numbers, a list of frequencies, and aerial intel pictures of the
city of Hit. His neatly trimmed mustache paired his perfectly faded high and
tight—both of which were graying. His clean and pressed cammies contrasted
with those scruffy, dirty, and detached marines before him.

"Based on intel gathered from Operation Blood Hound, and confirmed by
the spotter Sgt. Grimm's squad brought in, we have a high-value target operating
in our area," he said with enthusiasm.

JP and Joey stood together jotting down the details of this new mission,
Operation Night Hawk, sketched in big red letters on the mobile chalkboard
beside Major Taylor. It was a quickly organized and approved task handed down
straight from an overzealous Battalion Commander. A chatty BC who craved the
excitement of relishing in his battalion's achievements at the officer's lounge at
Al-Asad, the chow hall, or wherever he found someone to stay still long enough
to listen.

The mission briefing was just that, *brief.* And to JP and Joey, the whole thing
seemed rushed and full of flaws.

Sgt. Grimm's mind rummaged through all the holes and scenarios plaguing
this poorly put together operation.

*A mounted patrol? Their spotters will see us coming a mile out. And why would we extract
an HVT from the same route we took going into the city? Doesn't that just beg for an ambush?
IEDs, landmines, RPGs…if they take out the lead tank on route Raspberry, we're fucked
from the start. Why the hell don't we have a better assessment of the size and strength of
resistance. And Air on standby? A bunch of bullshit!*

Joey held his tongue until he was clear of anyone higher ranking than the two
disgruntled squad leaders.

"Air, twenty minutes out on standby? You gotta be shittin' me!" he
murmured as they scuffed their way out of the stale briefing room with their
rifles slung cross-breasted.

JP stopped and leaned against the HESCO barriers——the wire and fabric
cages full of dirt making a safe corridor for transporting gear and information
back and forth between the three concrete buildings. He slapped his notepad
against his palm and looked up at the clear night sky. The amount of sparkles in

the dark purple and fuzzy sea above his head amazed him. The beauty of that vast violet and diamond display overwhelmed him every time.

"Yeah. Another clusterfuck."

His teeth clenched as he ran through the most recent gaffs and *fuckups* that nearly ended him or his men. Like the time his squad was tasked with cleaning out garbage from the old machine-gun pits, where the mortars would land near the front entrance of the FOB—and of course, his men had to dive for cover when bombs rained down from the sky. Or like the time they had to borrow AA batteries for their NVGs from second squad for a night patrol to Zulu Sector just outside the city because someone in charge of supplies forgot to put batteries on the resupply list. But the most memorable? When they all stood down while a civilian convoy was ambushed outside the city, which forced them to listen to the gunfire and explosions from the FOB.

"We can't go all half-assed into a firefight," he remembered their CO saying when pressed for action. And when permission to leave the wire and respond to the firefight finally arrived, it was too late. All that was left of the convoy were smoking vehicles and smoldering bones still sitting in the driver's seats of their SUVs.

That was a hard one for JP to swallow—a painful blow to the whole company and maybe the pivotal moment when Sgt. Grimm realized that nothing made sense anymore, that he was losing what little control he had left of the angry beast inside him.

"I don't like it, Joey. It's bullshit," he said, staring at the bright cluster of stars to the West. He had named the brightest two Adin and Lisa. Often, he would stand outside while Joey smoked behind the HESCOs and they'd *bullshit* about their lives, their families, or the differences between New York City life and the hills of East Ohio. Each time before they came in, JP looked up at those same two bright spots in the darkness, said a little prayer, and sent them up a kiss goodnight. But tonight, a glimmer of green reached out from the northern horizon. JP blinked as his eyes adjusted to the soft jade hue barely rippling at the edges of the horizon. *Strange*, he thought. *I didn't know the Northern Lights happened in Iraq.*

"Dude, you see that?" He nodded at the shimmer of green stretching out and arcing like ripples on a calm lake.

"What? You've never seen the Northern Lights?"

"Not in Iraq!"

"Hm. Well, maybe it's a sign. Maybe the world's ending," Joey teased, sarcastically.

JP snorted. "Yeah, definitely."

A long silence left the two gazing off into the distant, emerald embers rolling across the horizon.

"Look, man, we gotta watch each other's backs out there, Jay," Joey spoke softly at the night, before pulling out a half-smoked cigarette. He let it hang on his lip as he pulled out his American flag Zippo lighter, cupped his hand around the flame, and pulled away with a glowing cherry and a puff of smoke. Then, like an ornery older brother trying to stir the pot, he blew the smoke in JP's face.

JP jerked his head away and waved the cloud from his eyes. "C'mon, man! You know I hate that." Blinking out the blur and sting, he slugged Joey in the shoulder. "You keep doing shit like that, and I'll let the poor bastards take ya."

They were grinning like two pals back home, hanging out and jabbing at each other with their friends. For a moment, the war didn't exist. No rockets or bombs exploding midthought, burning away young men—or old children—from their mothers' dreams and their girlfriends' arms. But under those stars, everything had a hidden intent. Death was just an old friend you'd bump into at the store or gas station and ask, "How's everything going?" before you both walked away, wondering when you'd meet again.

Joey sucked in a long drag to the filter, flicked the butt to the dirt, and let it smolder where it landed. "Hell, they'd just give me right back," he choked out, exhaling a cloud into the sky.

JP turned to face the HESCO and wrapped his fingers through the stiff wire mesh. With a groan, he stretched back and let his spine pop and crack, releasing some of the tension in his shoulders. He rolled his head from side to side and tried to relax with a loud sigh.

"Yeah. I can't blame 'em. You're pretty damn annoying." He studied Joey's face. "Remember that time at Pendleton when you hid Gunny's beanie in Sgt. Brown's pack, and Gunny made everyone empty all their shit until it turned up?"

Joey smirked. "Yeah, what about it? Sgt. Brown was a dick."

JP chuckled. "Yeah, he was. Remember how pissed he got when you told him it was you? How many swings did he try to take before you dropped him? Two? Three?"

They snickered in unison.

"Hell, I thought he was trying to slap me!"

They shook with muffled laughter.

"How do you always get away with that shit?" JP asked.

"What?"

"You know, just…pushing everyone's buttons until they snap."

"Ah, well, it's just one of my many talents. I wear many hats. I mean, you should hear me rap battle."

JP wiped at his eyes. "I think we've all seen that shitshow. You can keep that talent to yourself."

"Fuckin' hater." Joey's thick accent blended with a quick backhand to Sgt. Grimm's chest.

Their laughter brought out First Sergeant from the briefing room.

"Finish up out here, gents, and call it a night!" His rusty voice was drenched in discontent.

"*Roger that, First Sergeant!*" Joey's sarcasm nearly made JP lose his composure.

Once clear, JP just shook his head. "See. Only *you* can get away with shit like that."

"It's cause I'm from the streets, yo!" Joey postured up and pretended to box with JP.

"Stop. Stop it. C'mon! Joey! Quit!" JP dodged his light blows.

Hearing the faint roar of an F35 soaring through the cool desert air, JP looked back to the stars and leaned on the HESCO once more.

"You think we'll make it outta here?" he asked with a rare sense of dread.

"I mean, I will. I don't know about your pansy ass, though."

"Fair enough." JP shifted his eyes to the desert dust while lightly kicking a trench with the tip of his boot.

Joey spat in the dirt and watched the green flicker of the Northern Lights. "Look, we both know you're the better marine. Hell, you're better at everything. If anyone is going to make it out of here, it would be you." He placed his hand on his shoulder and squeezed. "Besides, you got a family to take care of. You have a reason to go home."

"Well, you do have a point there." JP brimmed with pride.

Joey grunted and nodded. "Me, I couldn't care less either way whether or not I soak this dirt with my blood." He leaned his back against the wire mesh. "It doesn't matter either way to me. You can't outflank Death, Jay. If I had a choice, I'd like to go out with a bang. You know, the whole fire and brimstone kind of shit." A sort of sorrow glazed his eyes. "Just let me burn, baby. Let me burrrn."

JP adjusted his rifle dangling from his chest, gripped the handle, and spit in the sand. "Shit. I won't let a damn thing happen to ya, bud." He softly kicked at the wet spot where he spat. "Nothin' to none of us. You got that?"

A slivered moon touched the horizon as night began to creep over the sulfured plains and rocky plateaus that stretched out from each side of the Euphrates. The lights from the city sparkled in the distance. An odd chill hung in the desert air. It reminded JP of those summer nights as a kid when he pushed the limits of his nine o'clock bedtime, begging his grandparents for five more minutes as he crept around the barn, gunning down the enemy with a bright toy gun and making explosion sounds when he threw rocks into the loft. But *this* enemy was real, armed with contempt and shrapnel, and their glory was death and destruction.

Sgt. Grimm had spent the day preparing his men for the mission: capture a high-ranking ISIS commander operating from within the comforts of the city. His squad's responsibility was to provide security, while Joey's squad assaulted the building where the HVT was supposed to be hiding. He made a terrain model of the city in the sand—complete with MRE cardboard for houses, 550 cord for streets, and rocks marking known enemy lookout positions—crafted with care and precision for his marines to visualize their tasks, routes, and targets. Third squad spent the rest of the day prepping their gear and doing dry-run rehearsals in the courtyard. But still, JP couldn't shake the nagging feeling that they were all ill-prepared and uninformed, heading blindly into the bowels of Hell and being tasked with keeping the ice from melting.

"Third squad is set," Cpl. Richardson relayed through the radio, kneeling in the doorway of their rooftop overwatch position.

"Roger. Waiting for the go-ahead, and then we'll push up to the objective. Standby," Second squad's radioman replied.

"Copy."

"They're waiting for go," he relayed to Sgt. Grimm, who peered over the near corner ledge and down the quiet street.

The city was calm, settled with a strange peace, at 0200 hours. It had a certain beauty about it: the orange glow of streetlamps under the mask of midnight made the city seem less lethal and more like the small towns JP grew to know. The night shrunk things, like turning open desert roads into narrow corridors of ultraviolet light, or reshaping big backyard squares into grainy, yellow haloes of lamplight. At this early hour—before the trash-lined streets filled with speeding and honking Hyundai sedans; before the market doors and windows hinged opened with old Iraqi men and young children selling prayer rugs, candy, and foreign electronics; before crowds of people cluttered the stillness; before the potshots cracked down the alleyways or another IED painted the streets and walls red; before the dead came back again at first light—the city was just another place where people lived together.

The city curfew—strict and rarely broken—made it easy for one to feel alone in the threshold of shadows, where thoughts of home and *what-they-are-doing-nows?* twisted in the silk. Occasionally, quiet night patrols let JP's mind drift back to the times he and Lisa were blanket-wrapped on the patio swing overlooking the porch-lit village of Barnesville. Hand-in-hand, they shared their shooting star wishes out loud. But not tonight.

Sgt. Grimm had divided his squad into three teams, each with its own sectors of fire. Team One gathered behind the child-high wall of a flat-roofed, two-story home. They provided overwatch security with an attachment of a four-man team of machine gunners aiming in on the complex a hundred meters ahead of them. Team Two sat at street-level, covering the South and West. Team Three patrolled the North and East sections of fire down on the pavement. Each had a team of machine gunners in the prone position behind their M240 muzzles pointing down the road. Sgt. Grimm and Cpl. Richardson chose the rooftop with Team One, which provided the best vantage point of the complex, the main road, and the narrow alleyways webbing out around them.

Crouching behind the ledge, Sgt. Grimm observed the objective: a quaint, corner complex surrounded by a beige concrete wall high enough to keep prying eyes out of the barred, bottom windows of the two-story home. Like others, it had a flat rooftop with a chest-high ledge all the way around. The tarpaper roofs of a few shed-like structures, lime trees, and shaggy bushes were sharp, black masses for men to hide. A nicer home for the city, it had a cream-colored exterior, marbled steps, concrete statues in the courtyard, and a green, ornate front gate with high, sharp pillars on each side. All was dark in the complex except for the glare of a corner streetlamp leaving long shadows in the dirt.

Between him and the target, a handful of houses lined the main road and secondary streets. All quiet and undisturbed. It was the richer part of the city, with bursts of colored lights and an occasional working streetlamp. Blues and greens, whites and pinks; different hues dotted the bleak and bland tan that spread across the jagged landscape. Though sparse, even the propaganda graffiti on the walls seemed to be spray-painted neatly.

"They're moving." Cpl. Richardson reached up for his handset still tucked into his helmet strap and listened carefully.

Sgt. Grimm pressed his own radio. "Be ready. They're Oscar Mike. Send me the all clear."

One by one, his team leaders reported back a simple "all clear." He raised his scope and searched the complex for movement. From the open, second-floor windows to the square rooftop and back down to the lime trees and white-flowered bushes in the courtyard. Nothing. All calm. All clear. If there were sentries, they were well hidden or inside the house.

"No movement. All clear," he said to Cpl. Richardson, who relayed it over his radio.

They watched as Joey's squad moved like shadows over the wall, entered the complex, and disappeared into the blanket of darkness that covered the corner of the courtyard.

"Approaching the door," Cpl. Richardson said, sitting at Sgt. Grimm's side with his back pressed against the ledge.

"Breaching. Standby." Sgt. Grimm was low behind his scope resting on the ledge, blending in with the backdrop of the city. His men flanked him in each corner of the roof. All watched and waited, silent, as four dark masses moved to the side door of the main building. There, the engineers rigged up the C4 explosives to the green metal door.

"Fire in the hole," Cpl. Richardson whispered to JP, who repeated into his squad's ear as they all leaned tight to the ledge.

A few moments later, a tremendous boom and flash exploded into the desert. It vibrated through the concrete and into their bones, into their ears. They felt it deep in their chests, as smoke and fire briefly filled the night.

Two more explosions immediately followed—grenades tossed by a marine on each side of the hole—splashing the inside of the house with shrapnel, noise, and light. Through the haze, beams of light on the barrels of the black-rifled hellhounds flooded the house.

A brief silence settled in the dark. Then, gun shots boomed through the house. A barrage of the distinct AK47 bursts cracked from the flickering windows. A moment later, a flashbang erupted upstairs, followed by the snapping of several rifled double-taps that swept through the second floor like firecrackers.

Sgt. Grimm scoped in on the windows anxiously. He scanned the black rooftop with his muzzle and scoured the shaded courtyard. Nothing. The thought crossed his mind that maybe no one was left. Everything was going as planned. And that sent a silver tingle down his spine.

Shouting came from inside the house. Right away, JP recognized Joey's irate New York accent.

"Show me your hands, mother fucker! Show me your hands! Shut up! Shut the fuck up! Get down!"

House lights started to dot the night. The single-story house to the right of JP flicked on. A dreary man in a black gown stuck his head out the front door.

"Get back inside!" JP yelled, startling the man, who quickly slammed the door and flicked off his light.

Machine gun fire from Team Two lit up the main road to the south. Tracer rounds skipped off the pavement and curved up into the darkness, like fireflies in the backyard. *So much for a calm night,* he thought.

"SITREP!" Sgt. Grimm demanded into his mic.

"Truck wouldn't stop," his second team leader replied. "It's stopped now."

"All quiet over here," Team Three's team leader responded.

"Stay alert! There's gotta be more than this!" Sgt. Grimm commanded.

Suddenly, gunfire exploded from the rear of the complex. Its amplified melody matched the roar of half a dozen angry Kalashnikovs. That choppy thump of automatic fire had long been engraved into JP's mind.

"Shit!" He scampered to the right corner of the roof, Cpl. Richardson in tow, and kneeled beside two baby-faced lance corporals who had come in with the reinforcements two weeks earlier. Though they were behind their sights, they had not yet fired a single shot. He aimed in on the back corner of the complex, where the flashes ricocheted off the walls and pillars. Two black-clad men squatted behind the corner and fired blindly into the courtyard. Sgt. Grimm buckled them face-first into the dirt with four well-placed shots.

Headlights lit up the alley fifty meters to his front left. A handful of men with rifles and RPGs loaded into the back of a small truck. Just as quickly as the lights flicked on, the machine gunners in the left-hand corner of the roof ripped into the truck. The gunners ended them in a heap of bloodied bodies in the back.

Black dots behind flashing muzzles crest over the rooftop ledges around them. Sgt. Grimm pointed to a pair on the rooftop to his right. Their weapons strobed in the dark, lighting their shaded positions like a nightclub dance floor.

"There!" He pointed for his young marines to fire. "Pull the trigger, damn it!" He shouted as rounds sprayed past them. Each marine unloaded a full magazine in a fit of fearful rage until the rooftop fell silent.

Sgt. Grimm smacked the closest one on the helmet, making him flinch as if he were just shot. "Good work!" He shouted into the chaos of the battle around him, but the pale marine's eyes were hazy and lost. Sgt. Grimm slapped him hard on the back. "But you gotta breathe, damn it!"

The marine exhausted his lungs and heaved in the dusty air. He nodded as he came out of the fog, shook it off, and got back into the fight.

From a rooftop adjacent to the complex, a man fired an RPG at their position. It landed low, but the explosion rocked Sgt. Grimm to his back, dazing him and his men. He shook off the ringing in his ears, wiped the smoke and debris from his face with his sleeve, and quickly gathered himself to his knee, pressing his rifle firmly into his shoulder. Three well-placed shots slumped the man with the RPG over the edge of the roof. His limp body dangled for a moment in Sgt. Grimm's scope before it slid over the top to the concrete below with a sickening smack that JP could *feel* more than *hear*.

More headlights flooded in from the south. They bounced rapidly along the road. Soon enraged men would spill from those lights, slinging rounds from their hips or over their heads at the marines engaged with their comrades. Only seven minutes had ticked by since Joey's squad flooded the house with tactical lights, grenades, and hot lead. Sgt Grimm knew the longer they engaged in the firefight, the more time it allowed the enemy to organize their reaping response.

We need air support! He screamed in his head.

"Do we have Air on station yet?" He hollered at Cpl. Richardson, who was squatting like a loyal dog beside him. Richardson spoke into his headset, paused, and then shook his head grimly. "Ten mikes out."

"Shit!" He shook his head and shouted into the radio. "Hey! Conserve your ammo! It could be a long fight if Air doesn't get here soon."

Sgt. Grimm peeked over the ledge. First squad sat just a hundred meters outside his position. Tanks and rockets engaged vehicles and enemy machine gunners behind him. Their deep thunder shook JP's chest. Sparks flew through the fog and ricocheted off the roads and buildings. Where they ended up, he didn't know. But bright spots—trucks and buildings ablaze, their occupants smoldering beside them or burning within them—flickered around the city. Dust, smoke, and muzzle flashes filled the air. A ghostly haze lit like the underbelly of a thunderstorm when splinters of lightning shattered the sky. A cloud of the deceased hovered.

"They're coming out! Covering fire!" Sgt. Grimm hollered until the roof looked like flames in the corners, spilling over the edges, flaring down on the town like lava stones. Where their muzzles pointed and flashed, destruction followed. Roaring like beasts spitting flames, their weapons thundered through the night.

Searching the rooftops and windows through his scope, Sgt. Grimm saw Joey's squad exiting the front door. He cracked shots at a shadow around the corner of the shed until it crumbled into the earth. It left a blood splatter on the wall behind the shadowed man's head.

"Let's go!" JP yelled, running around the roof and smacking his marines on the shoulders as they each peeled their men away and down the stairs into the street to provide security for the extract.

Bounding across the road from corner to corner, Sgt. Grimm's unit engaged targets as the enemy lit their barrels and made themselves known in the shadows. His squad moved into position with muzzles flaring for covering fire like a greased machine meant to flame and move forward. They kneeled behind parked cars, crouched in trenches and around corners, holding their ground for Joey's squad to move up the street.

Joey tugged on the arm of a limping and bloody man in flex-cuffs. JP scoured the backdrop of buildings and allies from behind a bullet-holed truck across the street. The men moved like muddy water on a windshield, coming together as one, with only a four-laned road between them.

Sgt. Grimm's men mirrored Joey's squad as they kneeled along the street and fired at flashes in the shadows and headlights on the pavement. The marines on either side pointed their muzzles in all directions. Joey crouched with his radioman and the battered HVT behind the concrete base of a streetlamp. Sgt. Grimm and Cpl. Richardson pushed ahead behind a white sedan directly across from Joey. Their marines picked off targets until there was nothing left to shoot, until the only gunfire was on the outskirts of town, where the snipers picked off the men fleeing the battleground.

Both Joey and JP were determined to get their men to the armored vehicles two blocks away. Joey's hand chopped the air signaling he was about to move across the road toward JP. Joey smirked when they locked eyes. He had won and wanted him to know it. His arrogance was comforting, although JP still flipped him the bird before he motioned for him to cross over.

The block had settled to a damp dead zone. Bodies and blood painted the burning streets. Concrete rubble and smoking cars littered the neighborhood. The black smoke waving through the air stung JP's nose. It made it harder for the enemy to see them move, and he was thankful for that. But just as Joey stood, out of the corner of JP's eye, he saw movement coming out of the black footpath across the street.

Is that someone crawling? A dog?

From around the rear bumper, he snapped his rifle to his shoulder and pierced the shade with his scope. It wasn't a man, nor a dog. It was a child. A boy emerged from the darkness. A singed and fret little boy in a bulky, black Thor T-shirt with a red hammer in the center, like a target on his little chest. *Thor.* His son's favorite superhero. A child no older than Adin, himself.

What the hell's he doing?

JP hesitated, his finger on the trigger. *Is he a threat?* Sgt. Grimm knew what he *should* do as the boy moved closer to Joey. But he couldn't. With thunder and lightning cracking in the city around him, with war striking at all of his senses, all he could focus on was that little boy's face, so twisted and determined, yet so helpless and afraid. *Hazel eyes, like Adin's.* Arms outstretched, cautious steps, like treading barefoot on gravel for a goodbye hug, the boy moved from the dark static of a concealed footpath directly toward Joey and his bounty.

Is that the guy's son? What's he doing? Trying to reach his father?

And for a moment, through the blurry haze, JP didn't see an Iraqi boy in the chaos of a littered battlefield. No, JP didn't see Iraq at all. JP saw his own son begging for him not to leave, his own son's petrified face when his father told him it was time for him to go away.

Adin? Jesus, he looks just like Adin. JP thought as he lowered his rifle just a tilt and squinted through the smoke and fire flashing against the walls.

Wait. There's something under his shirt? Is he injured, or is that a vest?

In that frozen moment, when Joey rose from his knee and stepped out from behind the concrete base of that lamppost, his baffled eyes found JP gazing into the darkness. But JP wasn't staring at Joey; he was stuck on the fire eyes of that frightened, frail boy. He was mesmerized, enthralled, seized by the child that resembled his son. And all he could do in those pausing seconds was stare stupidly as the boy took another step closer. Closer. One shaking step. Two. Three.

Joey and his men were in the open, exposed. Fresh sparks of gunfire rattled down the alley and his men returned fire, pulling Sgt. Grimm from his slumber. He snapped out of it with a jerk and felt the weight of the rifle in his hands and the grit under his knee as he leaned around the back bumper of the sedan.

"Allahu Akbar!" The boy yelled.

Now focused, he pulled his rifle into his shoulder and sighted in on the boy. Clutched in his tiny hand was a small black remote. *Shit!* The chaos muted as they locked eyes from across the street. A golden-brown shade. Dark and light. Hazel eyes. Adin's eyes. So afraid. So helpless. So desperate. *So deadly.*

JP's finger pressed against his trigger. But it was too late. A blinding bolt of lightning and a ringing roar of thunder exploded from the child's chest.

And the firestorm swept away the men that Sgt. Grimm promised to protect.

<u>Chapter Four</u>

Death Letter

On this green, issued, sweat-stained cot,
in salt-stiff desert cammies,

I drip words from my pores, like blood
from shrapnel wounds.

It is hot.
And thoughts of you steam my blood.

To say goodbye to smiles in a pile of pictures

is prison.

But, *here,* there are no visiting hours
no holiday breaks to touch your skin.

I am captive in this foreign land
a slave to a unit number
a digit in a media war.

I'm a piece of paper to a brass paper weight
filled with training checkmarks, achievements,

and next of kin.

No amount of wind will let me fly.

I am chained in this sand, blindfolded and bound,
as useful as a rotting corpse

without life…without soul.

And I am days away from that kind of death.

Or maybe minutes, or hours,
or even the seconds that tic loudly by
on this olive drab, sun-faded watch.

I'm writing to say goodbye,
because, by now,

I have accepted it.

Sgt. Grimm grunted as he leaned back in his front row, bottom bunk of tent three at Al-Asad Air Force Base. It was a tent big enough to house his whole platoon, though, with the excited noise and chatter of home, he wished it was only for himself. His lower back still felt like needles and his heavy head throbbed as he rested it on his folded digital blouse. "Bed rest." Doc had ordered after the explosion several weeks ago. Now, as the deployment was coming to an end, and they had left FOB Hit behind them, the marines of Kilo 3/25 decompressed by playing football out front in the dirt, lifting weights at the Al-Asad gym, grabbing hot-chow seconds at the chow hall, or spending hours at the phone center calling home. For many, the morale was high.

But JP awoke that morning with another migraine and blurry vision. They'd be headed Stateside in less than two weeks, and he wondered what it would be like to face Joey's family or tell them how he died—if they asked. Those thoughts kept him in bed all morning. Joey was the only marine who could piss him off more than First Sergeant, but still make him laugh until he forgot about the war. He needed that now, more than anything. But Joey wasn't there to settle him anymore. Instead, his friend had been shredded by shrapnel at the hand of a bronze-eyed, six-year-old boy. The same six-year-old boy JP knew he should have shot when he had the chance.

But how the fuck are you supposed to take a child's life? How can you kill someone that looks just like your own son?

Sgt. Grimm had plenty of time to replay the last few seconds of his friend's life.

I should've killed him. I should've shot that kid right between the eyes. Dropped him. Ended him. Removed him from this Hell. Stopped him from creating mine.

He pinched the bridge of his nose and tried to relieve the pain throbbing at the back of his eyes.

But how? How could I? How could anyone?

JP had wrestled with a million questions flinging themselves, one after the other, against his pounding skull. He had wrestled them all and failed to pin them down. It was *his fault*, and no one could tell him any different.

He needed to keep his mind distracted. Busy work. Something to do with his hands to keep his mind from wandering, to keep from drowning in self-inflicted misery. Sgt. Grimm needed to feel useful again. And he tried, painfully shoving on his boots and blouse when his Platoon Sergeant—the *large-and-in-charge* Gunny Smith—burst through the open flap and asked for volunteers.

"I don't think so, Sgt. Grimm! Back in the bunk. And that's an order," he scolded, rubbing the sweat from his bald head with his sleeve.

"Gunny, I can supervise," JP pleaded.

"Negative, Grimm. That is, unless you can magically shit out a chit from Doc Demler clearing you from bed rest?" Gunny placed his hands on his hips like he meant business.

JP rubbed the back of his head, gritting his teeth. *This is bullshit!*

He sighed. "I could probably come up with one if you turn your head for a few minutes."

"Damn it, Grimm, I'm not joking around. Get your ass back in the rack, and I don't want to see your face again today—unless it's to tell me you've been cleared for duty."

Gunny Smith squeezed JP's shoulder and his tone softened. "Look, I know you want to get back out there and do something, but we need you healthy and clearheaded," Gunny pressed his lips together, looked down for a moment, and then back up into his eyes, "*I need you healthy and clearheaded.* Understand? Just get some rest, Grimm. There'll be plenty for you to do at Lejeune."

JP backed down, flung off his cammies, kicked off his boots, and crumbled back into the bottom bunk. It was the first bed in row one of the four perfectly aligned rows of bunk beds, where daypacks, flak jackets, rifles, and ballistic helmets dangled from the bed poles. "The Bootcamp Bunks," is what the PFCs had called them the first day. But they were Heaven compared to the stiff foldout cots and the hard, rocky ground they were used to sleeping on.

Other than a few NCOs and three *voluntold* lance corporals on fire-watch, JP was left to himself to rest and relax—to clear his head of all the demons creeping out from the dark corners of his frayed mentality.

He was just settling in with his feet crossed and hands behind his head, coming down from his frustrations, when he heard Cpl. Richardson holler from his top bunk beside him.

"Damn it! What the fuck?!" Cpl. Richardson shook his computer, punched the buttons, and then slammed it shut. "Seriously? No connection on Al-Asad? I thought this place was supposed to have the best Wi-Fi in country. Bullshit." He tossed his computer to the bed.

A few other NCOs joined his frustration as their own computers disconnected from the Wi-Fi. All closing their computers and cursing out their frustrations.

A few moments later, Richardson hobbled over and plopped down on the edge of JP's bed. "How ya holdin' up, Sgt. Grimm? Need anything?" He said, leaning the crutches he hardly used against the frame and adjusting the black eyepatch over the fresh gauze at his brow. Doc made him wear it since his left eye was still hypersensitive to light after getting sandblasted and gashed by shrapnel in the explosion.

JP barely moved his head to answer. "Nah, I'm good. You?"

"Ready to take this damn thing off. I feel like a fucking pirate."

JP cracked a short-lived smile. Any other time, and he'd let him have it: *Yeah, a butt-pirate.* Or, *where's your parrot, Captain Hook?* But today, he wasn't in the mood. Instead, he scooched his legs over for Richardson to sit and thought about how close his radioman came to losing his eye. "When's it come off?"

Cpl. Richardson, still fidgeting with his patch, finally gave up on making it comfortable and instead opened a Maxim magazine seemingly left over from the previous wars. "Well, would've been a week ago if I didn't rip out the stitches trying to carry my pack the other day. I'm an idiot. A stubborn asshole," he said, reminiscing about trying to look tough and pull his own weight, even after he sprained his ankle in the explosion. "Doc said a couple more days, probably just before we leave for Tent City."

Can you even read that thing? JP wanted to ask but held back. "Well, at least you won't have to wear it home. Right?"

Richardson flipped through the pages of the Hometown Hottie contest. "Yeah. I'm just ready to be done with the pirate jokes, you know." He shrugged. "You guys need new content; the same jokes are lame."

JP chuckled, sighed heavily, and picked at the gray paint on the metal bar above him. "Look, man…I'm really sorry." His chest shuddered, and his eyes glossed over. A sudden rush of emotion came over him. He sniffed and wiped his nose on his sleeve. "They'd all still be here if it wasn't for me," he mumbled to the chipped-paint bed frame above him.

"Bullshit."

Just then, Sgt. Kovo, First squad's squad leader, ripped open the flap to the tent and ducked as he darted in. Grimm and Richardson caught his eye. Kovo's thick chest swelled, and he grinned from just one side of his mouth—a thing he did when he was thinking of something ornery to say. His bright blond hair shined as he walked from the desert light into the shade of the tent.

"You pussies done milkin' it yet?" he jabbed as he got closer. "Listen, y'all gotta come see this! There's a *huge* sand storm rolling in. Lightning like you've never seen. Flocks of birds flyin' around running into shit and droppin' like geese on a huntin' pond. It's crazy!" His country boy accent got a lot of attention during his four years in the Corps. "Looks a shit-ton worse than the last—"

Richardson's glare wiped the happiness from Kovo's face. And when Kovo was close enough to see tears in JP's eyes, he realized that he was, once again, sticking his huge foot in his mouth.

"Oh, shit. My bad," he said as he eased his long strides to a stop, holding up both hands. "Don't mind me; I'm a dumbass." He lifted his chin. "You guys good? Need anything?"

JP wiped at his face, and they both shook their heads. "No, we're good," Cpl. Richardson said, giving him a head nod toward the exit.

"All right" Sgt. Kovo put his desert cover back on his sunburned head. "Well, I'm gonna have a smoke before shit hits the fan out here. Just holler if you need me." He winked, and an eerie gray blotted out the afternoon sun as he swiped the green flap open and let it swing behind him as he left.

A swirl of wind blew dust and a cigarette butt across the floor, as Sgt. Kovo popped his red neck back in. He caught a side-eye from Cpl. Richardson. "I know. I know." He awkwardly snorted, holding up a dead bird in his hand. "'Bout took off my head. I'm just gonna go ahead and pull the flap shut. For you guys…because I love ya…even if you are milkin' it!" He tossed the dead bird by their boots and laughed before he disappeared, still laughing as he told someone outside what he did.

Both marines stared at the dead bird and shook their heads. JP sniffed again and turned away on his side. Cpl. Richardson folded the magazine and smacked JP on the leg. "Dude, come on. None of this was your fault. Don't be an idiot."

JP sighed heavily.

"If anything, you saved lives that day."

Sgt. Grimm snapped his head back at Richardson. "The fuck I did! I killed 'em! I'm the reason they're dead! Meee!" He pounded his chest. "Me, damn it! I'm the one who didn't do his damn job! I'm the one who didn't pull the fucking trigger! Not you! Not Hound Dog! Me!" A tear trickled down the side of his face and left a dot on the tan sheet.

Cpl. Richardson looked away, fighting his own urge to cry. When he turned back around, he slapped the magazine nervously in his hand before he spoke. "Look, man, there'd be three other KIAs if you hadn't crawled over and stopped the bleeding. We'd never have gotten that intel from the HTV if you hadn't put the tourniquet on his leg. Think of how many lives that saved! Taking out that bomb factory, their lead bomb maker—you did that when you saved that piece of shit's life! *You* did. You saved lives when you saved his!"

"It's not fair! Goddamn it! It's not!" JP pounded the frame with his fist. "Why's that son of a bitch get to live when the others didn't? Why'd it have to be them? Why not someone else? Why not *me*?" He ripped his blouse from under his head and screamed into it until his throat hurt. He was red-faced and exhausted when he pulled it away. "Why couldn't I have just pulled the trigger?" he whimpered.

By the time the sandstorm had ended, they finished their conversation. Cpl. Richardson left to see Doc about removing his eye patch, giving JP some time to sulk and regain some energy. He stared out the open tent flap at the marines playing football in the dust and wished he could join them. Instead, he thought of home, his family, and his wife. Wiping the sweat from his forehead, he reached into his blouse pocket and pulled out a folded letter. He had asked Lisa to write as often as she could. And while the other marines poked fun about the letters, he enjoyed the nostalgia and old-fashioned, personal touch of reading his wife's handwriting and being able to hold it in his hand. It was like he could feel his wife's fingertips when he brushed his thumb over her neatly inked words. He plucked the letter from its dirt-smudged envelope. The paper still smelled like Lisa's lilac perfume when he unfolded it for the third time.

Darling—

I hope this letter reaches you in time. Four weeks! Ahhhh! I can't believe I'll have your strong arms wrapped around me in one month! If only I could fall asleep and wake up four weeks from now. Although, I'm not sure if Adin would survive on cereal and Easy Mac for that long. And he'd probably wake me up for the 100th time to ask me how many days until you'd be home. But, if only...

Needless to say, we miss you terribly.

Adin lost another tooth the other day. There's no doubt that he's your kid. He was running around the house with a bloody mouth, pretending to be a vampire. And, I'm sorry, I tried to get it out, but there's still a small stain on the collar of your Black Rifle Coffee shirt from where he tried to bite me. Oops, busted. I've been wearing it to bed every night. It even still smells like you, sort of.

But anyway. Things are still going well here. Well, as well as they can be with how weird the weather's been lately. It hasn't rained in, like, two months. Your grandmother is getting worried. Mostly about your grandfather. But you know how he is—still out there busting his back in the fields. Why do men have to be so damned stubborn? I swear it's going to kill him one of these days. The dust is getting to us all, but especially him. He's had a bit of a cough lately, and it's making him short of breath. And honestly, I think if the farm doesn't kill him, then your grandmother will. So, there's that.

I had a dream about you the other night, and I wondered if I should say anything at all about it, but it was so real, as if you were right here beside me. And now I smile every time I think about it. So maybe you will too. (And listen! You better not share this with anyone, or I will NEVER tell you about one of my dreams again! Jay! I mean it! Don't make me have to put you on the couch!)

All right, so it was the first night that you were home (I've been thinking about it so much, lately). And I was making your favorite dish (chicken stir-fry, in case you forget how much you looove my cooking!) and for some reason...I was wearing nothing, <u>absolutely nothing</u>, but my red knock-off stilettos and that silly apron you got me when I said I was going to learn how to bake pies like your grandmother.

Yeah, I know...okay, so it sounds like one of YOUR dreams. But what can I say? I aim to please.

So, picture me in nothing but heels and that "shut your pie-hole" apron you got me (Ha! Ha! Asshole!). I had the apron tied in a big bow in the back, and you were watching me from the doorway of the kitchen. I was putting on a show. You know, the whole nine yards—bending over extra far, swaying my hips back and forth, winking all sexy-like. And you were just taking it all in with the biggest smile on your face.

Then, you walked over to me, caressed my cheek, brushed my hair aside, and kissed my neck. I could literally feel the shivers and tickle just below my ear—that warm gush of "hell yes!" that makes my eyes close and my breath shake. Then you pushed me up against the counter, and we legit made out like we were back in school. You reached behind me and untied the string, slowly lifting it over my hair. I felt so powerful and sexy as you looked me up and down. That's when you picked me up and plopped me down on the counter. You started kissing my thighs, gently. I could feel them tingle. You slowly made your way up to my hips—and then back down! I wanted you so bad, and you knew it! You used it against me! But the teasing was just what I needed. You did that little thing with your tongue that, you know, drives me wild! Mmmm! I was on fire!

Then you flipped me around and bent me over the counter...

The way we made love was like...well, it was like how we used to do it—you know, back BEFORE we got married! God, it felt so real! I could feel you. Allll of you. It was as if you had never left—like we had never made it past twenty-two, and like the world wasn't falling apart.

But then, when I woke up and reached for your scruffy face, you weren't there. And my heart sank, knowing that it would still be weeks before I could feel you.

Babe, I'm so proud of you. A little pissed off too. But mostly, I just love you so damn much for being the man that you are. You know, for fighting for all of us back here. For standing up for our freedom and way of life. I don't think I tell you that enough. But I'm going to start telling you more. I want to do better for you.

You know, I was afraid of what this time away might do to our connection. Honestly, I was petrified that we'd be different. But I've never loved you as much as I do right now!

Now, hurry up and get that beautiful bubble-butt back home to me!

I miss you. I need you. I love you.

See you soon...ish?

MUUUUAH!

Lis—

JP lifted the letter up to his nose and let his wife's scent fill him with joy. He stared at the ink, smiling like a fool for a few moments, letting its warmth take away all the cold that had settled on his soul. Then, he carefully folded it back along the creases, gently placed it back into the envelope, and tucked it away in his front breast pocket.

He rummaged in his pack beside the bed and pulled out his notebook and a pen. There was so much he wanted to tell her, so much he wished she knew. With the swirl of marines and joy around him, he began to write her back.

Babe—

I can't even begin to tell you how much your last letter made me want you. But that was your point, right? You're slick! But I'm onto you (in a few weeks. Get it?? Haha!). Anyway, I've read your letter three or four times today. And I'll probably read it a few more before bed. (Who knows, maybe it'll inspire some dreams of my own? Wink. Wink.)

I love you more than you could ever imagine. I think about you more than I really should. You're on my mind constantly. You and...and...our son. Adin. I...

The pen fell to the pad and rolled across his gut to the damp sheets underneath. He rubbed his face with both hands, letting the stress and emotion blow from his lips. Staring off into nowhere at the gray metal bed frame in front of him, he let every emotion flood through his veins. He needed more than anything for her to know what happened to him.

But how do you start that conversation out of nowhere? How can you push that kind of torment and anguish onto someone you love?

He gripped the sheets tight and squeezed until his fingers turned white. He exhaled, picked up the pen, and started writing again.

I killed Joey. I know that's no way to start a conversation, but how else am I supposed to say it? I got my men blown up because I couldn't do my job. I failed. I hesitated. I was weak. Because I saw my son in that little boy's face. The boy with the bomb. The bomb that blew up my brothers. I did that. I let that happen. Me. Your faithful husband. Your marine. The man that you're so proud of. I killed them.

And now, all I want to do is reach out my furious hands at anyone and everyone and everything around me…and rip out their fucking eyes for judging me. I want to strangle the life right out of them. I can feel their hate when they look at me. They won't say it, but I know it's there. And GOOD! Cause I hate me too.

Maybe I should start with the shattered eyes looking back at me in the mirror?

Sgt. Grimm bit the end of the pen as he examined what he wrote. His face contorted as he read through it. Biting harder and harder as he read until the pen cracked between his teeth.

He yanked it from his mouth and studied it as he spit out the plastic shards. *Idiot!*

Looking around to see if anyone was watching him, he tucked the broken pen under his mattress, ripped apart the letter into tiny pieces, crumbled them into his fist, and stuffed them into his right hip pocket.

Then, with a deep breath and satisfied smirk, he swept his legs to the edge of the bed, sat up, laced his boots, and boldly walked out of the tent to help his fellow marines do work.

<u>Chapter Five</u>

Post-Traumatic Stress Disorder

It was obvious in that
still
jerk-tight grip,

and that
still
wide-eyed yank hard left
of that fresh sweat and ArmorAll
sticky steering wheel

that time
that I rattled my shining jeep
through a cold,
shallow mud
and dead leaf ditch

still

still

still searching back-road garbage for wires
and IEDs
in the third week back home
from those shit and death streets.

It's right there in that
take-cover jolt
and ready-to-swing clenching
of a rough shovel handle
at the crack
of each tailgate Boom
from dad's old dirt-and-rust dump truck.

Or, on that whiff of black cloud exhaust
from a tired diesel engine
fast rolling those screeching tracks

and I'd be back
to up-gunning
that machine gun
again;

dark bandana over my breath
on a squinting, peppered face,
scanning for the dead
in the sand and sulfur
of a death land.

And it's there just as obvious,
in my cousin's shock-and-awe face
while hunting for deer,
when I dropped
to a raised-gun knee
instincts aiming in
behind the cover of a fallen tree
as a camouflaged hunter's nearby shot

rallied up from the gully.

The Welcome Home party was great—a little overwhelming, but *great*. Everyone gathered at the farm on a hot October afternoon. Everyone was there: family, old high school buddies, and all the small-town friends that showed up when they knew someone who knew someone. Even Mayor Todd *graced them with his presence*.

Lisa had been glued to his side all day, squeezing his hand to see if he wanted to escape whenever the questions dug too deep. But he stayed there, as sturdy as he could muster, trying not to let anyone see the bloody movie reel flashing in his eyes each time they asked, "What's it like over there?" She was his rock, rubbing the tension from his neck when he was forced to listen to his buddy, Ben, complain about how exhausted he was from working another fifty-hour week out on the road. Lisa quelled the anger that swirled inside of him when Chris had changed the discussion from his impending divorce to his belligerent opinion that *this war* was just another pointless war on a long list of pointless wars in the Middle East. She was there to lead him away and back to the table of strawberry pies when he told Mayor Todd to "kiss his ass" after he suggested all returning vets should get a mental evaluation.

And when Adin slammed the barn door, and JP lit into him like Hellfire, she saw the damage inside of him. It was only her calm words, gentle embrace, and tender kisses that brought him back down from boiling after his reaming of their confused little boy. *Stress,* she thought, from over-stimulation, the noise, the people, the excitement. Even as she caressed the back of his neck and stared into his, *I'm so sorry* eyes, she was steady, firm, and a sturdy place for him to fall.

He *was* sorry. She knew that. But as bright as the sun shined down on their family and friends, something rigid, something sharp, something *dangerous* lurked where the soft folds of JP's laughter used to be. Something quite different from the husband and father she used to know. Something that kept a discerning distance from the excited little boy who tugged on his daddy's arm when he refused to go hunt snakes with him in the barn. Surely, she thought, it was just JP's way of adjusting to the months, space, and tragedies that came between them while he was away.

But now, another sleepless night later, lying awake during the moans, screams, and jerks of her damp husband, she wondered why the father of her child has been avoiding their son. Keeping them both far from peaceful dreams, she was finally ready to ask him what made him sweat and shake at night.

He stood at the window with a flashlight in his hand scanning the night with slow strokes.

"Babe, what are you looking at?" She came in from the bathroom and set her phone on the nightstand.

"Huh? Oh…uh, nothing, I guess. Just looking."

"I guess you really missed this place, that view, huh?" She folded back the sheets.

"Uh, yeah. Yeah, ya know…it looks a little different than it did in my thoughts and dreams. Looks a little edgier. Darker. Maybe? I don't know."

He clicked off the flashlight, letting the curtain swing back into place, and turned to watch her slide out of his blue, flannel shirt. She let it drop to the floor where she flung it to the corner with her toes.

He watched her elegant form melt into the sheets of their pine-wood bed in the glow of the nightstand lamp. *How could a guy like me land a goddess like this?* he thought, as she opened the sheets for him to join her.

"I love you, so much," he whispered, climbing in and kissing her forehead.

She gleamed in heavy thought, knowing the measure of that love, but now wondering where that same magnitude had gone for his son.

"I love you," she whispered back, rubbing his muscular chest and gazing into the far corner of their rustic cabin home, gifted to them when they wed by his grandparents.

It was a quiet little home on the back five acres of his grandfather's farm, where the woods and pines met the golden fields. How surprised they were when his grandparents had revealed that the cabin and the land were theirs—as long as they helped with the farm. "Because good land needs good roots," his grandfather had answered when JP questioned why they had given them such a big gift.

Good roots, she thought. *To reap what you sow.* She chewed at the inside of her lip, not noticing the length between her last words and the next. "And Adin loves you too." She looked up from his shoulder to study his face. The sadness and pain surprised her. Where she thought she'd see joy, she found shame. Struck cold by his storming eyes, she propped herself up on the pillow, while he took the space as a chance to turn away toward the window.

"JP…" Her fingertips grazed his shoulder. "I know that I'll never be able to understand what you went through, but I'm here when you need me. Please know that." She left a long kiss on the arch of his shoulder and felt his deep, shaking breath. "I can tell something's bothering you, and if you don't want to talk about it, I understand. But I just want to help where I can. I just want to be here for you. Okay?" She pressed up against him. His skin was cold and sticky. She tried to wrap him in her warmth.

He stared at the red numbers of the alarm clock on the pine nightstand. The red began to blur and flicker, matching his breath. After a moment, he cleared his throat, still facing the alarm. "Some terrible things happened over there. I can't tell you what or why or how. But I want you to know that I love you. I love you *both* very much. I just…I just need to get it all figured out. You know?"

Squeezing him, she held onto his every word and swallowed down the urge to cry before she spoke softly. "I'm so sorry, babe. I really am. I just wish there was something I could do to help." She stretched her arm across his chest, and he took her hand in his. She could feel the dampness of his palm on top of hers. "I just want you to know how much we love and care about you, Adin and I. We missed you like crazy and can't wait to spend all our time with you…whether you like it or not," she added with a forced chuckle, hoping to lighten the mood.

They laid like that for a while, in silence, both deep in thought and grief.

"What about Adin?" She finally found the courage to ask.

His chest rose and fell. "What about him?" he said.

She wasn't sure what to say next. She had no idea how to move forward—should she tread lightly or force the issue? He was still so far away when he was with his son. She could see it, and she was terrified that Adin could see it too. She wanted them to be like they used to—playing and cackling together, so close, best buddies. But they'd hardly done any of that in the few days since he'd been home. What did that mean?

"Babe, you've barely been around him since you've been back," she finally said in the high, gentle voice she used to deescalate uncomfortable situations.

He flexed, and although she couldn't see his face, she felt it twisting with thought.

"I'm sorry," he finally forced out.

And all she could do was hold him and let him know she loved him. Because honestly, she didn't know what else to do. This was new territory—a new thorn bush on their path back to normal. Like a mosquito buzzing in her ear, she wanted nothing more than to slap it away and enjoy the rest of their time together.

The next morning, he shuttered awake with a gasp in wet sheets. Laying in them, he knew his wife was right. He needed to make more of an effort. And those were the first thoughts he fumbled with while trying to distract himself from his death dreams. Before his feet even hit the cold hardwood floor, he decided today he was going to *do better.*

Lisa and JP were holding each other around the waist next to the hickory kitchen table when Adin—with brown, bedhead hair and a toothless grin—hurried down the stairs and rounded the corner. The emergence of his son from the stairway shadows sent a sudden pinch into his chest. Lisa felt him flinch and push away slightly. Caught off guard, she tried to catch his eyes. But they only darted away. So, she matched his deep breath and forced a smile. Quickly, they both brushed it away with laughter as Adin, proud in his camouflaged pajamas, twisted his hips this way and that, showing them off. Adin was so much like his great-grandmother—a morning person, full of giggles and energy, a showboat with an attitude—he even made the sun want to come out and play.

"Will you take me to school today, Dad? Pleeease?" He wiggled back and forth, eyes closed, hands behind his back, and grinning as hard as he could.

JP's face lit up. "Better yet, how about I take you to the park instead?"

Lisa snapped her gaze to meet her husband's arching brows. She cocked her head in thought, smiled, and nodded her approval.

"What about school?" Adin asked.

"Ah, school will be there tomorrow," JP said and shrugged. "How about me and you go do some father and son stuff out on the town? How's that sound?"

"Father and son stuff?" Adin's lip curled.

"Yeah, you know, go exploring through the park, go spend too much money on toys and tools at Walmart, orrr I don't know, maybe go on an adventure to Salt Fork? Hit the trails and try to find Bigfoot? What do ya think? You want to catch Bigfoot today, buddy?"

"Bigfoot! We're gonna catch Bigfoot?" Adin jumped around the kitchen, his voice high and excited as he whooped and hollered.

JP shrugged and nodded his head. "I mean, if we can find a net big enough?" He shot a look at Lisa that made her flush and filled her heart with warmth. To finally see her husband and son bond like they used to, made all the difference. She loved to watch them play together. There was something so beautiful and natural about it, something so pure and loving about the way the two bonded over "guy stuff," and she knew they had lots of catching up to do.

Before they knew it, Adin was off and running up the stairs, shouting, "We're gonna catch Bigfoot! Oh my gosh! We're gonna catch Bigfoot!" And then came the sound of opening and closing drawers and tossed toys as he got ready for the day's adventures. JP and Lisa snorted at each other, flinching and making faces at the various thumps and thuds coming from their son's bedroom.

"I don't think he's excited at all," Lisa said with a bright face.

"Not even a little bit. Also, *not it* on cleaning up that pigsty when we get back." JP touched the tip of his index finger to his nose.

"Ah! That's not even fair! You didn't give me a chance!"

"Well, ya gotta be quicker than that. Or are you getting slower in your old age?" he jabbed.

She smacked him on the shoulder and laughed, pretending to squirm away when he tried to take her in his loving, teasing arms.

"I hate you so much, right now." She squinted at him, trying to hide the mischief in her eyes, and then scooted forward a touch, aiming for his lips.

His lips stretched while rubbing the tip of his nose against hers. "No, ya don't," he whispered, just out of reach of her puckered lips. He lingered there a moment, just long enough for her to feel his teasing. Then, he pulled her into him with gentle but strong arms and caressed the skin below her ear with his warm fingertips. "I love you," he whispered before they pressed their lips together for a long kiss.

"Ewww!" Adin moaned, standing at the bottom of the stairs with a disgusted look on his face and his arms full of toy guns, camo clothes, a bug net, and a set of binoculars.

JP could feel Lisa's smile against his own as he pulled away, grabbing one last peck before they separated.

"Wow, Bud," he said, looking Adin up and down. "You look like you're ready to go Squatchin'."

His face lit up with excitement. "Yeah!" He shouted. "Yeah, I'm ready to go squashin'!"

~

"You can't stuff a Bigfoot in the back of a Jeep," Adin said scrunching his dark brows.

His father chuckled. "Okay then, the truck it is."

The sun was in and out, throwing shadows across the drive and into the truck. It gleamed and sparkled, at times, catching some piece of metal or glare on the window. They hadn't made it out of the driveway before the sun had streamed into the truck and lit up his son's eyes. Golden, like fire and sparks in the night. A breathtaking color for many. Breathtaking or *breathless.*

JP cleared his throat, "kinda bright out here today, huh? Here, why don't you put these on? Keep the sun out of your eyes."

He handed his son a pair of huge, aviator sunglasses. Adin took them but hesitated to put them on.

"It's not that bad, Dad."

JP glanced his way as they bumped down the drive. "Yeah, but think of how cool you'll look. Plus, your mom would want you to wear them. Right?"

Adin grinned, nodded, and put them on as his father watched out of the corner of his eye.

"There, that's better. Right?"

"They're a little big, Dad. We should've grabbed mine out of the Jeep." Adin struggled to keep them on his nose.

"Aw, no way! They look cool!"

"Where's yours?" Adin's forehead wrinkled.

JP reached across the console, pulled another pair from the glove box, and put them on. "How do I look? Am I as cool as you?"

"Daaad, you'll *never* be as cool as me!"

JP's red Silverado cruised down the chip and sealed back road blaring a country station turned up loud, at Adin's request. Both in their matching sunglasses, Mossy Oak camo jackets Lisa gave them last Christmas, and jeans. It had only taken Adin three tries to finally find an *old* pair of jeans, while JP was surprised to find that his favorite faded pair actually fit, although he had to stab another hole in his belt with the large knife on his hip. And his old hunting boots were a comfortable switch from the combat boots he had been cramming his soggy feet in for the last year or so. Being in something other than his uniform calmed him. He was an *individual* again, like he had his identity back, the freedom to move around and do whatever he wanted, which was a pleasant responsibility.

His heart jumped when he adjusted his seat and reach for his M4 rifle, which wasn't there. Although almost two weeks had passed since he had handed it over to the armorer at Camp Lejeune, a tightness in his chest still existed whenever he went to grab what wasn't there. It had been an extension of his body and being. He carried it wherever he went. He ate with it dangling from his back, slept with it tucked in his sleeping bag or under his cot. It even joined him in the port-a-john, leaning in the corner beside the leftover adult magazines for the marines to share. Without it, he was naked, useless, and wrong. After almost two weeks, he still felt less than whole, less than what he used to be when he had it. Flawed and exposed, he couldn't leave the house without tucking his pistol between the seats.

With the local country music station up loud enough to keep them from talking, Adin's large hazel eyes were glued to the window with thoughts of what he might do if they caught a Bigfoot. *What would he say? What would he look like? Sound like? Smell like?* Amazing adventures filled his head while he daydreamed about making Bigfoot his best friend. He kept a watchful eye out the window, at his father's request, surveying the fields and woods bouncing by, hoping to catch sight of a Sasquatch before they even made it to the Bigfoot capitol of Guernsey County, Ohio: Salt Fork State Park.

Out the window, magical colors swooshed by as they blazed down the winding back roads. It was one of the things JP loved about this time of year in Ohio—when the leaves crinkled and burned to a red, yellow, or orange glow. The final cut of the season had huge bales of hay dotting the fields, which opened up between the woods and hills that made this region one of the best to down an Ohio Big Buck. The bucks were in rut and moving; brown herds clumped in the fields and spooked does darted dangerously from the tree line now and then. Like always, during the colorful crispiness of fall, JP remained extra vigilant for wildlife along the road.

The radio cut from the music to a news update. "Another bizarre mass whale beaching has closed Myrtle Beach, South Carolina—a popular tourist destination for many Ohioans—for the remainder of the season. This marks an unprecedented *third* mass beaching in South Carolina this month. NOAA officials have released another emergency statement about the mass beachings all along the east coast this year."

JP shook his head and turned the radio down. "So, what are you going to do if you see a Bigfoot?" He asked with large eyes.

Adin didn't budge from the window or miss a beat. "Uhhh, try and catch it," he shrugged.

"Catch it? How you gonna do that?"

Adin looked at his father and cocked his head to the side in thought. "Well, I could use you for bait!" he exclaimed, showing the tip of his new front tooth starting to fill in the empty gap.

"Ohhh. Okaaay. I see how this is gonna go down. Just throw old Dad under the bus, huh? Just like that?"

JP reached out and messed up Adin's hair. Since he'd been home, he couldn't stop touching his family. Grandma's warm embrace, Grandpa's leather handshake, the little brushes across Lisa's back in the kitchen as she prepared dinner, or the snuggles on the couch watching TV. JP had missed that small, intimate contact with the ones he loved. And now, as he rubbed his son's head, making his brown hair stand up, he gleamed at the thought of finally being home where he belonged.

Ya know, I can do this. I can hang out with my son. No big deal. I got this.

"Dad, you're a *marine.* You'll know what to do," Adin said, pulling away from his father's hand and stretching out to try to mess up his father's short, sandy hair.

JP leaned toward the window, just out of his son's reach. "Hey now! Don't be messin' with my *fro!*"

Adin laughed. "That's not a fro, Dad. You barely have anything there."

"Gee, thanks. I love you too, *son,*" he tittered.

JP focused back on the curvy road. Up ahead, loose trash piled beside the ditch. His heart jumped as he squeezed the wheel. Without any thought, he swerved sharply to avoid it, making Adin grab hold of the armrest to steady himself.

They rounded the next pot-holed curve in the road, and JP's eyes grew large at all the trash scattered along the right-hand side. Black and white bags, beer cans, and tires tainted the ditch and roadside. It was like spilled paint on a scenic country painting, a scar on the landscape, a black-and-white gash in the beautiful crimson-and-gold carpet that lined their country drive.

His head snapped to the right as he sucked in the dusty wind around him. His boot tapped the brake before mashing down the accelerator, squealing the back tires. The truck swerved sharply to the other lane, speeding toward the cluster of garbage that littered their rustic corridor in a loud cloud of engine and smoke.

"Whoa!" Adin gasped, grabbing hold of the armrest again as his body swayed back and forth.

His father continued accelerating, the exhaust revving as he clung to the left edge of the road. Up ahead, a white plastic bag, stuffed full of *something*, leaned just into the gravel at the edge of the road. JP whipped the wheel again, sending his mud tires down into the shallow ditch. They bumped through the trench, JP stiff in his seat and focused, Adin with each hand on an armrest, bracing himself the best he could.

As soon as they cleared the trash, JP tugged the wheel and swerved his truck back onto the pebbled road. He decelerated both the truck and his heart. His grip on the wheel loosened, as he swallowed the tension in his throat, and took in a breath. But, JP didn't say a thing. He just continued on as if nothing out of the ordinary had happened.

Adin, still clinging to the armrest, took a couple of deep breaths. "Dad, are you drunk!"

JP looked at his son, slightly confused. "What, Bud?"

"Are you drunk? You're swerving all over the road!"

His father's eyes showed a glimpse of panic as he realized what he had just done. That reaction was routine in the world of war he had just come from. But *here*, at home, there were no IEDs or roadside bombs for one to swerve around. At home, there was no kill zone to accelerate through.

Embarrassment filled his face. "Oh! Uhhh, yeah, that…well there was a deer," he said almost convincingly. "You didn't see it?"

"Where?"

"Back there. It jumped out of nowhere." He sounded sure of himself now. "Luckily, we just missed it."

"We did?" Adin was on the edge of believing him.

"Yup. Totally missed it. But, hey! Wasn't that fun?" His face lit up.

Adin's eyes grew larger. "Yeah! Let's do it again!"

"Uhhh, maybe on the way home. Well, only if you promise not to tell your mother." His father winked and smiled.

They finally pulled into the empty, twelve-spaced parking lot at the head of Morgan's Knob Loop trail. JP put the truck in park and turned off the engine. For a moment, they sat there and looked at the painted forest before them. Although JP had *mostly* lost his adolescent excitement for what mysterious things may lurk beyond the safety of open spaces—what dangers and adventures arise from deep down in the crowded belly of the woods—Adin's glowing eyes were wide with wonder.

"Wooow!" he whispered, taking in the tall, rusty trees with the leaves fluttering to the ground.

"Excited?" JP asked. The sparkle on his child's face enthralled him.

"Bigfoot lives in *there?*" Adin asked, taking off his glasses and pressing his nose to the glass.

JP nodded and shrugged. "That's what they say. You ready to go find out?"

"Let's go!" Adin flung open his door, ready to jump out.

"Wait. Wait. Wait. Hold on, I got a little something for ya first."

Adin twisted back into his seat. "Huh? You got me something?"

His father dug into the console for a moment but paused before he pulled his hand out. "Close your eyes."

"Daaaad."

"Come on. Close 'em. No peeking."

"Fiiiine." Adin rolled his eyes before he covered them with a loose hand, unable to contain his toothless grin.

"Adin! I can see you peeking."

His son growled with a frustrated excitement, but then placed both hands tightly over his eyes, overly exaggerating his compliance. His father's face sparkled.

Ornery little shit. "Just like his father." JP heard his wife's teasing voice in his head. He pulled out his hand and held it in front of Adin.

"Can I look?!"

"Not yet."

"Errr." Adin wiggled, barely able to contain himself.

"Wait…. Aw, maaan! I must've left it at home. I guess we'll just have to go back and get it later," he teased.

"Not Funny, Dad!" Adin slowly spread his fingers, seeing something slender in his father's hand. Then he jerked his hands away from his face with a high-pitch squeal. "A knife! You got me a knife!"

A three-inch, black, folding blade on a matching handle and nylon sheath lay in JP's hand.

Adin held out his vibrating hands and waited for his father to give him the knife.

"Now wait a minute, Bud. There's rules," JP said, pulling it back a smidge. "Number one: this is a weapon. You will treat it as such, meaning that you will *not* play with it. Number two: this is a tool. So, treat it like one. This means that you will take care of it, clean it, and make sure that you put it away somewhere safe when you are done with it. And number three: don't hurt yourself! Or your mother will hurt me. Got it?"

Adin's cheeks flushed with excitement. "Got it! I promise! Now can I hold it?"

"Careful, it's sharp." JP placed the knife into his son's hands and admired him as he admired it. "All right. It goes in *and stays in* the sheath, and the sheath goes on your belt."

Adin sheathed the knife and looped it on his belt, staring down at it like it was a piece of gold on his hip. Brimming with happiness, he looked up to his father, who beamed with pride.

"I love it, Dad!" He reached across the seat and hugged his father tightly. "Thank you. Thank you. Thank you. I love you, so much!"

"I love you, too, Little Buddy."

They embraced, hesitant at first. But JP slowly unwound, allowing his son to once again reach his heart with a wistful smile.

"Can we go find Bigfoot now?" Adin pleaded as he let go.

JP glowed as he rubbed his son's head.

"Yeah, let's go get him."

The trail was muddy from a month of above-average autumn rain—a stark contrast to the summer drought that agonized his grandfather and his fields of hay and corn. Many trees had fallen during those recent storms. The chainsawed remnants marked the side of the path in mounds and stacks. Twisted and snapped treetops stuck out like hawk breasts among the limbs, a ripping reminder of what the wind will sometimes do.

Above them, several stubborn leaves, their rustic tinge warm and cozy, barely held onto their limbs. Ahead of JP and Adin, colorful leaflets paved the small path. Adin thought they looked like scraps of construction paper from his Halloween project in school. But to JP, the scattered leaves swirled and fluttered like the trash in the streets of Iraq—only brighter, with a more welcomed and earthy smell.

Adin lagged behind, carefully jumping and stomping his boots beside his father's footprints, with one hand resting on his sheathed knife. Nearly twenty minutes into the woods, and he was already bored from the lack of Bigfoot activity.

"How big do you think Bigfoot's feet are?" Adin asked, noting his were half the size of his father's.

"Well, I don't know, Buddy," JP responded, scanning ahead of them intently. "How big do you think they are?"

Adin jumped forward and landed in his father's muddy treads. "I don't know. Maybe as big as yours, or even bigger?" He squatted and analyzed their tracks.

"You think his foot is *that* big?"

"Dad, he's Bigfoot," Adin declared.

"Okay. Okay." JP nodded, still walking. "But, wait…then maybe *I'm* Bigfoot." He puffed out his chest and stretched his arms to the sky, spinning around like he was suddenly possessed by the spirit of Sasquatch.

But Adin was not all that amused. Instead, he shook his head and rolled his eyes as his father laughed at his own joke.

They continued on the cut path, trekking deeper into the woods. All the noises surrounding him—the shaking leaves, the cracking and bending trees, the squirrels preparing for winter, the flashing birds in his peripheral vision—added to the stress of his hypersensitivity. Even in the woods, Sgt. Grimm couldn't shake the feeling he was on patrol through the dirty streets he'd just come home from. The leaves were trash tumbling across the pavement, or the dark dirt before him. The trees waved and let the sun stream down in columns, like a spotlight for all to see, in the same way the palms shuttered the high sun, with just enough holes in the canopy to burn his heated skin. The deeper they went, the more JP's mind churned up the daunting past.

As squirrels darted from tree trunk to tree trunk, Sgt. Grimm kept his hand close to his knife handle, soon, scolding himself for not carrying his pistol on the trail. He had an eerie feeling they were being watched or followed. *It's all in your head, you idiot*, he thought. But the noises behind him tugged at his imagination. The way the sun and shadows played and danced across the ground took him back to the palm groves along the river. He looked over his shoulder every few steps, not knowing what to expect—an insurgent with a machine gun or a little boy with a grin.

You're with your son in the woods. He arched his back and stretched his neck, trying to shake off the past and feel the present. *You're enjoying the day with him.* That's what he needed to focus on—his son.

"Hey Dad, are Bigfeet dangerous?" Adin asked, right on cue.

"Well, that depends if you're trying to run down the stairs or not." His dad jokes weren't as amusing for his son, but they gave JP a bit of joy.

"Daaaad. I'm serious."

For a moment he imagined what he might do if somehow, someway, a Bigfoot actually jumped out of the brush and attacked them. His hand gripped his knife handle. *I'd kill it.*

"Not as dangerous as me, Buddy." He immediately regretted his words. "So, tell me what all you did while I was away," he said quickly.

"I don't know. Nothin'." Adin jabbed at the mud with a small stick as they walked.

"Nothin'?" He turned with his hands on his hips. "So, you're telling me that you just sat in your room for seven months and did *nothin'?*"

Adin looked up from the mud, bright-eyed, and nodded.

JP snorted and started up the hill in front of them. "Man, that must've been *boring.*"

"No, I just slept the whole time," Adin joked.

"For seven months? Wow! No wonder you've stayed up past your bedtime all week."

Just then, up the hill and beyond their sight, a large branch snapped, startling them both. They froze. Instinctively, Sgt. Grimm raised his closed fist—the signal to freeze while on patrol.

"What was that?" Adin whispered.

"Shhh" Sgt. Grimm's gaze scanned the hilltop.

They hadn't seen another person the whole time they'd been walking. JP figured they were alone in the woods. But uphill, less than a football field away, something big, something heavy lurked, and JP could feel it waiting for them. He reached for his knife and unsheathed it, adjusting a tight grip. Crouching down and peering ahead of them through the trunks and leaves, he saw nothing. No movement up ahead. The woods had fallen into a quiet chill, with only the fall breeze tickling at the back of his neck. He motioned for Adin to crouch down without taking his eyes off the hilltop ahead.

Adin followed his lead, pulling his knife from his sheath and kneeling in the mud with wide eyes and a tight chest. For him, the first ten minutes of the hike, every noise had been Bigfoot. But then, after Adin had yelled "Bigfoot!" for the twenty-eighth time as a squirrel skittered across the leaves, his father had said, "When Bigfoot wants you to know he's around, then you will *know* he's around."

A tingle rose on JP's shoulders as footsteps came from the top of the hill. *Or was it thrashing? A deer? No, too loud for a deer. A squirrel? Couldn't be. No, those are definitely footsteps.* And then, a low murmur, perhaps a growl.

The adrenaline pumped through JP as he crept behind a tree, Adin tucked behind him. It was like the time in the desert when they climbed a small, rocky hill and heard movement on the other side of the crest. At the top, with sweat pouring and hearts thumping, they found an ISIS machine-gun team setting up in the dirt overlooking the village below. Sgt. Grimm's hot lead had shredded their flesh, turning their brown skin red in the glowing sun.

It's an ambush! It's definitely an ambush!

"Stay close," he said to Adin through gritted teeth, turning to look at his son.

Adin didn't recognize his sharp, mean face, and slivered eyes. He returned his gaze with a blank stare.

Adin's oval eyes and open mouth reminded JP of PFC Smalls. Fresh from the School of Infantry, Smalls had frozen during his first firefight instead of taking cover behind the wall. Back then, Sgt. Grimm had to pull him down to the dirt and shout some sense into his head.

Now, Sgt. Grimm grabbed Adin's arm and pulled him ahead to a bigger tree trunk. "Don't look at me like that!" he snapped. "Wipe that look off your face and come on!"

"Dad! What is it?" Adin cried in a whisper.

"Shhh, they're coming." Sgt. Grimm ducked low behind the tree with his knife gripped tight in his hand and his son pressed behind him with his other.

The footsteps came closer. Louder. Only ten yards away and coming down the hill toward them. Sgt. Grimm bent lower, crouched, and readied himself to pounce, if he needed to. He was concealed behind the trunk, just off the path, waiting for them to pass, or to turn and fight.

Tears began to well in Adin's eyes, but Sgt. Grimm didn't notice as the voices were nearly upon them.

The footsteps came to a shuffled stop. "Hey!" a man's voice yelled. "Hey! You! What are you doing?"

Sgt. Grimm trembled with rage and hate. His knuckles glowed white and red as they squeezed down on the blade's handle. He shut his eyes and leaned his head back against the tree, his breath troubled and edgy.

"Hey! Hey, are you okay?" the man's rusty voice shouted.

"Oh, my God! He's hurt, Tim. Help him!" a woman shrieked.

"Dad! Dad!" Adin shook his father's shoulder.

But Sgt. Grimm was in another place. A place where death was a day's work, and blood was the color in their eyes. A place where everything was a threat, even the trash, the trail they walked, or the scuffling of shoes along a path—it was all poison, and his head was pumping it full into his heart. With his eyes squeezed shut, his breath labored, JP pressed himself deep into the tree, as if it were a bunker he needed to burrow into.

"Sir, are you okay?" The graying man was hesitant but reached out for JP's shoulder.

JP banged the back of his head off of the tree with his pulse. He didn't respond or acknowledge the present situation. He simply and methodically thrust his head against the bark like the beat of a drum.

Adin stood up, crying. "Stop! Stop it, Dad!" He grabbed for his father's head to keep it from hitting the tree.

"Hey, Buddy, what's wrong? Do you need some help?" The man reached out to take the knife from JP's hand.

Sgt. Grimm's eyes flung open. "Don't touch it!"

The words startled the gentleman, and he stumbled back with his hands up. "Okay. Okay. I'm sorry. I just thought you needed some help," he said, still backing away. "You're okay then? Should I call someone?"

Confused, JP looked around at the trees swaying in the wind, and the yellow-ribboned leaves swishing all around him. He searched his body with his hands, patting his chest, arms, and legs. Nothing amiss. When he looked over at Adin, still crying, the blood drained from his face. His chest flexed with anger and embarrassment. "Uh, yeah. Yeah. I'm sorry. I'm good," he stuttered out, reaching for his boy's face and wiping away his tears. Blinking, he looked down at the knife in his hand, bit the inside of his lip, and quickly sheathed it. With a deep breath, he labored to his feet and brushed himself off.

"Yeah. Yeah, I'm fine," he forced a friendly smile. "Thanks. It's uhh, it's my asthma. I forgot my inhaler." He kicked at leaves, rubbing the back of his head.

"Dad?" Adin sniffled and wrapped himself around his father's leg, squeezing for dear life.

"Sorry about that, Buddy. My asthma…" his voice trailed off as he brushed his son's hair back off his forehead.

Chapter Six

Beer with Grandpa

We stood like soldiers there in
the chill of November's morning,
guarding our feast with loaded cans
aiming to kill the boredom. I was still
shaking off the clouds of late night
rompings; you were just getting started.

But the Bud Lights went down like
the bottled water that Grandma said we
should've had, their nipping cans biting
at our fingers. I watched you pull out
the work gloves from both sides of your
flannel jacket, and I slid the camouflaged
koozie from my torn jeans' back pocket.
We both grinned with our preparedness.

Around us was your home, my playground;
twelve acres of woods and rolling hills, all
gray with the coming winter. In back, the
raspberry patch we nibble in midsummer's
heat; where you had once laughed when I
unfolded the knife from my left hip pocket
and picked at the seeds in my teeth.

Down the hill stood the chicken coop we
built. And when the wind blew South, we
could smell your cherished brood. But there
between us, the deep fryer was warm, fifty
feet from your stained brown wraparound
porch. The peanut oil bubbling, smoking,
and blending with our breath; It smelled of
fall, family, and giving.

We talked of the days we both could
remember; all our cars and trucks that you
fixed, the chickens we plucked from the
pines at night, the front porch coons you

shot and the one that you missed (and
stubbornly, you still say that I fouled up
those sights of that old twenty-two, which
now sits on the top notch of my built-it-
myself gun rack).

Later, when we stand around a full table of
bread, and I call on you and you call on me
to give our grace, I will bow my head and
listen as you thank Him for our food, family,
and freedom, while I silently give thanks for
you and this morning's company.

"I don't know, Grandpa. Maybe I'm just losing it?" JP took a swig from his
camouflaged, koozie-covered Bud Light and then picked at the tab back and
forth. "I mean, I really scared Adin…those people…myself."

Grandpa lounged on the front-porch swing in his red flannel jacket with a
greasy work glove wrapped around a can of sweating Bud Light. JP, in a hooded
Brown's sweatshirt and backward camo hat, sat at the foldout table that was days
away from being put away in the attic for winter. Although it was a warm night,
JP was still adjusting to the climate swap, and to him, fifty-five degrees wasn't far
off from freezing.

Grandpa's glasses reflected the sparkle of the setting sun. His high-and-tight
flattop haircut hadn't changed since his two tours in Vietnam. Matter of fact, the
picture of him on the mantle above the downstairs fireplace in his dress blues
first perked JP's interest in the marines. That and one of his grandpa's old war
stories, which stuck with him, especially on the day he raised his right hand and
swore his own oath to support and defend the Constitution of the United States.
It was a story about the time his platoon fought off a company of Vietcong from
overrunning a small village that had shown favor to him and his men. JP never
forgot the emotion in his grandfather's eyes and the firmness of his voice, though
it cracked just a little every time he'd say "And not one damned innocent soul
was lost that day in the village. Not one. But Hell was paid for with blood and
grit, I can promise you that." Back then, JP would believe anything his
grandfather told him, and his story of protecting the innocent was one which
inspired him to enlist.

His grandpa gulped down a big swallow and gazed at the different tools nailed
to the dark wood siding of the porch area: two long scythes, one to each side of
the storm door, like welcoming pillars; a ribbed washboard; a rusty corn grinder;
several sizes of handsaws—some with big teeth, some with small, some with one
handle and some made for two; rusty hammers for nailing; hammers for clawing;

and hammers for pounding metal into the ground. All antique hand tools from a time when hands were harder and wills were stronger. His grandfather had used every single one of them building the farm. But as they grew old and tired, much like himself, he nailed them to the wall to honor their service of building his Heaven on Earth. Unlike those retired tools, his grandfather refused to hang himself up to be admired.

Even so, JP admired him and sought nothing more than a little conversation with a man who had so much to tell with only a few words.

"You see that right there?" Grandpa lifted his chin toward a sickle with a small, taped, wooden handle and a thin crescent blade with a hint of patina.

"What? The hand saw?" JP sipped his beer, intent on listening to some of his grandfather's old wisdom and advice.

"No. No, that beautiful sickle there beside it," he said, pointing with his beer.

"Uh-huh. Yeah." He studied it for a moment. "Wait, isn't that one of the tools you told me never to touch again, back when Danny would come over, and we'd chop down saplings and build tree forts?"

His grandfather chuckled. "Yeah. Yeah, it is. But I'm pretty sure, at one time or another, I said that about *all* my tools."

They laughed and took a drink. The swing moaned as the old war veteran rocked gently back and forth. JP leaned forward, one hand on his beer, the other holding his head up. A barn owl hooted from the loft of the old barn, and the doves whistled as they took flight from the under the bird feeders, chased off by the outside cat that caught more birds than mice and chipmunks. The clink of dishes being put away chimed down the stairs from the kitchen, where his grandmother was cleaning up from dinner. The hens roosted in the coop as the evening faded, the dark edges of the curtain closing on another day. Another chance to reap what they had sown, one more opportunity to forgive the debts of those who did them wrong, to laugh with family, to sit and converse about the weather, the good beer, the old times, or those rusty tools. The day was ending, but not without one last lesson before the lamp turned out.

"That there was a gift," Grandpa started slowly.

The reminiscent stare and glow of his grandfather in thought prepared JP for another one of his stories. He was ready for that. Matter of fact, JP *needed it.*

"Some friend that was," JP quipped.

His grandfather snorted and took a drink. "Well, you see, it was in Vietnam. My last tour of duty. We were a month away from going home…."

JP stiffened, an unconscious action of respect that may have been drilled into him by his drill instructors, or probably even before that, by his grandparents.

His grandfather inhaled deeply, coughed out the air, and labored it back in. "You all right?"

"Yeah, I'm fine. This damn weather." He tipped his head back and guzzled half his beer. "Anyway, as I was saying, we were about a month away from coming home. We had already lost so many men, so many young men." His eyes glazed over in thought. "There was this village. Just a small village, only a dozen huts or so tucked in between two hills. Well, they were good people. They shared their food, their shelter," he leaned forward with a whisper and a wink, "their women."

"Grandpaaa. C'mon." JP shook his head, smiling. "Nobody wants to hear about that!"

The old man bounced in his seat, laughing quietly. Then, he looked off into the night a moment before he spoke again. "Now, I never found any comfort in the arms of another woman, even in the face of death. No. That wasn't me." He paused and winked. "But boy, I sure did enjoy those stories!" He finished off his beer and crinkled the can, an unspoken request for another one.

"Grandpa!" JP chuckled, finished his beer, and stood up. "I'll get it."

The storm door screeched as he pulled it open, walked inside, and grabbed two more beers from the fridge along the wall.

"Didn't you already tell me about the village, like a thousand times?" JP pushed the door open with his back.

"Well, I haven't told you this part." Grandpa reached out for the beer, a sadness lingering around his gray brows. "I never told you *everything*."

JP offered to crack open his beer.

"No, I got it." He pulled the folding penknife from his jacket pocket and cracked the tab open, pulling it the rest of the way up with a shaky hand. "I haven't completely told you the truth about that," he admitted as JP sat back down and sipped his beer. "You were just a kid back then. I couldn't tell you the full story." He took a long drink. "But now, now I think you might be ready to hear it."

JP wiggled to the edge of his seat. *Had grandpa lied about the one story that resonated with me all through my childhood? What didn't he tell me? What did he leave out?* His mind sped through what could be different about the story that inspired him to follow in his grandfather's footsteps. *Did Grandpa lie about the village? Was there even a village at all? What the hell, Grandpa?*

"Wait a minute, Grandpa. You didn't lie to me about the village, did you?"

His grandfather leaned back in the swing with one arm stretched across the back, the other holding his beer on his belly. He crossed one leg over the dirty hand streaks glaring in the porch light as the laces of his dusty work boots nearly reaching the sole—they sort of just waved at JP as he rocked back and forth. Grandpa's gaze studied the old, rustic sickle sitting on bent nails. His hazy blue eyes seemed sad, hurt even, and a bit misty in the corners.

He cleared his throat. "Her name was Quang. It meant *pure* in Vietnamese— couldn't have been much older than eleven or twelve. She would chase our patrol with her friends, laughing the whole way when we came through. Sometimes, she would pass out Lotus flowers whenever we stopped to gather intel." His gaze shifted around a moment until it fell on his beer, where it stayed even after he took another drink. "When we found her down by the river, washed up not far from where we had stopped for chow, she was barely alive and completely naked. They had beaten her bloody, raped her, and slit her throat. Her feet were cut to hell, shredded in her escape."

JP shuttered as he sucked in the evening air. He couldn't imagine the courage and strength of that little girl to endure what she did and make it as far as she had. "Damn," he whispered, scratching at the top of his beer with a dirty fingernail.

His grandfather had stopped swinging, and now his leg shook up and down. "The corpsman patched her up the best he could, and I carried her the whole way back to the village. The look on her father's face, her mother's cries, their grief, and sorrow…" His chest shivered as he breathed. "It broke me. Something inside of me snapped."

JP exhaled. "Completely understandable. I think it would break any decent human being, Grandpa."

The can of beer in his grandfather's hand cracked and popped as he squeezed it. "You don't understand," he said in a deep, edgy whisper. "*I snapped.* I lost my composure. I saw red. Rage. I lost a little part of me, seeing what they did to that little girl…seeing her bloody, limp, naked body, knowing what they did to her…I lost whatever good was still inside of me, JP."

"That's not true at all, Grandpa! You're the best man I know! Raising me the way you did, loving Lisa as your own, giving us a place to live, love, and hope. Grandpa, you give us *love* and *hope*. You *are* a good man. And there's nothing that you could do or could've done that would change that."

His grandfather finished his beer and just stared past his grandson into the coming darkness. His face was tired, as if it had seen a lifetime of fighting. And he wasn't talking to JP when he spoke next, more like he was confessing to the Lord. Or maybe he was just letting it be heard out loud, as if that may have lifted the burden from his chest and freed him from the pull and tug of all the pain.

"We tracked them all. Slaughtered them. Cut them down with hot lead and steel. All but one. That poor bastard we dragged back to Quang's father. I watched as he took his sickle and hacked at that young man until his head rolled free from his shoulders." He wiped a tear from his eye.

"Well deserved, if you ask me." JP tipped back his beer, finished it, and clanked it down.

His grandfather glared at the sickle once more, took in a deep breath, coughed, and tried to contain it. He wiped his mouth on his sleeve and nodded at the dull tool. "He gave me that sickle as a *thank you*," his grandfather's raspy voice admitted. He huffed and shook his head. "It didn't matter one damn bit, anyway. A week later, the whole village was gunned down by an enemy patrol that found the body and the bandages the corpsman left behind." His jaw flexed as he crushed his can.

JP sat still and quiet. He had never seen his grandfather like this before. Although they were close, his grandfather had never revealed this side of the war to his grandson, never shared this kind of pain with him. Besides, Grandpa was a man's man, as durable as leather, as tough as iron, gritty and solid. But it wasn't like he didn't show emotion. Or that he didn't have a soft side. Matter of fact, JP had never known a man more loving and caring. Like the time he picked through his gun safe and sold his old M1 Garand the summer JP came up a little short to buy the rusty Chevy he'd worked so hard for. Or when JP busted that bully in the nose for constantly tormenting one of the freshmen nerds in his gym class, and instead of getting punished at home, his grandpa told him a story about what a sheepdog is used for. His grandfather was a part of a rare and dying breed, and one that JP hoped to become someday.

But now he studied the old man's face, full of anguish and regret. Each wrinkled line represented a scar across his humbled heart from years of carrying around more responsibility than most could muster. His eyes, a deep blue, flowed like the Pacific. His chin was scratched and bristled, aged in the wind and dust of his crop fields. His ears were red and chilled, not as clear as they used to be, but still able to hear the call of the wild or Mother Nature's stern warnings. And on his face shimmered a tear. A soft, sparkling drop of the past that made its way past his glasses and over his five o'clock shadow, until he caught it with the back of his wrist.

"You know," he said without looking up over the creak of the swing. "I often pass by that blade and see a glimpse of the past that still quickens my breath to this day. Maybe I should've taken it down years ago. But it just didn't seem right to run from the things that made me who I am."

JP flinched and glared at the table. Those words struck a nerve. And when he finally looked up again, his grandfather was pleading with mercy in his eyes.

"JP, we can't change the things we've done or seen." His voice was gaining strength. "And it doesn't matter one bit if we could. That's not why we're here. We're here to learn from our wounds. You understand?" He cocked his head and waited.

JP didn't know if his grandfather wanted him to answer or not. So, he slowly nodded his head as he thought about the meaning of his words. *Learn from my wounds. What the hell am I supposed to learn from not protecting Joey and my brothers? What could I possibly learn from failing to do my duty?*

His grandfather noticed the tremble in the corners of his grandson's clenched jaw, the painful squint of his glistening bloodshot eyes. "Son, you'll never grow old and wise if you don't allow things to pass. There's a reason behind every single thing that happens in our lives. I can promise you that."

JP's throat tingled. "How can there be a reason for so much pain? So much *guilt?*"

Grandpa nodded. "It's good to feel the pain. That lets you know you're still capable of feeling. And *guilt?* Hell, we're all guilty of *something*. We're all just the sum of the things we should've done or should not have done. We're all just stocks of grain in the wind, JP. We go where we go, we bend where we bend, and if it's our time to break, then we break. But you can't just let yourself bleed out because you think that you deserve it."

"I do!" JP slapped the table with his fist. "I do deserve it! Why should I be alive? Why should I be the one to come home when better men didn't? Why? Why me?" He paused to choose his words more carefully and bring the volume down a notch. "Grandpa, why did I hesitate? Why didn't I just pull the damn trigger like I'd done so many times before? Why wasn't I strong enough to trust my gut and take that child's life before he took theirs?" JP held his head in his hands and sobbed.

His grandfather grunted and coughed his way out of the swing and over to the table where he sat down. He clenched JP's hand in his. "You feel that?" he said, squeezing as tight as he could until JP jerked his hand back in pain.

"Yeah! Yeah, I can feel it! What the hell, Grandpa?" he replied, rubbing his hand, confused.

"Good. Then you know you're still alive. You know you still have a purpose. Don't you dare let them die in vain," he said with a thick finger in his face. "That's how you get by. That's how you get through it. You honor them by doing better…by doing all the things they can no longer do. You raise a family, you love, you give, you be kind and firm. You do *good.* Because doing anything less than that is like spitting on their grave. You got it?"

Through his watery eyes, JP glimpsed the sincerity on the face of the man who taught him to be the best *him* he could be. The man who would not settle nor let *him* settle for anything less than the best version of himself. For a moment, JP felt ashamed, like he had let his grandfather down or that he was too weak to be able to be the man that he'd raised him to be.

But his grandfather, always able to read JP like clouds in the sky, reassured him. "Son, do you have any idea how proud I am of you?" He met him eye to eye with a firm hand on his shoulder. "I'm so proud of you. I'm so proud of the man you became. I need you to know that. To know that I love you. That I always will. No matter what you've done, or what you haven't done, or what you think you *should've done.* It doesn't matter one damn bit to me. I will always love you for the man I know you are, for the man I raised you to be. Understand?"

JP stood up slowly, arms stretching out toward his grandfather, who on weary feet was ready to catch him. Right there, under the rising crescent moon and pinhole stars, two men, two generations, two warfighters, two marines, and two aching hearts embraced.

When they finally pulled apart, both had damp, red faces. They wiped at them like men do when they don't want their feelings to show.

"Damn it, how about we go see if Grandma saved us any pie?" Grandpa said.

JP held the door for the old man, who bent slightly at the waist as he worked his way into the hefty, two-story farmhouse.

He patted his grandfather on the back as he went by. "I'll grab us another beer."

"No. No. I'm fine, thanks. Grandma would have my ass if I had another one."

From the kitchen at the top of the stairs, JP's grandmother hollered, "You're damn right, I would! No more beer, Grandpa!"

His grandfather turned back from the bottom of the stairs with a sly grin. "See. I can't get away with anything." And he winked as he disappeared around the staircase wall and creaked his way up the hardwood steps.

JP shook his head in amazement at his grandparents and their lasting marriage. Nearly sixty years together, and they were still best friends, still knew each other better than they knew themselves. He warmed with the thought of wanting that same kind of lasting marriage and loving, silly relationship with his wife when they got old and ornery.

"Well, I'm gonna have one more," he said loud enough for both his grandparents to hear. "Because I'm not whipped like Grandpa!"

He cheesed from ear to ear, opened the fridge to a full bottom shelf of neatly lined Bud Light cans, and pulled out his fourth of the night.

Ain't nobody gonna tell me how many beers I can have. He sassed to himself.

Chapter Seven

Where We Come From

Mostly empty Old Milwaukee cans, stashed in the garage
behind the WD-40 and lined quarts of oil,
clamor from this year's litter of curious Calico kittens.

And there's new, stubborn, Slovak blood
rolling down the old stains on Grandpa's smeared
and greasy knuckles.

But he just grunts like the buck at the backyard apple tree,
where he built cousin Ju-Ju's square plywood tree fort
that now gives shelter to a lost Nerf football and a few
forgotten G.I. JOE army men;

there was a time,
back before he had us grandkids searching faithfully
for "purple-assed-buzzards,"
that he would have cursed at the pain of a slipped wrench
on a buddy's rusted old Chevy,

back when the pain of hard labor could still make new scars,
like the blizzard of '77, when the water pipes froze solid
and he lumbered out into the wind and fury, both before
and after work, to stretch a garden hose across the driveway
in order for his little girls to take a cold shower.

Or, back when Grandma's open heart would carry in
another stray animal, or another friend without a place to go,
back when the guest bedroom was always full, and no mouth
would go unfed, unless it was hers or his;

A cursing time, but a blessing time;
when he taught little girls how to feed the horses, peacocks,
and chickens before school, so that they could run off to class
learning how to live with the shit on their shoes;

or how to get dirt and blisters on their hands,
shoveling out the chicken coop into five-gallon buckets

to fertilize the sweet peas and cabbage;

or plucking bloody feathers from a freshly axed hen for dinner,
and standing on a bucket at the sink in the garage
washing out the gizzards and thumbing off dried shit from
those brown speckled eggs with a grease bubbled bar of Lava soap.

The same eggs that were gathered on the ice or in the mud,
both morning and night. Then, sending them off in saved cartons
to church, neighbors, or school, to those who needed them more
than a house of half-full stomachs.

"There is always someone who is less fortunate than you."

I remember Grandma would often remind us, while ignoring another
one of my temper tantrums on the floor of Kroger's candy aisle
as we filled church Christmas baskets; or, back then, when she had
to cash in her silver certificates in order to buy Pamra's new braces.

But now, here in the garage, Grandpa's new greasy bubbles,
on the same green bar of soap, turn my small, dirty-fingernailed
hands gray while I watch him wipe that still stubborn, Slovak blood
dry on Aunt Penny's new birthday flannel.

And the dogs are barking at mom walking across the hill,
while Grandma is sweeping leaves from the chairs and swing
on the patio, as more familiar faces sling gravel up the drive;

their hatches filled with homemade pie, pagachi, and corn on the cob
for the fire. The cousins are dressed too nicely in their collared shirts
and bright sneakers;

and later, we will be scolded for our creek-soaked shoes
and grass-stained jeans, swinging at lightning bugs with sticks,
and bragging about sleeping in the tent all night,

but waking up, instead, at the foot of Grandpa's snoring bed
in Aunt Patti's old basketball sweats.

As JP stomped his way up the stairs and into his grandmother's kitchen, the
warm scent of cinnamon and apples took him back to his after-school bartering

days when he'd sweet-talk Grandma into a slice of pie before dinner—as long as he promised not to tell Grandpa. The childhood smell stirred a memory of the time he and his buddies busted out the window of an old abandoned home down the lane and stole some rusty hand tools from the basement. She made him return the tools, clean up the glass, nail a piece of plywood over the hole, and handwrite an apology letter to Mrs. Patterson's daughter in Akron. Although Mrs. Patterson's daughter never replied, the lesson about the consequences of his actions was never forgotten.

The stairway led into the dining room, which blended between the open kitchen and living room. The scarlet and pearl-dotted wallpaper was as old as the creaking kitchen table that gave a little whenever someone leaned on it. Not much had changed since his childhood, except for the long wall to his right, which was covered in family pictures of vacations, sports, and birthdays. Various farm-themed knickknacks and wall-hangers or grandparent quotables filled the spaces between the photos. His favorites were the two hand-painted, pallet-wood signs he picked up at the Buffalo Trade Days flea market, which read: *There's no love like that of a Grandma*, and *I get my hard head from my Grandpa*.

Over the years, they had amassed many walls of gifts such as those from JP, his humble attempt at showing his appreciation for the way they pushed their grief aside to take on his own after the tragic death of his parents. They absorbed his anger, pain, confusion, and tantrums from a desolate child who couldn't understand why his friends were able to have young, active parents who would take them to the park and play, when *his* mostly worked long, hard hours on the farm.

His heart fluttered each time he climbed those noisy stairs and strolled along the wall of memories, smiling at old photographs of the family that taught him how to love when hate was all he knew. It was a custom that often overtook him by habit and nostalgia before he'd settle into his spot at the dining room table across from the wall. A table that showed its age in scars, but which held a vast understanding of all the stories, tears, and love that had been shared around it.

JP set his beer down at *his spot* above the rooster placemat at the end of the oval table and kept walking. Sliding his fingers along the chipped curve of the wood grain, he drifted toward the drywall beside the closet door where his height was marked in blue and black ink. A reminiscent grunt escaped his pinched lips as he remembered the last time his grandmother made him stand with his back against the wall, as she slid a blue pen across the top of his head. It was the day before he left for bootcamp. Even though he had tried to convince her he was too old for such a silly thing, she insisted, and he obliged. Then two inches above the blue line, she wrote in red pen, *Must be THIS tall to complain to Grandma*. Standing there now, he turned and pressed his back against the wall, stretched his neck high, and marked the top of his head with his finger, turning again to chuckle at the phrase.

"Well?" his grandmother challenged as she pulled the steaming pie from the oven and hurried it to the stovetop. The brown juices bubbled from the fork holes as she waved away the steam with a green, knitted pot holder her daughter had made for her in high school. Even with wrinkled skin and thinning, dyed hair, she was still a beautiful woman. Her round face and kind, hazel eyes invited all to feel welcomed and loved. Her purpose came from caring for others, especially in the kitchen. An active woman, even in her seventies, she enjoyed walks down the gravel drive to the end of the lane, where she would pick colorful weeds along the creek bank and call them "flowers." Classic in every sense and quick-witted, she made the rules at the Grimm Farm, though Grandpa denied it.

"Just a hair short." He winked, walking back into the kitchen, and leaned over the stove, sniffing in the steam rising above the brown-spotted crust. "But who could complain about something as wonderful as this?"

"Hey! Get outta there!" She slapped him playfully with the pot holder. "Aren't you forgetting something, young man?" She presented her cheek and tapped it for him to kiss.

"Oh yeah. Hey, Grandma, I didn't even see you there," he joked before pecking her cheek.

"Uh-huh. Sure." She smacked him again and shooed him away. "Go. Get out of here. Have a seat with Grandpa. I'll bring you a slice."

"Well, you *definitely* won't hear me complain about that."

He chuckled as he walked to his seat. Grandpa emerged from the hallway, coughing and clearing his throat after washing his hands, which he was still drying on his black and gray flannel shirt.

"That's not sounding so good, Grandpa," JP stated, blindly cracking open his beer and placing it in his camo koozie.

"Ahh." His grandfather waved him off, taking a seat opposite him. "It's just a little cough. I'll be fine."

"It's not *just a little cough*," Grandma scolded, setting down a piece of pie and scoop of melting vanilla ice cream in front of JP. "He's been hacking all through the night, keeping this poor woman wide awake while I lay there thinking about maybe smothering him with my pillow." She scooped a smaller slice of pie on a plate and carried it over to Grandpa. As he reached for it, she pulled the plate away and tapped her precious cheek until he leaned in and kissed it.

"I'm just kidding, darling. I could *never* do that to you." She smirked and winked across the table at her grandson, who shook his head and laughed to himself at their back-and-forth teasing.

"Hey, woman!" Grandpa grunted back. "Where's *my* ice cream?"

Grandma was already at the stove and cutting herself a slice before she responded. "A man as sweet as yourself doesn't need any ice cream, Dear."

Grandpa grumbled, huffed, and dug into his pie with his fork, letting the steam twist above the oozing apple filling.

JP, still chuckling, quickly wiped the smile from his face. "Wait. Then how come I got ice cream?"

Grandma shrugged, bringing red faces to them all.

Just then, JP's phone rang. Pulling it from his pocket, he read Lovely Lisa on the screen. For the first time all evening, he felt like he was in trouble.

"It's the wife. Just a minute," he announced, gulping down the rest of his beer before lifting the phone to his ear.

From the stove, Grandma shared a concerned glance with Grandpa. After all these years, it wasn't difficult to know what the other was thinking. After all, she had lived her husband's "drinking days" right along with him after the war. She saw that same spirit in the man sitting across from her husband now. And her sad eyes showed her heartache for the broken man that drank at her table.

"Hey, Babe." His words were overdone.

"Hey," her soft, sweet voice rang with concern. "Where are you?"

"Shit! I forgot to tell ya, didn't I? I'm at Grandpa's. Finished the chores a little early, wanted to chit chat."

Grandma pressed her hand gently on his shoulder and kissed the top of his head. "Tell her hello for us."

He glanced up as she sat down at the table between him and his grandfather, who was happily shoving pie into his face. "They say hello."

"Heyyy," she said, still treading lightly around the circumstance of her husband disappearing without saying a word.

His grandfather coughed deeply, a rattle within his chest, and he gasped for air afterward. "Is everything okay over there?" Lisa asked.

JP silently questioned his grandfather with arching brows, but Grandpa waved him off as he caught his breath and wiped his mouth clean on a napkin. Shaking his head at his grandfather, JP just shoved another bite of pie into his mouth. With closed eyes of pure joy, he savored the moment before he answered. "Yeah, everything's fine. Why?" He mumbled.

"I could hear him hacking up a lung over there," she paused, and JP sensed there was more, so he simply chewed and listened. "And, well, I was worried. I wasn't sure where you were. And, I guess, after the other day…I was just a little worried, that's all."

He swallowed loudly. "I'm sorry. I completely forgot to let you know."

She sighed. "No worries! Are you coming back anytime soon? Dinner's ready."

Even in the blurred edges of a few beers, JP knew her tone meant more than her words. Reloading his mouth, his chewing slowed as he looked down at what was left of his pie and tried to swallow half the bite so he could answer. "Dinner?"

"Yeah. Dinner. Remember? I told you I was making stir-fry. To, you know, cheer you up from the other day." Her choppy words marked a tinge of agitation.

"You did?" JP set his fork down and it made a loud clatter.

"JP! Are you eating right now?"

He looked around at Grandma and Grandpa for help, but they were doing their best to stay focused on their own plates.

"Uhmm. Nooo?"

"JP!"

"Okay. Okay. *Maybe*. All right, yes! I'm sorry. Grandma made me."

Grandma scorned him with a side-glance.

"She made pie!" He got defensive and then apologetic. "You know it's my kryptonite. Want me to bring some home? I can. I will. I love you."

"Baaabe, are you even still hungry? Should we start without you?"

Again, he pleaded to his grandparents with a playful but desperate look, hoping they would save him. But they stayed clear. They knew better.

"No. No. It's okay. I'll be right over."

"Okay. Well, hurry while it's hot."

"Babe, I'll be right there. I'm leaving now. Don't worry."

"All right. See you in a minute. Love you."

"You too." He hung up and instantly regretted his last choice of words.

Grabbing his plate, he stood up, knocking his chair to the floor as he stumbled out of it. "Whoops," he bent down to grab it and dropped his fork to the floor. "Whoops, again," he giggled to himself and teetered to the sink, where he stuffed the last couple bites into a full mouth before splashing his plate with a spurt of water.

As he turned away from the sink, his grandmother cleared her throat with a motherly exaggeration.

He stopped in his tracks and spun back around. "Oh yeah, my bad," he said, before rinsing his plate properly and putting it in the dishwasher.

"I gotta go. Dinner's ready." He wiped his hands on the towel beneath the sink but had trouble placing it back on the rod. Grandma's glance at Grandpa had concern all over it as JP walked over to the table, shook his empty beer can, and frowned. "Okay if I grab one for the road?" he asked.

His grandfather swallowed hard and pointed at the clock on the wall with his fork. "I think you've had plenty for the night, don't you?"

"Oh great. Now *you're* gonna get on my case too? I thought we were on the sssame team?" he slurred.

"I'm just–" The cough came on strong this time, growing deep and long, concerning both Grandma and JP. Grandma dropped her fork and pat Grandpa on the back. It didn't help. Grandpa held a napkin to his mouth, trying to hold back the deep rumble in his chest. His face grew red as he hacked and wheezed, looking like he struggled to breathe.

"You all right? You okay, Grandpa? Jesus. Do we need to call someone?" JP stood at his side, trying to comfort him.

"Just breathe, honey. Breathe for me. Come on," Grandma encouraged him, patting his back to no prevail.

The veins stood out on his neck and head. His body shook. His bloodshot eyes bulged. He gasped for air.

"I'm calling 9-1-1!" Grandma rushed to grab her phone from the white countertop.

JP stayed by his grandfather's side as he sucked in shallow air and wheezed it back out again.

"Twenty minutes?" Grandma shouted into the phone. "That's the best you can do?" One hand trembled at her brow and the other pressed the phone to her ear. She surveyed her husband and shook her head. "No. No. Twenty minutes won't work! He can barely breathe!" she yelled into the phone. And then: "I am calm!"

"We can't wait," JP said, balancing himself on the back of the chair beside his grandfather, who seemed to have backed away from the verge of explosion, but he still couldn't catch his breath. "I'll take him. It'll be quicker."

"No, you've been drinking!" his grandmother barked, and then aimlessly ended the call so she could be more in control and tend to her husband.

"I'm fine," JP said. "Help me get him up."

Together, they carefully helped Grandpa down the stairs and out into JP's truck. The coughing fit had left him weak and short of breath. He laid his head back against the head rest, too tired to talk and his breath labored.

"You be careful!" Grandma instructed as she hugged her grandson. "I'll be there shortly."

JP hit the gas, and gravel flung against the porch steps as he peeled out of the drive. A cloud of red taillight dust billowed behind his Silverado as they bounced over potholes and slid around the bends on loose gravel. His grip was tight, his focus on point. But his timing was off, his vision delayed, and he didn't see the deer beside the road until it jumped out in front of his headlights.

He slammed the brakes and jerked the wheel. His grandfather, not harnessed with a seatbelt, flung forward but caught himself with his arm against the dash. The truck started to fishtail, and the ripping tires spit gravel from side to side. Before either of them could react, JP skidded to the side and slammed bumper-first into the ditch. The truck came to a hard rest with its front bumper buried in the bank.

Among the fall crickets and sparkling stars pinpricking the purple darkness above, the red truck fell still in the middle of a steamy, dirty fog. His headlights glared against the bank and a cluster of trees stood like a wall between the gravel road and the countryside. Dust poured through the beams, making tiny specks, like glitter, flickering brightly in the black night. Only the melody of the evening crickets and the groaning of both men gave life to the night. They stirred and shifted back into their seats.

"Aww shit! You okay, Grandpa?" JP grunted and rubbed at the lump forming on the side of his head.

His grandfather hacked at the dust filtering in through the cracks and vents of the truck tilted front first into the roadside ditch. "Jesus Christ!" he forced between the grimacing and clutching of his convulsing chest.

"These fucking deer! I wish we could shoot 'em all!" JP flexed his jaw, and the hostility pinched on his face glowed in the dashboard lights. He ripped his gearshift into reverse and stomped on the gas. His tires spun, and the truck jerked backward. It hesitated and rocked forward when it couldn't clear the ditch. "God dammit!" JP jerked his shifter into drive and crept up against the bank before jamming it into reverse and stomping on the pedal once again. The truck spun backward a little farther than the last time, but it stopped and rolled forward when he let off the accelerator.

In the passenger seat, his grandfather tightly gripped the seatbelt strap, now across his chest, as he struggled to take in air. His face turned red again as he coughed and focused on trying to catch his breath.

JP growled in frustration. "Hang on, Grandpa! Come on now! Hang on!"

Determined, JP coasted the truck forward a little quicker for momentum, and just as his bumper banged against the bank, he shifted and hit the gas. The tires spit gravel and dirt that rattled off the wheel-well and splattered across the road. His truck arched up over the bank until it freed itself from the ditch. JP stomped the brakes and whipped the wheel, shining the headlights back down the dusty road. His engine roared, jerking the truck forward, as a black plume billowed from the tailpipe.

<u>Chapter Eight</u>

Living Out Loud

Life—

how quiet
we are
at a time
when disturbance

is needed.

The hospital was an ugly place. A square concrete building with square rooms and sharp corners. White walls as bare and as blank as the look of death. Like hollow eyes on a bland, adjustable bed, unbiased, with handrails and white sheets—where the last fruitful visions were of a blurry halo from a dim ceiling light and a dull chorus of sobs and beeping machines.

It was like any other hospital where the ill come to die, or to live, or to wish for life and pray for peace. It's a painful place, sad and sorrowful. Floors stacked on top of floors, room beside room, coughing and crying, long, hard hallways that lead to nowhere great and sometimes, to no one at all. It's an evening visit with friends and family that ends too soon and without resolve—a place where one is left flipping through the channels on a corner TV, wasting away with the hours and new faces that come with shift changes.

It is desolate and dim, where hope comes to suffer, and curses echo from wall to matching wall. All parallel and uniform for the elderly to lose their way and ask kindly of an unfamiliar face, *which way to room 339, please and thank you?*

JP hated the hospital. He hated the sounds of it—the beeping and the blaring, the fluttering of scrubs and flashing coats down the hall to another room. He couldn't stand the smell of it—the scent of sickness in the air, a decay no sanitizer or lemon-scented bleach could scrub clean. He could taste it, hanging in the back of his throat like a bitter spoonful of unseasoned lima beans. Yes, the hospital was a Styrofoam bowl of lima beans, and JP had a sweet tooth. He cared more for the desserts of life, like laughter and love, rather than the bitter truth of goodbyes and fading eyes. He was a romantic, and the hospital a dagger in a tragic play. He avoided those blank walls and flickering, florescent lightbulbs as best he could. But this morning, he sat in the corner chair beside his grandfather, watching the gauges and monitors tell him that his grandfather, though intubated, was still alive.

The door swung open. Lisa, Adin, and his grandmother walked in carrying breakfast in a Styrofoam box.

"How is he?" Lisa asked, rubbing the back of her husband's head.

JP had been there all night, a light sleep in the corner chair. Despite the doctor's and his wife's advice, he refused to go home for the night.

"There's nothing we can do but wait," a middle-aged man in a lab coat had said after several hours of tests and frustrating questions. But JP insisted he would do his waiting *there*, beside his grandfather's rising and falling chest.

JP's tired sigh said enough, but he answered anyway.

"No change," he mumbled, resting his chin on folded hands.

"Well, there's nothing you can do sulking around here all day," his grandmother said, holding out his breakfast. "Here, eat."

He shook it off with gloomy eyes and a wave of his hand.

"She's right." Lisa leaned down and kissed the throbbing vein beside his bloodshot eyes. "You don't look like you slept at all last night. Why don't you go get some rest, and we'll stay with him for the day?" She caressed his cheek and rubbed her thumb along his ear, feeling the tension in his rigid jaw.

He leaned into her fingers with closed eyes, letting her tenderness comfort him after a hard night. He placed a gentle kiss on her hand and turned to look up at her. Her soft smile brought color to the pale room. She filled the space with a purity that inspired him to hang on and to be strong. He needed that. He needed *her*.

Adin, who hid behind his mother and stood on his tippy toes to see his great-grandfather, ducked his head behind Lisa again. Repulsed, he clung to his mother's leg.

"Come here, Buddy," JP reached out, and after a moment of hesitation, Adin joined his father and mother for a hug.

"What's wrong with Gramps?" Adin asked studying the hose and IV coming out of his resting body.

Lisa rubbed her husband's back as she pulled away from his resisting arms and bent down to Adin's level. "Gramps is sick. Very sick. But the best place for him is here at the hospital where they can try to make him better."

When she stood up, JP wrapped his arm around her thin waist. Her purple silk blouse felt comforting against his tired hands. He held onto her as though she were keeping him afloat. Because they were right, he hadn't slept. Trying to sleep in the corner chair was hopeless. But he stayed. Even against the doctor's advice, even when he knew there was nothing he could do to help his grandfather breathe on his own, he stayed. He stayed because he didn't know what else to do; because it was the only thing he *could* do. He had hoped that maybe somehow his being there would be beneficial—that his presence in the corner would inspire his grandfather to keep fighting, to somehow magically heal himself, wake up, and bitch and moan about the tubes and needles jabbed into his leather skin. He hoped his being there would be enough to bring his grandfather back from wherever he had gone, that maybe his existence, curled into a ball, sideways in the hard chair all night long, would be the prayer that eased his grandfather's pain and let him be *him* again.

If only his hardheaded mentor would wake up and drag that tube from his throat, yank that needle from his wrinkled skin, yell at the nurse for poking him in the first place (and promptly apologize with his gentle blue eyes), and curse the bare room and thin bed for keeping him from his farm. If only *that* man would stir from his medically induced sleep, turn to his beloved and loyal grandson, and like a bandit in the passenger seat of his getaway car, demand that they "get out of here!" It was *that man* JP stayed uncomfortably in the corner for all night. The man that had a way of inspiring the weakest hearts to stand strong against the pain. A man that led by example—whether he meant to or not—such that softer men would follow wherever he went, waiting for his next move, hoping to emulate his grandeur, to stand in his shadow, and be thankful for the shade.

That's what his grandfather was capable of—stirring those who crossed his path to be a stronger person, to be a *better* person. He had that kind of power. As JP gripped Lisa's hand, he thought about the story Grandma liked to tell about Grandpa talking a knife out of an angry drunk's hand in the parking lot of the Hi-Li Bar a few years after the war. He stood between the drunkard's blade and an arrogant young man who didn't know how to shut his own mouth. Grandpa fearlessly and selflessly approached the scuffle two cars down from their stepside Chevy the night they celebrated his thirtieth birthday. He could have destroyed that drunk man's life in a blink of an eye and a thrust of his scarred, seasoned hand. But instead, he found the words to bring the sense back into the drunkard's mind. He said what needed to be said in order to prevent the slashing and stabbing of a swift-tongued imbecile.

"There won't be a death tonight, unless it's your own," he'd said. "But I'd rather leave here and go home with my beautiful wife without her having to see a drunk man's silly ending of a short and useless life. Instead, let me say a prayer for you and buy you a drink, friend. You can tell me about your family, your kids, or your wife. Hell, you can tell me all about the things you wish you would've done differently. Like perhaps tonight, instead of killing, or dying, or going to prison, you can share a few jokes with a war-weary Marine and his elegant wife." Then, with a confident glow and a fire in his eyes, they went back inside the bar and made a new friend over a tall Pabst Blue Ribbon.

And although Grandpa was quick to dispute his wife's "embellished" recalling of the "whole damn thing," he never once took recognition for the bravery and heroics he displayed that night. Because to him, it was the right thing to do, and that was all the reason he needed to step between life and death, sharpened steel and a dull-headed man. That was the man JP prayed for all night.

"I need to be here when he wakes up," JP said with fatigue in his voice.

His wife's loud sigh blew against his temple before she leaned down and kissed it again. "You Grimms are a stubborn breed."

"Ain't that the truth," his grandmother chimed in, adjusting the sheets and tucking in her husband as lovingly as a mother would a sick child.

"Well, at least be useful and tell us what the Doctor said," Lisa smirked.

"Well, the follow-up tests all confirmed it; lung cancer. So, nothing's changed there. But the doc says that surgery may be an option. But with his age, it's extremely risky. Last I heard, we're still waiting on a decision from the VA."

"Figures," his grandmother said roughly. "The VA operates about as well as your grandfather's old John Deere. And he's been tinkering with that thing for years," she rebuked.

"What's the *GA?*" Adin's slivered eyes looked to his father.

JP snorted. "The VA, Buddy. *V. A.* They're supposed to help people who went to war. We need them to pay for expensive surgeries or treatments for your great grandfather."

"So, what are they waiting for?" Adin asked, innocently.

"That's one of the best damn questions I've ever heard." He reached out and rubbed his son's dark hair until it stood up from the static.

"So, what do we do now, then?" Lisa said.

A short, begruntled pause. JP looked to his grandfather's gentle body, all still and quiet, except for the deep rise in his chest every couple of seconds after the noisy *pshhh* from the breathing machine. He skimmed his hand over his thin hair to the back of his scalp, where it slowly slid down his neck and wrapped under his chin for his heavy head to rest upon.

"I don't know. Raise Hell until they make a move, I guess."

Just then, a middle-aged nurse, who looked just as strung out as him, entered the room with a quick knock. Her pink eyes and frizzy brown hair suggested she had been up most of the night as well.

"Hello. I just need to check his meds and vitals real quick. Did he wake up at all?" She moved around the bed, flicking the IV bag, checking the machines, and writing new numbers on the dry-erase board on the wall.

"No. He's been out the whole time. Hasn't even moved. Except for a few flinches here and there." JP adjusted his body in his chair, anxious for some news. "So, what's the next step? Doc said surgery?"

She pressed a syringe into the valve of the IV drip and squeezed in more medication. "To help keep him asleep," she said without looking up. Once she had finished, she checked his chart and scribbled some notes.

"Well?" JP didn't hide his frustration.

Her tired eyes looked over the top of the chart board in her hand. "Whatever the doctor said is all I know. He'll be in later this morning to give an update."

"When?"

Her shoulders sunk, and she started clicking the ballpoint pen in her hand. *What was she hiding? Or is she just too preoccupied to care?*

"Honestly, I don't know." Her clicking stopped. "He can get pretty busy in the mornings while he's making his rounds. But don't worry, he'll get to you as soon as possible."

And with that, she turned and started out the door.

"Well, that's not good enough!" JP's voice had turned to ice.

She stopped in her tracks and spun around. Lisa rubbed at his tense shoulders, sensing the anger turning his face hot.

"I'm sorry, sir. It's been a long night. I don't mean to seem insensitive. I apologize. It's just, honestly, I can't predict the doctor's schedule. And I don't want to give you the wrong time. All I can tell you is that he will be in later this morning, and then you can ask all the questions you want." Her brows raised, and JP couldn't tell if she was being condescending or if it was just the way she was after a long night of work. "Is there anything else I can help you with?"

JP bounced out of his chair, desperate for more than what he was getting.

"Yeah! Yeah, Godda—"

"No!" Lisa's hand pulled at JP's arm as she spoke over him. "No. But thank you. We appreciate all you've done. We're just curious about what's next and what we can do to help." Her voice softened. "If there's *anything* we can do, please let us know."

The nurse offered a weary smile. "Absolutely. Thank you." Then she was out the door just as quickly as she had entered.

JP pulled away from his wife's grasp and walked toward the window. The sun was still quite low, but bright, as its rays stretched out over the trees and rooftops of the nearby businesses. The thick morning traffic sped by without a second glance. Below the window of their third-story room, white gravel covered the roof of the emergency room section.

He looked out at the bright day rising over Cambridge, Ohio, and wondered what life might be like without his grandfather around. The thought stirred a bubble of emotion that pinched the back of his throat. The fury boiled hot, like a volcano, in his gut. His crossed arms hid his clenched fists. He squeezed them tightly against his lungs. But the pressure on his chest only made him think more about how hard it was for his grandfather to breathe. He thought about the cancer, like a small army swarming and fighting in his grandpa's lungs. Terrorists. Extremists. Tiny insurgents plaguing and disturbing an otherwise peaceful place. He was outraged. He was tired. And he was losing control.

"Nothing's going to change staring out the window," his grandmother said, her usual sass lacing the sympathy in her voice.

Her words broke his concentration, and he was glad for the interruption. He turned to look at his family, who all watched him steam and vent in front of the sun.

"Babe, go home. Rest. We can take it from here." His wife pleaded with her eyes and gentle tone.

JP thought for a moment and then shook off the notion. Picking up the remote and clicking on the TV, he scooted the chair back into the corner and plopped down on it. "Nah, I'm fine right here. I'll just watch a little TV and crash when I can."

"Well at least eat. You're looking like one of those meth-heads all over the news."

"Grandma!" JP rolled his eyes and turned up the volume.

The morning news opened on the flatscreen TV. The female news anchor's distressed voice filled the room. They all turned their attention to her.

"Yes, what we're looking at now, I'm being told, is another electrical storm in Northern Michigan," the anxious news anchor said.

Scenes of burning buildings, scorched power lines, and lightning ripping through the darkened early morning sky flashed on the screen. As the alarming pictures and videos divulged the seriousness of the situation, shock filled their faces.

"Oh my God." Lisa's hand covered her gaping mouth.

"Jesus." JP sat up and leaned forward.

"Okay," the anchor woman said with her hand to her ear. "I'm being told now that we have someone live on scene. Hello? Terry, can you hear me?"

A man in a blue, hooded jacket and dust mask came onto the screen. "Yes! Yes, I hear you!" He shouted over the noise of sirens in the background as he stood in front of a burning residential city block. He raised his arm to shield his face from the heat and smoke.

"I'm here in Marquette, a once beautiful town of about twenty-five thousand." He looked around at the burning house fires and black smoke billowing into the sky. "But now, now as you all can see, it is completely engulfed in flames—just like several other northern towns over the last several months— it's a horror that many woke up to in the early morning hours. Oh my God," he said as one of the burning, two-story houses collapsed to the ground. "That's just terrible. Awful," He turned back to the camera. "As you can see, it's a war zone here. If anyone is watching this and is in or near the surrounding area, please…please get out and get to safety."

"Dad, what happened?" Adin leaned against his father's knee.

"Shhh."

The fraught newswoman observed the damage from a helicopter live shot. "Wow. Just…heart-breaking. What can you tell us about the situation down there?" she asked the reporter.

"Honestly, all I know right now is that they are calling it an electrical storm." He pressed one hand to his ear and nodded his head. "My producer is telling me it started with multiple lightning strikes concentrated over the town. Yes, folks, *lightning.* Unlike anything they've ever seen, here in Marquette. But, unfortunately, much like the many other electrical storms and fires that have become frequent around the country recently. And, well, obviously, it has inflicted complete havoc here on this small town. Such a horrifying and sad—"

"Dad? Hey, Dad?"

"Shhh, Buddy. Not now."

"Dad?" Adin tugged at his father's knee.

"Quit. I'm trying to watch this."

"Adin, leave your father alone. Something terrible happened." Lisa tried to reason with their child. "Please honey, what do you need?"

"*Daaad!* What's an electrical storm!"

"Damn it, Adin! I said shut up! I'm trying to listen!" JP snapped, causing Lisa and his grandmother to glare at him, and then at each other with concern in their eyes.

"But, Dad?" Adin's glowing eyes shimmered up at his father.

JP looked at his son, into his eyes. He understood the images might be difficult for Adin to process. He knew his son needed comfort and an explanation. But JP saw more than just a city burning. He saw all the fire and death that comes with it when a five-hundred-pound bomb explodes among houses and scorches all that is near. JP saw Iraq. War. Carnage. In the flames and fury of that poor town, he saw the death and destruction of what happens when a little boy blows apart his suicide vest, sending fire and shrapnel into the bodies of his Marines, his friends.

"Shut up and get away from me!" JP roared. "Just do what you're told! I don't know what you got away with when I was gone, but damn it, Adin, when I say to do something, you do it!"

"JP! He's just curious and confused. Like we all are," his grandmother explained.

The scowl on JP's face was battle-ready and dangerous. He roasted in his heat for a moment before blinking away the past and bringing the present back into view. His son was wrapped around his mother's waist, sobbing.

"Unacceptable." Lisa's tight jaw and dagger eyes drew blood.

A rush of panic set in. "Adin," he said gently, nearly choking on the guilt.

Adin buried his face in his mother's stomach.

"Adin?" JP reached out to touch his shoulder, but he pulled away. "Bud, I'm sorry."

"What's gotten into you? He's just a boy," Grandma scolded. "Shame on you."

On the screen, the flames rose from the blazing windows, like fire in the Devil's eyes. The smoke, thick and dark, was like the haze creeping from the shadows of JP's mind. The sirens. The loud, flashing sirens. The whipping flames. The lightning. The roaring sound of the fire swirling in the wind. The heat. JP could feel his skin burning. Sweat beads dripped down the side of his head. Suddenly, he felt like the walls were caving in, and he was suffocating. He had to get out. He had to breathe. He had to escape the vice.

"I'm so sorry!" he said, jumping to his feet and wiping his head on his sleeve as he dashed out of the room, out from the flames and burning eyes.

Chapter Nine

Grandpa Dying

I cannot hear the distance
in your voice,

but I can smell the rotten
on your breath.

Your eyes have gone milky,
red and blue.

It reminds me of the patriot
in you,

and I wonder

if you can still see in me
the ornery blonde screamer, tree
climber and fighter

that I used to be.

And I hope
that you think of the stubbornness
that you spent years teaching me,

even
as you hold onto
these last long breaths.

JP flipped over onto his shoulder, pounding his pillow until it fluffed to his liking. The wind rattled the window across from him, whistling under the door at his feet as it permeated their cabin walls. He wondered if that was what had awoken him *this time* as he glanced at the blurry, red numbers glowing above the sharp outline of the black pistol on his nightstand: 3:33 a.m. *Unbelievable.*

Glancing at his restful wife to his left, he was thankful she was a heavy sleeper. For the last couple weeks, ever since the doctor informed him the VA denied his grandfather's surgery—because of his age and his high risk—he had found himself blinking sleepily at the same numbers he stared at now. Frustration climbed along his back and shoulders, which flexed with each whistle and rattle of the wind.

He didn't care much for whistles or rattles. Just months ago, in Iraq, the rattle of his sandbagged window meant impending danger: *BOOMS* and shrapnel that swallowed whole men in black smoke; the overhead whistle of enemy mortars walking their way closer to him and his men, bringing a cracking thunder that shook their chests, their lives. He whipped back his damp sheet, his heart thumping, and muffled the disturbing sounds with a pillow stuffed firmly against the windowsill.

A draft stirred from the large frame windows down in the living room, causing a chill in the air. It slinked up the steps to the loft and cooled the hardwood floor of the hallway. It fluttered the Grimm family pictures along the wall: smiling in their red flannel shirts, posing in front of the faded barn doors, the front porch rocking chairs, and among the golden fields of the farm. And tapping against the green drywall, they pulled JP from his room.

His bedroom door, at the end of the hall, squeaked open with a square pistol muzzle leading a shirtless man from the shadows and into the halo of his son's Superman nightlight by the bathroom door. The floor fussed with each slow footstep. Cursing the moans, he crept forward, cautiously— heel…toe…heel…toe—with dark eyes behind the green glowing night sights of his Glock 19. He was a sentry standing post, his senses alert, both ears and eyes keen, and a pistol ready to kill.

A small splint of light stretched out across the floorboards from his son's cracked-open door. Inside the room, Adin's soft snores reminded him of Joey and the way he would whistle when he slept in the rack beside his own. *How bizarre*, he thought, *the small things that make you think of the past.* He stood awash in the dresser lamp light, frozen at Adin's door and watching his dark-haired child sleep so softly. A sharp contrast to Sgt. Grimm, as he patrolled the hallways with his gun.

He swallowed one last look at his peaceful son: his camouflaged covers pulled up to his chin, which sparkled with drool on a damp spot of his pillowcase, his delicate hand hanging over the bed, poking out from under his sheet and twitching every now and then. He was beautiful. But the thoughts of his son soon brought with them a slight sting in his gut as his son's dark hair and shiny eyes resembled the one who took his friends away in a smoldering blast of black smoke and grit.

His neck was tight when he pulled away from that picture in his head and spun back toward the stairs, where an unnerving tap drummed from below. His feet were feathers as he descended the stairs with his pistol high at his chest and muzzle dipped but ready to blast if it needed to. His grip was comfortable and practiced. His eyes scanned the corners quickly. Down into the living room he inched, his finger confirming the trigger at each tap and scuffle against the outside wall. As one, him and the gun swept the room like a flashlight, searching the dark. But he wasn't shining, and tonight, nothing about him was bright.

Outside, the weather was turning. The heat of climate change brought in storms with the warming nights. They were storms that dazzled with displays of jagged bolts—sharp fingers reaching out across the sky or bright spears jabbing into the earth like the sky was at war with the ground. The wind rustled the leaves into corners and twigs along the walls. The moon was nothing more than a faint glow behind a black and gray curtain rolling in with the first true cold front of fall. Everything was shadows and blurs outside the window. JP and his pistol poked their heads around the blinds of the double window. During the day, it gave a view of Adin's swing set and jungle gym pushed back in the front yard against the corn stalks and high grass. But in the gray of the early morning, JP only saw shadows. Dark forms blending in with a sea of black around them. The trees in his yard—black monsters waving and mocking him. The leaves and twigs—coal-colored critters of the night. The cut fields and twisted corn stocks—Damascus blades. The raspberry bushes lined along the far side of the yard—jagged teeth against the black backdrop. Everything out his window was shady and dangerous. Only the security light from the telephone pole on the other side of the garage gave a true hint of what lurked about.

JP unlatched the door gently and grasped the handle. He tucked his pistol back into his armpit with a firm grip. Then, all at once, he yanked open the door, and thrust out into the darkness with his muzzle leading the way to his left, and smoothly swept back to his right. A stirring of debris and leaves rushed in. They blew past his bare feet and fuzzy WELCOME rug. But JP wasn't bothered by the leaves or twigs or dirt. He wasn't hunting the obvious. He was hunting the hidden—the prowlers and thieves that were out to steal the peace and silence. JP was hunting the demons inside his head.

His form followed smoothly along the porch, beyond the matching rocking chairs and porch swing, all moving with the wind, and out past the corner shrubs. His feet squished in the chill of the cold ground. He patrolled around the corner and then the next and the next, searching for a target to drop, an enemy to engage. He pointed his pistol around each bend and break in his line of sight until he popped around the edge of the porch to find nothing. *Nothing. Nothing?* Standing flat-footed outside the door, he glared out into his now filled and faded world, where scrapes and rustles are nothing, and large lumps of darkness are things without a threat. His gun hung at his side, saddened, and he shook the disappointment from his head.

"Next time," he mumbled to no one. And marched back into the house, locking up, before drifting to sleep in the armchair, facing the door, and cradling his Glock in his lap.

~

Before the morning sun streamed through the window, JP woke from a dream of his grandfather taking him to feed the chickens and gather the eggs when he was very young. They had been hand-in-hand, walking down the backyard slope along the concrete block path to the shed-sized chicken coop. JP felt the corn pellets in his tiny hand as he flung them out in front of him and squealed when the hens rushed the pile like kids to candy in a parade. He *heard* his grandfather's sweet laughter, and the joy of their bond filled him, as if he were four years old all over again.

But that was all just a distant memory. In the here and now, he sat in the gloomy stillness until the sun broke the trees, slipped through the window, and spotlighted the family portrait above the fireplace. He rose, determined to do *something* to help the situation his family found themselves in. By a quarter past nine, he'd been on the phone for an hour, trying to get through to the Veteran's Affairs office. Finally, someone picked up.

"Veteran's Affairs Main Office, Columbus, Ohio. Can you hold, please?

"No! No, I *cannot* hold, I've been—" *Click.* A droning hum followed on the other end of the phone as JP's white-knuckles squeezed the receiver. "Hello? Hello? Goddamn it!"

"Please remain on the line." An automated female voice replaced the hum. "Your call is important to us. All representatives are currently busy. We will get to your call in the order that it is received. There are **seven** calls ahead of you."

Please stay on the line—JP growled deep in his throat and slammed his phone down on the kitchen table. Leaning on his wooden chair, head down and hands folded in front of him, a boiling heat filled the room and his face. The loud bang brought Lisa, still in her flannel pajama pants and oversized Ohio State hoodie, into the room. The morning sunrays, like Maglite beams beneath the forest-green blinds, illuminated the dust in the air. The sunny mornings were a rare beauty this time of year, and Lisa greeted the blessing with a smile. Back before the war, when she woke before anyone else, she'd enjoy a cup of coffee as the sun spread its love over the land and bright treetops while she mixed batter for pancakes. But this morning, JP was first to rise and already dressed in his rough jeans and long-sleeved black flannel, ready to take on the day's responsibilities with vigor and joust.

"Any luck, Babe?" She asked, rounding the corner from the living room to the kitchen. His rigid form softened her eyes as she walked up behind him to rub his tense shoulders. Then, she wrapped her arms around him and rested her head on his back. It was hard and hot, and it vibrated. Her heart sank. She wanted so badly to take away his hurt and hostility, to turn him back from the seething, hurting man he'd become. But she had learned since his return that no amount of *want* would be enough to change what was.

She kissed the back of his neck, hoping to calm his seas. But he pulled away, shoving the chair against the table as he put distance between them. He stomped over to the gray, marbled counter, tossed his phone beside him, and pressed his backside against the edge with folded arms. Like any stubborn man, he refused to acknowledge that he was no longer in control—that he was no longer able to harness the frenzy that unraveled in his mind. He was *fine.* He was *okay.* He *knew what he was doing.* But he didn't. And she knew that more than anyone else. She *felt that* more than anyone else.

He was her father in these angry moments. A hard-nosed cop, he wanted nothing to do with anyone when he was heated; he just wanted his space and room to sour alone. That quality—emotional distance and hard walls placed between him and his loving family—was one she hoped to never find in another man. But JP was becoming her father, and it left a bitter, nagging scratch at the back of Lisa's throat.

"What did they say? Are they going to pay for the surgery or not?" she asked less softly this time. It had been over two weeks since his grandfather had been admitted into the hospital. A long time to wait for an urgent surgery.

His eyes pierced her when he looked up. Arrow-shaped and sharp, they ripped into her like she was the enemy. They accused her, cut into her like *she* was the one causing all his pain. They dug down deep into her heart and slashed away at her like a soldier in a trench fight.

"It's the fucking VA! What do you think?" he said coldly.

She frowned and crossed her arms, keeping her distance. "I don't know…that they'd do the right thing." She shivered as a draft blew across her bare feet.

"Hmp! Yeah. Right. The *right* thing." He rolled his eyes and huffed.

"Soooo? What do we do now?" Fear and confusion rumbled through her voice.

He leaned his head back, glaring at the ceiling. The dark knots in the stained wood panels resembled the scars on his wavering heart. "They said we have to file an appeal."

"An *appeal?* What the hell does that mean?"

"I don't know, Lisa! More paperwork. More time." He shrugged.

She looked on in disbelief. "JP, we don't have *time!* How long will that take?"

"That's a *damn* good question! One that I would *love* to get the answer to, if they'd ever answer their goddamned phone!" His voice cracked with emotion.

The intensity on his face and the tremble in his arms as he squeezed them together around his chest indicated he needed more, *more than she was giving.* Whatever it was, whatever was eating away at his sharp semblance, at his happiness and well-being, it was winning. Space wasn't working. He needed her, them, *his family.* He needed their love, their support, their care, and salvation. *To hell with giving him his distance,* she thought.

"Babe." Her eyes dampened and filled with sympathy as she approached him.

And his narrow eyes followed her gracious form as she reached out for his sharp, tight jaw pulling it down toward hers with strength and liberation. Her caress was passionate and pure while she kissed his burning lips. Then she kissed him again, and again, until his shoulders relaxed, until he surrendered, and his mouth accepted her love.

Deflated, his bulging arms wrapped around his wife, taking in her warmth and affection, her tenacity and devotion. And with a burst of regret and shame—right there against the cloudy, marbled countertop, underneath the crimson-lettered *Home Is Where The Heart Is* home décor hanging above the pearl-white cupboards—he wept upon her gentle shoulder.

His phone buzzed loudly on the countertop, and he flinched in Lisa's arms. He sniffed and wiped his face quickly with his hand before twisting to grab his phone. Without noticing who the call was from, he answered with a hasty "Hello!"

Lisa took a step back with her hand tracing her cheek, anxious to see who was calling this early on a Saturday morning.

"Yes, this is him," JP said, smearing the last of his tears across his cheek. "Who's this?"

"The Hospital? Oh, I was hoping you were one of those VA—what? Now? But he was doing just fine last night."

Lisa's hand jerked to her mouth.

JP pushed his backside away from the counter and stiffened. "Wait. I'm sorry. He's going in now? *Right now?* Okay. Okay. We're on our way. Thank you!"

Before he even ended the call, Lisa raced up the stairs to wake Adin.

JP sped off, trailing in her wake. The faster they all got ready, the quicker they'd make it to the hospital.

When the elevator came to a stop and dinged, JP caught sight of his grandmother from the corner of his eye as she waved them over to a few saved chairs beside her.

She sprung to her feet as they approached. JP wrapped his arms around her and squeezed gently. The dampness on her cheeks and green blouse meant she'd been crying.

The room was like any other small-town hospital waiting room: off-white walls, dark, fuzzy cushioned chairs lined in rows and scuffing the walls, tissues on the end tables, a TV in the corner playing The Price is Right reruns, and that sanitized smell that lingers in the nostrils even after an hour's wait. A variety of characters sat in groups. Some with children playing games on iPads and iPhones. A room full of solemn faces and ticking clocks. A room JP did his best to avoid. But there he was, immersed in the stench of the dying and lemon-scented bleach, saturated in the heavy somber air of sadness and worry.

"What happened?" he asked, backing away and letting Lisa and Adin hug her as well.

She took a second to compose herself. Her crossed arms held in her heart as she let out a deep, shaky breath, looked up to the ceiling as if she were asking God himself for strength, and settled her misty eyes back on JP's waiting stare.

"His lung collapsed. They rushed him back for emergency surgery. That was about an hour ago."

"Any updates?" Lisa rubbed his grandmother's upper arm, trying to comfort her.

Her head shook slowly as she spoke. "Just that the surgeon expected a two to three-hour operation."

"Here, sit. Sit," JP said, guiding her down by the elbow into the chair.

They all sat, sat and waited, just like any other worried family member sitting and waiting to hear when their loved one had made it out of surgery, if it was successful, or if they even survived. The time passed slowly. Adin had a hundred questions that received only partial answers until JP got frustrated and handed his phone to his son to play Call of Duty. They tried small talk and distractions. But it was futile. And when there was nothing else to say, they reminisced about the sturdy man whom they expected to see smirking on the other end of his successful surgery.

"I still remember the time he caught me shooting at crows in the corn with his old .22 from up in the hayloft." JP took his turn sharing a memory with a faint glimmer across his lips. "I couldn't have been much older than nine or ten. Still an ornery little shit, back then."

His grandmother patted him on the thigh. "The most wonderful ornery little shit I've ever had the pleasure to raise." Her sweet smile spread to Lisa and then JP.

JP sniffed and held his grandmother's hand. "I thought for sure that I'd get my ass beat for taking out the gun without asking, or maybe for shooting so close to the house and herd. I nearly choked on my heart when I saw the puff of his tractor shifting gears and chugging up the path toward me." He paused to reflect on the memory—chewing it, savoring it—he let it fill him up with life and love. Then, with a huge grin on his face, he continued. "I nearly pissed my pants when he yelled up into the loft, 'Hey! What the hell you doing, boy?'" JP looked at his grandmother's puffy but glowing face. "But you know what? He climbed up that ladder, saw me lying on the hay with his rifle beside me…and he just shook his head and laughed. Then, in his greasy overalls, he crawled over, laid down beside me, and said, 'You have to *squeeeeze* the trigger, not jerk it. Here, let me show ya.' And we stayed up there in that loft, picking off crows, talking about his own ornery childhood, and him coaching me on the fundamentals of marksmanship for, I don't know, it must've been at least a couple hours." He drifted in thought. "I'll never forget that," a ripple of emotion tingled his cheeks. "That man taught me more about life than anyone else ever could have."

His wife and grandmother dabbed at their own tears, and Grandma playfully slapped his arm. "Hey, I resent that! Knowing how to bake and cook is farrr more important than knowing how to kill!" She playfully stared him down.

A glow lit up his face as leaned in to kiss his grandmother on her wet, wrinkled cheek.

Just then, a young, thin nurse appeared from the automatic double doors and called out their name. "Grimm? Grimm?"

It startled them, and when JP answered "Yes!" it came out louder than he intended.

"If you'd all follow me, I'll take you back to the doctor," the nurse said as they lined their way to a small room where the doctor was waiting.

"How is he?" JP asked before they even took their seats.

The doctor, a bald black man in his fifties with a thick, gray mustache, adjusted his glasses and pulled a blue pen from his white jacket. He hesitated and acted as if he were checking some paperwork in a folder on the desk in front of him "Well, you know," he started.

"Listen, Doc, before you even try to feed us some sort of bullshit, just stop," JP said.

"JP!" Lisa scolded in a whisper.

He glanced her way and then returned a stern look at the doctor. "We're not in the mood to hear it. Understand?"

The doctor fidgeted with his pen and adjusted his glasses again quickly.

"Just shoot us straight, Doc. No BS." JP glanced at Lisa and shrugged her off when she squeezed his hand.

The doctor took a deep breath. "Well, all right then. I'll just, uhhh, give it to you straight." He looked around at the worried faces before him, then back at JP, who hadn't budged from his stern stare. "Look, your grandfather is an old man, and it was a risky surgery for someone of his age and health." He glanced at the paperwork and back at JP. "The surgery had a slim chance anyway, and…and I'm terribly sorry, but it was not successful. I'm so sorry."

His grandmother let out a soft cry as she gasped.

"What does that mean? Did you kill him? You son of a bitch! Did you kill my grandfather!" JP lunged forward, rigid and hard. Lisa grabbed his arm, holding him back.

The Doctor nearly fell back out of his chair. "No! No! I didn't kill your grandfather! He's in recovery!"

The room simmered and everyone adjusted in their seats.

"His body was just too weak. Once we got in there, he coded twice. We revived him, but…" The doctor took a deep breath. "It was too risky to keep going. Perhaps, if we were able to get in there a little earlier, then maybe…you know, maybe we could've done *something*. Again, I'm sorry." The doctor removed his glasses and pinched the bridge of his nose, rubbed his eyes, blinked wildly, and then put them back on.

"So, what does that mean for Grandpa?"

"Son–"

"Don't call me son!" JP growled, causing Lisa to squeeze his arm, slide her hand down to his, and interlock their fingers.

"My apologies. Sir, it means that his lung is still collapsed. He's not doing well. I'm not entirely sure how much longer he can hold on, quite honestly. He's a tough, stubborn man. But, even tough, stubborn men need to breathe."

"Jesus, how much time does he have left?"

The doctor leaned back in his chair. JP wasn't sure if it was to put more distance between them, or if he was just searching for the right words. "I'm afraid, not long."

With her other hand, Lisa wrapped her arm around Grandma and let her cry on her shoulder. "When can we see him?" Lisa asked softly.

"He should be waking up any minute. I'll have my nurse take you up to his room where you can say your goodbyes."

That comment broke them all, and they cried the entire way to his room.

The overhead light was dim and flickering when they walked in. It was the same room as before, but this time, it felt different, darker. It felt like death was crowding around them.

When Grandpa finally woke up, his voice was weak and rotten. One by one, they all leaned down and kissed him, spoke with him, and told him how much they loved him. His eyes were glazed over, his body was cold, and when he spoke, they could barely hear him.

But it was the last thing he said, that would stay with JP forever. He leaned down as his grandfather barely squeezed his hand. A tear dripped from his cheek and landed on the blue blanket pulled up to his grandfather's chin. He bent until his ear rested next to his grandfather's gray lips. And despite the faint, far voice of his grandfather, JP heard him loud and clear, as if Grandpa had opened up his very soul and shouted the words like thunder into his heart.

"Let go."

Chapter Ten

Dying in the Light

The shadows here are tall and mean.

A darker version of myself, armed and just
as dirty; stretching out toward home, or
freedom, or forgiveness; only to fall short
of that salvation.

A dark angel beside me, who looks like me,
who moves like me, but is able to bend along
these desert walls, hugging to the cover of
concrete and marble, if it wants to;

or fearless, poking out into the open streets;
daring poor bastards to fire, to expose their
hidden intentions, to invite in that kind of
death and destruction.

My shadow is a cold-blooded warrior;
faceless and stern. But in the heat of a flaring
sun, he still catches me when I fall.

The funeral was *nice*. That's what everyone said.

It brought a crowd of old friends and family to pay their last respects, an
honor guard and full military honors, and the playing of a soul-crushing TAPS on
the trumpet. The elders from the local VFW folded and presented the burial flag
to a tearful Mrs. Grimm, while their twenty-one-gun salute on wobbling knees
made Sgt. Grimm wince with each salvo.

It *was* nice. But for JP, it was the end of a noble man's life, one who inspired
many with insight and righteousness. For JP, it was the loss of a gentle, loving,
wise man who taught him how to brave the flames and embers of a burning life,
how to walk the *right* path, through the smoke and the heat, keeping a clear vision
and cool head on what's important and true.

For JP, it was a blade-deep bayonet piercing the ground on a black M4 rifle,
sticking muzzle down between a pair of combat boots and a combat helmet
propped on top, with Joey's dog tags dangling from the pistol grip in the desert

grit. It was the flinch and desperation of not having a weapon when the rifles fired into the air. And it was a chest-flexing agitation that rippled through the veins of a fading man.

As it closed in on midnight, he looked like a lost soul searching for his spark as he sat in the dark in his favorite plush armchair turned toward the door. In his lap, the weight of his pistol comforted him, as a nearly empty whiskey glass dripped on the end table.

Lisa had kissed him on the cheek well over an hour ago after she put Adin to bed and said goodnight. His grunt was not enough, but she let it go, allowing him to wallow in his whiskey thoughts. He had scoffed in anger as her soft steps made the floorboards moan, and his imagination stirred images of armed night crawlers creeping through the house. Upstairs, she lay awake wondering how to help the man she once knew.

The only glow in the room came from a full moon and the strategically placed nightlights plugged into scattered outlets around the house. The nights had turned to frost, and now the thud and hum of the furnace kicking on made JP curse his always-cold wife. After all, his black mesh shorts, green polyester T-shirt, and glass of Maker's Mark were plenty to keep him warm. His eyes, full and fearful, stayed fixed to the dark green curtain on the front door, which fluttered in a draft.

But he wasn't *thinking* about any of that. Instead, his thoughts were on the dead. The man who raised him, the men who fought with him, and the friend he let die in the dirty streets of Iraq. He was thinking about life's cruel and crippling punishments for the mistakes that are made.

With a hot gut, he stood and carried himself and his pistol to the window of the timbered front door. There, his quivering hand brushed aside the curtain, and he peered into the night. The moon cast long shadows like the sun in the desert. Even at home, he couldn't escape their reach.

He lifted his gun to the glass. A dull *clink* sounded when he pressed it against the pane. A sudden dread shimmered at his neck. His eyes narrowed while scanning the front yard and rolling corn stocks, chopped and twisted from the late summer's cut.

Someone's out there! he thought, feeling eyes upon him and switching the button on his tac-light mounted under his pistol. A bright beam flooded the front lawn. He pressed his forehead to the chilled glass and slid his light back and forth. *Nothing.* But a prowler still lurked around him. He searched as the light lit up the trees like statues in the yard. With each sweep, he thought he found the threat. But no. Only trees and toys and a truck.

His heavy breath blew waves into the curtain. He flicked off the light and let the curtain fall into place. The gun sunk to his side. His weary glare rose to the timber beams above him. "What am I doing?" he whispered.

With a moping drift, he made his way over to his chair and glass, slugged back the rest of the whiskey, and pulled up his text messages. He flicked past the long line of ignored texts from his hometown friends asking him to come out for a beer, to play cards, or just hang out for a while. But, he couldn't. He wasn't *that guy* anymore. So, he flipped briskly through the days, leaving those old memories alone, until he found Cpl. Richardson's name. He hammered the words with his thumb and sent them before he changed his mind.

"Call me. I need to talk."

Two minutes later, his phone rang. The buzzing made him jump before he snatched it from the stand. "Hello?"

"Grimm! You sack of shit! How the hell are ya?" Music and talking strummed in the background.

"Richardson, you asshat! What's up?" His words were on the verge of slurring—that moment just before the last drink, when thoughts are still calculated, words articulated. It wouldn't be long before they started piggybacking onto one another, mashing the syllables into new words and phrases, when the world spins faster and the tongue can't keep up.

"Hey. Hold on." The sound dampened, and Cpl. Richardson's voice seemed far away as he muttered something to someone. The music faded into the background before he spoke again. "All right, sorry. I'm at the bar." He paused, then in a slightly muffled voice, said, "Heyyy! What's up, Donnie! Yeah. Yeah, they're inside. All right. Yeah. I'll be in in a minute." His breath into the speaker made JP pull the phone away from his ear. "Shit. Sorry. It's a wild night, man!"

"Sounds like it. I can let you go, it's fine."

"Nooo. No way, man. It's cool. They can wait. What's up?"

The noise vanished from the background, and judging by his breathing, JP figured Richardson must be on the move.

"Ah, you know. Just life, brother."

"Aw, shit. Yeah. I hear ya." Phone breathing filled the awkward pause. "Look man, I'm real sorry to hear about your grandpa. I know how close you guys were. Is everything good? You all right?"

JP looked over at the empty whiskey glass, down at the handgun in his lap, and then at the door. "Yeah. Yeah, I'm good. Everything's good. You know…hey, hold on. I'm gonna pour another drink and head to the porch. I don't wanna wake Lisa."

He gathered himself up out of the chair, draped the Ohio State throw blanket over his shoulders, shuffled into the kitchen, and poured another full glass from a half-empty bottle on the counter.

"How is she by the way?" Richardson asked with an ornery tone.

JP chuckled. "You're just waiting for your opportunity to slide into her DMs aren't you, ya sand-baggin' sonofabitch." The door squeaked along with his laughs as he twisted the knob and headed outside to the back-porch railing.

"You know it! I wish you'd hurry up and get the hell outta the picture. She doesn't know what she's missing over here!" Richardson's laugh, open and friendly, reverberated over the line, and JP realized how much he missed talking to *the guys.* He had stayed in touch daily for a while. But as things fell back into place, and old routines became new again, their conversations spread further and further apart, until it was just text messages once or twice a week.

"What a dick," he blended with the slurping of his whiskey.

"And the kid?"

"What?" A bolt of panic webbed across his chest.

"Your boy. Adin? Right?"

"Oh. Yeah." A flush spread throughout his face, shame really, but the Maker's in his blood masked much of his embarrassment.

"Well, how is he? He's like, seven, eightish? Right?"

"Yeah. Yeah, he's…doing good. He's doing fine. Everything's fine. We're all *fine.*" JP shook his head. An internal growl rolled in the back of his throat. *Real convincing, dumbass!*

"Uhhh, okayyy? Well, that's good then. I'm happy to hear it." A horn blared in the background. "Whoa! Bout got smashed by some drunk asshole," he said nonchalantly.

They laughed in the way those who had faced death would laugh at the possibility of being done in in such a bullshit kind of way. Unheroic. Unpoetic. Like slipping on the ice and busting open their head or getting stung by a bee and having an allergic reaction. For them, death was only worthy if they went down fighting.

"So, what's on your mind, man? What's up?"

"I don't know…" JP made it sound like he had more to say, so Richardson waited. Then, in a low, dirty voice, Sgt. Grimm broke the silence. "Do you miss it?"

He didn't have to explain. It was a common question among vets. One they had tossed around over the last few months.

"Do I miss it? Fuck no! Why the hell would I miss getting my ass blown up or shot?" Cpl. Richardson said.

"Not at all?" JP pressed.

Richardson huffed as if he couldn't believe someone would ask such a ridiculous thing. "No."

"Like, nothing? Not even the way they'd look at you over there? Like how they knew what power we held, or what we were, like…fully capable of? Not even a little?"

"No, man," Richardson said with a short snicker. "I don't miss *anything* about it. I miss *this!* Going out with old friends and drinking until I can't stand. I miss the girls. I miss *fucking.* And you know what I *don't* miss? That godforsaken shithole of a country. Those gutless, worthless…*pathetic* pieces of shit who couldn't find the balls to stand up for their own people, for their own country. I don't miss the death for nothing." The flick and grind of a lighter torching a cigarette, and then the long exhale of a slow drag filled the silence.

The woods and pine rows surrounded JP's backyard. He listened to the coyotes sing in the back fields and adjusted the pistol tucked in his pants. A hard chill hung in the late-night air, and for a moment, he let it shake him. He shivered, peering out into the outstretched arms of the pines that rattled on the breeze and waved at him, mocking him, taunting him. He pulled the blanket tighter around his shoulders and scoffed at the thought of being so domestic, so homely, so peaceful. He considered heaving his glass in their direction.

When he spoke, his words were delicate, desperate, and demented. "But…we were gods…"

After the call, JP quietly headed up the stairs. His head was heavy and low, full of turbulence and turmoil. With pistol hanging in hand, he methodically watched his toes balance and creep across the thin, mahogany carpet. Until this dark moment, he hadn't paid much attention to the detail of the stairs. But now, the dark red reminded him of the bloodstains on the concrete in a distant Hell he couldn't seem to escape.

A flutter and a moan emerged from his son's room at the top of the stairs. His nerves were on end, and the hairs on his arms spiked. There was a muffled thud like something fell to the floor or someone bumped into something. His head snapped toward the doorway. *What was that? Adin? Is someone in his room?* The narrow gash of light protruding from the dark corner of a cracked-open door cut across the landing ahead of him. He listened for movement, for the black mass to show itself, but all was still and silent. *They're waiting to ambush me.* He raised his pistol to his chest, gripped it tightly in both hands, and started toward Adin's room.

The hardwood in the hallway was less forgiving than the carpet. It creaked and groaned with each tactical step. Again, a moan filtered out from the room. His steps quickened, louder this time, but he didn't care. He aimed the muzzle at the door as he got closer.

Another loud moan and rustle of the bed made him barrel for the door. His heavy, unbalanced steps shook the walls and rattled the picture frames. He lunged forward, shoulder first, muzzle second, into the door with a loud bang and rumble. It slammed against the wall and knocked down pictures in the hall.

His body and feet twisted as he scanned the room down the barrel of his Glock 19. Over top of the front sight post, Adin's room unfolded before him: his black, three-drawer dresser along the wall, his open closet doors full of school clothes, the Nerf guns lined up on a gun rack, the window, the bed, the desk where he drew pictures of marines fighting "bad guys." And Adin, sitting upright in his camo pajamas and screaming.

No intruder, no burglar, no enemy to do them harm. No awaiting death. No one, but his petrified little boy.

Fuck!

His gun dropped to his hip. "It's me! It's me, Buddy! It's Dad!" He flipped on the light.

Lisa was halfway down the hallway, still pulling on her hoodie, when she saw the light flick on and her armed husband standing drunkenly in the halo of their son's room.

"What? What happened? JP, what is it?" She scurried into the room to see nothing but the end result of a distorted mind—drunk and disabled.

Back in his own bedroom, JP stood at the window gazing into the night when Lisa finally came back to bed.

"What the hell was that all about?" she asked as she carefully shut the door and turned to face him.

But JP couldn't look her in the eyes. Not yet, not now. Instead, he stared out into the shadowed backyard, watching the breeze flick the pine boughs back and forth, catching the moonlight like glitter on black construction paper.

"I don't know."

She cut him off before he could say anymore. "You don't know? What the hell, Jay? What's gotten into you lately? You've been acting all…weird and stuff."

"I know! I know! *I'm sorry!*"

She crossed her arms and felt the anger rush to the tips of her fingers. "This is *not* okay! JP, this kind of behavior, whatever *this* is—the distance, the alcohol, the late hours, and the paranoia—the way you've avoided your son since you've been home…." Her voice pitched as emotion overtook her.

His shoulders slouched as his breath fogged up the window.

"Turn around and look at me. Please. JP. *Pleeease.*"

Like a scolded dog, he turned, but he couldn't hold her glare.

She studied him and his demeanor, both damaged and defeated.

He searched his fragile thoughts for the right words to say as he followed the lines on the hardwood floor. But he couldn't find them. Shame and embarrassment draped across him like the flag on a casket.

Although still upset, she was sympathetic. She brushed her golden hair out of her face and tucked it behind her ear. JP glanced her way, and remorse reflected in his eyes. She couldn't possibly understand what he was thinking or what he was going through. She *knew* that. But that didn't stop her from wanting to know more.

She took him in her arms and stroked the back of his head, trying to ease his tension. He was sweaty and smelled of whiskey. His rough stubble scraped her cheek like sandpaper. His arms dangled at his sides as if they were holding the weight of his past in each hand. But she held him. Even though he lacked affection. She held him. Even when he tried to pull away in shame. She held him. She held him until his body began to tremble like the lid on a steaming teapot. She held him as he tried to hold it all in.

At last, the dam burst, and his tears began to flow. Her eyes, too, were wet when he finally lifted his arms and hugged her like he used to. After a moment, she spoke like the loving mother she was. "Babe, I need you to talk to me. I need to know what's wrong. Please. I need to know how to help you." The hurt in her voice stung him.

He sniffed loudly and lifted his head from her shoulder, his face a mess of drunk tears and welled-up emotion. "I…I don't know. I don't know what's wrong with me." He forced out the words between gritted teeth.

She squeezed him into her chest and felt his thump against hers. Something inside was trying to get out, but he held it back with all he had.

"You can tell me, Jay. You can tell me anything—everything. I want to know it all, every detail of what happened to you over there. I want you to unload it and let *me* carry it for a while. Let *me* carry *you* for a while." She leaned back and took his face in her hands. When he wouldn't look her in the eyes, she gently guided his gaze to meet hers. "What can I do? How can I help?" He didn't answer. "JP, I love you! With everything I have, I love you." She sniffled as a teardrop glided down his puffy face. "All I wanted while you were away was for you to come back home to me. But now that you're home, there's some part of you, *something* that's still over there. I have you, but I don't have *all of you*." She burst into tears and rested her head against his chest while she cried.

He placed his chin on her head, and after a moment, he kissed it.

"I'm sorry. I don't know…I don't…know *anything*, anymore." This time, he was holding her and rocking smoothly back and forth. His voice drifted as he spoke. It was ghostly and gone, as if he were searching for something he had lost. His heart, his mind, his soul, maybe. "I don't…I don't know who I am, anymore. And that scares the hell out of me," he let the words drip from his mouth before letting go of her.

He froze in place, staring off into the distance. The moon blazed at his back and shadows dimmed his face. He was grim and pale, mouth agape, eyes shifting and unblinking.

Then, floating toward his bed, he followed his shadow, climbed on top of the mattress, and sank there for the night.

And for the first time since he'd been back, Lisa felt fear for the man in the moonlight staring up at the swirling black knots in the ceiling above their bed.

<u>Chapter Eleven</u>

Letting Go

For fuck's sake gentle souls,
breathe;
calm your dying hearts;
let it be.
It is.
You are.
I am.
Silence.
Stop wasting
your troubled thoughts
on nonsense.

We are here to be,
so be.

When the sun rises on a cold night, lifting the frost from the tips of crusted leaves and strokes of dying grass, one is reminded of the way the world works. A lesson exists in the stirrings of morning—when the rooster wakes and yodels his sunrise song, when the robin hops toward his breakfast, eying the earth in the bacon breeze, and the laughter of youthful innocence bounce on their beds until weary champions robe and wobble from their sacks to make pancakes. When the fog in the valley breaks, and the wiggle of the morning wind rattles the leaves like a tambourine, and that thankful kiss of daylight tingles on the skin, a thoughtful mind might wonder how much they could love the light of day if it was not for the dreadful chill of night.

JP awoke to sunrays on his face. It was a welcomed, simple pleasure, often ignored by those who don't know any better. But for him, the sunlight gave hope. It was the morning that ended the night—when beast and demon lurked from the shadows to feast upon the weary and weak-hearted. It was a coffee-mugged *cheers* to the morning glow from a porch rocking chair, a pleasing smile sweeping over the grassy fields of hay bales and cut corn stocks. For JP, the rising sun was something he could not go without.

For the last few weeks, JP had taken a more prominent role in working the farm. And on this pleasant winter morning, he enlisted his son to tag along. Beside the idling tractor in the drive, JP, clad in a tan Carhart jacket and his dirt-stained jeans, had his .22 revolver holstered low on his right hip and a knife sheathed on his left. He snorted when Adin scurried from the front porch in his boots and matching jacket, *his knife* looped through his belt beside a bright green Nerf gun tucked into his pants—all while holding his Red Rider BB gun in his right hand and a blueberry muffin in his left.

A sharp terror ripped up his spine at the sight of his bright-eyed son holding a rifle. He cursed himself and the bitter-tasting reflex. Embarrassed, he shook it away and forced a smile. *Well, there's no doubt he's mine,* he thought, enjoying his son's hands-full shuffle over to the John Deere tractor.

"You ready? You got everything you need?" JP teased.

"I think so," he said, with crumbs on his cheeks, looking over his gear to be sure.

"Well, it definitely looks like you're ready. What, uh…what exactly do you plan on Nerf gunning out here this morning?"

Adin shrugged with bright eyes. "Whatever I need to, I guess."

"All right then. Prepared for anything. I can't argue with that."

JP climbed up the hand-me-down John Deere his grandfather passed down to him when he bought a new one a few years ago. "Hop on up, Bud." He reached out his hand to help his son climb up on his lap. "Here, let me hold your rifle."

Adin stepped back and clinched the rifle to his chest. He looked up at his father with scrunched brows. "Dad, a marine *never* gives up his rifle!"

Taken aback by how much his son remembered his stories, JP smirked. "Well, *this marine better*, or it's gonna be a long walk to Gram Gram's for breakfast pie."

Adin's jaw dropped as he scowled. "Daaad!" Then, he contemplated the long walk of the gravel driveway cut between the hayfields and disappearing into the bright sky up the hill. With a missing-teeth grin, he surrendered his rifle to his father's outstretched hand. "Mmm, pieeee," he whispered climbing up onto his father's lap.

They chugged along the gravel drive with Adin at the wheel, bouncing up and down and swerving more than usual as they passed the pasture where the last half-dozen of Grandpa's herd roamed, and then around the bend of the hayfield. Soon, Grandma's yard opened up to a large fenced-in chicken coop and a gray, two-car garage. Or, as Grandpa called it, *his shop*. The brown farmhouse loomed ahead, with a red chimney and a screened-in front porch. The hay barn stood beside the path to the hayfield along the driveway.

But the first stop was Grandma's kitchen. Because the workday couldn't start without a fresh slice of Grandma's peach pie.

"Good morning!" Grandma shouted after hearing the screen door slam. She wore her pajamas and pink robe while wiping down the kitchen countertop.

"Gram Gram!" Adin was first up the stairs, nearly knocking her over with a hug.

JP followed, tossing his jacket on the bench by the door. "Mornin'. Damn, that smells good!"

"Language!" Grandma's scolding eyes darted from JP to Adin and back.

JP snorted as he rolled up his sleeves, moseyed over, and inspected the three pies lined on the counter, like a grocery shopper selecting fruit. "He's heard way worse from his mother," he chuckled as Adin joined him at the counter.

Grandma dropped her shoulders and tilted her head sarcastically. "In an ornery mood this morning, are we?"

"Always," he replied, grabbing a plate and jabbing a fork into the center pie.

Grandma cleared her throat. "Uh, not before you come over here and give your grandmother a hug and a kiss, mister!" She stood before him with her hands on her hips and a dish towel dangling from her right hand.

"Yeah, Dad! Give her a hug."

JP laughed and left the fork standing straight up in the pie. "What is this? Gang up on Dad day?" he said, leaning in to give his grandmother a hug and a kiss on the cheek. "Good morning, Grandma. How are you this beautiful morning?"

She swatted at his sarcasm with the dishtowel. "Get outta here, and go eat your pie, you heathen."

JP wrapped his arm around his grandmother and kissed her on the head. "How you doing?" he whispered as she leaned her weight into his chest.

She took a deep breath before she spoke. "About as good as anyone could expect."

JP rubbed her back and gave her a proper good morning hug.

Adin, on the other hand, stood on his toes, eyes barely over the pie crust, as he sawed out a third of the peach pie with a butter knife.

"Woah, Buddy." JP took the knife from his hand and cut that piece in two, giving himself the larger slice before motioning to Grandma if she wanted any. She waved him off and shook her head, dabbing at the corners of her eyes with a tissue.

"Heyyy!" Adin protested, as JP lowered his son's plate into his waiting hands.

"Eat that first, little piggy."

Adin giggled. "You're the piggy! A big, fat, smelly…dirty pig!" He exaggerated his laugh and nearly dropped his pie on the floor.

"Uh-huh. See. That's what you get for being an ornery little shit," JP said, licking the peach filling from the fork in his hand.

"You two are so bad," Grandma smirked and shook her head. Then she sat down at the table where the coffee mug was still steaming.

Adin was all giggles as he dragged out his chair and climbed behind his plate of pie.

"Where do you think we get it from?" JP winked, as he poured himself and Adin a glass of orange juice. Balancing his plate on both glasses, he carefully made his way to the table. But not before pausing in front of Grandpa's uniformed picture, folded flag, and medals on the wall. He dipped his chin in respect as the glow from his eyes faded before he sat down.

"What's on the list, today?" he asked before slurping his orange juice.

Grandma grabbed a napkin from the wooden rooster holder in the center of the table and tossed it to Adin. "You're supposed to get more in your mouth than on your face, Silly."

Adin grinned and presented his pie face proudly before wiping filling and crumbs from his chin.

She took a sip of coffee and folded her hands on the table in thought. "Well, the fence in the far corner of the big pasture needs mending. You could bring a few bales of hay into the barn. Check to make sure the water is still running to the center trough—it's been acting up a little in the winter." She looked out the kitchen window at the sunny day. "It'd be a good day to walk both fence lines and see what lumber we need before the ground freezes. Adin, you could feed and water the chickens, check the fence and make sure the fox or coyotes can't get in."

JP listened intently, visualizing each task in his head. He had helped his grandfather on the farm for as long as he could remember. He was familiar with the ins and outs of keeping the place from falling apart—even after Grandpa sold off most of the herd and downsized in his old age. But he refused to sell them all and *actually* retire. "I'll retire when I'm dead," he'd say in his deep grunting voice. *Well,* JP thought, *I hope you're kicked back in your armchair with your feet up, a cold brew in your hand, with endless seasons of the Browns on rerun—well, the winning seasons anyway.* That was the kind of Heaven JP envisioned for his grandfather. And now, he just wanted to make him proud by keeping alive the dream he had planted right there in those wooded hills and golden fields.

The chickens fluttered and flapped in their pen when Adin opened the door to the coop. He loved to feed the chickens, so when JP tasked him with that responsibility while he stacked bales in the barn, Adin was more than happy to get the job done. A trail of concrete blocks, submerged in the earth, led down the hill away from the house and behind the garage to the familiar stench of foul chickens in the coop.

The coop itself—about the size of a large shed—was unnecessarily big for the dwindling flock Grandpa let shrink a little more each year. A cluster of fruit and nut trees Grandpa planted nearly two decades ago dotted around it. Matter of fact, it looked more like the concession stand at the city park than a place to house chickens. Ornate with dull and dirty white siding, it had two push-out windows, one to each side of the man-sized door, covered with wire fencing to keep the predators out in the summer when the windows would stay open. The roof had shingles, rowed and lined like a mini-house, hand-nailed by Grandpa himself while a young JP handed him supplies from the raised tractor bucket. To each side and the rear were separate fenced-in areas, each as large as the coop itself. Adin had learned from his great-grandpa that it was wise to keep the mean chickens away from the others and to let the chicks grow separate from the flock until they were big enough to fend for themselves.

The ruckus and commotion of chickens being chickens tickled Adin's funny bone. Everything amused him—the escalating squawking, jerking, and bobbing of their heads, their beady eyes looking angry and afraid all at once. The way they ran away and then ran back when he tossed handfuls of corn.

"Stupid chickens," he gleamed, as they pecked at the gold ground and muck.

Ornery like his father, Adin was a chicken chaser. He'd even reluctantly admit it—his guilty grin gave him away each time he tried to deny it. And while he tossed out grubby handfuls of feed from an old soup pot, he made his own chicken noises above the brown, cackling brood.

Finished, he turned the pot upside down and smacked out the crumbs, and returned it to the trash can of feed—but not before beating out a loud tune in harmony with their squawking on his newfound drum. Giving long thought to whether he would brave the thumping beaks of laying hens, he decided he would leave the egg gathering for his father. Lastly, he twisted the faucet and filled a mason jar with fresh water before splashing it into the buckets through the wire fence.

After slamming the door shut and chasing down his father on the tractor, Adin was ready for the next chore. They chugged along on the John Deere with a fresh bale of hay stabbed to the front spear. Even the black exhaust couldn't dampen Adin's bright-as-the-sun, ear-to-ear smile. He sat on his father's lap while steering the green guzzler past the paint-chipped windmill, alongside the tattered barn, and down the path in the hayfield. When they stopped at the gate, he hopped off and swung the rusty metal open for his father to jiggle through.

Watching his son's excitement reminded JP of his own childhood. The whole shebang—the farm, woods, hills, chickens, cows, and fields—was an Arcadian experience. A simple, rustic pleasure: the joy of the open air, the breeze tickling his cheeks, the scent of earth turning over in the tread of his tractor tires, the sound of a perched crow crying out as it took flight, the whitetails flicking from the hillsides off into the woods, their cotton backsides flashing until they were swallowed whole by the pines. It was Heaven, and he was a happy hostage to the nature of it all, their roots, this land, their shared dream for peace. Freedom existed in this kind of life, and JP wanted that *now* more than ever.

Once Adin closed the gate, he hopped back up on his father's lap, took charge, and told his dad when to go and when to stop as they bumped up the hill in the pasture to feed the cows. The modest brown and black herd was already trotting their way when they crested the hill in the center of the olive-colored pasture. It flattened out for a bit where his grandfather had placed the round bale feeder and one of three water troughs toward the back corner. JP slowed the rig to a stop before the feeder.

"Can I do it?" Adin turned to ask with big eyes and red cheeks.

"You think you can handle it?"

"Heck yeah!"

"Well, all right then. Let's get 'er done." He pressed the clutch and shifted into first gear. "You remember which way to move the stick?"

He nodded with his tongue out and hand already on the knob, gingerly tapping it up and down to get a feel for the weight of the bale.

"Well look at you! When did you become such a pro?"

"Gramps," Adin simply replied, gazing over the wheel in concentration.

JP nodded his head up and down. "Go figure. That's how I learned too," he boasted, trying to bond as two students who learned under the same professor.

"Duh." Adin was having none of it. He was in his own little world with one hand on the easy-turn knob of the steering wheel and one hand on the joystick, as they crept closer to the circle feeder.

The cows mooed impatiently, eyeing the bale from a few yards beyond the feeder. A single brave *or dumb* one waddled up to the front of the tractor and pulled at the loose hay hanging from the bundle.

"Get outta here, you!" Adin yelled from the driver's seat, and the cow scampered back with the group, chewing on his prize. Like he was born to be a farmer, Adin lowered the bale down into the blue steel cage, tipped his spear, and let it slide off the end. Then he raised it back up over the edge of the feeder while his father backed the tractor out of the way. The cows took to it like they had never eaten, whipping their tails at the late-season flies. They watched a moment as they frenzied. Betsy, the large brown one, shoved a calf out of the way whenever it got too close.

"Stop it, Betsy!" Adin yelled, before they turned around and headed for the fence that separated the big pasture from the small pasture.

They chugged along a while, Adin driving as before, and still smiling wide.

"Betsy's mean!" he blurted out, as if he'd been thinking about her for the last couple of minutes.

"What? Oh. Yeah. Well, she's bigger. She can get away with it."

"That doesn't mean she should bully the others!" Adin yelled over the engine.

"You're right. I guess when you're big, you think you can do anything you want."

"Well, when I'm big, I'm going to help people, not hurt them."

That put a glossy sparkle in JP's eyes. He rubbed Adin's head with affection. "Good, Bud. That's the right thing to do." His heart fluttered as glanced up at the oak tree on the hill. *Good roots,* he thought. "Your mother must be doing something right," he said more to himself than Adin.

"Huh?" Adin yelled back.

"I said, your mother must be doing something right for you to think like that," JP said a little louder.

"Oh." His eyes were fixed on the path in front of him, making sure to stay in the tire marks. "Mom didn't teach me that! *You did*, Dad!" he hollered.

JP looked confused. "I did? When?"

This time Adin glanced back at his father and shrugged. "When you went to fight the bad guys."

JP's throat tingled. His chest warmed. And for the first time in a long time, he felt proud. He pulled his son's head into his chin and kissed it.

"Heyyy! I'm trying to drive!"

His father snorted. "My bad. My bad."

JP eased off the throttle as they came to the back fence that needed mending. A small tree had blown down during a recent storm and landed on the barbed wire, pulling it down with it and snapping a fence post. JP surveyed the site as the tractor idled low to a stop, and he shut it off.

"Well, we made it. Come on. Hop down."

Adin looked up as soon as his feet hit the ground. "I need my gun.".

"You do? What for? Is there something out there? A wolf? A bear? A tiger?" He tried to stir Adin's imagination in his fake, dramatic voice.

"No, Daaad. For security. So you fix the fence." Adin's tone indicated his father should have known that.

"Ohhh. Okay, I see." JP winked as he handed down his BB gun. "That's pretty smart. I could use someone watching my back while I work."

"I know. I got your seven."

JP chuckled. "Uhhh, you mean six?"

Adin thought for a moment. "Yeah, I got that too!"

JP pulled the small chainsaw from the toolbox Grandpa mounted behind the seat and got to work, diligently sawing off tree limbs, pulling them into a pile, and cutting the trunk into firewood.

Adin took turns sneaking up on birds with his BB gun, aiming and shooting, and then hanging his head when he missed. Adin reminded JP so much of himself. But the longer he worked, the more a nagging feeling urged him to be observant. For some reason, he couldn't help but feel a certain unease pricking the back of his neck as he worked, head down, in the noisy fog of the saw.

As the late morning sun reached higher in the sky, JP shed his Carhart down to his flannel and draped it over the fence. Stretching up toward the sunlight, he let its burn bathe his face. For just a moment, the glint of heat reminded him of the desert glare back in Iraq. He arched his back one last time and let a deep breath be his only break. *Too much work, too little time.* His grandfather's words echoed in his head—a blistering lesson he learned as a teen. Taking in the picturesque rolling hills, grassy fields, and surrounding woods, he thought about the times he rushed through his chores to hang out with friends, go hunting, four-wheeling, exploring, or drinking in the backwoods at the edge of the property.

He was thankful for those days, the ones that taught him about hard work and responsibility. Though he'd never admit it back then, he had learned so much under the guided direction of his grandfather. Like how to use a chainsaw. He had watched his grandfather cut wood for the fireplace for as long as he could remember. But it wasn't until his thirteenth birthday that Grandpa thought he could do it on his own. JP chuckled to himself as he remembered trying to think up a good story on the slow walk back to the barn to explain why Grandpa's chainsaw was pinched and bent in the trunk of a tree along the wood line.

Grandpa had simply paused under the hood of his old work truck and then continued to crank his wrench on a bolt. "Well, you better go get it unstuck, huh?" he grumbled without looking.

Back then, it took over an hour trying to free the bar from the tree. By then it was so bent beyond repair, he knew he'd be working the next few days for free to pay it off. Though he had been on trembling knees back then, now, JP chuckled and shook his head about how much he *thought* he knew and how much his grandfather still had to teach him.

JP was lost in thoughts about the past, reminiscing about his childhood on the farm, and carelessly stacking the wood into a pile beside the fence. Preoccupied, he wasn't paying much attention to his son sneaking around the tractor behind him.

Adin had become bored with the birds and turned on his father. Creeping behind the green machine, he poked his head out from beside the big tire with his Nerf gun in hand. His father piled logs like a robot—tossing them one by one and sometimes two-by-two onto the stack, where they fell neatly into place. *Dad's a lumberjack*, he thought. But today, he was an evil, enemy lumberjack building bunkers for his army to fire onto the make-believe town on the next hilltop over.

Adin took aim, arching his muzzle up into the air. He would need to lob the dart high into the sky for it to make it all the way to his father. With all his might and imagination, he screamed at the top of his lungs just before he fired.

"INCOMINGGG!"

Instinctively, Sgt. Grimm dove into the dirt and buried himself as low as he could, covering his head and neck and cradling into a ball. The sick feeling of death crept onto his skin. It tingled and burned like electricity. The anticipation of where the explosion would land, where the shrapnel would rip into his flesh— it all slowed down into a heavy cream of thoughts, like he was trapped in that grass, holding onto himself, awaiting death, and no matter how long it took for the blast to come, he could not unstick himself from where he had fallen. His body was heavy and immobile, foreign and uncontrollable. But his mind—his mind—tried to outrun the smoke and fire. A fire he could feel on his face, and a shock wave that turned in his gut. In his mind's eye, he could see the Hell before him. And yet still, he tried to bury himself deeper into the earth.

The Nerf dart landed on his shoulder, and he screamed out like molten steel had melted into his flesh. The dart bounced and rolled down his arm to the ground in front of his face. For a moment, he was confused, lost, baffled at the toy on his battlefield. Then, in an echo, he heard his son calling out.

"Dad! Dad! Are you okay?" Adin ran up to him and touched his shoulder.

JP jerked and groaned as if his son's fingers were blades ripping into him. "Dad? Dad, it's me!" He shook him. "Get up! Please get up. I'm sorry!"

His father blinked and unraveled from the fetal position. He turned and looked at Adin. *Is he real? Am I really home, or is this another twisted dream?*

Adin leaned into his father, his head pressed into his shoulder, and squeezed him with all the might of his love. "I'm sorry! I'm sorry! Daddy, please forgive me!" he sobbed.

JP rolled to his knees, pushed his son's fire eyes away, and wobbled to his feet. The tractor was real. The grass was real. The field and mooing cows were real. He *really was home.* Then anger replaced the embers, leaving the same kind of burning in his blood. "Goddamn it, Adin! What the fuck?" He roared at his son like a lion. "Why the fuck would you do that? Huh? Answer me!"

"I didn't mean to, I–"

JP's callused hand slapped across his son's cheek. "Don't talk back to me!"

He clenched his son's shoulder, shaking his finger in his face. "You didn't mean to what? Do something so stupid, so awful, so goddamned awful?" His anger blew from his mouth like a torch. "Why the hell would you do that? What's wrong with you?"

"I'm sorry! I'm sorry! I was just playing!" Adin's face recoiled, and his tears came fast and hard. He'd never heard his father's voice sound so threatening. He'd never seen such viciousness in his father's narrow eyes. Terrified, he began to bawl hysterically. He didn't know what to do. His father's rage, like a cannon in his face, roared and boomed before him. He had to get away. He had to leave. He had to run. The Nerf gun dropped in the brown grass at his feet, and off he dashed toward the house, calling out to his mother. "Mom! Mom! Dad's gone crazy! Mooom!"

Watching his son disappear through the field, JP's senses stirred back to him. All at once, he realized what had just happened, and it drained his face pale. "Adin, wait! I'm sorry! I'm sorry! Come back! I didn't mean to…"

But it was too late. His son was halfway to the house, to his mother.

And hearing his sobs fade away ripped into him like iron shrapnel. The breeze sent a chill through the air. His skin bumped up. He rubbed at his temples as shame and dread reverberated through his bones. *Oh God, what did I do?*

"*Fffuck!*" was all he could say.

Chapter Twelve

Mortar Us

I.

I can't see you from post three,
this dusty sandbagged bunker,
but I know you're out there. Hiding
behind your turban-wrapped face;
you think you're a bandit; Ali Baba;
thief; stealing the peace from the night.

II.

The hum of my thermals sucking white
figures from the darkness tickles my nose
and drones out the river's wind. Though faint
and far away, I can still see the palms sway,
pointing toward the cities few speckled lights.
The green one, a mosque, flickers on and off;
there must be bombing up North. The power
cuts from the stone houses across the river,
normal, I know, but boredom hopes for more.

More buzzing down past the dunes, past
the groves, another boat spotlighting fish,
fishermen catching trout, or whatever the
native fish is.

It's been seven hours since the last explosion,
when evening prayer brought out the loyals.
And I'll never get used to those concussions,
but I've learned that the whistling means it'll
land over there.

I pick up the range card, which is permanently
marked on leftover MRE cardboard. It's seven
hundred and fifty meters to the river. I click the
sights on my SAW to a thousand.

Stray dogs, matted, mangy, rabid
cousins of Brewskie back home, bark
at each other in a lust. It perks my eyes
to the East Ridge. It's all darkness now.
My NVGs can't penetrate the distance.
For a moment, I feel less of a killer;

vulnerable; blind. How did Hathcock do
it in the Jungle? I imagine that he slept with
Death, with the Devil, or some wicked charm
on fate. He must have been a smooth talker.
While here, I stutter on the radio.

III.

The thumps come in threes, sending red
headlamps running from the shitters. The
last one out, still holding to his trousers, is
swallowed up by the smoke. From this shelter,
I watch him die. Shrapnel to the throat, his
blood shinning scarlet in the Corpsman's
dim light. He couldn't even gargle his last words.

In sand and dust, you slither away; just like
that viper Phil found and let go at OP Paige;
you disappear into your oasis.

In sweat-stained letters back home to dad,
I tell him and God how much killing you
would make me happy. I wait weeks for
restitution. But it never comes. Dad only
talks of home, and God only listens.

"What the hell happened out there today? He was shaking when he came
inside." Lisa had kept her distance from JP when he came in for the evening,
offering him only a cold shoulder and sharp eyes with dinner. She waited until
Adin was asleep before she lit into her husband.

Out on the back porch, at her request to keep from waking their son, she
had her arms crossed and head tilted standing between him and the door. Her
cheek muscles flexed waiting for an answer.

He was backed against the rail, leaning on it for support with a drink in his hand and a weary face. "I know. I know. I messed up. I'm sorry." He took a sip of his whiskey and threw up his arms. "I don't know what you want me to say. I'm sorry!"

"JP, that's not good enough. I need more than that. You *owe me* more than that. He cried on my lap for ten minutes, trying to understand why you were so mad at him." Her eyes sliced at his cloak, trying to unveil whatever it was that he was hiding.

"I'm sorry. I don't know what else to say. He startled me. That's it." He took another drink. "Besides, I think it would do him some good to know the difference between a time to play and a time to work."

"You're kidding me, right?" She growled through her teeth. "You're going to blame this on a seven-year-old child? You're the adult! He looks up to you. He wants to be *just like you.*" She exhaled. *"You hit him."*

"I disciplined him."

"For what? Being a kid!?"

"For being disrespectful and talking back."

"Jesus, JP. This isn't the marines. He's just a kid. He didn't even know what he did wrong. He was terrified."

JP searched his glass for help, then the deck floor, and then the pines, before exhaling a long, deep breath. "I know. I *know.* But he's fine. He said he was okay and he forgives me." The ice rattled as he tipped his glass back against his lips, and he wiped his mouth with his arm.

She stared him down, trying to choose her words wisely, tactically. "That's not the point!"

His guilt turned defensive. "You know how many times I've had someone yell at me like that? How many times Grandma and Grandpa slapped my face for talking back? And look at me!" He pounded his chest and swung his arms out as if to show his lack of damage. "I'm just fine!"

"Fine? You think you're *fine?*" She shook her head, dismissed him. Then walked to the corner of the porch, where she let her emotions overtake her, and she sobbed.

JP started for the door. He was low on whiskey and words but still hesitated with his hand on the handle before going inside. He returned with a blanket and a glass full to the rim.

She was hugging herself, letting the tears roll freely down her cheeks. The night air nipped at her damp face while she searched the whispering pines for answers. She pulled her hoodie tighter when she heard the door open. When her husband walked out with ice clinking against the glass, she blinked hard, took a deep breath, and swallowed the rising resentment. She dabbed the tears with her sleeve as he approached her from behind.

Sitting his drink down on the railing beside her, he wrapped the blanket over her shoulders. Then he tried rubbing the warmth back into them, but she pulled away. So, he leaned against the railing.

"Lisa, I'm sorry. I really am. I lost it. I lost my cool, and I apologize. To him and to you. I shouldn't have done what I did, and I'm really ashamed of it. Embarrassed even, to be honest." His words were sincere. But she just sniffled and slid her sleeve across her nose.

When she didn't reply, he knew she deserved more, and the urge to help her understand pulsed through him. "Look, I don't...I don't know..." He trailed off, searching for the words. She tilted her head toward him, waiting for his confession.

He crossed his arms, squeezing his chest and his jaw. He wanted so badly to take another drink, but he knew he had to give his wife *something, some kind* of explanation, *some reason* for his behavior.

His head shook as he exhaled loudly. "There's something...*wrong*. I just..." He stared at his glass, the beads of water dripping down like tears, and he reached for it.

She could *feel* his struggle, tangible in the tension, in her words, his tone, his trembling. She wanted to help him get it out. "You're different," she said, turning around and causing him to freeze with his whiskey halfway to his lips.

"What do you mean *different?*"

Her big blue eyes sparkled in the starlight. Filled with sorrow and concern, they pierced his heart. It was a look he had only seen one time before, back when his drinking was excessive, and he crashed his truck into a tree on Old 21. It was *that* look which begged him to put the bottle down. And he did, for a long time. Until the war wiped that promise from his memory, and he leaned on the whiskey to chase away his fears.

"You're not *you,* anymore. You never used to explode like that." A tear stung her eye and streaked down her face.

He set the glass back down without taking a sip and wiped her cheek with the back of his finger.

She stared at his glass. "You're not the same man who left. And I know—I *knew*—you wouldn't be. I mean, they told us all about it, how the war would change you. They sent us a damn video that explained *what to expect from your marine.*"

She shook her head and looked up at the pin-prick stars. "*Your marine,*" she huffed. "Even in the video, they couldn't call you my husband. I should have known it then, that you would come back as more of a *marine* than the gentle, loving man you were before you left."

This time, he welcomed that sip of whiskey like a cold drink to a dry mouth. "Lisa, I'm *still* your loving husband. I'm *still* me. I'm just...hurting."

Her lip quivered. The emotion tingled at the back of her nose and eyes until all at once, she let loose, and her tears flowed freely down her scrunched, and grieving face. She tried to cover her *ugly* with the sleeve of her hoodie, embarrassed by the emotional outburst.

He watched just for a moment, not sure what she wanted him to do, not sure if he should give her space or close the gap between them.

But the space between them had been long and wide for long enough. Reaching out, he opened his heart for her to climb on in. And she did, as she leaned into him and sobbed into his chest. He held her. And she unraveled. She wept. And he untangled. With wet eyes, her head under his chin, and the faint glow through the window of the candle on the table, they swayed together in the light, in each other's arms.

A few minutes went by, and he broke the soft whimpering silence with a kiss to her forehead. "I need you. More *now* than ever—I need you." His voice cracked. "I'm broken. I can feel it like a poison inside of me. There's so much rage and anger and pain that's burning a hole into my head."

She leaned back to look into his eyes. "Jay. I'm *here*. I'm here *with* you. Babe, you don't have to do this on your own. Whatever *this* is—we can fight it together. We can get through it together." She kissed his cheek, and then his shivering lips. "But I need you to let me in. Damn it, Jay. You stubborn, stubborn man. I need you to talk to me, to tell me what you feel, to tell me how to help you." Her tone reverberated inside of him. "Because I don't know how to. Baby, I don't know how to heal you if you won't tell me what's hurting you."

The sickness was making its way to the surface, and he felt ill. Not sure if it was the whiskey or the poison that he buried inside of him, he began to sweat and tingle. His body was hard and tense, and then he shuttered like a sick dog.

She rubbed at his neck, his arms loosely around her, their hips still together, but he was in another place. He was away, distant, lost in the far reaches of his razor-wired mind. He waded through the blood and bodies buried in his memories. The persecution on his face, the pain of the past—it unfolded before her, crushing her. How badly she wanted to take that nightmare away from him was paralyzing.

"It was me," he said in a daze. "It was *meee*. *My* fault. *I did it.* I hesitated. I didn't pull the goddamn trigger when I should have!" He spoke like someone else was reading his story. Like it was some judge reading his verdict, his sentence. From behind the hard bars of his own prison, he confessed. "I didn't shoot the kid. I couldn't. I *should've fucking shot him!* Now they're dead. I got them killed. *I* killed them! *I fucking killed Joey!*"

~

That night, his sleep was restless and noisy. Explosions, rockets, and body parts painted his dreams. JP found himself in the desert. But it wasn't the kind of desert he experienced in Iraq—this was the movie kind of desert. Golden, sandy dunes rolled on as far as he could see. Rippled heat waves rose from their crests. There was no vegetation, only a white-hot sky, gritty sand, and a flaming sun.

And the sun—it was more than just a bright circle in the sky; it was fire, red coals, and flames licking out at JP's face. He felt the sting of it all, like he was the main dish roasting in an oven, like he was being cooked alive.

Yes, that was the feeling: he was being broiled, baked, and browned. He spun on a spit over an open flame in a sand and stone-lined firepit. The glowing embers and coals strobed red, white, and blue. He tried to free himself from the heat, but his hands and feet were zip-tied together. He was bound and trapped. Spinning and cooking, burning and baking, he felt his flesh melting and dripping from his bones.

He tried to scream. He tried to call for help—for his squad, for his men, for Joey. But no matter how loud he screamed, his voice was puny and weak, one which only he could hear.

Suddenly, he was in a room—cold tile squares were gritty under his bare feet. There was a hood over his head. The taste of dirt and burlap dabbed his lips. His hands were bound behind him on a steel folding chair. His toenailed scraped at the grooves and mortar between tiles.

Someone entered the room, their boots thumping closer and closer until the person's magnitude blotted the front of him, until the man's breath fluttered against the hood. But the man didn't speak. Instead, he smothered JP with his presence, towering over him, right up against him, a mere nose-length away from his face. Intimidating, frightful, and uncomfortable. JP squirmed to get away, to get free, but the heavy shadow of the man stayed with him, over him, on him, *in him.*

The room faded away to darkness. Sgt. Grimm felt the weight of a weapon in his hand and the grind of earth on his elbows, knees, and stomach. The lack of visibility was frustrating, infuriating, the anticipation agonizing as he waited, belly down, to ambush the enemy. He reached for his night-vision goggles mounted to his helmet. The weight of his gear pounded him into the dirt when he tried to rise. He groaned, grunted in anger, and stretched his arm out, desperately trying to reach his goggles. *I NEED them!* he thought. *I have to have them!* He stretched with all his might until his fingers touched their round, hard plastic. Accomplishment, relief, and hope filled him as he flipped them down over his eyes. But nothing. Only darkness. He'd given his last two batteries to his point man so he could watch for IEDs.

His heart sank. His gut turned. *How am I going to see the enemy without my NVGs?* Anger overwhelmed him; the last resupply had not brought enough batteries for them all. Then a shot rang out in the night. He raised his rifle at the flash but didn't fire. He *couldn't* fire. No matter how fiercely he wanted to pull his trigger, he was frozen, unable, and completely helpless.

A flash illuminated the night, and a *poof* sounded in the distance. Sgt. Grimm was now in the sandbagged guard tower on top of the concrete building where his company slept. Anxiety rushed through his blood, pounding like a ticking clock in his temples. He searched the Iraqi desolate land fading in from the haze surrounding him: the speckled lights across the river popped into existence, the tops of the palms a few hundred meters away were sharp and swaying, the rocky hills beyond the river were jagged shadows against the starry sky. Two more flashes, two more *thuds* bashing the silent night. He heard them. He saw them. He *felt* them.

Then, the whistling overhead screeched into his eardrums like a bottle rocket. He looked down into the courtyard at his friends mingling about: happy and laughing, joking, looking at a Playboy magazine, and throwing bayonets into a sandbag with a turban wrapped around it and a beard scratched on with a Sharpie. None of them had their gear on. They were just hanging out, out in the open, out in the danger zone, exposed and unprotected in the impact area.

Some played cards at a table in the dirt: Joey, Cpl. Richardson, the high-value target from the raid, Joey's radioman, and the little brown-haired, bright-eyed boy who blew up Joey's squad. They laughed and played together. Buddies. Bros. Best friends. But Sgt. Grimm had to warn them. He *had* to protect Joey!

"Incoming! Incoming! Incoming!" he shouted at the top of his lungs.

No one moved. *No one cared.* They just laughed, joked, talked, threw knives, and played cards.

JP jumped up and down in his bunker, waving his arms and yelling. Finally, Joey saw him, and looked up with his shit-stirring smirk and waved. *He fucking waved!*

"No! No! No! No!" JP called out. "INCOMING! Get down! Take cover!"

But Joey just grinned and waved as if they were neighbors at their mailboxes greeting each other across the street.

Then, the little Iraqi boy turned his gaze to Sgt. Grimm. Their eyes met and locked. JP could see the different swirls of brown, tan, and gold in his eyes. He was smiling, but it wasn't a happy smile. It was a desperate smile, a twisted smile. To Sgt. Grimm, it was a taunting, evil smile.

Suddenly, everything stopped: the laughter, Joey waving and grinning, the moving and talking. Everyone stared up at Sgt. Grimm in his bunker, their stares stabbing him all over. They judged him, hated him for being under shelter and safety.

But the little boy moved; he walked through the middle of their darkened faces wearing the same bulky Thor T-shirt, black with a red hammer in the center. A spotlight cast a bright halo around him, like he was the lead actor in some tragic play. His shadow was long and narrow and followed him as the sea of men parted, giving way for him to maneuver. He was heading straight for Joey and sneering up at JP.

In his hand was a small, black remote. He held it above his head proudly, smirking like he was hoisting a trophy after a victory. No one would stop him. No one would stand in his way. No one, but Sgt. Grimm, knew what the little boy was capable of.

"No! Stop! Stop him! Somebody stop that kid!" JP hollered from his bunker.

And then, standing among flames, as bright as the sun itself, the boy turned into Adin. Quickly, his glimmer faded into terror, despair, wide-eyed fear, and fluster. Screeching and screaming in the sandy courtyard shattered the silence as Adin searched the burning faces around him in horror.

All at once, every sound ceased to a *swooshing* stop. In a slow-motion, fiery explosion, Adin's head snapped up, and he drilled his speckled eyes into his father's as he uttered one simple word—

"Boom."

Lisa shook JP awake. "Baby! Baby, wake up! JP! Wake up!"

Thrashing, he blinked and stared up at the ceiling fan humming above him like a helicopter propeller.

"No! No! Adin! Don't!" he hollered in a blurry haze.

Lisa combed back his hair and hushed his sweaty, trembling form with her tender touch. "Shh. It was just a bad dream. Baby, it's okay. I'm here. Everything's fine. You're okay."

He kicked the debris, the loose covers to the floor, and gripped the sheet beneath him like it was the earth between his fingers.

Lisa folded her arm around him and snuggled up to his damp chest. His heart thumped against it like a sledgehammer on a concrete floor. "Just breathe, baby. Breathe with me. Nice and slow. In and out. That's it. You're doing great. Everything's fine. You're fine now. You're home."

His body, still tense from the images of his nightmare throbbing in his brain, flinched as it flexed. He moved to push her away, like she was a lifeless body on top of him. He felt smothered and on fire.

But she held on tight, pulling him back into her body. Kissing his wet cheek, she pulled his face to meet hers. His eyes were lost and hollow. The light had not yet filled their darkness. She caressed him and kissed him, not knowing what else to do.

He rubbed at his eyes and let out a vibrating breath, stepping back from the ledge and into reality. His grip loosened on the soaked sheet. His hard body started to relax.

"Lisa?" he asked, confused.

"Yeah, baby, it's me. I'm right here. I got you. It's okay."

His eyes and fingers scanned her face as if he didn't believe he was really at home in bed with his beautiful wife. Then all at once, he saw her. He felt her. And his whole being filled with humiliation. He crumbled into tears and shame.

"No, baby!" She pleaded with emotion jerking at her throat. "Don't. It's okay. I understand." Tears crept into the corners of her eyes.

He turned away to face the window. She snuggled up against his sopping back and cuddled him, rubbing his arm and shoulder with her gentle hand.

And then footsteps creaked in the hall. JP's body flexed and jerked as the door squeaked open. He darted for the gun beside his glass on his nightstand and swung it toward the door.

"JP, no!" His wife screamed.

But it was too late. JP stared down the glowing sights of his pistol aimed directly at the center of his son's chest.

Chapter Thirteen

The Pistol on My Nightstand

I wake, fist clenched and damp.
The reflection of headlights, like flares
across my room, catch the fading words
of some lost sentence. Such a strange voice,
scared and mean; I haven't heard its tone
in years.

But now, eyes blinking and confused; there is
no sand, no sun, no warm wind stinging at my
cheeks. In the mixed glow of a quarter moon
and red alarm, I search the corners of my room.
But I see no threat, no danger; only a ceiling fan
buzzing low and sheets heavy, binding at my ankles.

To my left, mounted to the wall, my gun rack,
made of oak and cherry when I was a boy. The
different calibers make shadows like fingers
reaching out for me.

Under my mattress sticks a blade fixed to a
wooden handle. And at times I test its angle,
try its slicing steel; I feel for it before I sleep.

But on these nights, when thunder creeps in
from the West and shakes these walls, pulling
me from my past, I reach for the pistol on my
nightstand, feel its weight, its power, its comfort.

I pull the slide to the rear, let it go, hear the
clink of metal on brass and chamber a round.
I imagine the cavity in your chest; blood and
flesh burned; pearl shards of bone; life smoking
from your holes. Death. Justice.

Then, barefoot and shirtless, I walk this house
armed until the morning sun.

JP's knee shook up and down like a jackhammer when the therapist finally entered room four. Dressed in a polo and clean jeans, which Lisa had laid out for him, they both sat waiting for what seemed like an hour. But glancing at his phone again, only thirteen minutes had ticked away.

The morning after JP's colossal nightmare, Lisa had dialed the therapist's number and handed her husband the phone. A sleepless December had come and gone, waiting for the VA to set up an appointment. And January's bitter cold had nipped at their noses as they marched into the Cambridge Veteran's Affairs Medical Facility.

The room wasn't set up for couples. The only extra chair was a black cushioned folding chair in the far corner that had a stack of educational books indenting the padding. JP set the books on the floor and dragged the chair beside him at the oval table along the wall. The buzzing overhead lights and the occasional coughing down the hall broke through the quiet and calm as JP took in the scene. A desk in the corner with a computer and keyboard, a brown swivel chair, and an American flag tin holding various colors of pens and pencils. Several small stacks of pamphlets in pastel colors were on the corner of the desk. Lisa stuffed a stack in her purse while they waited. Pearl walls decorated in veteran-themed pictures, informationals—one about mental health, complete with arrows and explanations—and inspirational quotes or photos, each meant to encourage and enlighten. But for JP, it felt more like elementary school, where the teachers had tried too hard to create the perfect learning environment.

Lisa grabbed his hand when the door opened, and a large man in a black Under Armour polo walked in with a white placard nametag that read: Dr. Clatterson. JP stood up, letting Lisa's hand fall back into her lap as he shook Dr. Clatterson's hand, which seemed more like they were competing for *The Firmest Handshake Award* than a simple introduction.

"JP? Dr. Clatterson." His deep voice matched his large frame, graying stubble, and dark hair. "Does JP stand for something, orrr?"

"*Jäger, please.* My dad was drunk when he named me."

Lisa laughed and smacked his arm. "Stop it!"

JP cracked a smile, and Dr. Clatterson, looking confused for a moment, grunted as he stood back holding his clipboard and pen. "Well, make it two, if you're buying." He chuckled boisterously, reaching out his hand to shake Lisa's. "You must be his wife?" he said with a wink.

"Yes, Lisa. Nice to meet you. Should I just let you two head off to the bar for this appointment, orrr?"

"No. No. No. Gave it up a few years ago. My wife would kill me, probably quite literally." He laughed out loud and motioned toward the chairs. "Please, have a seat." He wheeled his chair from the desk and sat across from JP at the long ends of the table.

"So, should we get started?" He flipped the top page on his chart, skimming the information that the nurse scribbled nearly twenty minutes ago during her initial interview. Then he pulled out a few clean sheets of computer paper from the bottom of the stack on his clipboard and snapped them on the top. "I like to doodle when I talk, do you mind?"

"Uhhh, nope. Not at all. Doodle away, dude."

"All right, good. Thank you." Dr. Clatterson slid a pen from the bottom button of his V-neck shirt and clicked it open.

JP shimmied and shuffled in his chair, not able to find a comfortable position. So, he sat up straight as if he were at a job interview and clasped his hands together atop the table.

"Relax. Relax. The first few questions are the easy ones," Dr. Clatterson winked. "Marines, huh?"

"Yep."

Dr. Clatterson raised his sleeve to show off his eagle, globe, and anchor tattoo on his shoulder.

"Nice." JP tried to sound interested.

"Not really." Dr. Clatterson grunted. "I was eighteen, drunk at Lejeune, and paid half of what a *good* artist would have charged. Lesson learned. Semper Fi."

"Semper Fi."

"What was your MOS?"

"Infantry." JP side-glanced his wife.

She was studying him and his reactions, ready to offer support when she could. "I think he's been infantry since the day he was born." She winked at her husband.

He shrugged in return. "Raised by a Grunt. What can I say?"

"Oh, your father's a marine too?"

The light faded from JP's face as his eyes shifted. He quickly found interest in the diagram of the central nervous system pushed against the wall. "No."

The patch of skin between Dr. Clatterson's eyes wrinkled.

"No," JP continued. "My father died on 9/11. I was raised by my grandparents." He fidgeted with his thumbs, and Lisa reached across to pat them sympathetically.

"His grandparents are…*were* the sweetest. He was very fortunate to have such loving and caring people take him in and raise him to be the *wonderful* man he is today."

"Oh, I'm sorry. Are they no longer living?"

JP cleared his throat. "My grandpa passed away not too long ago. But Grandma is still baking pies and bossing us around on the farm." He tried to smile, but found it exhausting and let his shoulders fall instead.

"I see. Helluva generation. To make it through Vietnam and the Cold War. Scary times. I can still remember practicing nuclear attack drills in grade school. You know, back when they thought a school desk would protect you from a nuclear bomb." Dr. Clatterson leaned across the desk with a smirk. "More like learning how to bend over and kiss your ass goodbye, if you ask me."

"Yeah, I couldn't even imagine. Grandpa used to tell me about those times when I was younger. What a world to grow up in." He pinched his lips together and shook his head.

"Yeah, but look at us," Lisa offered. "We had 9/11, Afghanistan, Iraq—*three times*, ISIS…*and social media*!" She tilted her head. "We've done our share of messing the world up too."

JP rolled his eyes at how hard his wife was trying to be a part of the conversation. "All right. All right. Fair enough."

"So, JP…" Dr. Clatterson leaned back in his chair, folded his arms, and searched the ceiling in thought. "Why are we here today?"

JP raised his eyebrows at his wife, a sign for her to speak up.

"Well, he recently returned home from deployment, about a few months ago, and well, I know they told us—the wives and such—to keep an eye out for signs of PTSD." She looked over at her husband with *sorry* in her eyes. "Well, my husband, JP…he's been…"

JP cleared his throat. "I've gone off on my son a few times." He blurted out.

Lisa studied her husband again. She wasn't sure if he was truly apologetic, or if this was all just some sort of joke to him. She got the sense that he *wanted* to get help, but she could tell he wasn't sure how to accept it. "And the nightmares," she added.

Dr. Clatterson, still leaning back in his chair, rubbed his chin, taking it all in. JP looked past him at the door.

"He hasn't been the same since he's been back. He's not the person he was when he left." Lisa sounded as though she were pleading for help, and it made her husband shift uncomfortably. "He sleeps with a loaded gun on his nightstand."

Dr. Clatterson shook his head knowingly. "That's pretty typical with returning veterans. They've had a weapon glued to their hands for a year. It's been their lifeblood, like an extension of their body. Hell, they even *sleep* with the damn thing. So, it's not that unusual for him to feel like he needs it."

"He keeps it beside the flashlight he uses to shine out the window before he climbs into bed. It's like he's searching for something—or for someone. I don't know." She threw her hands up, half expecting her husband to chime in. But he didn't.

Dr. Clatterson leaned forward, focusing on the center of the table between him and JP, finding his words deliberately. He was familiar with this type of behavior, not just because he himself had experienced the same thing from his two tours to Afghanistan, but because it was quite typical for combat veterans to come home and still feel like they needed to fight off some sort of enemy. It was common for them to feel that the things they loved were under constant threat.

"JP, there's no one out there. Who are you searching for?" He folded his hands on the table and met JP's shifting eyes. "Son, the enemy's gone. You won. You're back home now. It's time to drop your pack."

Taking a deep breath, JP aimlessly searched the ceiling corners before he spoke. "Look, I can appreciate what you're trying to do. But I'm going to do whatever I have to do to protect my family. And if that means I have to search outside the windows or look a little crazy doing it, then so be it. At least they'll be safe with me patrolling the house." A faint wince came with the last few words, and he hoped nobody noticed.

"I can respect that, a man who wants to protect his family. But at what point does the behavior go from rational to irrational? Have you thought about that?" Dr. Clatterson scribbled and traced two circles on the mostly blank sheet of paper and connected them with arrows.

"You see, when we display a bold behavior such as keeping a loaded gun unsecured on the nightstand or searching the yard with a flashlight before we can go to sleep—when we do these things, we have to be able to set some kind of limit. Would you agree? Do we not have to keep ourselves in check?"

JP nodded. "I agree."

"Well then, where's your line? You said you *patrol the house?* Is that something you did before the war orrr?" He trailed off with a shrug.

A tingle sparked in JP's fingertips. The dampness under his arms was uncomfortable and embarrassing. *Why am I being attacked? Am I wrong for trying to protect my family? Hell no, I'm not! I'd do whatever it takes to keep them safe!* He slouched a little farther back into his chair.

"Okay, Doc, you've made your point. Not that it's going to change anything, but you made your point." He caught Lisa's concern out of the corner of his eye.

"Fair enough," Dr. Clatterson scribbled out his circles and started etching a dark box below them. "So, let's say that your mind is a box, right? It could be a cardboard box, maybe a footlocker, or toolbox—maybe a package your wife ordered from Amazon." He winked at Lisa. "And in this box…is *everything*." He scribbled and jabbed his pen inside the square on the paper.

"Okay." JP shrugged.

"Right. So, you stuff everything inside this box—your family, your finances, your choices, your emotions, your thoughts about the future, your dreams, your problems, your past—*everything*. Well, before too long, this box is stuffed so tightly it begins to tear at the seams. You understand?"

JP bit his lip. "Uh-huh." Lisa nodded beside him, fully invested, probably more involved in what Dr. Clatterson was saying than him. This was her way of *helping*.

"Great. So, what do we do when the box becomes too full? You understand?" He drew little blue scribbles and dots overflowing the shaded square and tapped his pen against it. "Some things just can't stay inside the box. We have to unpack them, you see? Otherwise, our box will explode, and everything will come tumbling out. We'll have a mess on our hands, JP. Does that make sense?" His head was cocked slightly, and his eyebrows arched.

Lisa was still nodding and slurping it all in when JP glanced at her. "Well, it looks like it makes a lot of sense to my wife." He cracked a smile as she smacked him on the arm.

"JP, be serious!" A shimmer teased on her lips. "We want to help. Please. For me?"

"All right. All right." He sat up in his chair, leaned forward on his elbows, and stared down Dr. Clatterson. "What should I unpack?"

"Hm." He raised his hands off the table. "Well, that's up to you. You tell me."

They listened as JP explained his desire to keep his family safe, his feelings of uneasiness at night, how he was still getting used to the sounds of the house while not having to worry about things exploding all around him.

Lisa stared at him the whole time while he let it all out. Her hand on his leg for support, happy he was at least trying—proud that he was even talking. But he failed to confess or address some of the biggest issues at hand. He was short on words, short on admissions. Ultimately, he came up short of confronting his sins.

The light buzzed in the pause after he finished. They were all waiting for something more. But Lisa felt cheated. Unsatisfied. He had skirted around his most serious behaviors. She felt desperate to confront them right then. *This was her chance.* And it might be the only one she got.

"He drinks! A lot!" She spilled like she was ratting out a playground bully. "He drinks. Like, every night and the mornings, too, sometimes." She paused. Maybe JP wanted to explain or jump in to defend himself. Anything would have been better than just sitting there like a hard rock, unphased, unmoved. "He's distant, he snaps and gets angry easily." She was looking at Dr. Clatterson but turned to JP, who was sitting with his arms crossed as if he were being accused of stealing something. She rubbed the back of his head, trying to let him know that she was doing it all because she loved him.

"And our son…he…some days JP treats him like the enemy. And other days, like they're best friends. I just don't get it. Dr. Clatterson, I'm scared. *We're* scared. We're scared *for* him." She bit her lip and searched the tabletop. "We're scared *of* him!"

There it was—the stake to the heart.

For the first time during the whole session, JP looked as though he was going to cry or fight or maybe thrust his fist through a wall. He looked like a sad and lonely child sitting there listening to his parents accuse and scold him for misbehaving. He looked hurt and afraid, confused and angry, ashamed and upset—and *sorry*. He looked so *sorry* sitting there, listening to his wife label him a lunatic, pointing out his flaws, calling him out on his issues, poking fun at his problems, accusing him of being crazy.

Unbelievable. My wife thinks I'm some maniac madman with a psycho death wish and desire to harm everyone and everything in my path. For fuck's sake. I've just got some shit to deal with, okay? Like we all don't have some shit to deal with. And now her too. Shit, the whole fucking world is against me.

That's how he perceived the situation, anyway. His irrational rationalization was purely defensive. A twisted defensive mechanism triggered by the shame and rebuke brought on by the things that he had become.

How did I let it get to this? How did I become such a fuckup?

He hated himself for that. He hated himself for becoming another statistic, another *tic* or *tally* on a chart full of disorders. He hated himself, so he started to hate everything else.

The chair shifted. It creaked as he leaned away from his wife, as if that small extra distance would be just enough space for him to deflect the arrows she was shooting right through him. That's how he saw it. Arrows. She was an archer, and he was her target. He felt punctured, slashed, stabbed—the life draining from him like corn spilling from the red center of a hanging burlap sack.

"What are you thinking about, right now, JP?" Dr. Clatterson asked what was on his mind, but his tone suggested that he already knew.

JP's stone-cold reply said all. "Nothin'."

Defiance. Ignorance. A hardheaded man with an iron shield. He stacked his walls high as their unsatisfied eyes burned his cheeks with waiting glares. His gaze settled on the mental health placard sitting on the table. He skimmed the explanations for the reasons why he was the way he was.

- Defense Mechanisms - behaviors people use to avoid unpleasant events, actions, or thoughts. Some common defense mechanisms are: Denial, Repression, Projection, Regression, and Rationalization. Defense Mechanisms are controlled by the frontal lobe of the brain.

"JP? What are you feeling right now?" Dr. Clatterson asked with his hand at his chin and a fat finger tapping his cheek. "Your wife has mentioned some troubling behaviors. Do you have anything to add to that?" It was as if he were talking to a child, which made JP want to reach across the table, grab him by the shirt collar, and bust him in his stupid face.

JP's slicing eyes met Dr. Clatterson's. "I think it's bullshit!"

Lisa's head snapped around.

"All of it," he said, crossing his arms and shrugging. He shook his head and swept the room with shifty eyes. "All *this. This* is bullshit." He pointed a jagged finger at Doctor Clatterson. "*You're* bullshit!" And finished by pounding his fists on the table.

"Okay. Okay. I can understand where you're coming from. Let's try to keep a level head here and just give this a chance. All I want to do, JP, is just open up a dialogue." Dr. Clatterson was quick to ease the tension. The session had turned, and he didn't want JP to close up and shut the gate. He wanted to help. He wanted JP to understand that all they wanted, he and Lisa, was to *help*.

"Babe." Lisa put her hand on his fist; it tightened and trembled in her palm. "We just want to help. Please talk to us. Tell us what you're thinking. Let us *help you! Please!*" she begged.

For the first time in several minutes, JP looked into his wife's face. She was truly pleading with him. He could see that. He felt it. A stiffness and aching in his chest wanted to give her what she needed. But he couldn't. He couldn't talk about *everything*. Not like this. Not *here*, in *this* place. He felt guilty. Crazy. *Psychotic.* He felt weak and judged just for being there. And that's not who he was. He wasn't weak. He wasn't *crazy*. There was *nothing* wrong. He just needed some time to get it all figured out. *Yeah, just time to figure it out.* It wasn't something a doctor or therapist could change. It was only up to *him* to control his own behavior. No one could do it for him. No one could make him. It was *his* fight to fight.

He searched her face, every line, every curve and crinkle, every red vein in her eyes—her beautiful blue eyes that were now puffy and red all because of him. Shame. That was his weight. His burden. *How can I do this to my wife? To my family? What kind of man makes his wife cry like this?* He retreated into the shady corners of his mind, where the solitude and shadows he once wanted to flee now started to feel more comfortable and fitting. Like during Defense Week in the School of Infantry, when by the third day of cold and rain—when his gear, clothes, and fighting hole were soaked and muddy, when *The Suck* became so miserable—he actually started to embrace it, to own it, to become it. And he was the one caked in mud for camouflage, hidden in the dirt when the line was attacked, and he jumped up out of his brown crust and captured a whole squad by himself.

"JP?" Dr. Clatterson's deep voice interrupted his thoughts. "Do you think that your son is…*the enemy?*"

It was the way he said it—like he wanted to push JP's buttons. It was as if he wanted to stir the pot, to break his seal.

But JP's glare gave him the clarification he was looking for. Dr. Clatterson knew there was something bigger, something deeper and more troubling at hand. He had seen the same flesh decomposing so many times before with so many veterans who sat across the very same table, in the very same seat, with the very same look of destruction in their eyes.

With one big breath, JP kicked his chair back out from under him and popped up. He was done, over it. This wasn't going to be the day to crack his shell. He would figure it out on his own. He wanted nothing more to do with that place, that office, that therapist—that *stupid placard* telling him who he was and why he wasn't. He wasn't having any of it today.

"I think we're done here. Lisa, let's go. I have a farm to look after."

And before he would hear another word, he was out the door and stomping down the hall toward the dull, gray light misting in through the glass double doors of an overcast sky.

Chapter Fourteen

Love, My Sword

I've yet to discover a blade
as sharp as Love.

A mighty sword in battle,
slicing down my enemies.

And, yet, such a fine,
shining steel to fall upon.

"Mom? Why's Dad hate me?" Adin played Call of Duty on his phone while aimlessly following his mother through the grocery store. He looked up, heartbroken after his character died in an explosion. His mother had picked him up from school while she was out running errands, and now he was the tagalong to her grocery shopping adventure. It always seemed to be an adventure, squeaking a cart full of food—*enough to feed an army*, she always said—down the narrow aisles and around lingering shelf-browsers and near-miss collisions. Adin wasn't a fan, and neither was Lisa. But somebody had to feed the family; if it were up to her husband, they'd eat pizza and carry-out every night.

Lisa pushed the cart through the canned vegetable aisle and skimmed the shelves for green beans to make green bean casserole later that evening. JP loved it, and she'd been on a mission to make up for the distressing doctor's appointment with the VA therapist. Her son's question didn't register right away, as she leaned back for a better view of the selection. "What, buddy?"

Adin scrolled through his game. "Why's Dad hate me?" He posed the question as if he were asking about dinner, or school, or why there were so many different brands of beans.

"What? Honey, your dad doesn't hate you!" She rubbed the back of his head, still holding a can of beans. "Sweetheart, what would make you think your father hates you?" She bent down to his level and everything else faded out of perception. Her chest tightened as she took in the dimensions of such a question.

Adin shrugged, still stuck to his game. "I don't know. I just do."

Lisa exhaled and took the phone from him.

"Heyyy! I was winning!"

"You can *win* some other time. Right now, I want you to tell me why you think your father hates you."

He shrugged, again.

"Adin?" Her voice was a little louder this time. "Tell me."

Adin's golden eyes shifted to the tiled floor. He swayed nervously, fidgeting with his jeans' pockets.

"I don't know. He doesn't do stuff with me like Johnathan's dad does."

"Johnathan Maley?"

Adin nodded his head but refused to look at her directly.

"Like what? What's Johnathan's dad do that yours doesn't?"

"I don't know. Like *stuff*. Football, baseball, video games. His dad plays Call of Duty with him. He even bought them both new VR guns and headsets." He looked up at Lisa, his eyes bright but sad. "Dad doesn't even watch TV with me…all he wants to do is sip from his cup and farm all day. He's not fun like he used to be."

An elderly woman an aisle over shouted to her husband about what type of soup he wanted. Her husband's inability to hear her and her repeated shouts down the aisle made Adin and his mother giggle to each other.

Lisa put her finger to her stretched lips. "Shhh. It's not nice to laugh at people," she said.

Giggling, Adin tried to cover his mouth with his sleeve. "Then why are you laughing?" he asked.

Lisa tried to wipe the smile from her face as the old man finally hollered back. "Hell, I don't care, Ellen! Get whatever you want! It's all crap, anyway!"

Adin and his mother busted out in laughter, and Lisa quickly tried to hush them both. When they settled, she shook her head and gave her little man a hug. "Buddy, your father doesn't hate you. He's just…he has a lot on his mind right now, and he just needs time to get it all figured out. You know, like when you have tons of homework and you get all frustrated and throw a fit like a four-year-old?" She raised her brows.

"I do not!"

She *booped* him on the nose before she stood up. "Yes, you do."

He rolled his eyes. "Can I have my phone back now?"

She started to push the cart past the beans and looked over her shoulder. "Maybe if you tell me something your father does to show you how much he loves you."

"Aww, *Moooom!*" He followed with his head rolled back toward the ceiling.

"Think about it. Think of everything your dad does for you, all the things he's taught you, the games he buys, the knife he got you, *without asking*." She rounded the corner and scanned the cereal boxes. "Come on, tell me something."

Adin thought as he inspected the different colors and kinds of cereal. "I don't know, Mom. Can I just have my phone, *pleeease?*"

"What kind of cereal do you want?" She pulled out a box of strawberry toasted oats. "You liked these, last time, didn't you?"

"Eww, gross!" Adin caught up to her as she rolled her eyes, put the box back, and strolled up the aisle. "Ooo, this one!"

She turned: he held up a box of sugar puffs with colorful marshmallows. "Umm, no. I don't know think so. Put it back."

"Aww. Mooom!" He pouted, but to no prevail. Her stern expression was firm. "Fine!" He said, moping back to the cart.

"How about this?" She held up a box of oats, nuts, and fruit to his disgusted face. "Great! A nice healthy choice." She tossed the box into the cart. "Moving on."

"Whatever." He dragged his feet as he followed her.

They rolled into the chip aisle, and Adin's eyes widened at the different flavors lined up around him.

"BBQ!" he shouted before his mother could even ask.

She grabbed a bag and tossed them in the cart. "Still waiting," she called out over her shoulder, heading for the milk.

Adin let out a loud sigh and growl. "He taught me how to shoot a gun! He said it's in case I need to protect you when he isn't there. He takes me hunting, to Salt Fork, riding on the tractor, shows me how to run the farm, lets me feed the chickens—*buys me the kind of cereal I like!*"

"Watch it, buddy," she said with squinted eyes, perusing the yogurt selection.

"Lisa! Oh. My. God! Is that you? It's been forever!" A shrill voice came from up ahead.

"Amanda? Oh, my gosh! How are you?" They both embraced beside their carts.

"Good. Good. How have you been?" Amanda asked. "And look at you, big guy! You were just a tiny little thing the last time I saw you. Ahh! It's so good to see you guys!"

Lisa scooted her cart out of the way for other shoppers to pass.

"We've been good. You know, just doing the mom and wife thing. How about you? How's Nick? The kids? Everyone?"

Amanda's smile faded.

"I'm sorry. Did I say something wrong?" Lisa placed her hand on Amanda's shoulder.

"Nooo, no. I'm sorry." Amanda took Lisa's hand in hers with sad eyes. "Nick and I…well, it's been all over Facebook, anyway. We're splitting up."

"Oh, no! Seriously? But you guys were so happy! What happened?"

Amanda leaned in and cupped her hand around her mouth. "Well, he couldn't keep his damn dick out of other women," she whispered.

Lisa rolled her eyes. "So typical. What an asshole."

"Mom! Language!" Adin said, picking through the different bags of doughnuts on the shelf.

"How about you stop listening and get away from the junk food?" She glared at him, and he got the point.

"How are the kids taking it? What are they…nine and ten now?"

"Ten and eleven. But they're, you know, sad about it all. But most of their friends have single parents, anyway. It's nothing that crazy to them, I guess. Jake even bragged about getting twice as many presents. That little shit."

"No way? Wow, girl, what kind of world are we living in?"

"I know, right?"

"Well, I'm so sorry to hear that. It's terrible. You guys had been together since, what…senior year?"

"Junior."

Lisa shook her head. "Unbelievable. It's so sad."

"I know. I know. But, it's for the best. To be honest, it was getting hard to stand the man, anyway."

"Wow. Really? Well, hey, if you need anything, let me know. We should go do something sometime if you're back in town. Same number?"

"Yeah. Yeah, same number. And I'd like that. Thank you."

Lisa made her way to the checkout line, Adin a few steps behind, pouting about not getting his doughnuts. Once in line, his eyes scanned the candy stacked beside him. But his mother shot down every candy bar he picked up. So, he flipped through the tabloids on the end of the aisle, waiting for his mom to put her groceries on the conveyer belt.

"Hey Mom, look!" He held up a magazine with an apocalyptic scene of the sun shooting flames at the burning earth. Adin sounded out the headline on the cover. "The. End. Of the…world. Is…com–ing. Mom! Can we get it? For Dad? I think he'd like it."

"Huh? What?" She scanned the magazine and read the subheading to herself. *The Earth is due for a major solar flare.* "Buddy, put that down," she chuckled. "That's garbage. Just nonsense to sell copies. Come on, help me unload the cart."

"Aw, Mooom."

It was dark by the time JP finished the chores. He kicked off his muddy boots on the porch and walked inside to the smell of baked chicken and green bean casserole.

"Man, that smells good!"

"Thank you!" Lisa hollered from the kitchen. "Let me get you a beer!"

JP cocked his head to the side as he peeled off his jacket and hung it by the door. *"Oookay,"* he said. "I won't argue about that. Thanks."

"Babe." Lisa rounded the corner with a cold beer in a camo koozie, sat it on the coffee table in front of the couch, and opened it for her tired husband.

"You'll never guess who I saw at the store," she said, leaning against the wood-trim corner of the kitchen.

"Oh yeah?" JP peeked out the window. "Taylor Swift? One of the Kardashians? Miley Cyrus?"

"What? No!" Lisa laughed. "Is she even still alive?"

JP shrugged his way to his beer and took a drink, taking the time to savor the first gulp before swallowing and letting out a satisfying *Ahhh*. "Hell if I know."

He leaned against the back of the sofa and waited with a sparkle in his eye. "Amanda!"

JP looked confused. "Amanda Cain?"

She rolled her eyes and scoffed as if that was the silliest answer ever. "No."

"Well, I can't keep up with who your friends with this week, or who hates who because of something they posted, or their new shoes, or whatever you women get mad at each other about these days." He flashed his ornery look her way.

She dropped her shoulders and stared at him like she wasn't amused. But he knew deep down, she enjoyed his jabs.

"Amanda Sears."

"Who?" JP joked.

"Quit it," she said, tilting her head and throwing her dishtowel at him.

He flinched and tossed it back. "Well, that's cool. How's her and Nick?"

Lisa took a deep breath. "Not so good, apparently. She said they're getting a divorce."

"Wow. Really?" He took a drink and let that news sink in, shaking his head. "If anyone was going to stick it out and last, I thought it would be them. Hm."

He thought back to high school, when Nick and Amanda first got together. They were so in love, so wild, and reckless. He remembered the time the four of them skipped class and went out to Seneca lake in May. The water was still cold, but Nick and JP talked the girls into it—and then out of their bikinis.

"Yeah. Me too." She, too, drifted off into thoughts about their old friends and all the parties they used to go to together. Nick was a bit of a fighter—a *shit-talker*, as Lisa would call him. He was always getting them into trouble, which they joked about years later.

"So, what's for dinner?" JP asked after a moment.

Lisa pushed herself from the corner, and swayed her hips back into the kitchen, taking one lip-biting peek over her shoulder before she disappeared.

"Well, come on over here and take a look, Mr. Grimm." Notes of *sexy* wafted from her lips, her voice sultry.

Like a love-struck teen, he followed her trail without hesitation.

Dinner and the evening were pleasant. And after JP secured the shed, the garage, and patrolled his property one last time, he gave a quick *goodnight* to Adin while Lisa read him a bedtime story about a boy who emerged from a bunker to save his father and town during a war in America's Midwest.

JP was in bed, reading the news on his phone—something about the electrical charges in the atmosphere and the impacts on the electrical grid in the future—when his wife finally came to bed.

"He's out cold, Nerf gun tucked in beside him and all."

The night shimmered in the glow of a three-quarter moon. The stars flickered like candle flames against the navy blue sky. A fever hung in the air—some excitement, electricity. It had been building since before dinner, when Lisa set her snare and her husband willingly walked right into it. They both knew what was coming next. JP made sure to remind her after saying goodnight to Adin by stroking her neck with his fingertips as he leaned down to kiss her before heading off to bed. Her embers still smoldered from that little stunt.

But now it was her turn. Now, she would set the mood in the glow of the nightstand light. She slid off her pajama pants and sweatshirt, revealing her new pink-laced bra and panties she was more than excited to show off for her husband.

JP let his phone slowly fall to his chest as she undressed. Lisa was perfect, more beautiful than he deserved, and he knew it. Her thin, tone waist and legs glistened in the lamp's soft haze. He took in her darling form as she slowly undid her bra and tossed it to the corner. He swallowed and realized he was holding his breath. *Funny how much she still gets to me.* Then he tossed his phone beside his pistol on the nightstand.

Taking pleasure in knowing she had his full attention, she stood there stretching her body, rubbing her neck, and letting the day's tension release from her shoulders. The light skimmed over her curves, like the sun kissing flower petals.

He sat up a little as she rolled her panties from her thighs down her ankles and kicked them off the tips of her toes beside her bra. His heart rumbled like a snare drum. His body shimmered and tingled. It had been so many days since they last made love, and he had not thought much about its absence until now. His blood pumped and warmed him as she waltzed around to his side of the bed.

She placed her hand on the inside of his thigh, making his legs spread apart while she leaned down, stopping short of his lips, until he stretched up to meet hers. They kissed. Just an appetizer kiss—a small, sweet, barely lingering kiss to get things started. It was playful. Much like their love, it was teasing and ornery.

His hand reached the side of her face, slid around her earlobe, behind it, and down the side of her neck, making the hairs stand erect on her skin. Her hand slid up his leg. A shiver shimmied through him, and he pulled her down into his lips and his open mouth. She leaned over him, powerful, elegant, with her yellow hair draping down her shoulders and tickling his chest. His fingers lingered sweetly at the side of her neck, his open legs and body nearly lifting from the bed with anticipation, as if Heaven was calling him home.

She climbed on top of him.

He slid up higher in the bed and bent in to kiss her neck. His lips moved down to her collarbone, her shoulder. Then down her chest to her breasts, where he suckled them until she let out a breathy moan and tilted her head to the ceiling.

They made love. More deeply than when he first came home. More passionate than the times before he left—they shared themselves completely, absolutely, honestly. They shared themselves until they collapsed, exhausted, in a damp heap of skin and sheets.

With her tired head heavy on his hard chest, JP played with her golden hair until she drifted peacefully to sleep. His thoughts skittered all over the place, running his calloused hands through her soft hair. But they all circled back to one stamped and chiseled thought: he loved her with all he had, all his might, all his strength, and breath. He loved her as the wind loves the leaves on a bright autumn day. He loved her as the day loves the sun and the stars love a clear, midnight sky. His glow broadened as he thought of her and the farm. And laughing through his nose at the thought of loving her like his cows love seeing his tractor crest the hill with a fresh bale of hay bouncing on the front spear.

But his wife's flinching on his chest soon disturbed his pleasant thoughts. She twitched and jerked, subtle at first, but then she yanked her head out from under his hand with a groan.

"Babe?" He whispered.

She didn't reply.

"Babe? You all right?"

Nothing. She just nuzzled her chin into his gut as if all were fine and well. And he put his hand back gently on her head, stroking it again to calm her.

A moment went by before she jolted again.

"No!" She blurted out.

He jerked his hand from her hair, thinking he had upset her. "What? What I do?" he asked, barely above a whisper.

"No! Stop!"

He froze.

"Don't hurt him!" She twitched. "Adin! Adin!"

"Babe. Sweetheart, wake up!" He thought about shaking her shoulder. "You're having a bad dream."

She jerked and mumbled. "No! Put the gun down!"

It hit him hard in the gut and drained the blood from his face.

"Lisa, wake up."

He reached down to shake her shoulder, and as his hand met her skin, she cried out.

"Let him go! He's your son!"

Chapter Fifteen

The Consolation Prize

How many breasts have been painted purple
at a time when purple means red and red is blood
and blood means sacrifice?

Too many can talk of sacrifice.
A story for each tear. Roadside bombs,
Rockets from the sky, Double-Stacked Mines…

The Purple Heart;
a blood-soaked medal to replace
your arm, your leg, your life.

"Congratulations marine, you've been injured."

"Thank you, Mr. President,
as soon as I learn to walk again, I'm going
straight home to place this up high on my mantle."

Grandma sat at her kitchen table with the phone to her ear, watching the early morning deer nibble at branches along the back-pasture fence. The sun had just crested the hills and sparkled the frost on the grass. Another pot of coffee brewed as she sipped her cup and listened to Lisa on the other end of the line.

"Honestly, I just don't know what to do, Barbara. I'm on the edge over here. I don't know how to reach him." Lisa spoke quickly and quietly. "The drinking, the mood swings, the nightmares…" her voice quivered. "I'm scared I'm losing him. I need your help."

"Oh, sweetheart. I'm here. I'm always here whenever you need me. You and Adin mean the world to him. Even as he's pushing you away, he still needs you."

"I know. I know. But he's just so damn stubborn! And I feel so helpless. I mean, I try to give him space and that doesn't work. I tried to get the VA involved, *what a disaster*, and I try to get him to open up to me, but…" her heavy sigh was felt in Grandma's bones.

"Trust me, dear, I know! His grandfather was just as hardheaded when he got home from the war. And he kept that side of him locked up tighter than a chicken coop on a fox farm."

"Then what do I do? Please, just tell me what works so I can do it. I'm falling apart. It's killing me to see him hurting like this." Her voice softened. "And it's killing *us* to feel it too."

"Love, darling."

"Love?"

"Yes, love. Love and time are the only two things that can heal him."

Just then, the porch door squeaked open and closed way too loud for 7:00 a.m.

"He's here. I better let you go. We can talk any time you'd like, honey. Just give me a ring and I'd be happy to listen."

"Thank you. You're the best, Barbara. We're so lucky to have you."

A few minutes later, JP and his grandmother shared the kitchen table and a pot of coffee.

"You look like shit!" Grandma exclaimed before slurping her mug.

"Gee, thanks, Grandma," he said, wiping his face with his dirty hand and grasping his white, *Chicken Shit* inscribed mug in the other. His four-day-old stubble sounded like Velcro as he brushed against it. He hadn't had a haircut in over two weeks, and it reminded his grandmother of his days before the marines, when he tried so hard to look manly with a beard and shaggy hair.

But now, he only looked debilitated and detached, like a hobo with nowhere to drift, as he lifted his white mug to his lips and slurped in that hot, morning nectar. With his eyes closed, the rich aroma perked his weary mind. It was his third cup that morning, but he savored it as much as the first.

"Well, you do." She shrugged, lifting her head from her hand and elbow. "Rough night?" He brought the cup up to his chin and let it linger a moment, warming his nose and tingling his lips before he sipped. He could never understand why, but Grandma's coffee always seemed to be better than his own, and he'd be content just sitting there with her and his coffee the rest of the day if he could.

"One of many," he said, leaving her waiting for an explanation with her eyebrows raised. He swallowed another gulp and shook his head. "You don't need to be burdened with any of my troubles. It'll be just fine. Don't worry about it."

"Ah, bullshit!" She leaned back in her chair with crossed arms.

"Grandma! What's gotten into you?" He laughed. "A little feisty this morning, aren't we? You feeling all right?"

"Apparently better than you." She smirked.

JP just let her win. He was too tired to engage in their typical banter. Besides, he felt like shit, so he assumed her words weren't far from the truth. His wife's nightmare had chafed his mind for nearly a week. It crept into his dreams, his morning thoughts, and lingered in the lull between chores: *What have I done to my family? How could I let this happen? What can I do to fix it?* His mind spun in the muck like a tractor tire.

"Well?" Grandma pressed.

"You're not gonna let this go, are you?"

"You should know me better than that. I could read you like a book ever since you were a child. How do you think I always knew when you were lying?" She winked.

He shook his head, grinning and thinking back to the lies he couldn't get away with: The party he and Dan went to when they said they were staying at each other's houses, the barn window he shot out with the BB gun, and the beer cans she found stuffed under a bale of hay. None of which he could talk his way out of. She knew him well because they shared the same wild soul.

"I guess you got me there." He shrugged.

"So, what is it? What's on your mind?"

"Just…" He bit his lip and sighed. "*Everything.*"

"Hmm. That sounds heavy," she teased.

He rolled his eyes. "Well, it is. And I think it's starting to get the best of me."

"Is that right? Wouldn't have anything to do with hardheaded men branching from the Grimm family tree, would it?"

Rubbing over his stretched lips with a callused hand, he wasn't sure if he wanted her advice. Or if he wanted to burden her with his problems. Or maybe, he was just too exhausted to explain it. *Might feel good to get it all out. Maybe I should just spill it all?*

"Have I ever told you about the first year your grandfather was home from the war?"

His focus shifted to the ceiling. "Well, yeah, sure. Plenty of times…the farm, the tree, the bars, and dance halls."

She squinted. "But did I ever tell you about the *other stuff?*"

"What do you mean? Like, the bar fights? The drinking?"

"No. More than that. I mean, the bitterness and eruptive behavior. The nightmares. The time he got rough with me, and I left for a week." She stared past her grandson but suddenly shifted, gauging his reaction, which was shock. "Went to stay with my sister in Marietta. Kept it all quiet from the family. But maybe now's a good time to bring it up."

He sat up straighter. "No. No, I had no idea. What happened?"

She squeezed her lips together, looked down at her cup, and shook her head. "Oh, you know, he was drunk one night and going on and on about some village in the jungle. There was rage on his tongue and it only made it worse that I wasn't understanding the significance of it all. Apparently, I just didn't grasp what it meant to him. I don't really remember. But it was just like with most of his other stories, he rambled on, slurring his words in some drunken stupor until I could barely understand him. Those were typical nights, after the war. Sound familiar at all?"

Her words slashed into JP, and he shuddered at the thought of his own drinking habits. "Maybe."

"Well, let's just say that it was one of those nights where he *needed* me to understand his story. And the fact that I just couldn't comprehend the importance of it all, well, that just got him worked up even more. That damn heathen started throwing my good china against the wall, yelling something about it all being worthless." She paused to dab at a tear with her napkin. "That was my mother's fine china, one of the only things of value she left for me."

"I'm so sorry. I had no idea. What happened next?"

"I told him if he didn't get himself under control, I was going to leave him. He dared me, so I packed my things and headed for the door. That only made him worse. Like I said, he *needed* me to understand. But he was too drunk to make any sense. So, he grabbed me by the arm, harder than I think he intended, but it jerked me backward. I stumbled, got tangled up with his feet somehow, and we tripped, fell backward, and I hit my head on the floor. Left a pretty nasty bump for a few days." She rubbed the back of her head as if the bump was still there.

"Jesus. I'm so sorry. I had no idea."

"It wasn't that bad." She waved her hand at him. "Well, looking back on it now, it wasn't that bad. Honestly, at the time, I was pretty upset. I didn't know if I could live with a man that drank like that, with a man who might hurt me. Even if he did beg for mine and God's mercy every day for what seemed like an entire year." She sniffed, swallowed, and took a drink from her mug.

JP took her hand in his across the table. "I'm so sorry that happened to you, Grandma. I'm sure he didn't mean it. I know how much he loved you. He'd never want to hurt you like that."

She smiled and tears rolled down her cheeks. "Oh, I know. You're sweet. Just like him. I'm glad you got that part of him." She patted his hand. "But anyway, after that, I left and stayed with my sister. I told him to get sober, or it was over. He called every day to apologize and confess his love for me. And honestly, I knew that he didn't mean what he did. I knew that it was somewhat of an accident and that he was terribly sorry. But I needed him to understand that it would *never* happen again."

"Absolutely," JP agreed.

"Things were rough for a little while, awkward, uncomfortable—you know, hard. But, he tried, he did. He tried to quit drinking for me. And, he was able to give up the liquor, but we both agreed that a beer or two every now and then was probably a *good thing* for him."

"Well, beer *is* a good thing," JP quipped.

She smacked his hand, and he pulled away.

"Ouch."

"Yeah, ouch is right! I'll do it again, too, if you keep it up." They both snorted.

But her light faded and a solemn demeanor spread over her face. "JP, it was after that incident that I talked him into getting some help. He needed someone to talk to, to get it all out, to sort through the mess inside his head. And for the next twelve years, he went to group therapy. Even admitted it was the best decision he ever made—*well, besides marrying me, of course.*" She winked.

"I didn't know that. I didn't know he went to therapy."

"Not many did. He wasn't the type of man who liked to admit he needed help. *Sound familiar?*" She glared at him. "But that's exactly what he needed. And I thank God that he was able to get it." She looked out the window with a deep breath and then back at her grandson. "Which leads me to my next point. When are you going to quit being a stubborn ass and do something to help yourself?"

The question caught him off guard. It was the way she said it, the wording—the *knowing.* "Uh, I mean…well, I did go see a therapist the other day with Lisa. Her idea," he said, ashamed. "But I went."

"And how'd it go?"

"Uhhh."

"JP! If you don't do something to take care of yourself, it's just going to get worse. Trust me. Talk to someone."

He let it sink in. She had experience. She knew the ticking time bomb inside him, and though vulnerable, he was also relieved. A tinge of comfort came from having someone recognize and know the kind of storm that brewed within him.

He nodded. "Okay. I will."

"Soon. Before it's too late."

"Okay. Okay." He held up his hands. "I promise, I will."

He downed his coffee, stood up, popping and cracking with the table, and stretched. "But right now, I need to go feed my heifers before they wither away to nothing. I love you," he said, leaning down to kiss her wrinkled forehead.

As he pulled away, she grabbed his face with both cold hands so that she could stare him in the eyes. "And I love you, young man. But if you don't get your ass to a therapist, I'm gonna have to kick it."

Later that afternoon, sometime while hauling firewood from the fallen trees along the fence line to the pile of logs that still needed to be split beside the barn, JP missed a call from Cpl. Richardson. He shook his head and hit the green button, half-expecting to ring in on a college kegger or one of Richardson's bro-love "miss you" sessions.

"Heyyy, you son of a bitch! How's it going?" Richardson said.

The ball-busting brotherhood that bonded combat marines like best friends made JP grin. "You sack of shit. How the hell are ya?"

"Ah, you know. Just spending time with all these beautiful women and my buddies Jim, Jack, and Mr. Cuervo."

"Right. Right. How's that going for ya?"

"Gives me a damn headache!" Richardson laughed.

"I bet." JP chuckled. "So, what's up?" JP could *feel* the mood change on the other end of the phone. An eerie shudder vibrated his bones. *Fuck, what happened now?*

"Well," Richardson finally said somberly, "have you heard yet?"

"Heard what?" JP walked away from the tractor and barn and started down the tire-tread path into the field so he could concentrate better.

"About Kerns?"

"No. What about him? What happened?" JP stopped and stared blankly over the brown, grassy slope toward the dark trees on the horizon. His mind raced. But ultimately his gut knew what Richardson was going to say.

There was a pause. Richardson cleared his throat; his breathing quivered on the other end.

"He killed himself, man."

There it was—the dark thought he buried every time one of his marine brothers called him. It left a tightness in his throat—a sad, sick anger.

"Shit. When?"

Richardson cleared his throat again. *Or was he choking back tears?* "Saturday night."

"Damn." Visions of Kerns and his stupid smirk floated in JP's memories. He kneeled and picked at the pale grass. Ripping out a long, dying blade, he rubbed it between his fingers. It was dry and rough, sharp on the edges. *Much like life*, he thought, before throwing it down and sitting on the hump between the two tire ruts. "How?"

"Apparently, he found out his girlfriend cheated on him while we were deployed. He fucking kidnapped her, man! Went crazy. I guess he drove her out to the middle of nowhere and made her watch as he shot himself. How fucked up is that?"

"Jesus. You serious? What the fuck, man?"

"Yeah, I know. I guess, I don't know, I guess we all have a little bit of psycho in us. And let's be honest, Kerns wasn't all that stable, to begin with, right?"

It was a joke, but one that carried with it all the seriousness of the situation.

"No, you're right. He was one crazy motherfucker, wasn't he?" He sort of laughed, sort of breathed heavy. "Then again, I guess we had to be, you know…to do what we did."

"Abso-fucking-lutely."

They shared a silence as they each reminisced about one of their own.

"Hey, man." Richardson chuckled. "Remember the time he made that MRE bomb out at OP Tomahawk, even though you warned him not to do it?"

His cheeks wrinkled and his eyes lit up. "Yeah. That dumbass!"

"Gunny Smith reamed your ass so hard after the FOB thought we took incoming and sent out the QRF." He snorted. "How many sandbags did you have Kerns fill that day? Two hundred? Three hundred?"

JP rubbed above his eyes, smiling at the memory but hurting inside. "I think he ended up with about five hundred by the time he had radio watch."

"That's hilarious. Only Kerns could fill that many sandbags in four or five hours. He was special."

"Yeah. *Real special.*"

Their breathy laughter blew through the speakers. Afterward, another long pause.

"I'll miss that dumb son of a bitch," Richardson finally said.

"Yeah, me too, man. Me too." JP tried to swallow back his shock, his grief.

"You all right man?"

He sniffed. "Yeah. Yeah, I just…" He shook his head, trying to find the words. "I just…goddamnit! *Why?* You know? Why, after all the shit we went through, after all the times we cheated death, why did it take an unfaithful woman, a broken heart, to take his life? It's bullshit, man. It's *all* bullshit."

"It *is* bullshit. And I'm tired of losing so many brothers *after* we got back home. I mean, I heard a few weeks ago, that three from Lima had already done it—killed themselves. I just can't believe it."

A flock of starlings fluttered from a cluster of leafless trees over by the corn. They flew across the field to another cluster of leafless trees at the edge of the wood line, passed the pasture. The clouds hung gray and dark. The grass was dead or dying. The trees, bare from the last storm that came through, tossed the last of the bronze leaves from their branches. He hated winter. He hated the ugliness, the dullness, the gray and dim. He needed the light. The world was dying around him, and it was pulling him down into its gloomy grave.

Then, over the southern horizon blurred a dark mass. It pulled JP's eyes toward the tree line across the field. As the dark tide swept over the sky, JP realized what it was—Canadian geese *honking* north in droves. Like a storm cloud directly above the farm, the whole sky seemed to be filled with flocking birds. An eerie sight and sound whistling overhead sickened JP's mind and gut. *What the fuck?* He thought. *It's still winter. What the hell are they doing?* The mass moved with urgency—an agitated jerking and weaving JP had never seen before. V-shaped arrows migrating to frozen lands, zigzagging like drunkards on ice. The bizarre scene lasted for only a minute before the skies over the field cleared again. *That was weird as hell.* His emotions swirled like the birds in the sky.

"It's fucked up. The whole world's fucked up. You know?" JP sniffed. "I don't know. I don't know what to say."

"Me either, bro. I don't know if there's anything we could say, you know?"

"Yeah. Well look, I'm gonna get off here and go get some shit done. I appreciate you calling and letting me know. If you need anything, just get a hold of me. I'm here, bud."

"Same with you, brother. Take it easy."

"Yeah, you too. Later."

After JP hung up, he sat there on the path and watched the limbs of the trees sway in the breeze. He listened to the call of the crows in the cornfield and breathed in the smell of dirt and manure. This was life. This was *his* life. And if he was going to live it, then he needed to embrace all that it was. The good and the bad. The just and the unfair. The happiness and the heartbreak.

He spent the next several hours splitting firewood by hand until blisters formed, busted, and bled through his gloves. It was going to be a rough night, and he needed something painful to pull his mind from the darkness to which it was retreating.

Chapter Sixteen

I Still Sleep with This Gun

I still sleep with this gun.

Reaching out to adjust it on
this nightstand, the rear sight's
green glowing eyes
meeting mine,

that's how I like it,
intimate and piercing,
looking into the shaded corners
of this cracked shell of reason;
where ambushing nightmares
of a whistling mortar's thunder
still wait in the black haze
of my room;

I clear them out with a mounted
tactical light.
The shaking hiss of my breath
blowing truth
against these walls.

With it in my hand,
I stand a chance,
its weight grounding my conscience,
pulling me back from shaded places.

It is rough,
heavy,
and cold.

It is perfect and comfortable.

Lisa knew something was wrong when JP walked in and slammed the front door. Shaking her head, she grit her teeth and checked on the chicken casserole. It was starting to burn. She rushed it out of the oven, burning her hand in the process, and let it drop heavily on the counter beside the fridge.

"Errrr." She threw the potholders against the wall and leaned on the counter taking in deep breaths beside the brown chicken casserole. Her day had been worthy of a door slam too.

Of course, she cared about JP and whatever it was that had put him in the kind of mood that made him toss his boots around and slam doors. But her afternoon was rough too. Where was *her* sympathy? Still fuming from her overly dramatic boss not listening to her input about the *unfeasible* client expectations on her digital marketing project and *still* bumping up the timeline, she just wasn't in the mood for the extra drama tonight.

Besides that, Adin was acting out, refused to clean his room, broke the end table lamp horsing around, and had an attitude the size of his imagination.

So, dinner was slightly burned, Lisa was "over it," Adin was grounded for life, and JP was a hornet about to stir up the beehive.

He rounded the corner into the smoky kitchen. "What happened to the lamp? And what's this?" He held up three mental health pamphlets Lisa took from the therapist's office and waved the smoke from his face. "Geez. What happened in here?"

Lisa huffed, turned on the oven fan, and stirred the green beans, but didn't bother turning around. "What's what? And you'll have to ask your son about the lamp?"

"Well, if you'd turn around and look at me, you'd see."

She spun around with teary eyes and the spoon still in her hand.

"Why do you have all these pamphlets out?" He asked.

"Oh. Those." She turned back to her beans. "Because I've been reading them."

"Why?"

"Why do you think, JP?" She sniffed.

"Are you crying? What's wrong?" He leaned against the corner of the timber-trimmed archway.

"Don't worry about it. I'm fine." She stayed busy with the food.

JP let her agitated words digest for a moment. "Hm. All right, then." He tossed the pamphlets on the counter under the hanging wine glasses, headed straight for the fridge, grabbed a beer, and rattled the door shut.

He let it splash as he cracked it open and downed half the can just before the fire alarm in the staircase started blaring.

"Goddamnit!" He rushed over to snatch it down, ripped out the batteries, and tossed it on the couch. "Adin! Adin! Get down here!

Adin's door creaked open, and he tiptoed to the edge of the steps.

"Adin! Now!" JP walked back into the kitchen and surveyed dinner as he drank his beer. "What happened to the casserole?" He asked, half-joking.

But it struck a nerve with his already stretched-thin wife, and the spoon clanked in the pot when she let it go. "You don't have to eat it if you don't want to!"

Amused, JP fought a smile. "Whoa, whoa, whoa. That's a bit dramatic, isn't it?" He leaned against the counter, crossed his arms, and drank his beer.

"This whole house is dramatic!" She shot back, wiping up the juice that splattered from the beans.

JP laughed. "Well, it is *now*." He leaned his head toward the stairs. "Adin! I'm not saying it again! *Now!* 5…4…3…2!"

Adin ran down the steps. "Okay! Okay! I'm here. *Geeeez!*"

JP cocked his head to the side and looked back at his wife.

"*Yeah*. All afternoon. I think he needs an attitude adjustment."

"No, I *don't!*"

His father scrunched his face. "Having a rough day, are we?"

"*Nooo!*" Adin defiantly kept his distance at the bottom of the stairs.

"You can drop the attitude," JP said with arched brows.

"I don't have an attitude!"

"All right, I'm gonna need another beer for this." JP headed for the fridge and caught his wife shaking her head at the sink.

"What?"

"You think a beer's gonna help?"

He reached the silver door and swung it open. The light splashed his face. A tinge of agitation pulled at the corners of his eyes. "Well, it damn sure ain't gonna hurt." He snatched a can from the bottom shelf. "Now, Adin, you want to tell me what happened to the lamp?" He turned to read his son's face.

Adin paused to gather his thoughts holding onto the pine banister. "It fell."

"It *fell?*"

Adin nodded with confidence.

Lisa slammed a fork in the sink and spun around. "It didn't just *fall*, Adin! You knocked it off the stand when you were horsing around and not minding me!"

"Nu-uh!" Adin protested.

JP gulped his beer and leaned against the counter by the sliding deck door.

"Adin, come here." His father's tone had turned more serious, and Adin's gaze stayed on the floor as he inched toward his father.

"Look at me."

Adin looked up, sort of.

"Did you break the lamp?"

"Well…it—"

"No! I don't want excuses!" JP leaned forward, towering over Adin.

His face crumpled. "I didn't mean to!" he yelled with tears burning his eyes.

Lisa joined her husband's side with her arms crossed. "Well maybe if you would've been cleaning your room like I asked you, *fifty million times*, instead of rolling around on the couch, then the lamp wouldn't have been broken."

"Adin, what do you have to say?"

Adin looked up at his father but said nothing.

"Adin?" His mother echoed.

Adin exhaled and slouched his shoulders. "I'm *sorry!*"

"Say it like you mean it this time!" JP slugged back his beer.

Adin acted as though the words would kill him. "I'm…" His voice shook. "Sssorry." He swallowed, and a tear wet his cheek.

"All right. Thank you. That's all you had to do. Just apologize and act like you know how to behave. We raised you better than that, right?"

JP was being more reasonable than Lisa had imagined. Perhaps he was too exhausted to fight or too angry to care, but she found a little hope in the way he just parented his child. For a moment, she thought that maybe *she* was being the unreasonable one.

Adin nodded his head.

"Okay. Good. Now run upstairs and start cleaning your room until the rolls are done."

Adin pouted as he turned and slowly made his way up the stairs.

JP gloated with a simple shrug, which Lisa met with rolled eyes and a playful middle finger.

But Adin wasn't done. He found courage in the distance at the top of the stairs. Bold and loud, he let the whole house know how he felt. "Well, maybe if you would be around to play with me more often, then I wouldn't have to play by myself and break things!"

~

With the sting of the evening's revelations waning and the booze bringing on a numbing comfort, JP sat in his chair in the living room, staring at the images of intense lightning, transformer fires, and the swirling Northern Lights above Cleveland. This room—a comforting, roomy, and open space—had always been one of Lisa's favorite parts of the house. The fireplace and stained wood gave the cabin a rustic feel that reminded her of summer vacations in the Smokey Mountains of Tennessee. The cabin was her dream home, decorated in a homey antler theme with a touch of feminine charm: rugs and drapes in dark red or green, patriotic knickknacks and Americana, an antler chandelier, pinecone wreath, piney and earthy candles that made the house smell like a forest on a sunny day. She even allowed JP to stretch out a bear rug in front of the fireplace. Cliché, but they laughed when he tried to seduce her with his shirtless "sexy poses" sprawled out on top of it the night he brought it home from a small gun store in West Virginia.

The fire in the hearth blazed, but on the couch, Lisa was still wrapped in her red Ohio State blanket. She had agreed to put her phone away and stop worrying about work. Instead, she watched her favorite dating show. And while JP considered it laughable, he compromised by switching to the news stories about the bizarre and fiery effects of Earth's weakening magnetic field during commercials. Adin had calmed and given an apology—full of hugs and kisses that strummed the heartstrings of his mother. JP had pushed Kerns's suicide to the back of his mind, where he kept a chest full of stressful things locked down the best he could.

With a glass of red wine in her hand and the fireplace glare on her cheek, Lisa had finally unwound from her stressful day. "Babe, come snuggle with me," she pleaded with her husband.

He was doing his best not to pay attention to her show and instead peeked out the windows at the distant flashes of heat lightning splashing the hills with a faint licking of light.

"Huh? What?" JP snapped out of his daze and admired his wife, with her hair in a messy bun and red cheeks, all wrapped up like a butterfly in a cocoon.

"Come sit with me, pleeeease," she begged with a pouty lip.

He grinned. She knew his weakness—her cute puffy lip. The way her eyes shined and twinkled with joy made his heart melt. He was a sucker for her simple, youthful beauty and charm that took over on nights like these.

"Over there? Like, with *you?* Ugh! That's absurd! How could you ask me to do such a thing?"

Her head tilt and unamused blinking made him smirk. "Shut up and get your fine ass over here." She unraveled the blanket and held it open like a door for him to enter.

"Well, if you're gonna put it like that. You win. I'll come join you in your sauna." As he stood, he wobbled slightly. "I'm grabbing a beer—more wine?"

Lisa hesitated. He'd been drinking since dinner, and although she thought anything other than alcohol would be a better choice for them both, she didn't want to ruin their evening with another argument about drinking. Not tonight. Tonight, she wanted her husband to hold her. "Why yes, my dear, that would be lovely," she said in her *upper-class* voice while holding out her mostly empty glass.

"Oh please." He rolled his eyes and started toward the kitchen. But as he passed the end table where the broken antlered lamp used to stand, his barefoot struck something hard and sharp. "Ah! Shit!" He hobbled to the corner of the couch to balance himself.

"What? What happened?"

He lifted his foot to his knee. A drop of blood oozed from the padding of his big toe. Instantly, a fire filled him. "Goddammit! I stepped on glass," he growled, wobbling back and forth with one hand holding up his leg and the other grabbing the corner of the couch.

Lisa threw off the blanket. "It's okay. I'll get a needle and tweezers, just sit down and relax. I'll get it."

Before he could react, she had burst from her cocoon and was heading up the stairs toward the bathroom closet.

In that moment alone, JP boiled. And all the day's stress he'd stuffed inside his box now threatened to burst from the seams. A switch flipped. Not a reasonable switch, but one with a glaring, scarlet light—and he saw red. His body vibrated as his mind flipped through all the events that led up to this moment—this small, insignificant moment that quickly blew up to be monumental. "Adin! Damn it! Adin, get your ass down here! *Now!*" he hollered at the steps.

Searching through the bathroom closet, Lisa felt the fire in her husband's voice. She gritted her teeth, grabbed the first-aid kit, and rushed out of the bathroom in time to see Adin lurk down the stairs.

"JP…" Her guarded tone was a warning he ignored.

"Come here!" he shouted as Adin rounded the banister into the living room.

With fear wrinkling his forehead, and his father backlit by fire, Adin approached cautiously.

"Look at this! You see this!" JP wobbled to show Adin his bloody foot. "This is *your* fault!"

The urge to cry contorted Adin's terrified face.

Lisa hurried down the stairs, but JP was locked in on their son.

"Come here!"

Adin inched closer.

"Now!"

He hovered at arm's length, with Lisa not far behind.

Suddenly, JP reached out and grabbed his son by the shirt collar. It caught them all off guard. Surprise and concern ripped across their faces as JP shoved his son's nose down toward his foot.

"You see that! That's glass in my fucking foot!"

"Dad! Dad! Please!" Adin cried out.

"JP! Stop it! Let him go!" Lisa dropped the first-aid kit and rushed to her son's defense.

JP clenched the back of Adin's neck and held his trembling cheeks inches from his dripping foot. "This is what happens when you don't listen! People get hurt! You understand? People get—"

But before he could finish his thought, his knee wobbled, his foot twisted, and down they fell—both him and his son—crashing to the ground. The thump of Adin's head against the hardwood floor made Lisa's stomach turn upside down. Instantly, Adin wrapped his hands around the back of his head, wailing.

The jolt of it all struck JP like an electric bolt to a tree trunk. His face exploded with shock and horror. "Oh, my God! Adin! You okay!" JP rolled to his knees to check on Adin, but Lisa was already there.

"Get away from me!" Adin shouted to his father.

Lisa swept him up into her arms and scowled at her husband before carrying her crying boy upstairs to the bathroom.

JP wiggled to his feet, feeling evil and disgusting. *What the hell, JP! What are you doing? What have you become?* "Buddy, you okay?" he yelled up the stairs with a shaky voice.

"Leave me alone!" Adin yelled back from his mother's arms as she soothed him.

"Adin—I'm sorry. I…I didn't mean to."

Lisa murmured to her son in the bathroom light. "It's okay, buddy. It's just a little bump. You'll be alright. You're as tough as a marine!"

Disdain filled her child's eyes. "I don't want to be a *stupid marine*!

"Is he okay? Lisa? Is he alright? Adin? Buddy?" But this time, he sounded desperate and deflated, like the life was being sucked out of him.

Adin sniffled, wiped at a tear, and gathered an arsenal on his breath. "I wish you never came back! I wish you were still at war!"

Lisa glared down at her husband and shook her head from the bathroom loft. "Unbelievable." She mouthed as her glare faded and transformed to match the remorse oozing from JP's gloomy eyes. The man withered and sunk into himself as she slowly shut the bathroom door.

~

After staring at her husband's pulsating back for over an hour, Lisa finally rolled over and tried to sleep. But her thoughts swelled with images of the happy and loving family she fantasied about when she was young. A sad sparkle glistened in her eyes as she reminisced about the pink bonnet baby doll she'd have tucked under her arm wherever she'd go. She pushed it in a stroller, sat with it at dinner, and made it a crib out of one of her mother's discarded Amazon boxes. Her childhood fantasies of what a family would be like were just that— fantasies. She never imagined it would get so hard or that she would have to be so strong for them all.

And that night, she dreamt of her baby doll. But in her dreams, the baby doll wore Adin's face and bronze eyes. The baby wailed out of control, terrifying young Lisa that she had done something to hurt her baby. Frantically and with a tremendous sense of dread, she pushed her infant down a path in the woods, searching for her father. A frenzied barking came from the distance as she pushed faster and faster. But she couldn't outrun it. The barking and growling were all around her, booming and echoing, following her as she ran. Then, silence. She stopped and turned to see a shaggy black dog snarling back at her. Petrified by its fangs and sharp green eyes, she knew he was after her baby.

She tried to talk calmly, rationalizing that it was just an innocent baby. But the dog only showed his teeth. She wanted distance between them, but no matter where she ran, the wild dog was right behind her. At last, she picked up a large stick and a stone, warning that she would do whatever it took to save her child. But the hound didn't care about her warnings. All he wanted was to silence her shrieking child with one monstrous chomp. Spiked and gnarled, the dog leaped for the stroller. Young Lisa swung the stick with all her might. But just as the

141

stick splintered across the growling dog's face, it transformed into her husband. She jerked awake with his betrayed and tragic eyes still etched in her mind.

In his room, Adin, too, was having a nightmare. One where his father was leaving to go fight another war. But instead of hugging him goodbye, Adin hid under his bed while his father pleaded for him to come out. But Adin felt afraid. He knew his father would get *mean* while away at war. So, he hid under his bed, wishing and hoping that his dad would just leave and never come back. That's when Adin found himself at his father's funeral—just like those on TV. Marines dressed in their Dress Blues. His father's coffin draped with an American flag. But this flag had blood on it, his daddy's blood. And then the men began to lower his father down into the grave. He didn't feel sorrow, or pain, or an overwhelming sadness. Instead, the thing that woke Adin up, the thing that made him cry and hyperventilate, was the uncontrolled, satisfying smile that had swept over his bitter face.

He jumped out of bed and grabbed the stuffed Gunny Bear JP bought him before he went to war. Squeezing it with both arms, he sobbed down the hallway, fearing that he had caused his father's death. And not sure what all he'd say when he opened his parents' door, he was certain he'd start with how much he loved and missed his best friend—his dad.

In a sweat and trembling from his own dreams, JP also wrestled with his demons. Sgt. Grimm came alive under the full weight of his combat gear, but he wasn't in Iraq. Matter of fact, Sgt. Grimm was at home in his living room with a loaded M4 and a flak jacket heavy with hand grenades and full magazines. But he could feel the enemy was near. An overwhelming sense of being watched or followed descended upon him, like he was about to be ambushed and overrun.

On a knee beside the couch, he scanned the half-home, half-combat zone and tried to gather his senses. But none of it made sense, and he questioned his reality. The living room fire was blazing hot, but it wasn't the fireplace, it was a burning Humvee. Suddenly, Sgt. Grimm realized his men were burning alive inside. He tried to move, but his knee stuck like mortar to the floor. Helpless, useless, worthless, his mind struggled to understand. He felt weak, ashamed, and pitiful. And for the first time since being home, he wished not to be alive.

Then, from around the flaming vehicle, stepped the boy who killed his friends. On his face stretched a first-place grin. His face lit up as he walked by the flames, both in glee and in light. JP knew the boy was basking in his victory—that the child had outplayed Sgt. Grimm and won the battle. That feeling of fury and resentment burned in JP's gut like whiskey. But no matter how hard he tried to move from that spot beside the couch, the weight was too heavy for him to bear.

Sgt. Grimm gave in. Defeated, he threw down his rifle in a fit. If his men were going to die because of him, then he wanted to be dead too. He opened his flak jacket and let it fall with a hefty jingle. With his arms stretched out and head to the sky, he gave himself up to the encroaching child. Death was coming, and JP felt its shadow on his face. It crawled all over him, biting at his skin like fire ants latching onto him.

But just before the boy reached the couch, he lifted up his Thor shirt. A suicide vest strapped to his body glimmered in the dim light. The boy's complexion changed, fright and panic in his glowing eyes, and for a tic of time, JP felt sorrow and compassion for his enemy. Resistance quivered on the child's lip—the boy wanted no part of their Holy war—and his hazel eyes pleaded for JP to help him.

Sgt. Grimm reached out his bloody hand with empathy. And in that moment of stretched fingers and fear, shade swept the boy's face with an evil smirk. His coined eyes sparked in the flames. A head-tilting, roaring laughter ripped from his belly like machine guns.

Enraged, JP chewed on betrayal—*outsmarted by a child, and made a fool.*

Then, the boy raised his hand, holding the detonator like a torch.

Panic poured into Sgt. Grimm's veins. His family filled his thoughts. The shame of letting them down soured his mind, and he imagined his wife and son learning how to live without him: Lisa raising a fatherless child, Adin growing to resent the dad that never came back home, their regret and remorse for loving a man of war—their disappointment in loving a warrior who couldn't keep a promise.

Such an overflowing frenzy of fury and rampage rushed through the heart and soul of Sgt. Grimm. Such a force of mania and madness betook him, that he became the torrents and tornados that lashed and ripped apart his being. Sgt. Grimm turned to the violence that made him—he became the gale and cyclone that spun beneath the love in his heart. And he let it loose like an opened door to a hurricane.

His grimy hand stretched for his gun. It was time. Finally, he would slaughter this child—this memory—and end the misery and mayhem conjured up from the depths of Hell, from war. The rage set Sgt. Grimm free from the weight holding him in place. As the horned fiend flashed his tiny jagged teeth, smiling at his prisoner's torment, Sgt. Grimm sprung from his knee and dove for his rifle. The weight and comfort in his hands soothed him as he pulled it into his shoulder. He was a *good* man, the *better* man, as he zeroed in on the child's contorted and scarlet skin through his sights. A devil was the boy, with flames licking at the wires of his suicide vest. But Sgt. Grimm felt no fear. *He* was Death. *He* was the warrior. And it was *his* shot to take.

His finger fit into the curve of the cold, steel trigger, like both were carved from the same metal. And as he pulled back and pressed the switch that would end his torment and nightmares, a loud creak stirred him from his sleep.

Gasping for breath and spitting sweat from his lip, JP sprung for the gun on his nightstand and swung its glowing sights at the opened door.

"Daddy, I love–"

CRACK!

One shot rang out and shook the house. One shot burst through the stillness of the night and woke the world. One raging flame roared from the end of a barrel and set ablaze the tinderbox which they called *home*.

Chapter Seventeen

Hole in the Wall

I told myself that I wouldn't do this again.

Well, I lied.

To me, and to you. For saying that I didn't
care.

And now, it's just me and this wall patch and
scraper, these left-handed strokes of sandpaper.

We're nothing more than falling pixie dust
in a fairytale,

and

I'm just making a mess on the floor.

"Oh my God, JP! What did you do?" Lisa leaped from the bed and rushed to her ghost-white son standing in the doorway. A bullet hole splintered the doorframe next to him.

JP tossed the gun to the bed as if it were crawling in his hand. His stomach turned and bubbled. The blood filled his head and face until it felt like they would pop. A vibration reverberated through his flesh, making him weak, unstable, and unable to move. Then, he remembered to breathe. It gushed out hot and fast as he sank to the bed, soaking in his steam, hoping to burn alive.

"Are you okay, baby?" Lisa spun her child, looking for blood. "Are you hurt? Did he hit you? Let me see!" Finding nothing, she smothered him in her arms and wept, kissing his damp hair and head until he complained of her squeezing too tight. Once more, Lisa held him with both hands at arm's length, kneeling on the floor at eye level, and for a moment the thought of her child not being in her life crushed her. She squeezed him again and snuggled his dark hair under her chin.

Finally, she turned toward her husband, who was shaking on the bed. *"This has **got** to stop!"*

But JP wasn't there. He was inside that bullet hole in the wall, faded from the present, and back in his wet uniform and bulky gear, clearing houses in the city. His feet touched the cold floor, and like a shirtless zombie approaching a fresh brain to feast upon, he dragged his feet, *swishing* with each step, his quivering hand extended, reaching out for the splintered door frame. So focused. So tuned in to the fine splinters and pale peeling of the wood's dark stain. He was mesmerized, traumatized, and couldn't process his wife's sharp words. Nor could he sense his son's soft whimpering as he approached the hot hole in the wood. All he heard was the ringing in his ears from gunshots and screams of the dying as his hand met the gritty frame.

With gentle fingers, as if each splinter told its own tragic story, he groped the bullet hole. It was sharp and fresh, deep and endless, like his misery. He stuck his finger inside and wiggled it slowly, like it was the first time he had witnessed such a mysterious portal to another world. A world where death was a field of blooming flowers, and the wind was glass shards in the skin.

"JP! What is wrong with you? Hey! Do you hear me!" Lisa shouted. But as his daze unfolded before her, his incredible delirium devouring his mental state, her ire melted into fear and sorrow. There her husband stood. A shirtless, glossy man in his shorts and muscular frame—a man she no longer knew but still loved—a stranger in her house, petting the wall like it was a damn dog. *Oh, my God! I have to get out of here!* Her wincing thoughts stirred her adrenaline as she clenched her son against her.

She shot up from her knees and rushed to the closet, flinging aside hangers and snatching an armful of clothes. Changed, she jerked her phone from the wall.

"We're leaving! I'll call you in the morning." And with Adin's hand clasped in hers, she stomped down the hall to his room and then out the front door, slamming it as the night took her away.

But JP didn't notice, he was off fighting battles for his country. With his mouth agape and eyes fixed on the way the wood twisted and split into spikes and splinters—like a tornado through the pines—he merely blinked when the door banged shut. The bullet hole glared back at him like a beast with an open mouth full of dagger teeth. He tried to wipe it away, to erase it with his fingertips. Gently at first, like he was learning as he went. But then viciously, like a maniac, a lunatic—a desperate scrub at a stubborn bloodstain. The splinters jabbed into his skin like needles. They ripped and tore at his flesh. Still, his hand whipped faster, scrubbing harder until blood smeared the wood. He gazed at his hand as if it had betrayed him. The crimson on the tips of his fingers was eerily comforting. The way the blood built and bubbled, dotting his skin like drips of wax, was compelling. In a daze, he circled the blood with his thumb until it painted his fingers red. Then, as he searched for what to do with the mess in his hand, he brought it closer to his face, observing, examining, contriving—completely fascinated. His touch was tender as he pressed the damp tips to his forehead, and brushed the blood in sweet, scarlet stripes down his face.

~

JP flinched from his slumber on the living room rug, rattling the empty Southern Comfort bottle next to him. The fire he started had burned down to smoldering embers as the morning light beamed through the near window and cast a spotlight onto a distressing scene. He was half-naked, sloppy drunk, with his only companion—the cold blue steel of his grandfather's loaded 1911 handgun—snuggled beside him on the floor. The green drapes he pulled down for a blanket were tangled around his legs and waist. A pool of vomit, rank and putrid, soaked the corner of the crimson rug. His hand swiped through the mess when his eyes caught the light, which shot a groaning pain through his forehead. The blood streaks on his face were dry and crusted. They flaked when he brushed the blur from his eyes.

If there was ever a time when faith was needed, it would be today. As he rolled over onto the sharp pistol, the memory of what he had done the night before hit him. "Holy shit," he moaned as he rose to his hands and knees. The dizziness held him down like the rocking of a boat on rough waters. The earth moved faster. The floor came closer and closer to his drool-dried cheek until he collapsed back onto the vomit-stained couch cushion he had pulled to the floor.

Sleep came in spells. His dreams were vivid and psychotic. At times, his mind couldn't grasp what was real and what was nightmare. But the one heavy stone he held to be true—he was alone, he was empty, and he was hurting more than just the enormous vice wrenching down on his temples.

The buzzing of his cellphone finally woke him. By then, the morning had turned to day and day to late afternoon. The sun was on its way toward the prickly horizon. Somehow, he had made it to the couch, where half a glass of water sat next to his head on the end table. Pushing himself to the sitting position, he pressed his back into the fuzzy cushion and reached out an off-target arm toward the glass. Once in his grasp, he finished it off and carelessly let it roll from his hand to the floor.

The buzzing came again. It vibrated the hardwood like thunder. It startled him at first, shooting blood to his pounding head and stealing the breath from his foul mouth. He wiped at his eyes and lips. He was still thirsty, but the sink was so far away, and his feet were slow and clumsy. Stumbling from the couch, he staggered his way past the buzzing phone and into the kitchen, where he opened the fridge door to a sharp, pointing light. With one eye shut and leaning on the door, he snatched out a can of Bud Light. Pressing it against his head, he wobbled over to grab his phone before plopping down at the kitchen table.

He sank down into the chair, his head in one hand as he cracked open the beer with the other, and he forced half of it down in one simple tip of the can. Shivering while he exhaled, he spun his phone to read the screen. Grandma had called and left a message. *Shit. I didn't feed today.* He held the can to his forehead as he scrolled through the missed calls and text messages from his wife. She was worried. Well, so was he.

His thumb hovered over the green call button. *What the hell do I even say?* He hesitated. *That I'm a piece of shit and a horrible father? That I'm fucked up? That I need help?* His thumb trembled. *That I love them more than life itself. More than me. More than anything?*

The phone shook in his hand until it darkened. Glaring at it didn't help, so he slid to the other end of the table. *I'll wait,* he thought. He'd wait until he had the words to say to save himself, until he could explain everything. *But how do you explain shooting at your son?* His anguish and despair tumbled inside of him like rocks in a tin can. It was hopeless. It was useless. *How could I explain it to them, if I can't fucking understand it himself?*

A grinding and shaving feeling cut into his chest, like shrapnel to the torso that caused a sucking chest wound. A bullet hole where his heart had been. He slugged back the rest of the beer and threw the can against the wall. Its clatter—the *tink* against the wood and onto the floor—rattled his mind to darker places. *Fuck! Fuck! Fuck! Fuck it all!*

He flung the chair out from under him. It slid across the floor and crashed into the countertop, knocking over the family picture on the counter. Its glass shattered and splashed to the floor. *You fucking idiot!* It only angered him more, as he flexed and shook.

"Ahhhhh!" He hollered. "Whyyy! Why?!" He yelled at his reflection in the glass door. The dried blood on his face had faded, war paint on a stranger looking back at him. The enemy. He *was* at war—at war with himself—and losing.

His fingers squeezed his aching head. There was fire in his hands as he clawed at his face. Then he slapped himself like a lunatic, harder and harder, until his vision blurred and his feet stumbled. The hurt felt good, a different kind of pain, the kind that he could control. He steadied himself against the table, reached up under the ledge, and flung it into the air, flipping it against the wall.

The crash was loud and powerful. His screams were even more.

Manic eyes searched the room for things to throw, to destroy: The plant he bought to apologize for the last time he went mad. The stack of bills on the counter. The pictures on the wall. The dishes in the sink. The *Live, Laugh, Love* decorations leaning and hanging in his wife's cooking space. All hurled against the wall. All slung and shattered. All destroyed and messed. All broken. All broken. All broken.

He put his fist through the wall beside the picture of him in his Dress Blues at last year's Marine Corps. ball. It bloodied his knuckles but made him happy—something other than him had a hole in it. The damage was good company.

There, he sank to the floor and buried his head in his hands. JP was spent, exhausted, and contemplating giving up for the day. Then his phone buzzed again. His weary head lifted to try to find it in the mess and debris. It shook from under one of the overturned chairs tossed into the corner. By the fifth buzz, he picked it up.

"Hello?" His voice was rusty and deep.

"JP? Where are you? Is everything okay?" His grandmother's sweet, worried voice settled his heart for a moment.

He cleared his throat. "Uh, yeah. Sorry. I…uh, I'm not feeling the greatest today. I won't be able to feed."

"*Today?* I hate to break it to ya, Bud, but the day's already over. Darlin', it's six o'clock."

JP looked out the window at the evening gray that settled in over the backyard.

"Oh. Yeah. Sorry, again. I should've called."

"You're damn right you should have!" His grandmother's scorn was crisp and concerned. "Are you all right? You need anything? Where's Lisa?"

JP examined the destruction he created in the kitchen: glass and picture frames scattered across the floor, table and chairs overturned, decorations and mail littered the room. But the wrinkled hole in the wall was solid.

"Yeah. Yeah, I'm fine. No need to worry. Lisa's out getting medicine right now. I'm sorry I let you down." His gaze shifted to the crumbled drywall and dust sprinkled on the hardwood floor. "I'm sorry I let everyone down," he mumbled.

"What? What do you mean?"

"Nothing. I'm good. How about you? You need help with anything?"

"No, don't worry about it. I took care of the feeding. Listen, I may look a little frail and fragile, but I still have a lot of fight left in these damn, old bones."

JP nodded. "Yes, you do, Grandma. Yes, you do."

"Don't patronize me," she said, half teasing. "You're still on my shit-list, young man."

Her labored breathing wheezed through the line.

"Grandma, are you okay? Seriously?"

"Yes, I'm fine. But you should know better. You got an old woman out here doing all the work for you. You ought to be ashamed of yourself." She meant it as a teasing jab, but as soon as she said it, she cringed.

His heavy breath let her know just how sharp her words were. "Well, I am." His voice weak and shaky.

"I'm sorry, hun. I didn't really mean that. You're a wonderful man, and I couldn't do any of this without you. You know that, right? You keep this farm alive. You keep *me* alive." Her breath was loud as she waited for his response. When it didn't come, she continued. "And I love you so much for that. You hear me, JP? Even if you'll always be an ornery little shit, I still love you to Hell and back."

"Thanks, Grandma. I love you, too."

"So, when do you expect your wife to be home? I have something I'd like to ask her." His grandmother was a sly woman, an intuitive woman. She knew there was more to the story than JP was letting on. She had seen him work all day in the driving rain when he had the flu. She knew that something more serious was afoot.

"I don't know. Maybe later on?"

"Around eight?"

"Maybe. Sure. Who knows?"

A heavy silence hung on the line. His grandmother was giving him a chance to confess. But he hoped she would just let it be.

"Well. Okay, then. Maybe I'll just call back later."

"All right. That'll work."

"Or…." Her voice had that tone it always had when she tried to give him a chance to admit he'd done something wrong.

"Or?" He echoed.

"Or…you could just tell me what's going on?"

He thought on that for longer than he meant to.

"JP?"

"Huh?"

"Call your wife. Talk to her. Tell her everything. But most of all, tell her how much you love her. Please."

His skin bumped. Grandma knew him too well. Sometimes he thought that maybe they shared the same kind of soul. That maybe they had some sort of higher connection, too powerful to understand. They were of the same being, and when he hurt, she knew it. And when she hurt, he could feel it too.

"I love you, Grandma," was his only reply.

When JP agreed with Lisa that she should come over to talk, he had no intention of cleaning up the destruction in the kitchen beforehand. *Maybe she'll see the mess and understand the mayhem inside of me,* he thought. But when she walked in the front door and caught a glimpse of the chaos he created, sympathy wasn't the look on her face.

"Oh my God, JP!" She gasped. "What the hell happened?"

His fist clenched, his eye twitched, as he shrunk inside. "Nothin'. Don't worry about it. I'll clean it up."

"My pictures! Nooo. Damn it, JP! Why?"

She stepped over the debris and zigzagged her way to the counter where the shattered five-piece frame holding the family pictures lay in pieces. Picking up the photo of the four of them making goofy faces in front of the barn, she covered her mouth at the damage he had done.

"*Why?* Why would you do this?" Her voice breathy.

He deflated and shrugged.

"JP?"

"Well, it doesn't even matter now."

"It doesn't matter?" Her eyes burned into him as she shook the photo in his face. "How could *this* not matter?"

He scavenged the room for some sort of salvation, but he had busted it, too, with the rest of their things. "I don't know. I'm sorry."

"You're sorry? That's all I get?"

"You wouldn't understand. How could you?"

"Really? Well, you could at least try."

"Damn it, I don't know what to say! How do I put *this* into words? Huh? I'm a disaster. I fucked up…*I'm* fucked up…and I'm sorry."

"JP, *sorry's* not good enough anymore. JP, you *shot at our son! You nearly killed our baby!*" She leaned on the counter with her hands above her brows, rubbing out the pressure building there. "*This*…this isn't going to work," she finally said as he stood in the chaos behind her, wondering how to defend himself.

Her glassy eyes fixed on the rough, grainy puncture in the wall left from one of the many picture frames he had thrown across the room. The jagged hole was exactly how she felt inside. "I can't do this. *We* can't do this."

The words pinched, but he still didn't know what to say to make it right. He inched closer and reached for her shoulder.

"No." She dipped away but turned to meet his pitiful gaze.

"JP, I'm scared." The tears in her eyes were close to falling. "Adin's scared. Your grandmother's scared. We're *all* scared. Jay, we're scared of…of *you*."

He stepped back, crunching glass under his boot. His lungs burned with the breath he was holding. *She's right. You're a hazard to them all. How could let this happen? How'd you let it get this far?* The whole mess, the kitchen, the broken decorations, the shattered glass and loose pictures scattered about, this was his mind—*his mess*—and how dare he bring that home to them. He hated himself for being what they feared. He despised what he had become—*a danger*—a danger to himself and to all around him. A frenzy began to roll up to the surface. An eruption simmered, and the lava bubbled in his chest.

Lisa watched his face bend and mold, sculpt from hurt to hate to heated. His emotions rolled over his brows like waves of a red tide.

"JP. We love you. We love you so much, but…"

Yeah, there's always a but. His eyes stung. His underarms beaded with sweat, and his hands hung like sledgehammers.

"We have to do something about this," she insisted, watching his eyes fade in and out of the moment. "Do you hear me? JP, this can't continue. We *have* to get you help."

His chest puffed and settled. His throat was tense and dry. A vibration in his bones began as he tried to quell the monster clawing at its cage in the shadows. It was coming. He could feel it, the bitter sting of knowing what his wife was trying to say.

"Please, Jay," she begged. "Please, get some help. For *us*, for *you*. So we can fix *this*." She unfolded her arms and gestured toward the mayhem surrounding them.

His edges were dull and scruffy. His face contorted and tight. A terrible shaking nagged at his hands, and he squeezed them to steady his quiver.

She braced herself against the counter. It helped support her for what was coming.

He backed up another half-a-step. The more distance between them, the better.

"Are you gonna join in here or what? Talk to me. Tell me what's on your mind. Please…just. Say. Something."

His eyes said enough, more than what his mouth could muster. After all, what words could he say to change what had already been done? How could he explain something he didn't understand?

Her tone was more annoyed when she spoke next. "Well, I just think…I think it's…" She tilted her head toward the ceiling, examining her words. She swiped at the tears on her cheeks.

"I think it's best if we just, I don't know, spend-some-time-apart." She forced the words out quickly, as if the faster she said them, the less time she had to hear them and the less time they had to hurt her. "We can't keep living like this. We need a break. Some time. You know…some time for you to figure this thing out. I mean, look, it'd be different if it didn't involve Adin, if it were just you and me." Her arms formed a cocoon around her chest. "But damn it, JP, he's not safe *here*. He's not safe…" her voice faded out as she realized what she was going to say next.

With me. Her words were serrated and hot. *He's not safe…with me.* JP fought those words away, back peddling. He twisted and jerked from their grasp on him. Their weight crushed him. Their edges ripped into him. They branded his skin with his own horrible blame.

His eyes narrowed. The less he saw, the less he could remember. His body moved violently in tiny trembles. But still, he was silent. There were no words for him to say. And even if there were, he would probably fuck those up too.

She sniffed and caught a tear with her knuckle. "Listen, Adin and I can stay at my sister's for a little while." Her tone was softer this time, trying to reassure. "Just until things settle down, you know? Just until we get this, *whatever this is*, figured out. You know…until you get some proper help. I think it's best to just give you a little space to deal with *this.* "

She growled as she smeared the tears from her cheeks. "We're not abandoning you. Please don't think that. We're here. *I'm here.* We will walk through this thing together. Before it's too late, and you do something that you can't take back."

When his eyes darted up to meet hers, they were both dropping tears. His silent streaks made her chest shudder.

"Oh, *baby*…I still love you!" Tears zipped down her cheeks as she closed the distance, reaching out for him, taking his pitiful face into her warm hands. "Jay, I do. I love you so much. Adin loves you so much. We *all* do. But this *has to happen.*

Because of last night. Because of this. Because…" Her hand met his throbbing cheek. "I just…we just…" Her words ran dry as she pulled him into her and rested her head on his hard, thumping chest. "Love you," she whispered.

Love you more, his mind whispered back.

But he didn't budge. He didn't take her in his arms. He didn't kiss her forehead or tell her that everything was going to be fine. He didn't do *anything* but flex and tremble and drop tears from his cheekbones.

She embraced him, wetting his chest.

"I don't know what else to do. I don't know how to help you!"

She could feel his body shake against hers. When she pulled away to see his face, she brushed a tear from his stubble.

"No matter what happens, Jay, I'll never *stop* loving you. That's not what this is!" She leaned in and kissed his lifeless lips. "We'll get through this. We will," she whispered, hugging him with her head on his damp shirt. "We just need some time. It'll be okay. It will. I know it will."

His arms hung at his sides like a statue in her grasp. But he was too afraid to move, too petrified of what his body might do if he let it do anything at all. What would he destroy next, if he gave himself the chance? So, he just stood there, rigid and hard, damp and red. Shaking. Trembling. Breathing. And nothing. Doing…*nothing.*

And *that* may have angered him the most.

Chapter Eighteen

Humanity

How could you not see
that I was dying;

stumbling by with a
loaded bottle to my brain,

speaking to you in whispers,
about me in tongues,

dragging my anger behind
me like a dead dog on a leash?

I was tall when I was crawling,
but you stepped right over me

like a crack in the sidewalk.

"Girl, you have no idea!" Amanda said, flipping her brown hair with sass and giggling, before sipping her Starbucks coffee.

"Oh, my God!" Lisa rolled her eyes smiling. "You're such a *hooker!*"

Both ladies laughed in the sunshine, sitting at their whiskey barrel tabletop on the outside patio of The Pen, an Americana-themed restaurant in downtown Cambridge.

"How do you even find the time?" Lisa asked.

Amanda shrugged, her pink shoulders gleaming in her white tank top. Spring arrived hot and early, again—late March was the new early May. But there were no complaints, as downtown bustled and buzzed from crowds of happy faces out enjoying the late sunny morning.

"Well. Shared parenting, to be honest." Amanda took another sip. Her bright red lips, sun hat, and oversized sunglasses looked *overdone* for a lunch date with her friend. But Amanda loved attention, Lisa would be the first to tell you that. And she was getting it too, from the business suits walking by.

"It's kind of nice having every other weekend free to go do…" she shook her head and shrugged playfully, "*adult* things."

"Wow." Lisa raised her brows. "I guess thirty really *is* the new twenty."

"Ugh, please! I've been twenty-nine for a few years now." She smiled and made eyes at a table of businessmen beside them.

"You better reel that in before you have too much on your plate to handle."

"No way! You know I can't help myself when there's a buffet!"

They both gleamed and sipped their drinks, waiting on their brunch.

"Aww, girl, this is nice. I needed this. Really. So, thank you." Lisa reached across the table and rubbed her friend's tan arm.

Amanda placed her hand on hers and patted it gently. "We both did. And we need to do it more often."

Lisa scowled playfully over her cup of coffee. "Oh, will you be able to make time for me between all your Tinder dates?"

"I hate you so much!"

Lisa blew her a kiss as they giggled.

The waitress, with her American flag tie, placed their breakfast in front of them.

"Mmm. Your buttermilk pancakes and bacon look amazing." Amanda pointed with her fork.

"Yeah, so does your, uh, fruit bowl and *salad?* Who eats a salad for breakfast? You're crazy! Wanna bite?"

"Don't tease me like that. I wouldn't be able to stop if I started. I guess the thing I hate most about dating again is the dieting and trying to look appealing. Damn, it's exhausting."

Lisa extended her cup across the table to *cheer*s her friend. "I wouldn't know. But good luck with that. I don't think I could *ever* give up pancakes and bacon."

"Yeah, and look at your perfect little figure. You make thick girls like me hate you."

"Oh, stop it. Girl, you got it going on. Just ask that table of guys over there that can't stop staring."

"Seriously?" Amanda glanced to the side to check them out.

"Well, they were."

Amanda rolled her eyes. "So," she said, covering her mouth with her hand as she chewed a strawberry. "How's everything with JP? How's he taking the whole *break* thing?"

Lisa finished chewing while she thought. "About as well as you would think. He's drunk more than he's sober." She took a drink of water. "But I really think he wants the help. He's trying. I just don't know if he knows how. You know what I mean? It's so hard." She took another bite and chewed a couple of times. "It's hard on all of us. Especially, Adin." She swallowed. "He just doesn't understand why we have to stay with my sister while all this is going on. He misses him. But we all talk every single day. I try to catch him before he starts drinking, but it's not always possible. He's hurting, Amanda. Not gonna lie, we all are."

"I couldn't even imagine," Amanda said. "I mean, Nick's dad had some issues from his army days, but he mostly just kept quiet and grumbled from his recliner. Nick said he used to have quite the temper. You know, before old age took away his energy. But I couldn't imagine having to deal with it like you are."

"What do you mean, *deal with it like I am?* How exactly am I *dealing* with it?" Lisa's voice sounded edgy and irritated, more so than she intended.

"Oh. No, I'm sorry. I didn't mean anything by that." Amanda touched Lisa's forearm, her fingertips warm and comforting. "I just mean…you know…how you and Adin had to leave."

"It wasn't an easy decision. Hell, I question it every single day. Honestly, it eats at me. To wake up in the middle of the night and reach for an empty pillow…it feels like JP is on deployment all over again." She stabbed at her pancakes and fluffed them around a bit. "And I miss him. I miss all of him. The good, the bad, the asshole, and the sweetheart. I miss my husband. But the man he is right now, *that man* is a dangerous man, whether he means it or not. And I *have* to keep Adin safe. If nothing else, it's for that simple fact—Adin isn't safe there right now.

"And I know that he loves us more than the world. *I know it.* He would *never* intentionally hurt either of us. That's just not who he is. Amanda, he's a good man. He's a good man dealing with bad experiences. And I wanted to help. I tried to help. But you know how he is. He's too damn stubborn to admit that he needs it. *Self-reliant,* he calls it." She rolled her eyes.

"Wow. I can't even imagine what you're going through or dealing with. I'm so sorry."

"Thanks." Lisa watched the sun glimmer from her drenched pancakes. Suddenly, she didn't feel that hungry. "I just wish he could find some peace. That *we all* could find some peace. I'm losing my mind worrying about what might set him off the *next* time. You know? Like, what will be the trigger that fires him off on either a sad, drunken bender or into a raging lunatic, flipping over furniture, punching holes in walls, and getting physical while yelling obscenities at our son."

She exhaled with sorrow tingling in her eyes.

"That's not him. That's not *Jay.* That's someone else—that's *something* else. And I don't know how to fix it. I thought he just needed time, but I think it got worse. Now, I don't know what to do, and I feel like I've failed. You know, like I gave up or something? But, I can't help him. Besides, he won't even open up about it. He won't even confront it." A tear zipped down each cheek.

Amanda nodded in the pause.

"I mean, how did it get *this* bad? You know?" Lisa thought for a moment. "Honestly, I guess the signs *were* there. I just didn't think it'd go this far. And I wish I would've done more." Her eyes sank to her plate.

"Sweetheart, it's not your fault." Amanda's eyes filled with sorrow. "You can't blame yourself."

"I don't know." Lisa slowly shook her head, inhaled a deep breath, and let it blow out through puckered lips. "All I can do is give him some space—even if it hurts. It's not like it's a *good* option. But it's the best one I have. Just give him space and keep trying to get him help before he ends up hurting someone." She swirled her fork in the puddle of syrup on her plate.

"Or himself."

~

Six drunk days had passed since JP nearly shot his son. He woke up on Cpl. Richardson's couch in the same wrinkled jeans and black hoodie he was wearing when he staggered out of the cabin, unable to handle his own company any longer, and drove almost two hours to Pittsburgh. He didn't know where else to go. He didn't know what else to do. But he knew he couldn't stay in that rank, empty house for another blackout night or hazy, head-throbbing day.

The dark brown couch, musty and damp, smelled of body odor and beer, but JP didn't care. Instead, he rolled over and grabbed a few empty beer cans that had wedged themselves underneath him while he slept and threw them to the floor. His phone was in the mix of half crushed and fallen over blue cans on the coffee table. He knocked over several, reaching for it. Twelve percent. His battery had never been that low before, and he felt both panic and relief that it would die soon. It took a few tries to unlock it as his balmy finger trembled across the print reader.

He had seven missed calls and four messages from his wife and one lengthy voicemail from his grandmother wondering where he'd been and if he was okay. His wife wanted to make sure he was still alive. And maybe he was, maybe he wasn't. Perhaps he was somewhere in between, where the hopelessness and worthlessness still stung in the mind, where time fermented and self-loathing thoughts blurred and dipped in darkness.

Leading the way down the stairs, shirtless, and holding the hand of a smeared make-up, last-call brunette he brought home last night, Richardson caught a whiff of JP's decay and scrunched his face. He rushed the charming young clubber outside with a quick kiss and a "don't call me, I'll call you" goodbye. Slamming the door and locking it, as if to lock out that memory from his life, he spun around to address the overpowering smell that filled his dank college apartment.

JP flinched at the slamming door and looked up from his phone. Richardson stood barefoot on the checkered linoleum entrance, arms on his hips, staring at his friend's mess in the living room.

"Damn, dude. Did you have a party last night?" He smirked.

JP rolled his bloodshot eyes, looked over at his blurry friend, and then back at his phone.

"Dude, seriously though, go take a damn shower. You smell like an eight-hour patrol through Haditha."

Richardson made his way into the small, simple kitchen with stains on the matching linoleum floor and dishes in the sink. "Coffee?"

It took a second, but JP groaned.

"I'll take that as a *yes*."

A minute later, Richardson walked into the living room with two cups of coffee. He swiped a beer can out of the way as he set JP's cup down on the coffee table. Then he sat in his *almost matching* recliner and kicked his feet up, sipping from his steaming cup.

Richardson stared thoughtfully at the one picture hanging on the wall—the flag being raised during the battle for Iwo Jima. "Hey man, you don't happen to remember that chick's name, do ya?" He reached for the remote and flicked on the flatscreen TV, which covered up several empty screw holes in the fingerprinted plaster walls. It was already on the news channel, so he pressed the volume down and sat the remote on the armrest.

JP clicked off his phone, let the stale air out of his lungs, and tried to sit up. He struggled, but made it to somewhat of a leaning and sitting position with his head resting on his hand. "I don't know man," he mumbled. "I think you called her a couple different names last night—Kelsey…Chelsea? Maybe Lacey?" He reached for the coffee, its weight too much right then, so he left it at the edge of the table with his hand gripping the handle.

"Well, shit." Richardson laughed and looked at his friend, who was struggling to hold himself up. JP forced a painful snicker.

On the TV, segments about beached whales all along the coast, flocks of birds smashing into buildings, and record-breaking lightening flicked by as a reporter showed charts and dates about the science of it all.

"What do you think about all this shit?" Richardson said. "They say Earth's magnetic shield is weakening. I guess it's down, like, I don't know, twenty-five percent or something from a hundred years ago. I don't really know what all that means, but it sounds kinda crazy, right?"

The reporter talked through images of the flaring sun releasing plasma, with animations of Coronal Mass Ejections hitting earth's magnetic field, and the Northern Lights visible in Southern Ohio for the first time in over one hundred and fifty years.

JP lifted his head and tried to focus on the screen. "The apocalypse—I hope."

"With zombies. That'd be cool."

"Yeah, really slow ones though, because I don't feel like moving fast today."

Richardson laughed at his older buddy. "Bro, you want a beer or something. A little hair of the dog wouldn't hurt."

JP swam through the clouds in his head for a moment, searching for a reason not to. He dwelled a moment on the thought of Lisa and Adin. And then: "Fuck it. Let's do it."

Three beers later, JP's phone buzzed on the coffee table. He glanced over from his Xbox controller annoyed that someone was bothering his Call of Duty battle with Richardson. He let it go to voicemail. But a few moments later, his phone buzzed again. This time he reached for it quickly, looked at the unidentified number, and swiped the red ignore button.

"Dude, c'mon! I'm getting lit up over here!" Richardson called out.

JP was back at the controls waiting for his character to respawn when his phone buzzed a third time.

"Bro, shut that damn thing off!"

But when he reached for it, he Lisa's name and hesitated. "It's Lisa."

"So, what?" Richardson's eyes never left the screen. "Call her back later. We're killin' shit."

He didn't answer, nor did he bother to look over when it buzzed from her long voicemail. But a few seconds later, his phone beeped with a chain of text messages. Distracted, annoyed, and curious, he set his controller down and picked up his phone.

"Really? You're just going to leave me hanging over here?" Richardson had yet to look away from the game.

"Just give me a minute. I need to see what's up."

"You haven't been much help all morning, anyway. I'm probably better off on my own."

JP opened the first text message. "Shut up," he methodically said as he read his wife's "Call me now!" and "It's important!" texts. He waved for Richardson to turn down the volume while he tapped the green button on his phone.

"What?" Richardson reached for the remote.

"Something's up. Turn it down."

Richardson muted the TV, set the controller down, and went into the kitchen to grab another beer. He offered a can to JP, but he shook his head, declining it.

On the fifth ring, his wife picked up. "Hey."

In that one simple word, JP could tell that something serious had happened. A panic tingled through him as he rushed through the possibilities of what it could be. *Is someone hurt? Does she want a divorce? Did someone hurt her or Adin? I'll rip their fucking throat out if they did!* He took a deep breath and braced for what she was about to tell him. "Hey. What happened?"

A commotion in the background filled his ear: a mumbled conversation, beeping noises, and an intercom paging someone. Shit, *she's at the hospital!* "Are you hurt? Is Adin? Are you at the hospital? C'mon, say something, please!"

Lisa's breath trembled on the other end. She was sobbing and trying to hold it in. He felt her trying to be strong, and that shook him to the core.

"Where have you been!?" she asked in tears. "We've been trying to get ahold of you all morning!"

Instantly, guilt stung his chest. He didn't know what had happened, but he felt responsible for it. He stood up and started pacing the living room.

Richardson saw the worry on his friend's face and took his beer outside to the front porch to give JP some privacy.

"I'm in Pitt, at Richardson's. Will you please just tell me what happened? You're scaring the hell outta me." JP's legs began to wobble as he paced. His body was hot and tingled with anxiety. Whatever had happened, he knew that he was too far away to help—and *that* made him sick to his stomach.

Lisa's sobs were noisy as she tried to talk. "It's…it's…you…weren't…here."

JP's pulse pinged loudly in his temples, as a thousand pins pricked his chest. *It was his fault. Whatever happened—it was because of him.* His eyes stung and watered. He wiped furiously at his cheeks.

"Please, Lisa, just say it. What happened?"

Someone on her end said something, and she pulled the phone away as they briefly spoke. When she got back on the phone, her sobs were more robust.

"Grandma. It's your Grandma!"

<u>Chapter Nineteen</u>

Gone

standing barefoot
in a muddy puddle
looking up

on a sunny summer's day

trying to evaporate
right along with it

and you

The colors were a blur on the way home as JP thought about the woman who had raised him, the woman who had taught him how to be both strong and gentle, to be brave in the face of uncertainty, and to love unconditionally. He thought about that sweet, sassy soul that loved to bake and cook homemade meals. The dear woman who ventured on walks through the pastures with him, orchestrated family picnics on the hill under the oak tree, and rarely lost a game of rummy on card nights. She was his grandmother, his mother, and his best friend.

Once, he and Lisa had snuck off from the basement, leaving their movie, *Friends with Benefits*, still playing on the only modern thing about the finished basement—a 52-inch flat-screen TV mounted to the drywall. His grandmother had called down to see if they wanted any warm chocolate chip cookies, and when no response came, she walked down to an empty basement. She wasn't dumb—she knew what teenagers did when they thought no one was looking. But she wasn't ready to be a Great Grandmother yet.

She stepped out onto the front porch and listened to the sounds of the night, which included faint wisps of laughter coming from the barn. With her blue kitchen towel still in hand, she made her way toward the sounds of two fifteen-year-olds giggling in the barn. JP remembered the shock and panic he felt when the sliding barndoor roared to life and let in the moonlight, spotlighting his bare bottom.

Whenever the conversation led to old sins, they argued about who was more embarrassed at the time. His grandmother had hollered out into the night, "Oh, my Lord! JP put some damn clothes on!"

Red-faced and fumbling for his pants, he tried to talk his way out of it. "It's not what it looks like, Grandma! I'm…we're…you see…what happened was…it was a medical emergency. Yeah. Yeah, she has…asthma."

He warmed as he reminisced about how much that story grew in ridiculousness each time his grandmother told it. Somehow, his version was always more innocent than how *she* told it. And that orneriness and bond he had with her were priceless.

With a head full of childhood recollections, he wandered in and out of snapshots of growing up on the farm. The late summer raspberry patch along the back-pasture fence, where his grandmother took him for walks when he was young. Carrying a stack of square green baskets and picking the ripe berries until each one was full. The taste of sweet and sour black raspberries, the smooshy sweetness of the plump red ones. He could still feel the seeds in his teeth remembering putting one in his mouth per every three in the basket. The sleepovers in the barn, when Grandma would bake treats for his friends and pass out spare flashlights when they tried to last all night in the hay. She even left the back door unlocked and a tray of chocolate chip cookies on the counter for a midnight snack when the yipping coyotes sent them running for the house, again.

JP wasn't sure how he made it from Pittsburgh to Cambridge in just over an hour, but that was the least of his worries. Seeing his grandmother sedated and tucked into her hospital bed with all the tubes and machines around her, he knew he didn't get there soon enough. And upon learning that his grandmother had suffered a stroke after working the farm while he was away drinking with his buddy, he broke down and cried at his wife's feet, beside his son, in the hospital hallway.

He slept in a chair in the corner of her room, like he'd done for his grandfather. As he drifted in and out of sleep, dreams, and nightmares, he wrestled with his decisions and failures of the last few months. And in the haze of sleep and stress, his grandmother came to him in his dreams—dreams that flipped like pages from a Berenstain Bear picture book his grandmother would read before bed.

A young JP chased chickens through the backyard in nothing but his superman undies and a stick in his hand. He squawked along with them, flapping his arms like wings and tilting his *caws* and *cock-a-doodle-dos* toward the blue sky. The feathers sprinkled the fresh-cut grass, like leaves in the fall. He could see himself as if it were someone else, like he was looking down on a movie screen. Out of body, but still able to feel what the child was feeling—pure euphoria. The glee and happiness, the giddiness and joy of romping through the yard, the freedom to be youthful, wild, and careless. A feeling like seeing his first live concert, playing fetch with his new pup in the sunshine, or holding hands with his high school love, riding the back roads at sixteen, untethered from life's anxious twists, free from worry in a wild world. Complete liberation.

But then the skies darkened, and the mood changed. Heavy, tumbling thunderheads roared over the tree line of the west hill. Its shadow edged its way toward the farmhouse. An eight-year-old JP sat among the chickens, tossing pellets of corn and seeing how close the hens would come to him. He dangled his hand outward for the hens to feed from.

But he didn't see the squall approaching. His focus was on the chickens. They crept and bobbed nearer, their red eyes cocking from side to side. Devilish, but he wanted them closer. One sharp foot at a time, one forked step forward, and then another. The closer they got, the bigger they became. There was no joy this time. Instead, he panicked as they enveloped him.

The storm's black clouds hung low, rolling and twisting above the brick chimney, blending with the fall fireplace smoke whipping in the wind. With angst, there was danger in the sky, and JP had to warn his younger self. His sleeping body jerked and snapped from side to side.

Suddenly, his view zoomed out, and he watched from the hilltop by the oak tree. Everything looked darker, jagged, and blurred in the dull haze of a gray sky. He screamed out his name. *JP! Hey, JP! There's a storm coming! Take cover!* His frantic voice sounded hollow and faint as he watched the clouds loom over his younger self. But it was no use. The mist thickened and rolled, spinning and lashing at the limbs of the apple trees in the pasture. The cold shadow crept against the child's back, darkness chilled his skin. It pricked at his neck like bristles from the hairbrush when his grandmother would try to tame his thin, wild hair. His skin bumped and tightened. He called out again, desperate this time.

The hens doubled in size with each flash of lightning. They pecked at his hands like knives into a feed sack. The boy cried out. JP cried out. All of a sudden, his grandmother's sweet voice rang from the back porch. "JP! JP, it's time! Come on in from the storm. Get out of the rain, you fool. You're going to catch yourself something horrible." But it was all too late. The black mass, the thundering bolts, and thrashing wind, swept down from the bubbling sky and sucked the boy up into the darkness.

His stomach flipped and turned. Restless, he shivered and pulled his knees to his chest in the chair, his breath short and shaky. His body weak, he floated between sleep and vivid dream.

Then, he was in his grandmother's kitchen, full of comforting chicken decor and country knickknacks on the walls. She was baking, humming to herself as she kneaded the dough with powdered hands. The dough turned into a bowl of batter for blueberry muffins, and JP could taste the sweetness as he licked the spoon. She wiped her hands on her chicken apron and moaned as she pulled the pie from the oven, poking it with a fork.

Grandpa sat at the table with a beer in his hand. JP was fifteen years old, dirty from the afternoon's chores and sipping sweet tea from the fresh batch in the window. Grandpa talked about the farm and "how things used to be back in the old days." Fifteen-year-old JP loved to listen to his grandfather reminisce about the struggles and hard work that was softened by the love of his grandmother.

"The love of a good woman will give a man the strength to do anything," his grandfather said as JP leaned in with intention, hanging onto his grandfather's words of wisdom.

All at once, JP was standing on his own front porch watching his wife drive off with their son in the jeep. In his hand, he held the heavy steel of his handgun. He turned it over in his palm, cursing it for what it had done to him and his family. Hysteria overcame him, and he heaved the gun above his shoulder, ready to throw it as far from him as he could. *Into the woods*, he thought, aiming it toward the dead branches where he would toss it away forever. But as he swung his arm forward, it wouldn't leave his grasp. He tried again, harder this time. But the gun remained clenched in his fingers. His anger roared from his throat as the taillights disappeared over the hill and around the bend, lifting a trail of dust on their way out of his life.

Desperate to end the pain, JP turned the gun to his temple and squeezed the trigger.

The bang woke him up, a burning sensation at his temple. As he came to, he felt the heat of his blood ooze down his cheek. He sprung from the chair rubbing at the side of his head. The moon sprinkled in from the hospital window onto his outstretched fingers. Nothing. There was no blood or brains or bullet. He checked his head again. Everything was intact. *Jesus! It was just a dream.* The steady ticking and beeping of the machines hooked to his grandmother sunk into his eardrums. He blinked, searching the corners of the room. Then he remembered where he was and what had happened. It was *his fault* Grandma was in the hospital. *Because of him*, she had a stroke. *He was to blame* for his family's suffering.

Exhausted and sweaty, he settled back into the fuzzy chair and stared at the door across the room. He thought of the bullet hole he put into his own bedroom doorframe several days before. The idea made him sick—sick of himself, sick about the man he had become. And the overwhelming, self-destructing thoughts brought about a tenacious dizziness that made him feel faint and nauseous. *How could I let myself get like this? How did things get so far out of control?* The room and shadows spun around him. His stomach flipped and turned. Physically ill, he wretched into the trashcan in the corner until he was drained and spent. Settling back into his chair, he wiped his chin on his forearm, rested his head on the cushioned arm, and faded back to sleep.

His grandmother hummed around him, but her form was washed out by the blackness that filled the room. Only the faint feelings of objects and familiarities of a place he had once been before lingered there. Wherever it was, he felt safe and secure, as though everything was going to be okay. His grandmother's soft humming soothed him and made him think of hot raspberry pie.

"Hello?" he called out, his voice deep and concerned. "Grandma?"

A candle flicked on in the darkness. The damp and dusty concrete room wrapped around him.

"We're here. It's okay, son." His grandfather's firm voice sounded trustworthy and solid.

As the candle grew brighter, he could make out his grandparents sitting on the floor and holding hands in front of him. Against his back was a shelf full of canned food, emergency meals, water, blankets, clothes, and survival gear. They were in the storm shelter under the farmhouse.

"What's happening?" JP asked.

"Everything will be okay, sweetie," his grandmother said, her voice echoing in the silence.

"It's just another storm. Don't worry, we've survived them before," his grandfather reassured.

"A storm?" JP's fear trembled in his words.

His grandmother smiled in the dancing light. "Just a storm."

"I don't like storms, Grandma!"

"Shhh. Calm down, now. It'll be okay. I promise."

His grandmother caressed his silky hair and kissed him on the forehead. Her actions helped comfort him at first, but then a rumble vibrated the shelves.

"No! Don't let it get me!" he shouted.

His grandfather scooted between him and the door. His grandmother followed and sat beside her husband, placing JP behind them both.

"You don't have to worry, son. We're right here. We'll protect you." His grandfather's dark eyes squinted and winked. His rough hand reached back and held onto his grandson's. Then his grandmother placed her hand on top of theirs.

"I'm scared."

"You don't have to face it alone," her gentle tone eased him.

"But it's *my* storm! And I don't want it to hurt anyone else!"

"Shhh." His grandmother placed her finger at his lips. "It's *our* storm."

"No, it's not, Grandma! It's *mine!* I don't want it to get you! Please get away from the door!" Young JP tugged on his grandparents' hands.

His grandmother slapped him on the cheek just hard enough to get his attention. "Stop it! Get your shit together!" she ordered.

The loving sting on his face helped him focus. He stared at her blankly, letting his understanding blink into his thick skull.

"What?" he asked.

She was eye to eye with him, her tight lips brave and unwavering, calm and steady, sassy and strong.

"I said…Get. Your. Shit. Together. Young man."

"But Grandma!"

"No! No buts, just actions. You have to hold it together for them." She pointed at the concrete wall, which was now transparent, showing his cabin bedroom where his wife held their sobbing son as she rubbed his quivering back.

JP was an adult again. "What's wrong with them? Why are they sad?"

"Because of you, son. You need to do better." Grandpa thundered.

The sorrow in his wife's eyes matched his own. "You're right. I'm not helping, am I?" JP could taste his son's tears on his lips. "I'm sorry. I'll do better, I promise."

When his grandfather spoke, it sounded like God was talking down from above.

"Son, sometimes you have to stand in the wind to know how deep your roots go. Sometimes you have to wait in the darkness in order to find the light. You understand?"

"I…I think so?" JP could feel his adult mind mulling the wisdom and churning it over and over in his head.

His grandmother wrapped him in her arms.

"You have to let love win."

"What?"

Her voice started to fade. "You have to let love *in*."

"Grandma! Wait! Where are you going?"

"Nowhere. I'm right here." Her boney finger poked JP in the chest. "Right *here*." Her voice faded to a faint whisper as the candle flickered out and the room shuttered in darkness.

"Grandma! Where are you! I need you! Come back! Pleeaasse!"

"Always…here…with…youuu."

Then the storm siren blasted above him as the tornado ripped his house apart.

He jerked awake with tears on his face as his grandmother's heart monitor blared the solid green line across the screen. Moments later, a nurse rushed into the room and pushed him back out of the way. Several nurses burst into the small space and worked to start his grandmother's heart again. He stood by, in the corner, watching it all pass as though it was still a part of his nightmares.

But as they frantically wheeled her bed out the door and down the hall, it sank in that his nightmares had finally become his reality. His best friend was gone.

<u>Chapter Twenty</u>

Pieces of Depression

There is something beautiful
about falling apart.

This dirty linen, darkest on the pillow,
permanent in the middle and heavy;
an ink blotch;
a Rorschach test,
a self-evaluation each morning by ten.

If you ask me,

I see a shadow of a man with a burned out
complexion, a smoldering disposition;

like those burned crumbs still comfortable
in last week's skillet
pushed to the back of a sticky stove;

like that familiar stench of old, rusty piss,
stagnate in this ring-stained toilet bowl.

I see spots of toothpaste on this half-closed
bathroom window, where I stand, and I stare,
and I listen,

waiting for inspiration, or direction,
or for the world to end,
as I scrub at my chipped tooth and bleeding gums.

I see the *what-fors* and the *how-comes*
and the *why-nots*
desperately interrogating
these *who-am-I* eyes
in this hand-streaked, clouded mirror—and broken.

Broken in the lower left corner, splintered
from the last time that I slammed it shut.

Broken from this horned fiend reflection,
from worshipping this deity of misery,
from these crumbling thoughts

of gun-muzzling this sickness,
of ending this agony.

But most of all,
broken from this monstrous conclusion:

that *I am <u>not</u> the hero that I need to be.*

And shattered
into scarlet and gray pieces of depression.

"Hello?" Lisa crinkled her nose as she closed the front door to the cabin behind her. "JP? Where are you?" The last few weeks, she made it a priority to check in on him when her phone call would go unanswered. Today, she brought Dr. Clatterson, but he waited for Lisa's thumbs-up outside in his blue pickup truck.

At just before noon, the house was a disaster and smelled of rotting food and beer. It looked as it did two days ago when she tried convincing him that cleaning up some of the mess would help clear his mind and maybe invite in good, clean thoughts. He brushed her off and yelled at her when she tried to do it herself. "I'm not a child!" he yelled, defiantly. His twisted point of view. One she tried not to take to heart. His hurt was a debilitating kind of pain, and she saw it, as he isolated himself from everything except the cows and chickens. If she had to be his punching bag for a bit until he could function on his own, then so be it. But his sadness was contagious and pungent. She couldn't stand to be in his filth for too long. So, when he insisted that he "was capable of cleaning up his own goddamned mess," she was obliged to let him have at it.

But clearly, he wasn't *capable*. She stumbled over his muddy boots and two pairs of crusty jeans piled by the door on the way in. And once she made it past that fuming scent, the sight of moldy pizza in opened boxes on the couch, coffee table, and recliner slapped her in the face. By the time she made it into the kitchen, the stale, fermented air of two-days-old beer was somewhat of a welcomed treat for her nose.

She'd never seen her husband live like this. *How?* She wondered. *How could anyone be okay with this? He's literally rotting away in his own filth. Unbelievable. Disgusting. Putrid. I'm not letting him sit here and decay. Not like this.* So, Lisa got to work, cleaning up his chaos and not caring what he'd say or how he'd feel about it. He'd be ashamed to live in this mess under any other circumstances. But he seemed cozy, wallowing in his filth and squalor like a pig. It was as if he hid behind the fear to live again, like he felt that wasting away and rotting in his cage was the kind of life he deserved.

"Well, I'm just going to start cleaning up then!" she hollered up the stairs as she slid dirty plates and utensils from the counter into the trashcan.

Upstairs, tangled in his crusty sheets, JP finally stirred from his drunken stupor. The clanging of the dishes brought him back to life in his sweat-stained bed.

She heard him stumble and bump into his nightstand, knocking his pistol onto the floor. She winced, wishing he'd just lock that damn thing up and stop carrying it around like a cellphone.

Tucking the pistol into the back of his shorts and without bothering to put on a shirt, he wobbled into the bathroom. The smell of stale urine hadn't bothered him in weeks. When he lifted the lid to the toilet, the stench reminded him of the port-a-johns at FOB Hit. He lived with it and preferred it to be that way, wishing he were back in that death land, taking fire and dying for something more than self-pity.

He stood by the window, speckled by spit and toothpaste as he brushed his teeth. Outside, a warm and sunny day beckoned, which he despised for all of its glory. *How can the day be so bright when the world is so dark?* He peered at the pines and thought about his time as a child playing army through the rows of trunks and crawling over soft brown needles in the fall. Never would he have imagined that being a warrior would be so hard.

"JP? Come give me a hand, would you?" Lisa hollered pinching her nose and dragging the heavy trashcan toward the back door.

His heavy feet clunked as he made his way down the stairs. With toothpaste and drool crusted in the corner of his lips and stubble, he sported a three-day-old beard, weeks-long hair, and an odor that demanded soap and water.

A homeless drunk—that's the first thing she thought when he rounded the corner all groggy and negligent with red, swollen eyes, flush cheeks, dropped shoulders, and a departed spirit. He was in rough shape, and she punished herself for that. She hadn't been able to save him, to help him, or to pull him hard enough out of the muck and mold of the decaying life he was wandering through.

"Jesus, JP," she said, covering her nose. "I don't know which smells worse, this kitchen or you."

She meant for it to be a teasing jab, to maybe lighten the dark cape he dragged with him down the stairs. But he didn't laugh. Instead, he sniffed at his underarms and cringed, embarrassed.

He smelled of something dying, a poetic irony of sorts. But his eyes said what his lips would not: *he was sorry*. In many ways, he was sorry. As sorry as a pitiful person could be when they imposed on a loved one's life, pulling them down too. He was sorry. Like the bearer of bad news on an otherwise perfect day, he felt responsible for the gloom, for the gray, and for the grief.

He moped over to the trashcan and dragged it to the door.

She seized the opportunity to recover from her jab that landed below the belt. With the can of air freshener in one hand and a dirty rag in the other, she aimed the can in his direction and sprayed him with three quick bursts. "There. Much better," she said.

He stopped in his slow path to the back door, drooping like an old man, and looked up at his wife's playful grin. JP wanted to smile back. He did. The ability seethed inside of him under the rubble and debris. He wanted to laugh. Hell, even his lips pulled just a little at the crusted corners and stayed that way for a second. But he couldn't sustain it. Instead, he nodded his approval at her efforts and then moseyed on out the back door with his stench lingering behind.

She cursed at the ceiling when he disappeared. It was hard to be a wife, a friend, a lover, and to be a protector and a fixer. She carried so much responsibility on her shoulders; the weight drained her. It exhausted her mentally and physically, but she still wanted to do more. And she wanted things to change. She desperately missed her best friend. She missed the back-and-forth teasing, the jokes, the laughter, the intimacy, and ornery grins. And she was less without that bliss.

When JP returned through the door, she hid her somber eyes by wiping down the counter. But he could see the suffering even in her strokes across the counter. He felt her damaged disposition, like a cold fog in the valley, as soon as he walked back through the door. And whatever bleak spark of life was still aflame within him burned out. *God, I'm so worthless. Pathetic. A wasted piece of flesh. She doesn't deserve this. And I don't deserve her.* His mind attacked itself until he gave in to the only comfort he had left: he lumbered over to the fridge, opened it like a case of bandages, and plucked out a blue can for breakfast.

"Already?" she asked, disappointed.

He cracked the can open and leaned against the crumb-covered countertop. "Who's that outside in the truck?" He asked after a long gulp.

Her shoulders dropped. "Well, I kind of wanted to warm you up a bit first." She recovered quickly with a more playful tone. "Buuut looks like the cat's outta the bag, huh? Any guesses?"

He scoffed. "Seriously, Lisa? I'm too hungover for games. Who is it?"

"Look, please don't be mad."

"It better not be who I think it is?"

"JP, please. Just talk to him. He just wants to help." JP shook his head as he downed his beer and crushed the can. *"Please? For me?"*

"Lisa," he sighed, grabbed another beer from the fridge, and let the suds spill over when he popped the top. "I can't."

"What do you mean *you can't?*"

"I just can't." His voice was rough, his face even rougher.

"Just give him a chance. We gotta do *something*. I mean, look at this place." She motioned to the surrounding disaster.

He scanned the filth, and sorrow sucked the last light from his eyes. "I can't. I'm sorry. Just make him leave."

"Just five minutes! Please, Jay! *Please!*" she begged.

But JP didn't say a word. He just made his way to the back porch, where he sat in his rocking chair and sipped his brunch with the late morning breeze and lustful birds.

Lisa watched him with tears in her eyes from the kitchen counter. He was a hollow shell of himself that she wished she could fill with love. But he was difficult and stubborn, a hard-headed man just like his grandfather. And she was still trying to find a way to get to him, to get him *back*—to pull him away from the ledge he had become so comfortable teetering upon.

Fine, she thought. *If he wants to live his life like this, then so be it.* She walked to the front door and waved Dr. Clatterson away. They shared a sad look before he left. Then she strode back inside, reached above the counter into the top cabinet, and pulled out a bottle of merlot. The dusty wine glass was fitting as she popped the cork and poured it to the rim. *If you can't beat 'em, join 'em.* She shrugged before she tipped the bottle to her lips and finished it.

She moved to the porch, letting the screen door slam behind her, plopped down beside her husband in the other rocking chair, spilling a bit of wine. Without hesitation, she gulped at the glass until it was half empty.

JP watched his wife as if she were a clown in big red shoes sent to entertain him. Unsure if he should laugh, clap, or feel sad for her, he just snorted and gleamed. "Atta-girl." he said, a playfulness in his tone, which made her feel like she made the right decision.

She wiped her lip with the back of her hand. "So, this is what you do all day then?"

His eyes glimmered, pressing the can to his lips, savoring the brew a moment in his mouth, before swallowing with a satisfying *ahhh*. "Yup."

She matched his pace, committed to the moment. "All right, then. Let's drink the day way." She kicked up her feet on the railing and settled in for the duration.

By two o'clock, she was wine drunk, and he had finally started to show signs of life. She was actually enjoying his company. "This whole day-drinking thing isn't all that bad."

"It has its perks." A smirk played at his lips.

"Hm." She smiled, staring out at the pines twinkling in the sun. Throwing the day's responsibilities in the wind and watching them blow far, far away made her feel youthful. Adin was at school, and her sister agreed to watch him afterward while she handled things at the farm. The freedom reminded her of the summer days they would spend together at the lake, just sucking in the moment, the sun, and each other. She thought of the time they snuck off from the fire and their friends and walked the dark shoreline until they found a secluded cove they could call their own. She could still feel the excitement in her chest when he reached behind her to untie the string to her black bathing suit.

That was the feeling she'd been missing the last several weeks. The lack of a love-thrilled heart had left her less of the woman she loved to be. Lost in her thoughts, she rubbed the cool wine glass against her neck and wished to feel those thrills again. The thrills that made her heart jump when he led her by the hand, bare-skinned and naked, into the crisp, chocolate waters.

"You remember when we used to do this out at the lake? Amanda and Nick? Dan and the guys?"

He nodded.

"Oh my gosh, those parties! What were we thinking?" She chuckled. "The slip-n-slide that summer when you cut your leg on a piece of glass, and I made you take off your trunks so I could nurse your wound. Remember how shy you were at first? Stumbling over your words in the camper as I cleaned and bandaged you up? You were adorable! Oh! And the fire that nearly burned down Dan's camper. The boat? You remember tubing every day until we couldn't lift our arms or barely hold a beer bottle?"

His face shined as she took him back to their youthful days.

"The late-night swims?" she said with a seductive grin.

"Oh yeah! You tried to tell me that you couldn't swim!" His voice raised with excitement as he remembered that day.

"Yeah! So, you'd hold me close, you idiot." She cocked her head. "Instead, you brought me those damn floaties!" She smacked his arm as they laughed.

"I guess I wasn't all that bright back then, was I?"

"*Back then?* You still don't know how to take a hint." She shoved his head playfully.

"Bullshit."

"My birthday? Two years ago?" She raised her brows.

He thought about it until it showed on his face. "Yeah, but—"

"Noooo. No, *yeah buts.*" It stimulated her to see him smiling.

"Hey, you said you were sick."

"So, you would take me home and ravish me! Not get me a puke-bucket and some Tylenol."

His embarrassment stood out in red blotches on his face. "Well." He shrugged. "You should've said something."

She rolled her eyes and finished her wine with bright cheeks. Pushing the hair away from her forehead, she reveled in the steam of the day. The heavy air smelled of pine needles and honeysuckle, and the afternoon sun placed a sparkle on the leaves and grass. Indeed, the springtime breeze held a certain magic, and with it came a twinkle and shimmer of light in her husband's face. *Where's that JP been? Damn, I hope that shine stays the rest of the day.*

They sat together on the porch, rocking and drinking, chitchatting now and then, soaking in the day, and each other. Lisa was determined to turn his sorrow into sunshine, and she let her hand wander and brush against his.

JP's hand jerked; he hadn't thought about intimacy in quite a while, and the electricity of his wife's touch shook him. His body resisted the urge to feel any pleasure; it would not allow him to take part in the things that made life worth living. *How can you allow yourself to feel good when all you've done is hurt everyone else?* His mind skittered into a small panic when her fingers stretched out to stroke his.

But she was cautious not to push too far, too fast. Though she yearned for her husband's loving touch, she wasn't sure if he was willing—or if he was even able. Perhaps it was the wine, perhaps the lustful mood of spring, but she was persistent in reaching him, and she was determined to start that spark with the soft tips of her fingers.

She stroked his index finger the full length of his hand. It sent a tickle up his arm and a charge into his chest. This time, he didn't pull away. As guilty as he felt, he held firm in his desire to feel something more than destruction. She traced up and down the back of each finger, one by one, eliciting little bumps onto his arms and neck. He inhaled the honey in the air while she laid back her head on the wooden chair and watched him come alive when she took his hand into hers.

The block of ice in his head dripped from her fire. He needed her. If there was ever a chance for him to come back from the darkness in which he had become so comfortable living in—to resurrect himself—then she was the flame that would light his way.

Lisa let him unravel. The way a tough man melts is all at once, dousing away his *macho* into a puddle on the floor. He was hers again. She pulled his arm around her as she climbed out of her chair and onto his lap. She took his scruffy face into her hands and guided it to her lips. A flutter glimmered inside of them—youthful butterflies—like what they were doing was something brand new. It stirred a nervousness, anticipation, a yearning for what the late afternoon would lead to, and a longing for it to last all night. If for nothing else but a moment, they were wild and free like their teenage days at the lake. And they were both ready to jump in.

She plucked him from the chair and led him by the hand into the house. The smell nearly quelled her appetite. But she pushed forward to the steps and paused at the top to peer into the bathroom. Her brows raised with her grin.

He tried to move past her to the bedroom.

"Not so fast, mister." She tugged at his arm. "How 'bout a team shower?" She winked.

His head cocked to the side. "You trying to say I smell or something?"

She chuckled. "Yes, actually. That's exactly what I'm saying. You're dirty. Now, come on." Her smile eased his embarrassment as they slid through the doorway.

Pausing in the mirror, the man staring back at him was red-eyed, wrinkled, and ashy. *Like a zombie*, he thought, trying to wash himself away by splashing water on his face while she got the shower ready.

While she undressed, he glared at the ghost in the mirror, cursing his crude reflection until the steam took it away. She interrupted his thoughts with her wet hand around his waist, taking his breath away in quivers. He leaned on the sink with both hands. The stimulation of her touch torched his skin. Paralyzed by her affection, he gripped the sink and gazed into the fog until she undressed him.

Still unsure of how to let go, he stayed hunched and firm near the mirror. But she ran her hands up and down his back until it loosened. She had always known how to touch him. And the golden strands of her pear-scented hair dangled against his skin as she rested her head on his back, holding onto him around his waist.

A woman's desire and affection inspires a man to become better. With an eager release, he let go of the sink, spun into her arms, and kissed her like he hadn't kissed her in years. In the rolling mist, they held onto one another and kissed until their skin was wet and steamy.

Then, she pulled him into the water like she was leading him to his baptism.

He rinsed as she lathered up the loofa. The first swipe across his back was gentle and tender. Her strokes were deliberate and pure. Mighty strokes— passionate and nurturing—scrubbing away the filth he'd been lugging around for days. The suds bubbled on his shoulders, streaked across his chest and arms. They rolled down to his waist, his thighs, and off his toes.

She soaped his entire body, spending time and care with each part, like preparing a king for a coronation. Diligent and tender brushes up and down, small circles of suds and sorrow spinning down the drain. She cleansed and restored him.

When she finished, he was new. He shined adoration, reverence. And with his wife's work done, he returned the favor.

But his quick strokes and sweeping suds bubbled with anticipation. He couldn't take it any longer. Before he could finish brushing her curves and breasts, he dropped the loofa and took her in his arms.

They made love like it could be the last time.

Afterward, a nap was in order. After all, they had exhausted all their strength and desire to hold themselves up for a while. So, they lay together in his dirty sheets that smelled of his bad decisions and late-night sweats. But she didn't mind. It was almost pleasant to smell him again as she slept, no matter how musky his odor might be. Besides, she cracked open his window before they settled into his stained satin.

Just when her eyes had finally fluttered closed, a late afternoon thunderstorm rolled in. And as the vibrations from the coming thunder shook inside of him, she awoke to his flailing squalls and trembling whimpers. Not wanting to wake him and experience the heat and sting that follows such horrid dreams, she laid there on the brink of tears as the explosions raged ahead and ever nearer.

In the flash and rumble of the hostile storm's assault, she questioned if he would ever be the same again. With each twitch and jerk, each quiver of his lip, the scowl of his brow, in each shutter and moan, each twist and groan, she lived his dreams along with him. His cries were her cries. His shuttering breath was her breath. Each explosion, each splash of metal into his skin, each gash and rip of his flesh—her blood would run, her lungs would burn, and her heart would break.

She watched him with tears in her eyes, begging God for mercy and grace. She watched and wondered what torment he must have been through and what torture he endured now. She watched him with pity, wanting to end his suffering with the smothering of her love. *If only my love were enough.* Powerless, she turned her shoulder and cried to the wall while he called out for Joey and his friends with each rumble in the sky.

He soon awoke to the echo of his own screams and the shaking windowpane. His body stuck to the wet fabric that peeled like tape when he sat up in the heat of his bewildered state to face the noises of the room.

His wife's sobs muffled as he moved. She sniffed and cleared her face with a swift hand. But he already noticed.

"Was I screaming?" Beads of sweat dotted his forehead. He smeared them with his forearm.

She took a moment to herself before she rolled over to face him. The whole while he stared at her smooth back and round shoulder. He wanted to reach out and touch it. He wanted to kiss it. But an uneasiness lingered in the room, and he knew it was because of him that she was crying.

Her puffy cheeks were pink when she forced a smile. "Just a little bit. But don't worry about it. It's okay." She tucked her hands between her cheek and the pillow, trying her best to look casual.

He wasn't buying it.

A clap of thunder stole his attention. He flinched and jerked toward the flash in the window. The pelting of rain on their shelter started slow and quickened with the wind. He watched as it marbled the window until he could no longer make out the edges of the pines. *Fitting,* he thought, *blur it all. All of it. Please! Blur it so I don't have to see it anymore!* His jaw flexed and he let out a gasp when she touched his damp shoulder.

"Babe. You all right?"

His shoulders shook as he inhaled and released it loudly. "No. Not at all." He turned to look at her reaction.

Her eyes said a thousand *sorrys.* They made his throat tighten with guilt. JP was ruining her picture-perfect life, and he knew it.

"It was just a dream. Everything's fine now." She lied right through her aching smile. "You're safe. You're here, at home, with me. It's okay."

Everything was *not okay*. She was lost and at the edge of giving up. She couldn't bear his trauma any longer. She had about as much as she could handle, without losing her own fragile mind. They were both in pieces. Neither one could reassemble the other. No matter how hard they tried, there was just no fixing what was shattered.

Lightning flashed in the dim room. JP jerked his head toward the nightstand, where his pistol gleamed in the low light. He reached out for it, and she shuttered. He clenched it in his sticky palm, and she squeezed the sheets in hers. Naked and armed, he drifted toward the cracked-open window, tapping the muzzle against his thigh.

He pressed his forehead on the cool glass. The murky swirls of different shades of green and gray dripped down the window with the streaks of rain. He closed his eyes for a moment. But all he could see were the body parts of his friends lying in scarlet pools of blood. The eyes of the boy in his scope, a blended hue of brown, green, and gold, daunting with deliverance, grieving, and desperate.

"JP? Please, put the gun down and come back to bed," his wife begged. "Babe, *please?*"

When he turned and his sad eyes met hers, he didn't speak. Instead, he gazed at her golden hair and smooth curves and wished her simple glamour would fill his dirty soul until he was cleansed of all his sins. She was his salvation—and his damnation.

She sat up and patted the wet sheets, surprised at how soaked they were. She glanced at the dampness gleaming on her palm. It was incomprehensible, what a fractured mind can do to a hard man. His pieces stuck to her hand like glitter. "It's okay, baby. You can cuddle up on my side with me. We can just hold each other. Okay?"

"I'm all wet," he said, tracing a streak of water down the window with his barrel. It squeaked against the glass, then settled back at his thigh, blending with the shadows of his hand, as though they were one.

"I don't care. I don't care about any of that. I just care about *you!* I just want *you!* Please, come be with me. Let me hold you and settle your mind. Just…please…hold *me* instead of the gun."

His hand twitched at the weight of the pistol. He had forgotten it was in his hand. It had become such a common comfort that he didn't even notice that it was still there. Its edges poked at him as he clenched it. Turning his palm up, he studied it as if it were connected to his bones, as if it were a part of him. He wanted to cut it off and toss it out the window. But it was stuck there. And as the thunder and lightning enveloped the cabin, it was the only thing that could keep him calm. "I'm sorry," he said with hurricane eyes. Then he headed out the door and down the steps to pour himself a glass of whiskey.

She scrutinized his every step further away in the late afternoon glow and glare of a shattering sky. He'd closed the door on the way out, and for the first time, she noticed it—the black duct tape stretched over the bullet hole in the bedroom doorframe. A simple *X* in black tape. *Why?* she wondered. *Why would he think that duct tape would fix a bullet hole?*

Several minutes passed before she dressed and followed him down. "What are you doing?" she asked, coming down the steps and tying up her hair.

JP was in his armchair with his whiskey glass in hand and gun in his naked lap, staring down the front door, as if the devil himself were about to burst through and steal his soul. "Hm?" His thoughts clouded his senses.

She walked into the kitchen to gather her things.

"What are you doing? Don't you need to feed?" she asked a little louder from the kitchen.

He didn't answer. Instead, he sipped loudly from his glass and banged it down on the stand beside him.

Did my question piss him off? He needed to tend to the farm. Someone needed to tend to the farm. Grabbing her jacket and purse from the couch, she paused. *Should I just do it? Should I just feed? Or will he blame me for making him feel inadequate again?* She huffed and lingered beside him a moment, playing with his still-damp hair and scratching the back of his head, as if to give him a chance to tell her what he wanted her to do.

"You want me to take care of it for you? I don't mind at all. It's no big deal."

He pulled away from her outstretched fingers, still burning down the door with his blowtorch glare.

She scratched her own head in frustration. "All right, well…I'll just take care of it then."

Instantly, he grabbed his whiskey and took a long drag, not returning it to the stand this time.

She huffed and shook her head, knowing that whatever this was—whatever reasoning was in his mind—it was outside her comprehension. And she didn't have enough energy left in her soul to deal with his dejection. The day had left her weak and exhausted. Drained, not just from the day drinking, lovemaking, and interrupted sleep—she was mentally deflated from the inability to tear down his brick walls, to comfort him, or to relieve any of the anguish tormenting him. Through all her efforts, she still hadn't found a way to fix *this*. So, she leaned down and kissed the top of his head.

With heavy steps, she headed for the door. When she reached it, she hesitated, still waiting for him to say something, *anything*. She just wanted him to be *there*, present, interact, connect, reach out, and unveil his inner-workings. Hell, she just wanted a damn response.

But nothing. Nothing verbal, anyway. He was gone again in the murky swamps and punji pits of his badlands and battlefields. And it shattered her like the silence in the room when the thunder would roar.

She shook her head. She needed her sanity. She needed to care for her child. *She needed her husband.* But he needed time, or maybe more than that. Facing the chill of the rain and bolts of the blackened sky, she walked out of the house and into the storm.

JP blinked with the wind and shuddered in its mist. Biting down on his lip, squeezing the glass in his hand, his body shook with resentment. *You're just going to let her go!? Why didn't you say something? Beg her not to go. Plead with her to stay. Ask her to come back. What the fuck is wrong with you!? Do something, you moron!*

Naked and not afraid of the elements, he shoved his drink aside, let his pistol fall to the floor, and ran after her. "Wait! Wait!" he called from the front porch.

She turned at the steps, saddened by the sight of his pitiful demise.

"Don't go! Please don't go!"

His words were a stake to her heart. The urge to melt burned in her chest. But she tried to hold it back. She tried to hold it in, because what she was going to say next would be enough to shatter her. "I can't stay, JP. I have to go."

The rain slashed at her silver Jeep in the drive. The large drops exploded like mortars at the curves and edges, like dunes and plateaus along the Euphrates, her shelter and his grim reaper.

"Why?" he yelled over the static of the rain.

She glanced at her Jeep as if it would save her. "I just can't," she yelled back. But it was her eyes that said it louder. "I'm exhausted. I'm just…JP, I'm drained. I have nothing left. I just," she exhaled loudly, *"can't."* The hood of her dark green jacket fluttered at her forehead. "If you're not going to help yourself, I can't help you."

He flinched. "Oh. Okay," he said. "I understand. No problem." He turned toward the door and stopped. "Same time, same place tomorrow, right?" He tried to grin, but his lips stretched into something more of a grimace.

Lisa's knees nearly buckled with the unfamiliar words that formed in her head and clamored in her mind. They scratched and pounded at her lips to get out. They knew what they were doing, but they still surprised her with how unfamiliar they were.

"I don't think so. I," she looked down at her boots, "I think we just need some time, some space."

"Oh. Okay, then." It was as though they were having a neighborly chat, and she just turned down his invite to the BBQ.

"JP? Are you going to be all right?"

The mist in the wind formed drops of water on his skin giving him goosebumps. He shivered and suddenly realized how cold he was. He wrapped his arms around himself. "Yeah. Yeah, I'll be fine," he said casually and reached for the doorknob. He stopped mid-twist. "So, maybe next week, then? Or, you know, whenever you want?"

"Maybe. But…I really just…" She bit her lip and crossed her arms, shivering in the wind. "No matter how hard I try, I can't reach you." She hung her head and tapped her toe in a puddle on the wood steps. "I can't put you back together, no matter how much I want to. I just can't fix you." When her blue eyes peered up at him, he wasn't sure if it was rain on her cheeks or tears. She cleared her throat and swallowed. "I think you need to go see Dr. Clatterson. You know, a professional. Someone who is better at this than I am. Because I don't…I just don't know what to do. And it's killing me." Her head titled as if the words were pulling her down into the ground.

With the door halfway open, ready to rescue him, to shelter him from the storm, he watched his wife torment herself with a decision she had been battling for a long time.

"Yeah. Maybe you're right," he agreed. "All right, well…stay dry. Love you."

And with that, he meandered through the threshold with his wavering hand extended—like a tired man in a dark room, searching for the light switch—until his fingers snatched hold of the icy burn in his sweating glass. And quick to his lips, he swallowed it all down. Deep. Deep. Deep down.

Chapter Twenty-One

Shadows in the Lamplight

The night is nothing more than
bad imagery and perspective:

Beer bottles loom like tombstones,
marking where dead worries lie.

Their shadows lean crooked and
bent by the dim lamplight.

A heavy head to a dirty pillow on a
dog-haired couch; what cares have I?

And if it wasn't so damned cliché, I'd
admit that she broke my humbled heart.

But in this moment of stale air and hatred,
the truth is easier to see; I broke it myself.

Jimmy wasn't Adin's best friend, but he was invited to the party, anyway. Matter of fact, Mrs. Morgan's whole second grade class got an invitation to Adin's birthday party two weeks before school let out for Easter break. Even at Adin's protests, his mother insisted on not leaving anyone out, because "You wouldn't like it if it happened to you. Right?"

But Jimmy wasn't the nice kid or the cool kid or even the athletic kid. No, Jimmy was the big kid with freckles and glasses who bullied the other kids whenever he had a chance. Lisa suggested maybe Jimmy just needed a friend. So, Adin put up with the behavior, *for his mother*, even if Jimmy often teased him about his father not being around.

The party was colorful, despite being camouflage-themed. Maybe the bright green, gray, and orange Nerf guns stood out the most as each kid ran around the Cambridge City Park yelling, "I got you! I got you!" at each other. Adin was all smiles and giggles, for the most part. Even if he did keep looking over at the parking lot beside his mother's Jeep, waiting for his father's red Chevy to pull in beside it. After a while, he got lost in the fun of chasing his friends and trying to include Jimmy, who had an attitude about the whole thing. The party wasn't "big enough" or "at the pool," and it "didn't have as many presents as *his* did." According to Jimmy, the party wasn't fun at all.

Then it was time for cake and presents. Lisa and the other parents did their best to wrangle all the children under the blue metal pavilion with gray plastic picnic tables to sing, eat, and open gifts.

But despite the birthday cheer, Adin strolled to the pavilion with his head down, his gun hanging from his grasp and his feet dragging through the grass.

"What's wrong?" Lisa asked.

"Nothin'."

She knew that it wasn't *nothin'*. Matter of fact, she knew exactly what bothered her eight-year-old child, because it was the same thing that bothered her. JP still wasn't there. She had stalled as long as she could, giving the children another half an hour to run around on the jungle gym and shoot foam Nerf darts at one another, until another argument sent one or two into *timeout* beside the fruit punch cooler. She looked at her quiet cell phone; it was time.

"Hey. Hey. Come here, buddy. What's wrong?" She guided his head back in her direction as he tried walking past her to the cake.

His pouty face said it all. "When's Dad coming?"

Lisa wanted to defend her husband. She wanted to believe he had a good reason for not being at his son's birthday party. The same birthday party she reminded him about for the last two weeks. But she knew the likely causes of his absence: beer, whiskey, and regret. "Maybe he's out getting you the biggest present ever!" She forced excitement into her voice.

Adin rolled his eyes. "Yeah, right. He probably forgot." Then he dropped his gun and moped over to the corner table, where he sat with his arms crossed.

Tears welled in her eyes. JP was the cause of her heartache and their son's, too. She pulled her phone from her shorts pocket and checked again for messages. She opened their thread and hammered out WHERE ARE YOU?!?! in all caps, but she hovered over the send button. *This was his last chance to prove himself, and damn it, he can't even make it to his son's birthday party. No! Nope! I'm not gonna do it! I'm not reminding him again. It's just something he's gonna have to learn the hard way.* She clicked her phone off and slid it into her pocket, message unsent. *Sooner or later, he'll feel the wrath of his decisions,* she thought, cursing his irresponsibility all the way over to the pavilion.

But before she made it to the waiting crowd, Amanda walked over and gave her a silent hug. As Lisa looked over Amanda's shoulder, she caught a glimpse of Adin and Jimmy messing around with their friends. *How sweet,* she thought, *they've become friends. Maybe Adin listens to me after all.*

But Lisa couldn't hear what Jimmy was saying and was too far away to recognize his vile intentions. Jimmy wasn't looking for friendship; he was looking for attention.

Jimmy picked through Adin's presents, shaking them and tossing the uninteresting boxes back under the picnic table. "Which one's mine?" he teased, shaking a heavy one. "Ooo, I like this one! I think I'll keep it."

More children gathered around the table; some shook presents with Jimmy, not really knowing any better, while Adin pouted in the corner, trying to ignore them. Then Jimmy started to open the big gift.

"Hey! That's mine! Put it down!" Adin demanded, getting to his feet.

Jimmy just laughed and tossed it to the ground. "Probably just boring school stuff, anyway. Nothing like the Xbox8 I got for *my* birthday."

"You got an Xbox8?" A blond-haired kid with a backward Brown's hat asked.

"Yeah," Jimmy glanced at the handful of kids watching him, "and you're all invited to come over and play too. Except for *Aaadin!* I only let friends with fathers come over to *my* house."

"Shut up! I have a father!"

"Where is he then? Probably off with his other family. I bet he has other kids he'd rather play with than be here at this stupid party, anyway!"

The other kids *ooohed* and snickered.

"Nu-uh! Shut up!"

Jimmy laughed in his face and shoved Adin's shoulder. "Your party sucks. My dad let us shoot BB guns at mine. It was way cooler than this."

"I don't care!" Adin's eyes were misty as Jimmy's teasing made him miss his father even more. "I didn't want you here, anyway! My mom made me invite you!" Adin shouted back.

The kids laughed, and Jimmy's face flushed. "Where's your *daaad*, Adin?" Jimmy teased. "He's a ghost dad, isn't he? Just like the other ghost dads." The kids giggled, wide-eyed and open-mouthed. "But I bet yours couldn't stand to be around you! That's why he's not here!"

Adin jumped to his feet and stared up at the big bully towering over him. "Stop it! No, he's not! He's not a *ghost dad!*"

"He probably doesn't even like you!" Jimmy sneered. "Ghost dad! Ghost dad! Ghost dad!" He turned to the kids behind him, trying to get them to chant along.

But they didn't. And when Jimmy turned back around to face Adin, he was met by the swift fist of an angry child and the bright red pain of learning life the hard way.

~

JP's legs slid from the edge of the couch to the floor. Their dead weight was enough to make a thud even on the thick living room rug. Instantly, his toes squished in something wet and slick. Repulsed, he looked down at the vomit on the carpet. He didn't recall putting it there, but that was a problem for another time. He scraped off the excess spew onto the plush rug and forced himself up onto wobbling legs. The late morning sun cast beer bottle shadows across the floor. He stumbled over them as he weaved his way into the half-bathroom under the staircase.

In the mirror, he saw a face he didn't recognize: pale skin, bloodshot eyes, and a scruffy beard. *Who the hell is that?* He twisted on the cold water and splashed his face. The jolt helped, but the fog lingered.

He let his face drip into the sink. *Is it Saturday? No. No, it's Sunday.* Something nagged at the back of his mind about Sunday. Splashing another handful of water onto his face, he carelessly spat the runoff onto the mirror. It squeaked as he ran his hand across it. *What the hell was I supposed to do on Sunday?* He dabbed his face with a crusty hand towel and tossed it into the corner with a rancid pair of old work socks.

Walking over to the fridge, his son's picture struck him. *Shit. Adin's birthday party is today! Did I even get him anything?* A nervous panic fizzed through him. It was one of the few chances his wife had given him to show up and be a father to his child, and the last thing he wanted to do was to ruin something again. He thought back to the day she told him about the party at Cambridge Park. She had so much fun planned for the day: a water balloon toss (and fight), a Nerf gun battle, fishing in the pond, and Wiffle ball. And then, when the afternoon sun flared too bright, they'd head over to the pool. It sounded amazing, and he was excited to go.

He opened the fridge and studied the last three bottles from the two twelve-packs he bought yesterday. *Hm. Maybe just one for the hangover?* His hand shook as he twisted the cap and tossed it near the overflowing trashcan. It *tinked* off the side and rolled until it hit the leg of the table, where it wobbled to a stop. *Ah, I'll get it later.*

The beeping from his phone's messages interrupted his wall staring. *Probably Lisa making sure I'm awake and getting ready. Ha! I'm already up. Boom! And she thought I'd mess this up, too. Phhft!*

Strolling into the living room, sucking on his cold brew and trying to avoid the light stinging through the windows, he found his phone among the beer bottles on the coffee table. He clicked the phone on—indeed, a missed call and voice message from his wife. The corner of his lips twitched as he imagined how good it would feel to call her back and let her know that he was "wide awake" and "getting ready for the party."

Finishing half his beer in a few gulps, he called her back without listening to the message. The phone rang several times. *She's probably getting ready,* he thought.

"Hello," a grumpy voice answered.

"Hey. What's wrong? Did I interrupt your eyeliner or something?"

"No."

"Uhh, okay then. Well, what's up? I'm awake. I'm up. I got it under control." He swirled the last few drinks of his breakfast around in his bottle. "I'm getting ready as we speak."

There was silence from the other end.

"Hello? You hear me? I'm getting ready. You didn't even have to remind me. Boom." He grinned.

A heavy breath blew into the speaker. "Ready for what?"

A shock zipped up his neck. "Uh, the *party*."

"Wow," Lisa retorted. "JP, the party was *yesterday*. You missed it. You weren't there for your son, *again*. And quite frankly, right now, I just don't want to talk to you. Didn't you get my message? I said not to call."

JP nearly crumbled to the floor. Panic bubbled up from his guts and into his chest. *She's lying. It's some sick joke to prove a point, right? She's getting even for all my recent failures. Or maybe she thinks it's amusing to fuck with me like this?* He squeezed the phone in his hand and slammed the beer bottle onto the coffee table. Several bottles clinked together and fell off onto the red, soiled rug.

"What!? C'mon! Quit it! Don't mess with me like that! I feel bad enough about myself without having you play some stupid joke on me. Do you want me to bring anything or not? A cake? Balloons? Beer?" He chuckled. "Just kidding on the beer. But seriously, what can I do to help. I *want* to help."

Her long, drawn-out breath was filled with both sadness and hopelessness. "I don't even…. Jesus, JP. I don't even know what to say. Look at your damn phone! It's Monday. I sent you, like, three texts yesterday and never heard a damn thing back! What is wrong with you?" She immediately regretted saying it and simmered in her own guilt.

Terrified, JP dropped the clothes in his hands and flipped the phone around. Suddenly, he felt ill. In his hand, on his phone, reality flipped him the bird and punched him in the gut. It was Monday. And he spun with the room until his legs gave out. Then, from his knees, he hurled into his dirty pile of work clothes.

"JP? JP? Hey! JP!" His wife yelled through the phone on the floor beside him.

He wiped his mouth on his forearm, picking it up. "Yeah? Yeah, I'm here," he said with a quivering lip.

"Did you just get sick? I could hear you."

"Uhhh, yeah. It's fine. Don't worry about it." He tried to lift himself from his knees, but the room whirled around him. So, he crouched with one hand, holding himself still, and the other pressing the phone to his sweating head. "I just…I just thought it was Sunday. I thought the party was today."

"*Dammit, Jay,* I told you over a week ago. You put it in your damn phone. How could you not know what day it is?"

His eyes shifted, trying to make sense of the new world he found himself in. The cold world that had turned on him in a blink of an eye. It was a lonely place when he realized that even his mind was against him. And devastation shook him: he had failed his family once again.

"I…uh…I don't know," he sounded disembodied. "I could've sworn it was today…I…" He sat down, leaning his back against the wall, and stared at the boot-tread clump of dirt on the floor. "I'm sorry. I'm so sorry."

On the other end of the phone, sitting at her work desk in front of her computer, in her sister's spare bedroom, Lisa closed her eyes and tried to find her strength. *I don't get it. How can a combat marine be so…untrustworthy? Don't they preach about being dependable?* She let her weary head rest in her hand propped up on the desk. She was at a true crossroads: on one hand, she was enraged by him disappointing their son, but on the other hand, she was heartbroken for the fractured man she couldn't fix. Pity found its path to the surface, and although she was afraid for what he might do, she was obligated to tell him what Adin did at the party.

"Look, I don't know what to say or what to do. Honestly, JP, I'm scared. *You* scare me. *This* scares me. You have to get some help, please. This is hurting us more than you know. It's hurting Adin, more than you know. I'm giving Dr. Clatterson a call later today. I don't know what else to do."

His choppy breathing puffed in the phone. "No. No, I'll do it when I'm…when I'm ready."

"Look, Adin got into a fight yesterday because of *you*," she said bluntly, pouring it on and hoping that it all sank into his heart.

"What? With who?"

"With some of his friends. They were teasing him. Making fun of him because you weren't there. JP, do you see what all of this is doing to us? Adin punched a kid in the mouth because he said you didn't love him. He called you a ghost dad."

"A *ghost dad?*"

"Yeah, I guess it's what they're calling fathers who aren't there for their kids. And Adin defended you. Can you believe that? Even after all the shit you've put him through. Even after the canyon you wedged between the two of you, he still loves you. He still defends you."

She knew her words gutted him, but she needed him to see the big picture. And she didn't let up. "Adin hit him in the mouth and gashed his lip open. He was on top of him, wailing away at the poor kid's face until I ran over and pulled him off. You should've seen the rage in his eyes. Honestly, it reminded me of you. He has your temper. He has your fight. And if we don't do something about all of this, then he's going to have your sickness too."

~

The afternoon was a river of whiskey through his veins. He had failed his family. He had failed his grandparents. But most of all, he had damned his wife and son to a life of torment and despair. He brought his war home to them. And for that, he was most ashamed and repulsed, appalled and distraught.

And in his whiskey bottle was the only salvation he could see. Death by self-destruction. Suicide. An end to the carnage. Defeat and extermination. In his distorted mind, in his deformed disposition, in his desperate and pathetic reflection, *death* was the only answer—*death* was his only savior.

JP sat on the concrete steps of the farmhouse. He slouched beside half a bottle of Jim Beam, his grandfather's Colt 1911A1 pistol and an old Amazon box sealed shut with black duct tape. The box, which he had dug out from underneath his desert combat boots in the back corner of his closet, was stuffed full of letters he had received in Iraq. He picked at the black duct tape, ripped it off, and unfolded the flaps.

The late afternoon sun gleamed across the white envelopes. JP squinted as his unsteady hand reached inside the box and lifted out the first envelope his fingers could grab. It was a pale envelope with dirty fingerprints still tattooed just below the long, handwritten address and black-inked stamps on the top. A letter from his grandmother.

My Dearest Rotten Boy,

I hope this letter finds you safe and well. We've been thinking about you every day and pray for you every night at supper. We even added your name to the prayer list down at the church. (By the way, Mr. and Mrs. Wamer wanted me to pass along their well wishes and hopes for your safe return.)

The corn's growing. I'd say it's about knee high now. It's about 7 p.m. here. You and Grandpa would be enjoying a beer down on the porch after the evening feeding. Hell, he's probably down there right now drinking one for you while I'm up here in my room at my desk. staring at your picture in your Dress Blues—so handsome! It makes me feel like you're here talking with me when I look at it and write. Silly, I know. But you always knew your grandmother was a lot of crazy in a little sack. (We have your grandfather to thank for that.)

The calves are getting along just fine. Three out of four made it. There's a really cute brown and white one. I think I'll name her Betsy. You should see them chase each other through the fields. I know! I know! You've seen it a hundred times! But it gets to me just like they were my own kids out there playing tag. It reminds me of you and your friends when you were just a calf with your blond cowlicked hair. Grandmothers and mothers don't forget those kinds of things.

Well anyway, the farm is still here, I'm still here, and your grandfather is still drinking beer. Nothing has changed, other than you being gone. Lisa, God bless her heart, has been a big help around here when she can. I know I tell you all the time, but you really picked a good one with her. (Even though she's way too good for you!) We talk about you every day. And no, I'm not going to tell you what about. That's just between me and her. Girl talk. Get over it.

Oh, before I go, your grandfather wanted me to tell you that he shot a coyote the other day with his 1911. He was awful proud and wanted to make sure I let you know that he's still got it—even for an "old son of a bitch." Pardon my French, or wherever "bitch" comes from.

I'll send out more cookies when I send this letter. You better be sharing with your buddies. I'll ask Joey when you guys get back home. And I'll give you the swift side of the fly swatter if you didn't share. Don't think you're too old to get whooped!

I love you with everything that makes me live. We miss you. We love you. And we want you back home in one piece. So, stay safe.

Love,

Your Old Folks.

His eyes glazed over picturing his ornery grandmother sitting at her desk beside her bed, refusing to use the computer, and handwriting her letters, because she "spent fourteen years learning how to write in cursive," and she'd "be damned" if she didn't use it until the day she died. He laughed at her antics and exaggerated hands when she got dramatic to prove her point. But JP didn't mind. Nor did he mind the cursive, handwritten letters he *sometimes* had to show his platoon commander, who studied historical languages and literature in college, just to decipher her words.

But now, he thought about how undeserving his wife was of him. Though he got a kick out of his grandmother's jabs back then, now they just seemed vicious and sharp because of how true those words turned out to be. His wife *was* way too good for him. And Joey never made it back home.

His hopeless eyes shifted from the dwindling whiskey to the shining slate steel of the pistol, and then to the rowed fields and green pastures. One of the cows, Betsy (of course), a brown heifer coming into her second year on the farm, was grinding grass happily beside the barbed wire fence down along the barn. JP watched her for a moment, wondering what it might be like to live life as a cow. *Would I know I was a cow? Would I know anything? Would I feel anything?*

A faint rumble, a low growl in the Westward sky, pinpricked his drifting mind. His attention scanned the busy horizon and looming, teal plumes puffing toward the heavens. A stone wall stretched the skyline. Its jagged rods pierced the green canopy below, sending a grumble across the sky like a battle horn sounding an attack. Just in time, the Devil had come to take him.

Great, he thought as the electricity filled his core and amplified the thud in his chest, *a perfect ending to it all.* Tossing his grandmother's letter back into the box, he shifted his attention to the bottle and pistol.

"Well guys, we better get to it. No one wants to die wet."

He wobbled as he gathered his gun, whiskey, and box of letters he intended on reading one last time before he ended the plague that sickened his family. It was an awkward load of companionship clinched between his arms, a heavy pack to carry for a drowning man.

As he stood atop the rough steps and gazed up toward the hilltop where he would do his deed, it was clear that his ground was not stable. And the concrete was too rugged for his clumsy feet. JP stumbled when he stepped, and like a football player holding tight to the ball, he never let go of his friends as he went down. The thud of his chest smashing the box of letters was the last thing he heard before his head smashed into the concrete walkway.

When he came to, a splotch of blood-soaked the concrete, his box was smashed, and the wall cloud above him stared down like a wolf keen on devouring its prey. He let the blood seep from his brow down between his eyes and drip from the tip of his nose.

"Son of a bitch!" From his knees, he examined the gun and bottle still clutched in his hands. "You guys all right? Okay. Good. Cause I need you."

He snatched a handful of letters from the broken box and teetered to his feet. But as the blood trickled down his face, so did the doubts into his mind. A swift wave of uncertainty and second thoughts shuddered up from his staggering legs to his stinging eyes. *Am I really gonna do this?* His hesitation prompted a second evaluation. And as the storm tumbled on ahead, bearing down on the twig he'd become, he decided to try his wife one last time.

The phone started its second ring and went straight to voicemail. *What the hell?*

He tried again. This time it barely rang before it was ignored. *Shit!*

Deflated, he gathered his only friends and started toward the oak tree. Then, as he paused for a swig at the base of the hill, he thought of Richardson. *Call whenever you need, bud! I don't care what time or what I'm doing. I'll answer or call back,* he remembered his friend telling him the other day.

The tree on the hill looked smaller than he remembered as he stared up at it from the bottom. It was a long climb to the top in the shape he was in. The appeal of his final stand felt less and less appealing as he rolled with the tall grass in the breeze. *Hell, why not? If he doesn't answer, then it's meant to be.*

Holding the phone to his ear, he wasn't sure what he'd say; he just hoped he could say anything at all. Maybe he would tell him he needed to be talked down from the ledge, or maybe Richardson would already know. Either way, *one last shot at hope.*

It rang once. Nerves tightened his throat. It rang twice. He yanked the phone from his ear, staring at the screen with his thumb hovering over the End Call button. It rang again, and he thought he heard someone answer, so he forced the phone back up to his ear. But all he heard was the silence before the fourth ring.

Then, a click and change of tone.

"Hello?" he said without much clarity. "Richardson?"

"Yo."

"Hey man—"

"You reached Richie-Rich, you know what to do. Leave it."

The phone beeped. But he didn't say a thing. All he did was breathe blood onto the receiver. In and out. In and out. He splattered red from his lips until his conclusion became clear. *Okay. Let's get it over with.*

The *pinging* in his head, silenced only by the thunder on his heels, followed him the whole way up the golden slope. At the top, he was welcomed with open arms by the brown and green figure waving *hello* in the wind. Thankful for its hospitality, he leaned on the trunk and rested his head against its ribs, staring at his grandparents' tombstones in the fluttering grass.

"I'm sorry I haven't visited more," he spoke to the gravestones. "I've been too ashamed to let you see me like this." The bottle tipped back. "But here I am...one final time."

It had been several gusts of wind before JP finally pulled out another letter from the stack: an army green envelope this time, big enough for a Hallmark card. He remembered it well. It was a birthday card from Lisa and Adin. He ran his fingers over the sandy glitter and glue Adin used to color in the marine on the front. Joey had made fun of him when he had opened it in April and walked around the barracks with glitter sparkling on his uniform all day. But back then, he had gleamed. Back then he was proud.

He tossed the card aside. *You don't deserve them. You're worthless. They're better off without you.* The clouds rumbled and flashed bolts to the hills on his left flank. The hairs stood up on his arms, and he eased them with two full slugs from the bottle of bourbon. *That's what I deserve.* He shook the bottle in his hand and swirled the last third into a whirlpool. A whirlpool which he held up to the growling storm and watched it spin with the churning clouds. *Yeah, that's what I need—to be swallowed up by the storm and blown away.*

Not long and the storm crashed upon him, roaring and flashing, as he read through the fibers of his existence. The letters scattered around him like flowers at a funeral. He swayed along with the wind, roared with the thunder, flashed in and out of existence with the lightning. He became the storm, his war. It was now or never. *No pistol tastes the same*, he thought, biting down on the muzzle. He just wanted a taste. He just wanted to know what the cold steel would bring when he pressed it against his tongue.

Hatred. Hatred is what he tasted. Remorse. Contempt. Scorn and damnation. He tasted the iron of gunpowder and blood.

His eyes closed, and he thought of home. But not of his house, his bed, or his front yard. He thought of the golden strands of hair that hung down his wife's playful grin after she teased him into confessing his love for her in random public places, like the grocery checkout line or hunting store. He thought of brushing those same golden strands from her glowing face each morning when he woke and kissed her good morning. He felt her hand in his, the tingle through him when they were young, back before they knew each other's bodies. He heard her voice, soft and sweet, calling out his name as they made love.

And he thought of Adin—his poor, innocent Adin—who would one day trace his father's footsteps and go off to war to fight for the freedom they both held so dear. He saw the wrinkled faces of Grandma and Grandpa. *Would they be proud looking down at me now? Or would they be ashamed?*

"AHHHH!" He growled and ripped the gun from his mouth.

"I can't live like this! God! Do you hear me!" The black rolling clouds absorbed his shouts. "I can't live like this!" The pistol shook at his temple. He pressed it hard into his skin. "You feel that, *don't ya?*" Harder and harder, he pressed, until his neck slanted toward the wind and rain. "Good. Cause it's the last pain you're ever gonna feel!"

The click of the safety sounded exactly like his M4. His gut churned as he let out a heavy breath, blowing pink rain from his lips. His finger shook with the thunder on his trigger. The cracking limbs above him pinched his chest. He closed his eyes and imagined what death would feel like. *Will it burn? Will I feel myself die? Will life drain slowly from my veins, or will it all end like the tug of the shoelace dangling from Grandpa's workbench light?*

The trigger crept back. It would all be over in an ember. The muzzle dug into the side of his head. He could feel the pulse in his temple.

Do it! Do it, now!

One last, long breath to blow away all the self-loathing from his lungs. The trigger met its breaking point. Then a study gust of wind rolled up the hill and brought with it his son's picture and message: Don't forget about me. Come home soon. Love, your best buddy Adin.

In an instant, a searing light scorched his charcoaled mind, like a flame to lighter fluid, its flare blazed all around him. Its heat licked at his cheeks and brain, and a mighty jolt shook him to the core—a deafening *BOOM* exploded through his cranium.

His body jerked with the shock, noise, and light. The gun fired, barely missing his flesh.

Instead, a spear of light and electricity, a bright strobe in the darkness, rose from the ground and shattered his intentions. An electrical discharge. Lightning. A force that rose from the tombstones before him and shattered up the tree into the sky.

The electricity tossed him against the tree. He tumbled below it, his body shaking and convulsing in one hot instant. The Earth had discharged its fury, and JP was nothing more than a grain of sand in the wind.

Chapter Twenty-Two

How to Hold Your Head Up

Stop watching where your feet go.

Aimless steps into the shadows
of a burned-out hallway light,
too high to reach,
too high to care,
tripping over angled hurdles placed there
by a careless moon; gilded
in the darkness
for the lost to find;
armored, and shining for your curses
and flying stones.

Aim high when you're desperate.

Potshots at the moon, at the sun,
both too bright for your dark thoughts.
Angry haymakers wild at a wall
that is there
to hold up
the shell that you are.
And now you swing holes into it,
like a lunatic
aiming to break,
you shatter.

Cold on the dark floor, you look up for help.

Lisa ended the call with her client sporting a happy face and a few sock-sliding dance moves across her sister's home office hardwood floor. She just closed the biggest deal of the year, and she was looking to celebrate. No matter how mad or disappointed she had been with her husband over the last several days, she still had the urge to call him. After all, anger doesn't void love.

Checking her phone to see how had beeped in during her call, she saw it was JP. A tinge of dread darkened her halo. Lately, his phone calls had brought nothing more than frustration and sorrow. He was a sad drunk when he called her, weeping or breaking things. Hoping he wasn't in that state this time, she wanted him to be sober enough to appreciate her accomplishment. And maybe even a dinner date to celebrate.

She twisted back and forth in the office chair waiting for JP's groggy voice to pick up. But it rang all the way to voicemail. The grandfather clock in the corner said 4:15 p.m. *A little early to be feeding. Maybe he laid down?* A pinch of worry sprung her from the chair as she tried calling again. This time, she paced the office as the long rings rang one by one until the automated voice told her to leave a message.

Hm. He just called ten minutes ago. Where'd he go? Whatever. He'll call back later.

And she left the office to talk her sister into an afternoon glass of wine to celebrate.

~

When JP came to in the mud, a few feet from the singed tree, he smelled burned hair. His hand snapped to his temple, his scalp, his face, and then he searched his entire body. Nothing. He had missed, and by the ringing in his ears and the fizz in his chest, he was clearly still alive. Battered, bruised, muddy, bloody, and sour—he was alive. But only by the breath in his lungs and the beat in his chest.

Jesus Christ! I can't even kill myself correctly. Pathetic.

But it soon dawned on him the significance of what had just happened. Lightning rose from the ground, up through his grandparents' gravestones, and splintered into the sky. He'd nearly been struck by lightning.

Holy shit, was that God? He joked to himself, because even in the darkest moments, marines still wave their humor around like a sword. *Was it them? Was that a sign? Did my grandparents literally just tell me to get my shit together? Maybe. Or maybe it was something more?* He wondered. *Maybe it's not my time to go? Maybe I do have a purpose?*

But with the heat of death still thick to his skin, he bent to his sopping knees, overwhelmed with emotion and a revived desire to live. Because life is fragile, fleeting; it is a thin glass in a windstorm, handwritten letters on the breeze. Life is a gift best enjoyed outside the box, and he was about to open his. Feeling enlightened, saved, rejuvenated by the signs of faith and his future, he kneeled in the muck and prayed to God.

"Dear God, please forgive me. Forgive me for not being the man you wanted me to be. I swear to you right now, here on this hilltop, broken, drunk, and empty—I swear to you that I will change. I promise to do better, to be a better man, father, and husband. If you would just give me the strength to move forward. If you would just fill me with courage, love, and wisdom, so help me God, I will make you proud."

But strength and courage only come in fragments, and wisdom to know change is a damned lesson to learn. Love is sharp, and getting help isn't as easy as it is to say or promise.

~

Pacing back and forth in his foul kitchen, phone clenched in his slippery hand, he searched for the strength to make the phone call to Dr. Clatterson. He left a trail of muddy water as he tramped from the fridge to the sliding deck door, contemplating what to say when someone answered, or whether he should drink another beer to calm his ravaged mind.

Pausing at the door, he scanned the backyard pines for a hint of inspiration. Instead, what looked like the Northern Lights glowed in the late-afternoon sky. *What the hell? In the daylight. In Ohio? What the hell's going on?*

He stood in awe as the green, red, and purple twisted and tangled like paint swirling down the drain. Like a double rainbow after a storm, which had moved on from the farm, he gazed at the colors. The absence of thunder left a peaceful drip on the branches and gave way for the sun to shine down onto his little cabin, filling his heart with a calming silence.

JP had forgotten how beautiful nature could be. After all, his wife's leaving left a huge void of color in his gray world. And seeing the flow and flicker of the earth's magnetic field made his worries feel small in comparison to the great wonders of the world. He was just a speck of dust on a windowpane, a roll of smoke drifting from a campfire; he was a memory in an old wise man's eye. And there were bigger plans at play than the ones he muddled in his mind.

How could I be so selfish to think that my troubles were any bigger than anybody else's? How could my hurt be more than those who feel just as much as me? How could I be so ignorant to a broader meaning—a deeper purpose—than what I thought I was meant to have?

His existence fluttered and tipped on the scales as he measured the man he *was* with the man he vowed to be. JP was a father, a husband, a veteran, and a friend. He had so much more to offer to this world than the prick of pain he inflicted on others. He was meant for something more. And gazing up at the emerald and lavender swirls of a grander life above him, at that moment of fear and fortitude, he found the desire to do more than just *be*. He discovered the grace and gall to take charge of his being and *push forward*.

But his hand still trembled as he dialed Dr. Clatterson's number. And he cleared his throat with every ring on the other line until somebody gallantly answered his call for help.

~

JP sat in his truck listening to the radio and nursing a freshly popped brew from his cooler on the passenger seat. It was his second since pulling into the far parking spot at the Cambridge Armory Gymnasium. He'd been checking out the situation, watching other vets trickle in, and still hadn't decided on whether to join them or leave.

Radio: And another series of solar flares are set to impact earth. NOAA reports indicate a moderate impact in the coming hours. And while experts say there's no real cause for concern at the moment, they do advise for everyone to have a safety plan, emergency supplies, and working flashlight for any type of severe weather situation.

His phone lit up on the console with a text from Lisa. He turned off the radio and sipped his beer while he read.

JP 6:22 p.m.: *I'm getting help. You were right. I'm sorry.*

Lisa 6:47 p.m.: *Are you? That's wonderful! I'm so proud of you! You can do this. I know you can.*

The words made him smile as he looked out his window. He counted the others as they filed past the dry-erase "Closed to the Public" sign affixed to a red pole stuck in a chipped-blue pail of old concrete. One by one, they passed by, some with missing limbs, others in camo hats and veteran T-shirts, and many lingered just outside the double doors to suck in that final drag from half a cigarette. JP knew the type. He was used to their bravado and demeanor. But he couldn't help but noticed the sorry eyes of the ones more broken than the rest. They matched his own in his review mirror.

He reread the text from his wife again before replying.

JP 6:50 p.m.: *Well, I'll give it a shot. Thanks. I appreciate your confidence. If you have a little extra, could you send it my way?*

One short and stocky kid, no older than twenty and gleaming from a fresh high-n-tight haircut, played on his phone while pacing in front doors like a sentry on guard duty. JP could see it without a second glance: new to this, just like him, and he was fresh from the field of war.

I'll stick with him. He thought, hoping the young man's skittish eyes and fidgeting hands would distract from his own disarray and sorry features. *Yep. That's him. That's the one.*

Lisa 6:52 p.m.: *You'll do great! Just have a beer before you go… "a beer," JP. That means one. I'll be sending you some positive vibes. Good luck!*

JP glanced at the beer in his hand and snickered. *She knows me too well.* His smile grew as he replied.

JP 6:53 p.m.: *Lisa, I don't even drink. How dare you suggest otherwise? But I love ya, anyway. Thanks for the support! Heading in now.*

He took another gulp before his phone lit up again.

Lisa 6:53 p.m.: *LOL shut up! I love you. You got this!*

His boot slid on the loose pebbles in the parking lot as he stepped out of his truck, head tilted back, finishing his beer. Then he crushed the can and tossed it in the bed. He wasn't drunk, but he wasn't quite sober either.

Who's gonna judge me? It'll be fine. Just get the first one over with. And then it will all be fine. He reassured himself one last time before he shut the truck door, adjusted his camo hat in the reflection of the window, and started toward the nervous kid by the door.

"Hey, Devil!" he hollered as he got closer. "You just get back or what?"

The young man stuffed his phone deep into his pocket and stiffened up a bit before he replied. "Yes, sir! Just got back, sir!"

"Where from?"

"Ramadi, sir!

"Okay, *Hard Charger. Relax.* No need for all that *sir* bullshit. Just call me JP or Grimm or whatever the hell you want, I don't care." JP offered a genuine smile in hopes to settle the young buck down before he stuttered out a moldy "Oorah!" or "Semper Fi."

He settled and stuck out his sweaty hand. "Lance Corporal David. You, uh, you a Marine too?"

JP shook his hand and grinned. "Not that obvious, is it?"

"Well, uh, I mean," he shrugged, "the beard and shaggy hair. I don't know, I almost pegged you for Army." He smirked and brightened up for the first time since JP laid his eyes on him.

"Aw, *fuck you.* Get outta here, boot."

They both grinned, and for that moment, an instant connection existed between them that only Marines or combat veterans could share.

"Roger that, Soldier."

JP punched him in the arm. "That'll be Sgt. Grimm from here on out, asshole."

David's smile faded quickly, and JP let him relish in the insecurity of proper military code of conduct to a senior NCO. And just as quickly, he slapped him on the back, laughed, and turned him toward the door. "Come on, Lance Corporal *Dick.* Let's go find a seat."

Inside, with his tie loosened, sleeves rolled up, and tattoos showing, Dr. Clatterson stood at the entrance of the gymnasium greeting everyone before they took their seats in one of the folding chairs in a circle at center court.

"Ah, the new kids," he said with a bright face, extending his hand. "Good to see you, John. JP." Their eyes met and he nodded before extending his hand.

"Wait, your name's John David?" JP asked.

"Yeah, why?"

JP chuckled, shaking his head. "No reason. Two first names. It makes sense now. I should've seen that coming."

"What does?" Dr. Clatterson asked.

"Nothin'. Just," he thumbed at David, "Nervous Nancy over here busting my balls for my awesome beard and sandy locks."

"I'm starting not to like you, Sgt. Grimm."

"JP. It's JP."

"I see you two jarheads are getting along nicely, already. We have a few other marines with us tonight, too." He paused and raised his brow. "Uh, no Mrs. JP tonight?"

Though he meant no harm, only a slight jab from one marine to another, the sting was the same. *No. No Mrs. JP tonight. Or tomorrow night. Or the night after. Matter of fact, Doc, I don't know when the fuck Mrs. JP will be joining me again. Thanks. Thanks for pointing that out.* But instead, he just shrugged. "Guess not. Maybe next time."

Doc motioned toward the two empty chairs next to each other and opposite of his more comfortable office chair. "All right. Well, I think you two are the last of the group. So, if you don't mind finding your seats, we'll go ahead and get started."

Chapter Twenty-Three

Truth

We spend all our lives
trying to hide from the truth.

But Death is a bright light
and Tomorrow
a stray cat.

The truth is
we all lie to ourselves.

The Armory gymnasium smelled of old towels and floor wax. JP pulled his hat down low as he found his seat in the circle. Above their metal chairs, which squeaked awkwardly as they shifted, an American flag dangled at center court. It vibrated when the air kicked on. If they spoke loud enough, their words would echo. Dr. Clatterson addressed the room before sitting in his office chair.

"It's the bond of war that has brought us all here today. But that's not the only thing we have in common. We know the price of our way of life. We all know the sacrifices. And unfortunately, that's not all that bonds us as brothers and sisters at arms." He folded his arms across his chest, leaned back in his chair, and spoke like the words were rehearsed. "It's the trauma. The death. The blood. The bombs. The loss of life and limbs. It's the toll war has taken from us that brings us here today. So please, let's all respect one another and listen to their stories. We've all been through something terrible that has pushed us through those double doors." He pointed to the entrance. "And maybe in sharing our stories, we can find some sort of peace."

He evaluated the room of somber-faced veterans before him: mixed calibers of men and women, some hard and solid, some glossy-eyed and staring at the floor. But they were all there for the same purpose: they weren't who they wanted to be or who they once were, and they needed Doc, and each other, to help find themselves again. All twelve were warriors imprisoned in their own minds. POWs. Prisoners of war. They were being held captive in the shadows and torments of the Hell inside of them.

"Would anyone like to go first?" Doc searched the room.

Most shifted and avoided eye contact. After a moment, a middle-aged, husky fellow with a scarred, scruffy face and bulging muscles popping out of a green

USMC T-shirt, spoke up. "Staff Sergeant Smith, USMC, retired, 0311." His voice was deep and rusty.

Everyone shifted their attention to him, and he cleared his throat.

"Since nobody wanted to pop the cherry tonight, I guess I'll do it. Short 'n sweet." He shifted until comfortable, folded his arms across his thick chest, and crossed his legs out in front of him. "As a young Sergeant, I was the acting Platoon Sergeant for second platoon, 3/1, Lima company. I was hot shit, you know? Made Sergeant before I re-upped. I knew my shit. I was good at what I did, and I was a helluva warfighter. The Iraq war." He paused and looked directly at JP. "Operation Iraqi Freedom. The *second* Iraq war."

JP nodded.

"Well, we were taking the city of Fallujah, a huge enemy stronghold—back in '04—when we came into direct contact with a squad-sized enemy element inside a compound in the heart of the city. My platoon was tasked with taking the compound. So, we did."

He spat tobacco juice into an empty Gatorade bottle. Brown saliva dribbled down his chin. The dip from his lower lip peppered his yellow teeth. "We took the compound," his eyes shifted down, "but not without casualties. Six KIAs later, including my 2nd squad leader, Sergeant Black, and a new boot fresh from SOI, the compound was ours." He spat again as his tough eyes went misty. "I ordered Sergeant Black and PFC Miller into a room rigged with an IED. I sent them to their death."

He cleared his throat, the noise echoing off the gym walls as he wiped his lip on the edge of the bottle and spit again.

"The hardest thing I ever had to do was confess to their families when we got back. The look on Sergeant Black's wife's face would've been enough to end the entire war as she leaned down and told her son, 'This is the man who killed your daddy.'"

Everyone in the room gasped.

"It was the look of pure, unfiltered hatred—both of 'em. And no matter what I do, I still can't get their angry faces out of my head." He swiped a rogue tear before it fell.

"Now, I'm scared to death to tell people what to do. I forget how to be a leader, even after I led marines in combat. I was a shit-hot warrior. And now," he stretched his neck to the side, "now, I sweep the floors and clean the toilets at McDonald's. I was in charge of *forty* warfighters. And now…" Shame ravished the man's wounded face. "A fucking toilet man at McDonald's."

He choked on his honesty, then jabbed his finger at center court. "That's why I'm here! That's why I do these groups! Because I lost it—that warrior spirit. I lose *me*. And I need help getting my confidence and leadership back."

The group locked in on his searching eyes. "I need you all to help me get *me* back before it's too late, and I end up on the streets again."

He sniffed and coughed to cover up his sudden burst of emotion. "I can't lose my family all over again. Not after I worked so hard to get them back. I need them. I need you. I need *this*."

A young athletic woman sat beside him, her lower left leg missing just below the knee. She patted him on the back and rubbed his shoulder. "We won't let that happen, Justin. I promise. We're in this thing together. We have each other." She looked around the room. "Right? We all have each other's backs here."

A murmur rushed through the room as she hugged the man. Then she sat down and leaned forward with her elbows on her knees.

"I guess I'll go next. Again, short and sweet, just like me." She barely snorted. "Well, army, here. I was the up-gunner on a hardback running route security. And I was a vigilant son of a bitch, too, calling out wires and disturbed dirt at forty-five miles an hour. I was good." She nodded around the circle.

"But what I wasn't good at was being in the driver's seat, being in control of the vehicle. Because, well, you know, some PFC boot drew the straw for that gig. I was just along for the ride." A frown scrunched her face. "And maybe that's what bothers me so much about *this*?" She used both hands to lift her leg and present her prosthetic.

"That dumbass never listened when I yelled for him to stop. It was plain as day, right there alongside the road. They didn't even bother covering it all the way up. They just kicked a little dirt on it and away they went. But that poor boot bastard didn't do a thing until we were right on top of it." Her head shook as she stared at the floor. "Then…*boom*. And just like that, I got a new leg." She shrugged. "Oh yeah, I'm used to it now. No big deal. One and a half good legs, right? But you know what I've never been able to get used to since I've been back? Someone else driving. Being a passenger. Having another person being in control of where I'm going. I just can't do it. My anxiety goes through the roof. Not being in control of where we go, how fast we go, when we break or stop— instant panic attack. It's inevitable." A sad grin spread over her face.

"Anyone else scream like a lunatic about swerving around trash piles, potholes, or other dumb shit in the road? I was really hard on my mom the first few doctor appointments. She nearly had a heart attack from all my yelling. And I nearly had one from all her driving, if you know what I mean." The room let out a slight titter.

"So that's my story. That's me, the freak who flips out when others try to drive. The crazy, loud lady who gets into screaming matches with friends and family when they insist on driving instead of me. I'm a burden. A psycho with a psycho problem. And none of them get it. I'm just *batshit crazy* to them. But judging by your faces, I think most of you understand. And I thank you for that. I appreciate it."

"Thanks for sharing." Doc leaned forward, making eye contact around the circle. "You see, this is the power of unity. This is why we do this. It's the support from one another that helps us to get through. And sometimes," he raised his brows, "sometimes that's all we have left. So please, don't hold back, don't assume someone is fine. Help each other. Be there for one another. Because you never know when you might be the only thing standing in the way of that person seeing another day or ending it all." He paused to let that sink in. "Who's next?"

A gray, balding gentleman in a camouflaged NRA hat stood up and removed his cap. Time had not been kind to him as he struggled to stand and keep his balance. He introduced himself as Chuck, special forces during Vietnam; he used the chair back to help steady himself as he spoke.

"I grew up just outside of Senecaville. My dad took us boys hunting all the time. Rabbit, squirrel, deer, it didn't matter. If it was meat, then it was fair game for the table. I remember my first gun—a single shot .22 rifle out of a Sears catalog on my seventh birthday. Man, you should've seen my face light up when I unwrapped it. Pure joy, let me tell ya. I was the happiest boy in the whole village." He paused to smile. "Hunting was a special time for us Grahams. It was an honest life-lesson experience for us. Our father would not only teach us about the significance of life in general but the responsibility that came along with taking a life. We didn't waste. We didn't kill for the hell of it. It was food. And it was a lesson about how to become a man. How to take care of each other, nature, life, and death. Self-sufficient, if you catch my drift.

"Well, after becoming a *hunter of men*, that joy and bond was ripped right out of me. My kids didn't grow up learning how to hunt. They didn't get that life lesson my father had passed down to me. I guess, after taking a human life, after seeing what war does to the body…well, I couldn't stand the thought of any more killing. I couldn't do it. I couldn't take my children hunting after the war."

His blue eyes became misty. "And I regret that still to this day. Because instead of hunting, I turned to substance abuse. I turned to alcohol. Which all led to me neglecting my boys. My poor boys…." His voice struggled through the emotion. "You see, my boys are no longer with us anymore. Both gone. Both dead." His chest shook as he inhaled. "Tyler, or *Tay*—as his neck tattoo said— was taken by gang violence up in Detroit. And well, Frankie—poor Frankie and his whore wife—he drank himself to death one night driving home from the bar."

He covered his heart with his hat while his eyes glared at his unlaced and dirty work boots. "I blame myself for that. I blame myself for failing as a father."

The gentleman beside him patted him on the back. And he turned to thank him.

"Somehow, and I know this might seem a little silly to you all, but I believe if I could have just taken them hunting, if I could have just shown them the importance of life and death instead of the anger found at the bottom of a bottle…well, then maybe they would still be here today."

He placed his hat back on his head before his closing words. "Yes…these damn wars took pieces from us all. For me, it took my love for the outdoors, the thrill of hunting, and the beauty of nature. For me, it took away my sons. And I've never forgiven myself for failing them." The tears flowed freely down his wrinkled cheeks as he took his seat and crossed his arms.

"Thank you, Chuck." Dr. Clatterson's solemn voice fell on a silent room. After a moment, he cleared his throat. "Who else would like to share?" He looked around at a few heads shaking back and forth. "Maybe one of the new guys?"

Lance Corporal David's breathing halted as he rapidly shook his head. Then Doc looked at JP, who avoided eye contact. "Anyone else? This is your chance to let it out, to work on the healing process. I encourage you all to at least try. Please."

A young woman with charcoal hair shifted and slowly stood. Makeup free and a few extra pounds around the midsection, still left her very attractive. She reminded JP of a first baseman in softball. He leaned in as she spoke to the peeling blue letters on the center court floor: Cambridge Armory.

"I…uh…my name is Rachel. I worked on a sub in the navy." She paused to collect her thoughts and, perhaps, her courage to keep going. "I was sexually assaulted several times on tour."

She nervously sat back down, but Doc raised his brow and nodded for her to continue. Her legs trembled when she stood again.

"Please continue, Rachel. I think your story could benefit several others here. Be their strength. I know you can do this," Doc reassured her.

Her gaze shifted around the room, meeting no one else's. Instead, she tried to find something comfortable to focus on. She settled for the chipped floorboard in front of her. "They encourage us *not* to talk about it. The command. The culture. Everyone." She bit her lip. "But I'm exhausted from carrying it around with me every day." Her head nodded as she spoke. "So, I'm going to tell my story. And hopefully, my story might be able to help someone here. So, I share this for you and for all the other survivors of sexual assault."

With her fists squeezed together, her eyes peeked to the sympathetic faces in the room. "He was an Officer. Married, of course. I don't know how it could get much worse than that. But he groomed me by passing off my duty to other sailors. At first, I felt special. I thought that maybe he respected my work ethic and leadership ability. But later, I found out the hard way that he just wanted to have sex with me.

"He would call me into his office and make me suck his dick under his desk while he did paperwork. I didn't want to. I resisted at first. But I was young and scared and didn't want to rock the boat, if you know what I mean. He also threatened to find something to NJP me for if I didn't. Then, after I complied out of fear—because I didn't know what else I could do—he started praising me and promised he'd fast-track my promotion."

She fidgeted with her hands in front of her. "It started feeling good. Like I was doing my part to help ship morale or whatever. And I know how crazy that sounds, but when you have to live with several men in closed spaces for months on end, sometimes you do things that you don't want to, just to make things less confrontational or edgy. Yes, looking back. I was young and dumb and naïve. I see that now. He even said I would make a great NCO because of my willingness to complete the mission." She huffed.

"And there were perks, I guess. I got extra chow, less duty, more sleep. Until someone spoke up about it. That's when he got paranoid and the verbal abuse started. Nothing I did was good enough: I was overweight, out of regs, and apparently, I didn't turn him on anymore." Pain clenched her face. "He started hitting me. Not like, punching me, but smacking me, whipping me with his belt, like he was my father or something. And when I complained, he threatened to send it up the chain that I was trying to come on to him. *Me…coming on to him!* Well, I never did tell anyone. I mean, what was I going to say? And who would believe me?"

Her voice was flat and defeated. The tone brought shivers to JP's spine.

"When I got back home, it ate at me like a piece of shrapnel buried beneath my skin. I went into a deep depression…put on weight…pushed everyone away. I was mad at everything and everyone. Then, well…I started dating men who treated me awful. Men who hit me, raped me, passed me around to their buddies. I thought that's what I deserved. I thought it was *my* fault, and that they were the best I could get. My self-esteem was nonexistent. I was at the bottom, and I didn't know what else to do." She rolled up her sleeve and showed the scars on her wrist. "So, I tried to end it all. I tried to kill myself." She took a deep breath. "That's when the VA sent me to Doc. That's when I started coming to these group sessions. That's when I discovered all of you who have been through so much trauma too. That's when I knew I wasn't alone. And it's because of all *your* strength that I can get up every morning and continue to improve. It's because of *your* support that I keep going, keep fighting, and keep coming here to get the help and care that I need. So, thank you. Thank you all for listening and not judging me for my mistakes."

When she sat down, the room stood up with a tear-jerking ovation. And the evening continued that way, each veteran sharing stories and getting support. Around the circle they went, describing their fear and anxiety of crowded spaces, loud noises, diesel engines, and Kia SUVs. Many spoke of the consequences of burying their anger and depression. Most talked about PTSD and how it damaged their families, friends, and their own lives. Even Lance Corporal David shared his story about the IEDs that took the limbs of his friends in Iraq and left him with a traumatic brain injury.

Everyone but JP told a story. And as he sat there with anticipating eyes upon him, he understood the importance to confront his demons. Looking around the room at mostly strangers——strangers he was certain would walk out of that building and fight tooth and nail for one another if asked—he realized that it was time to let it all go. It was time to face his failures and reconcile his faults.

The air kicked on and fluttered the flag above him as he sat in the flickering halogen lights. The beer on his breath hadn't faded, and no one cared. They didn't judge him for his disheveled appearance, red eyes, and hanging head. They didn't pester him, pry, or try to push him too far past his anxious limits. For the first time in months, he felt comfortable in his own skin. For the first time since he had been home, he believed in the power of unity and support.

Inspired, he nodded and cleared his throat with sharp intentions to lay it all out in the open for them to absorb and clean up. He didn't stand. Instead, he leaned on his knees, fidgeting with his hat in his hands.

"Hello, everyone. I'm JP. Err, uh, Sergeant Grimm. Or whatever you want to call me." He thumbed at Lance Corporal David. "Ask John. It doesn't matter to me, as long as it's not *Asshole*." He forced a laugh through his nose. "Marines. Grunt. Just got back from the sandbox last fall." His gaze darted to the rafters. "Welp, I guess that pretty much sums it up. Thank you."

Doc cleared his throat. "Uh, Sergeant Grimm, maybe you could tell us a little about what happened over there? You know, maybe tell us about those dreams?" His guidance was sincere, like a middle-grade history teacher prying answers from his students.

"Yeah. Yeah, okay, Doc. Well, uh…I dream a lot about my son."

A few grunted with understanding.

"I know. That doesn't sound so scary, does it? Well, unless you're a new parent, then I guess it's terrifying." He sort of chuckled and shifted nervously. "But, I guess, I mean…what I'm trying to say is…what happened was…" He looked at Doc for help.

"Go on. You're doing just fine. You're in a room with those who will understand. Share whatever you'd like. Just, you know, get it off your chest." Doc winked.

JP nodded, scratched his head, and rubbed at the back of his neck. A tension headache pulled at the base of his skull. His lungs deflated like an air valve releasing pressure. Then he just blurted it out.

"Because of me, my best friend and brothers were blown to pieces." He paused to breathe. "We were taking a high-value target in the city, and my squad was security. We took contact. Engaged. Did our fucking jobs. Did them well too. Until it was time to exfil."

He swallowed and blinked rapidly. "Second squad had the target. All they had to do was cross the street, to come to us, to get to our cover behind the vehicles, and get the hell out of there. But that's when I saw him." He grimaced at the memory. "A little boy, about the same age as my son, stepping out of the shadows…and…uh, for a moment, *he was my son.*"

JP bit his lip and bowed his head as he tried to put those scenes into words. "There was something off about him. His bulk. Something in his hand. I could see his bronze eyes burning in my scope. Terrified. Determined. They were my son's eyes. I froze. I couldn't shoot my son." He growled and raised his snarling eyes. "I couldn't shoot my son! Goddamnit!" His shoulders moved up and down with each breath. "I should've shot him! I should've shot him!"

Out of breath, he gasped a few moments before he spoke again. This time, more controlled. "His father had strapped him in a suicide vest. Trained him to blow it up if he was ever captured. I had him in my sights. I could've saved them all." JP chewed on his lip. "But I didn't. I hesitated. I just stood there with my rifle raised and finger on the trigger, watching *my* little boy walk toward Joey, his squad, and our target."

His shameful eyes walked the planks on the court floor.

"He blew them up. All of 'em. Right there in front of my dumb face. He blew them up into tiny pieces that rained down onto my skin, my face, my uniform, and rifle. Like a hard rain, hail, sand in a hurricane." He sucked in a much-needed, shaky breath. "I stepped on flesh when I ran to help the wounded. It squished under my boots with each step. Dear God," he cried, "I could feel it slide on the dirt like…like pizza sauce on the kitchen floor."

"Oh my, God!" the soldier with the prosthetic leg gasped, as the room shifted uncomfortably, and JP scanned the scuffed court in front of him for bits of flesh.

"Was it Joey?" He shrugged with glazed, red eyes. "Was I stepping on pieces of Joey? Did I trample my friend's flesh? Was it him that I squashed in the dirt like a rotten apple? Was it him that painted my face red and black? Was it a pink mist of Joey in the smoke and ash that I sucked in after each scream?"

His voice cut the room like a serrated knife, his hollow gaze ghostly and far away. "I don't know…maybe. Maybe there's still pieces of them stuck in me. I don't know. But what I *do* know…is that it was *my* fault! I know that it happened because I hesitated. Goddamnit! They died because I didn't pull the fucking trigger! Because I didn't do my job! I didn't keep my promise!"

A deep, shaky breath reverberated across the court. "And that's on me…just like their flesh and blood." His body quivered. "I might as well have just killed them myself. With these hands." He lifted them up, and they trembled. "These hands…these weak, pathetic, useless hands. *They* killed them. *I* killed them."

His chin met his chest as he sniffled and furiously rubbed his cheeks with the back of his wrists. The crowd of vets sat frozen in their chairs.

"But that's not all," he finally said. "You see, I wasn't done destroying things yet." He was looking at them now. "I brought all that shit home with me. All of it. Even the pieces of flesh that still stick to whatever I wear, that still streaks down my face like bloody tears. I brought it all home to my wife and son. And I tortured them with it. I tortured *them* because it was still torturing *me*."

His jaw and chest were flexed.

"So, when I dream…I dream of my son killing my friends. I dream of me killing my son. I dream of smoldering bodies. Fire and smoke. Thunder and lightning. I dream when it storms, and I storm when I dream."

His brows scrunched and sorrow filled his eyes.

"So, I drink. I drink and I drink and I drink. And…and I try to forget. But I can't. No matter what I do, their seared, pink body parts still stick to me." He casually wiped his arms as he squeezed them around his chest.

"Just looking at my son reminds me of death and destruction, fire and flesh. *And I hate him for it!*" He growled.

"Damn me! God damn me! No matter how hard I try, my son is still the enemy. And my wife? God bless my wife for all she's put up with, for all I've put her through. I mean, she's the *only* good thing about me. But now, now she's gone. They're both gone. My son and wife. They left me because I couldn't put the gun down, or the whiskey, or beer, or pain. They left me because I was a threat. Because I fired a shot at my son when he woke me up from a nightmare."

His words quivered with his body. "I'm a fucking bomb, wired to explode at any moment. And all I keep thinking is…is…I'm so glad they got away from me. Away from this monster, this beast I've become. And to be honest, I'm just ready to put it down. To put it *all* down. To either heal it…or kill it. Jesus Christ, I'm just waiting for *one more reason* to end it all." He buried his head in his hands and counted three slow breaths until he could face their misty eyes again.

When he came out of hiding, he felt lighter. Like the combat load he'd been carrying had been dropped. Like he set his pack down. Like he removed his flak jacket. He could breathe. Small slow breaths—but they *were* breaths. He *was* breathing. Facing the darkness, confronting his deepest sins, *didn't* kill him.

"Holy shit." He sniffed back the tears. "I needed that. *Jesus*, I needed to get that out of me. Thank you. Thank you all for that."

The room had started their applause, and JP beamed with a sense of pride for finally airing out his demons. For him, in that moment, there was a distant glow of hope on the horizon. And he inflated as he prepared to chase after it.

But it was all cut short by the flicker of the lights and the flash of the transformer out front as it blew with a tremendous flare, and squelched all the light from the buildings and street lamps. It left an eerie blanket of black under the yellow quarter moon hanging low over the blank peeks and pitches of the city. Cambridge had gone as dark as the demons inside each one of them.

Chapter Twenty-Four

To be the Westward Sky at Sunset

I want to be
the westward sky
at sunset, when
blues melt and trickle,
drip into fire, burn red
and glow orange;

warming to the eyes,
like wool mittens
in Montana's winter,
when frost-nipped
fingers go numb, tingle,
and turn pale white;

white as the sun streams
that break free from
the covering grey clouds,
when thunderheads build
over prairie-dog plains
and rocket through the sky
a web of busted dreams;

like when she twisted
this ring from her finger
and set it down on white paper,
as empty as the six syllables
that filled it:

"I have to find myself," it said.
And just as frankly, off she went
into the west fading sun.

Blackout Day 1

Welcome back! It's just after 9 a.m. on your Friday morning, and you're listening to 96 FM!

If you're on your way to work this morning, you might want to call ahead and see if they're still open. Widespread power outages and transformer fires have been reported across the area. Experts are blaming a series of solar flares fired off from the sun yesterday morning.

Stay tuned to 96 FM for all the latest updates. Be safe out there and enjoy your three-day weekend.

Now here's a new one from Taylor Swift.

JP cut the engine to his truck and dialed his wife's number.

"Heyyy."

He sensed a smidge more excitement in her voice than last night. "Hey. How's everything going over there now?" he asked, watching the sun glisten off the knee-high corn stalks.

"Power's still out. How 'bout you?"

"Yeah, same here. I guess it's pretty widespread. You been listening to the radio?"

"A little bit while I charge my phone—good idea, by the way—but it sounds kinda bad."

"I know, right? I might need more therapy after this." He cracked a smile.

"Oh, you liked it *that much*, huh?" A tinge of *I-told-you-so* teased in her voice.

"I mean, it *was* pretty therapeutic."

"*Therapeutic?* Did my husband really just use the word *therapeutic?* Do you even know what that means?" A breathy laugh blew through the phone.

"Shut up. I'm not a…well, okay, I *am* an idiot. But I *do* know what therapeutic means. Dick."

They giggled together, and for the first time in several days, they almost felt *normal.*

"Well, if it makes you feel any better, I'm still super proud of you. Seriously, I mean that."

"Thank you. I'm super proud of you too," he said, semi-sarcastically.

"Forrrr?"

"For being so smokin' hot all the time. Mm. Mm. Mmm. Momma's got it going *ooon!*"

"Oh, my God! I can't even stand you right now. Quit it." Her laughter bounced through her words.

"What? What I say? You're like, a solar flare, baby!"

"Stawwwp! Oh my God. You're ridiculous. I'm getting off here."

They both chuckled, and a warm feeling spread through JP's chest. It had been a while since he'd heard Lisa's laughter ring so free, so light. It was good to hear.

"All right, well hey, let's make this a thing. Same time, same place every morning? I'd like to make sure you guys are still doing all right? Deal?"

"Uhhh, yeah. Yeah, I'd like that," she replied.

"Great. Tell Adin to stay out of trouble. Love you guys."

"Will do. Love ya."

Blackout Day 3

Extensive. That's the latest report on the damage to the power grid from the recent solar flares. Expect at least one to two weeks before power can be restored.

Governor Maylee emphasized FEMA's latest advisory for all Ohioans to have enough food, water, medication, and other supplies to last at least three to four weeks.

In a prepared statement, Sherriff Barrett says a 10 p.m. curfew will be in effect for the rest of the week. Minor reports of vandalism and theft have been received in the last twenty-four hours. He advises all local residents to remain calm and stay safe.

Stay tuned to 96 FM for all the latest updates. Be safe out there, and please, stay civil. We're all in this together.

Now let's enjoy a classic from Thomas Rhett.

JP left his phone plugged into the charger as he spoke with Lisa. "Hey listen, I've been thinking, with the power being out and all, you think maybe it's a good idea to rally back here at the farm for a few days?"

"Hm. I don't know. Have you cleaned up any since the last time I was there? It smelled horrible."

JP's embarrassment lingered—she was absolutely right—but he tried to lighten the mood. "Well, I mean, a little. Maybe. Okay, I sprayed Febreze."

"JP!"

"What?"

"Will you please clean that place up?"

"Hey, I'm workin' on it. Sorta. Your candles smell quite lovely, by the way."

"What? Which ones?"

"I don't know, the snickerdoodle-berry-melon-flower or something like that."

"Oh, my gosh. *Quit it.*"

"Sooo, is that a *no* on the farm thing, orrr?"

She thought for a moment. "Why don't we wait it out a few more days and see what happens."

"Oh."

"Don't be sad, please."

"It's fine. It's fine. I get it. I just miss you guys. I mean, I could come there, if you want?"

"Why don't we all just stay put for now. We miss you too. And, look, I'm sooo freakin' happy and proud of you for trying to make things better. But I still think we need to go slow, you know?"

He side-glanced the .22 rifle in the passenger seat and the empty beer cans on the floorboard and envisioned the rotting food still in the fridge.

"No, I agree. You're right."

"Wait, what was that?"

He rolled his eyes, knowing full well she heard him just fine. "*Nothing.*"

"No, I'm pretty sure you said something. It sounded foreign, like, I don't know, maybe Latin or something."

"Oh, listen to you. You got jokes, huh? Great." He laughed and then caved. "I said, *you're right. Happy?*"

"A little bit."

"*Geeez.*"

"Listen, how about you just keep calling me every morning, tell me how much you cleaned, how much you miss us, and how the farm's doing—the cows, the chickens, and even all those damn crows—tell me how *you're* doing, and then we will see about 'rallying at the farm.' Okay?"

His heavy sigh was him giving in. "All right. All right. Fine. Hey, when Adin comes back in, let him know I miss him, please. Okay? Love you."

"Will do. Love you too."

Blackout Day 6

*Welcome back to 96.7 FM WCMJ. It's day **six** of the Midwest Solar Flare Blackout. Our emergency generators are still going strong, and we hope that yours are too.*

We'll get back to the music in just a bit, but first, an emergency update from AVC Communications:

NOAA and The National Space Weather Program confirmed that another solar flare and large release of plasma, known as a Coronal Mass Ejection, are on the way. Although large enough to potentially damage satellites, electronics, and power grids, they expect this CME to give just a glancing blow to Earth's magnetic field. They continue to warn that other strong flares and CMEs are still possible.

*Local power companies have **again** pushed back the timeline for repairs, this time, indefinitely. They ask all customers to please remain patient as they work around the clock to restore the power.*

President Anderson has now declared a state of emergency in two additional states — Virginia and Tennessee—adding to the list of Ohio, West Virginia, Pennsylvania, Michigan, Indiana, and New York. In his daily briefing, he encouraged the American people to stand together, remain strong, and be patient as help is on the way.

Governor Maylee reassured Ohioans she is working with Governor Jolie and Governor Arigyn, as well as other surrounding governors, to mobilize additional aid and supplies.

General Odin of the Ohio National Guard has issued a statement regarding local relief and aid as well as working with local authorities to assist against looting, vandalism, and other criminal acts.

Guernsey County's Sherriff Barrett stated additional looting and rioting would not be tolerated. He advised that due to undermanned staff and a depleted force, his department will only be responding to level three emergencies. He emphasized remaining calm, patient, and civil during these unprecedented times.

Several area churches are holding local food drives. If you'd like to donate or need assistance, please—

JP shook his head as he turned down the radio and checked his phone for charge. He was anxious to talk to Lisa and eagerly pressed on her number. "Hey. How's everything going?"

"Okay, I guess, considering," she said over the static on the line. "Tommy got the generator working again. So, we have that going for us."

"Good. Good. You thought any more about getting out of the city and heading for the farm?"

"Yeah. I mean, I think it's a good idea. It's just a little difficult to convince Tommy and Kristen to leave their home. You know?"

"Yeah, I get it. Understandable. But I think it'd be safer. Besides, we have food roaming around here in fences. Even Tommy could probably catch his own." JP chuckled.

"Well, I don't know about that, but he is pretty handy with fixing things. Maybe he could wrench a cow to death?"

"Ridiculous!" JP rolled his eyes. "All right. Well, keep trying, it's best to get out of there before things get too bad."

"Definitely. They're not that great right now, actually."

Static fuzzed the line.

"No? What's wrong?" Concern flared within him.

"Long story. People are crazy."

"Well, are you safe?" he asked.

Static.

"Huh?" Lisa said.

"Are you safe? You need me to come get you?"

"No…fine…them to leave."

"What? Babe, you're breaking up. What's going on?"

"They shot a man!"

JP grabbed his pistol. "What? Who?"

Static. "…not cops…."

"Huh? Babe, listen, I can't understand you, but if things get any worse, then I'm coming to get you—all of you. Tommy and Kristen too. I don't care. I'm worried about you."

Static overtook the line, and the call dropped.

Annoyed, he called back but got no answer. *No service? Worthless piece of shit!* He tossed his phone into the passenger seat. He slammed his door and flipped the sun the bird. Then, he stormed off to pack his gear, preparing to go into the city to get his family, if he had to.

Blackout Day 7

JP rolled out of bed with a list of things to get accomplished: try calling his wife again; feed; check the water barrels under the downspouts for damage; hunt; boil water; inventory ammunition, weapons, and gear. But when JP checked the time on his phone, the screen was dark and blank. "What the hell?"

He tried the power button. Nothing. He tried shaking it. Nothing. He yelled at it—didn't change a thing.

I know it was fully charged before I went to bed. He thought, shaking his head and lumbering toward the steps.

An ominous glow and fizzle popped in the morning sky when he stepped outside. The hair on his arms stood up as he approached his truck. An odd tingle traveled through him before he reached for the door, and it shocked him when he touched the handle. "Son-of-a-bitch!" He shook it off.

Inside the truck, the key swayed as his hand closed the distance. He twisted it, expecting the engine to come to life. But, instead, he got nothing. No matter how many times he turned the key or pumped the brakes or jimmied the shifter, he got nothing.

What the fuck is going on? He sat a moment in his truck, staring out the windshield at the sunrise, trying to figure out what was happening. *No phone. No truck. No power. No Lisa and Adin.* Gripping the wheel, he exhaled loudly before he got out.

He raised his hand to shield his eyes as he stared down the gleaming sun. "I guess it's just you and me, Big Guy. Friends or foes?" He squinted as the round ball of fire spread its rays through the sparse morning clouds. *Friends or foes?*

Turning toward the house, a low rumble and hiss coming from the opposite horizon caught his attention.

He lifted his head to the northwest sky, astonished by the gashing red, green, and purple lights on the horizon. They churned with the bubbling clouds and whispered through the morning glow like a colorful fire popping and cracking in the distant fog. A hole formed in the middle, like the atmosphere was giving way to outer space. And like the hand of God reaching down from the Heavens, the crackling lights poured in and rumbled through the sky.

What the fuck?

Then, it clicked—the radio report from yesterday.

They were wrong.

The CME didn't miss Earth. It was cracking it wide open.

Chapter Twenty-Five

She's Still Standing

She wasn't the hurricane,
or the loose and unfastened.

She wasn't the screaming wind
or the coming, ravenous waters.

She wasn't the squall.

She was the battered palm tree
that lasted.

Five minutes after CME

In a whirlwind, JP rushed back inside. He was ready for this. He had
prepared. Donning his desert fatigues and combat boots, he stuffed his camo
backpack with food, ammunition, water, and medical supplies. The setup was
familiar, comfortable, and useful. As a final touch, he added his "We the People"
dark blue and cream-colored hat.

Admiring himself in the corner mirror, JP was a warrior again. Transformed.
Refurbished. Suited up with a sense of purpose. He wore his pride like a badge
on his sleeve. Like the eagle, globe, and anchor on his chest pocket or the rank
on his collar, it was something that he earned. Stepping inside his camouflage
again, he could hide behind a sandy cloak, as if the uniform were made of magic
or mind-altering material. His dignity was layered in browns, tans, and sandstone.
When he donned his uniform, he suited up in armor. With it on, he was no
longer worthless. And like preparing to leave the wire, he checked the chamber
to his Glock before he slid it into his leg holster. Sgt. Grimm was ready to *rock 'n'
roll*, if the situation called for it. He was heading into the city to save his family,
and nothing or no one was going to stop him.

But the outside air seemed strange, charged, and full of energy. The ominous
red and green vapors rolled and flexed in the northwest sky. The smell of burned
plastic and metal stung his nose and guided his eyes to the fire-dripping
transformer on the power line pole beside the garage. *Damn!*

He turned and studied the sky with a sick feeling in his gut as the colors
churned and rolled. An eerie whistle and hum stirred about, low and muffled,
much like the buzz of electricity through the power lines that sagged from hill to

hill beyond the farm. To the west, the sky darkened, mixing with the red and green glow. It crackled and popped with electricity. The rumbles were like distant mortars exploding, walking their way closer to his position. For a moment, he questioned his whole decision to leave the house at all. *It's war out there, Sgt. Grimm. I hope you're ready.*

He passed his truck with a disappointed scowl as he headed for the garage and his grandmother's jeep. *Maybe it'll be all right since it was in the garage?*

But after he slid into the driver's seat, ready to roll, and twisted the key…nothing happened. It, too, was dead. *Maybe the whole world is dead?* Then, a percussion of thunder sent the hairs on his neck reaching up for the boiling sky.

He pumped the brake, jiggled the gear shift, and tried turning the ignition again. Nothing. *Damn it. Come on!* He turned it again and again, harder and faster, each time getting the same result. Nothing. No sound, no movement of the gauges, no fuel pumping, or firing in the engine. Dead. Not a single thing was alive in the vehicle but him—and he questioned as much as he racked his brain for understanding.

Did the CME kill everything? Like an electromagnetic pulse, right? Yeah, that's what they said. Computers and electronics? Useless. Fried. Dead. Shit. How the hell am I getting to Cambridge now?

He slid out and slammed the door, then searched the garage for ideas. *The four-wheeler? No. Electric. The tractor! Shit. No…no, that's too modern. Electronics would be fried.* His mind raced as he checked off each motorized option. *Hell, I could ride a cow? Where's Betsy?* He chuckled to himself, imagining the scene as he rolled up the street on a brown steer to rescue his family in stunning fashion. *You're an idiot.* Somehow, the marine in him always found humor in the darkest of situations. A coping mechanism, something marines needed to get through the hard times. Or maybe, marines were just demented. Either way, he found humor in the tragedy, and that led him to his next good idea.

The old tractor in the barn! It's from the '80s! It doesn't have a computer! He remembered helping his grandpa tinker on the old thing, thinking it was useless, getting frustrated when it wouldn't turn over, and complaining that they should just get a new one. But Grandpa told him it was special. The first new tractor Grandpa ever bought. It was faithful, tried, and true, and it had been reliable for more years than JP had been alive. A John Deere. Grandpa's baby, and he just scoffed when JP suggested it was time to move on. But that next spring, his grandfather was out there plowing the fields, grinning ear to ear on his old, faithful brute. *Damn, I hope it's still running,* he mulled, grabbing his gear and jogging toward the barn.

Meanwhile, the volcanic sky grumbled and shook, turning into storm clouds and flashing electric fingers far and wide—chasing him—getting closer, reaching out for him. He could feel them at the back of his neck as he ran down the gravel drive.

Ten minutes after CME

Halfway down the driveway, he startled a flock of mourning doves pecking at the bugs and seeds on the ground. They shot up into the fractured sky just feet in front of him, making his heart flutter with their wings. He jerked back and watched as they spun like a cyclone up toward the gray, red, and green waves. He had never seen them do something like that before. They twisted and turned as if they were lost. They circled, darting here and there, up and down like they had no place to go, even in the wide-open fields. Then in a panic, aroused and shedding feathers, they soared straight up into the sky, like a rocket. Faster and faster, with reckless abandon. *Where the hell they going?* Frozen in amazement, he glared up at the slate Heavens as they flew higher and higher until they were out of sight.

Then, a flash to his rear yanked his attention, and he turned back around, staring at the sky. *What the fuck?* One by one, the doves dropped like khaki-colored hail from the clouds and bounced with a sickening thud on the ground. They peppered all around him, popping when they hit the dust and gravel. He cowered and ducked in their storm as it rained down and filled the ground at his feet like puddles. *RUN! Run, you dumbass!* Using his bag as a shelter, he sprinted for the barn as the birds smacked off his pack and crunched as they rolled under his boots. But he made it. Out of breath and feeling like he was in some sort of horror movie, he yanked the barn doors open and disappeared into its gut.

Five minutes later, grinning wide for all the farm to see, JP bounced out of the white, sun-faded doors like a rugged cowboy on an old rusty horse, ready to rope and ride into town for some action. A thick, black smoke bubbled from the exhaust pipe protruding from the grass-green hood and puffed its way past JP's proud face. His husky tractor tires spewed gravel when he shifted into high gear and chug-a-lugged down the drive.

But before he disappeared around the timbered bend, he paused at the end just long enough to fend off the fighting memories of his past. Seeking glory and fidelity, he aimed his limping stallion west into the storm—west toward his family—west into the black and gold monster boiling over the treetops, as he bobbled his weary way the twenty-two miles to Cambridge.

One hour after CME

On the back way into the city, humming generators and spotty gunshots had his head on a swivel. Hunters, he assumed, but he still kept a watchful eye for trouble as he churned his way up Route 800 to Route 22 and into the city. It was a path he thought would be less crowded with panicked people displaced far from their homes, like which he expected to find if he traveled west on Interstate 70. And it was, as he tipped his hat to the boggled eyes that followed his diesel engine and gray tail dragging in the wind while he passed their useless cars steered to the side of the road after their computers fried and failed. Most were local, close to home, and for that, they were not as desperate to test his draw by taking the wheels which he found would roll when most others had stopped. But he kept his right hand rested comfortably on his pistol, either way.

Meanwhile, the black mass in the sky—more electric than anything—glowed in bright colors as the storm raged on. Though it lacked rain—a strange concept to behold from a thunderous bubbling and bolting sky. JP was happy to be dry, even though the wind was fierce and whipping him about like a sleepy toddler waddling down the hall. He weaved through the lanes, free from other moving parts, free from the holdbacks of stoplights and stop signs. Free to roam the yellow lines like a drunkard with a death wish.

Sgt. Grimm was all *Go*, no stopping, no looking back, no matter how sad and helpless those stranded people looked. He couldn't falter. He couldn't deviate from the mission. He was bound to his promise to fight on for love and family. So, he simply offered a sympathetic nod to the situation they found themselves in and thought mostly about his wife and son. *How are they holding up? Are there riots? Looting? Lawlessness or groups of armed men doing whatever they wanted to those who weren't?* The questions weighed him down as he anticipated what war he might face once he made it to town.

From afar, on the rural hilltops of the snaking Route 22, the city had an eerie stillness to it. Fire plumes and waving trees were the only dancing scenes as he neared the city limit sign. *Where are the people? The police? Why does it feel like I'm rolling into Haditha or an ambush?* He bumped past the notorious Mosser Glass building and instantly thought of the time he romped too hard for a little ninja and knocked over his grandmother's white, hand-crafted cake platter. He had watched helplessly as it splattered into a hundred pieces on the porch while he clenched a stick-sword in his tingling hands. He wondered if the city would be just as shattered.

The smoke pillars puffed into and mixed with the gray haze around them. *Food fires or arson?* Like fingers fluttering in murky water, lightning ripped through the air, giving him an apocalyptic feeling. *Maybe it's the end of the world? Judgment Day? The Second Coming? Maybe our sins have finally caught up with us?* Even the beauty of the yellow-and-white spring lilies whirling around, loose from their stems, were not enough to ease the dull veil of death that wrapped around the city of Cambridge.

Sgt. Grimm couldn't help but think back to the sandstorms of Iraq. In particular, the one that darkened the skies with a violent rampage right after an IED ripped apart third squad just outside of Hit. Then, the sand had stung his cheeks as his marines set a perimeter around the casualties and waited for a long-overdue medivac. He listened to their screams for a long, long hour while the corpsman used up his bag of tourniquets and bandages. Then, like now, the tentacles of lightning licked and whipped around them, reaching out for them, nearly snatching them from the rooftops where they provided security for the howling injured. And as it is now, the darkness, like a midnight fog, hung in the air, rolling over the city's ledges and clung to his skin like a poisonous gas. He felt the same anxiety, the same worry, and threat. The same helplessness, hopelessness, frustration, and fear. Now, just like then, he wondered what would become of them all.

It's the lack of reliable information that permeates the mind. It's the *what's going on's,* the *how come's,* and the *what to do's* that flood the senses. It's what the brain does to daunting voids that weigh us down. The space left to wander. The emptiness that makes us wonder. It's the mad conclusions we imagine that bring about our own destruction. The psychosis in the silence, the sustenance in the delusion, the painful satisfaction of the worst—it's the dread that pours full into our cups that poisons us.

But he had no time for mad conclusions as wind and thunder deafened him and a flash of light and voltage blinded him. The scent of smoldering buildings stung his nose. The taste of soot and sand made his tongue hard and bitter. All he could do was *feel.* And what he felt was a plague—a pandemic. It sickened him as he bumped closer to the streets and structures, the burned and littered houses and sidewalks.

A disease turned in his gut as the city closed in around him, bringing him back to Iraq. Back to battle. Back to the blood and heat and Hell that boiled in his bones. As the jagged city chomped down upon his limbs and swallowed him piece by piece, an urgent desire to escape—to run away—ran through him. As the trees gave way to brick and siding structures, concrete and paved surfaces, front yard flags, Easter decorations, and backyard playhouses, his courage was fleeting, his sanity was departing, and his will to push forward hinged in the wind. The warrior inside of him growled at the dainty voice calling out: *Turn back! Turn back!*

One hour twenty minutes after CME

Around the residential bend, a single row of houses on the righthand side gave warning: SLOW CHILDREN AT PLAY. The speed limit reduced to thirty-five miles per hour; JP chugged along at a solid fifteen. Up ahead, a brand-new, blue Ford F150 was on fire, half in the street, half on the sidewalk, just feet past the city limit sign. The owner stood by with a jug of lighter fluid in his hand, sporting a sinful grin as it billowed and bloomed into a fat, bright flame. He gave a satisfied salute and a friendly wave as JP passed. *How strange,* he thought. *But I bet that felt good.* He looked back over his shoulder at the man, who threw rocks at the brittle windshield. JP nodded, knowing the gratification that destruction brought with it.

But that nod turned to disgust when he remembered the steaming, silver, Nissan truck burning in some sandy alleyway of Iraq. A family had been inside the ransacked truck. Bullet holes and blood ravaged the shattered windshield. Tiny pebble-sized holes in the center of fractured webs his squad had inflicted when the truck refused to stop for their patrol. Bullet holes that came from his trigger finger when he sighted in on the bearded driver who damned his family to death. For a moment, both trucks burned in his eyes as he moved into the city.

The city was dirty. Trash had piled up from days of no service. Burn pits dotted the green backyards of two-story houses. The air smelled foul and crispy, full of plastic and spoiled food. He tried to weave around it, to hold his breath and put as much air as possible between him and the heaps of smoldering spoils. It took him to a place he wished not to go: Uniform sector in their AO back in Iraq. Filthy, it smelled of sewage, rot, and burned hair. A smell that lingered in the lungs well after he made it to fresh air. And the trash—it was the perfect place for fast IEDs and death. He searched the streets of Cambridge for wires as he drove by.

Such a strange scene he came upon in the sparse mix of muddled strangers walking aimlessly about, like the walking dead and delirious. They were ghosts in their own town, haunting their yards and streets, looking for answers to feast upon. And among them, a remarkable sight: a stunning, dark-haired, and sparkling woman in a midnight dress, flashing jewels and silver heels. She was dressed for the night, perhaps a ball or elegant evening, but bound by a chain leash to a thin, bony man in leather chaps and vest. She winked as she went by, proud of her bondage and bold look, strutting her whipping hips like a hypnotist's gold watch. The man in front waved as if all were perfectly normal. *What the actual fuck?* And when JP turned back to make sure he hadn't hallucinated, she blew him a red-lipped kiss. He blushed, laughed, and shook his head. *Weirrrd.* But who was he to judge what people did when things didn't make sense anymore?

And as he shook off the bizarre, the haunted crept in. The black dress reminded him of an Iraqi woman by the river, who fed them pita on patrol, before a villager sold her out to ISIS. They slit her throat and hanged her from a palm tree until JP's squad found her three days later and cut her down. The savageness of evil had painted scenery on the walls of his mind, and the apocalyptic triggers before him flashed light on them all.

White, tan, and blue houses seemed vacant as he passed, weaving around dead cars. If it wasn't for the trash thrown out the front door, he would wonder if anyone lived there at all. Other yards overflowed with gawking, bewildered eyes, staring at him and the sky. Too overwhelmed to move, too confused to do anything but watch as he continued down the double yellow line.

Cars lined the streets, many with broken windows and dented doors from children or men with a thirst for unrest and dangerous thrills. The flames of burning houses spit into the sky. With no way to pump water, the arsonists were free to claim their kills. JP hoped that no one had been inside when he passed the charred frame of an apartment building to his left. In the distance, countless plumes of smoke rose from structures no longer livable. Seeing the devastation of what civilization does when amenities are extinguished like a flicking spark, shot concern into the heart of him. *What if one of those plumes is my family?*

He bit down on his lip while the thunder and lightning exploded around him. He had not given up on what he came to do—rescue his family from the teeth of the city. He was more determined than ever not to lose the ones he loved.

A group of men in camouflaged fatigues and rifles huddled on the porch of a brown house with a Sheriff's patrol car parked in front. JP assumed it was some of the law enforcement discussing a plan to save the city. He waved as he went by, noticing their flustered eyes as large as scope lenses. But they weren't as friendly as he. Instead, they shouted, flailing about, and argued as they pointed at his tail of diesel fumes. He peered back; they had fumbled from the porch and into the street, their rifles raised in his direction. They shouted to stop and ran after him.

You gotta be kiddin' me! Sgt. Grimm searched ahead and planned his escape as he weaved down the hill around the cars and trash. Behind him, one young buck in digital green camo led the pack. The baby-faced man chased, outpacing the rest of them—gray beards and beer guts—until they all stopped but him. Sg Grimm knew what they wanted. They wanted what he had: the power to move, to push, and to pull, the power of diesel and John Deere. If he slowed, wrecked, or were thrown from the tractor, all would be lost, and the end would be bloody. He gripped his pistol as he throttled hard at the bottom of the hill.

Then one rifle fired in his direction. The snap of the bullet passing close by made him flinch at the familiar sound. One that he had learned very well in war. *But this wasn't war, was it?* If so, he was in no position to fire back or take cover. Sgt. Grimm ducked and dodged, whipping his tractor back and forth, clipping mirrors, trashcans, and mailboxes. He looked ahead, searching for cover, for escape, for a way out. If he could just crest the hill and disappear into the alleyways, he'd make it.

Peeking over his shoulder, he shuddered as a large older man snatched the rifle from the skinny one and scolded him for firing the shot. The group huddled in the street, gasping for air, except for the young gazelle streaking toward JP. They hollered and hooted for *Benji* to *get him!* But Sgt. Grimm grinned. *They wouldn't shoot again. There was no way they would risk hitting a tire or damaging the only thing moving in the city.* So, he sneered and waited for Benji to make his move.

His engine puffed black and growled up the hill, scraping by cars and trash. Behind him, the men yelled what they were going to do to him when they caught him. *Such brave words for old men with fat fingers and balding heads.* But when he looked back, Benji—the super-cop—was reaching out for the fender. Sgt. Grimm swerved, knocking the man off balance. But he regained his composure and charged with one last leap to board the tractor. Benji's fingers grabbed hold of the fender, and like a monkey, he swung to the foothold on the left side. *Crafty little bastard.* Sgt. Grimm drew his pistol and pointed it at the man's red, wet face and wide eyes.

"Happy Easter, mother fucker!" A warning shot blasted beside the man's head.

Petrified and deaf in one ear, Benji let go and tumbled when he hit the pavement. That's when the full weight of the situation landed on JP's chest.

If that was the law, and they were willing to fire at him to steal his tractor, then who was around to help all these terrified and troubled people?

One hour forty-five minutes after CME

Dubious faces swept aside curtains and pressed up against soot-dusted windows as JP bumped along the side streets with a vigilant hand squeezing his pistol. They were lost and hollow, confused and helpless, stupefied by the foreign land outside their homes. It was the same look he had seen so many times in the villages and towns he patrolled, sweeping for IEDs, weapons, and ISIS propaganda. These people clung to what they knew—their couch, their bed, their kitchen table, and dishes—afraid to face the things they couldn't understand. So, they did what they knew: chores, routines, the mundane way of living they were so satisfied in doing. When all the world around them was chaos and confusion, some chose to ignore it. One white-haired woman methodically swept the debris from her porch as the wind rustled it right back in its place. She didn't seem to mind. *I guess it gives her something to do? I guess we all cling to the things we're familiar with when everything else is chaos.* His eyes shifted to his hand resting on the black pistol grip holstered to his thigh. He felt a strong sympathy for their tragic stares and empty eyes that certainly wished for something more than just a man on a tractor bouncing by with a pistol strapped to his leg.

Their ghostly faces stuck with him, to him, as his black tail dissipated in his wake. Perhaps they thought he was help. Perhaps they thought he was their government come to rescue them from their demise. But he was neither of those things—just a conflicted man on a tractor, on a mission to save his family.

The scenes of war pricked at his mind like knife blades pitched into a sandbag. He let them linger until he turned on North 8th street, where Lisa's silver Jeep sat on the hill. Above swirled colors from the Northern Lights mixed with the gray mist and orange glow of electricity flashing its tantrum. An eerie, lively tingle turned JP hot as he climbed toward the top.

He finally pulled into the drive; the back window to the Jeep had been smashed in. Glass still peppered the concrete, as if no one even noticed or cared. *Animals. Hooligans. Thieves. Assholes.*

His legs buckled on the concrete drive as he stepped down from his green stallion. Nearly two hours on his steed left them weak and sore. He stretched and stood tall, looking around for what he had hoped would be a welcome party greeting him in the yard or at the front door of the white two-story home with black shutters. But nothing. No one. Not a peep from inside the house. *Had they already fled to another part of town? Or maybe they were on foot, heading to the farm, and he missed them.* Instantly, he scolded himself for not taking the interstate. He prayed to God his family was safe somewhere instead of out on the road in all *this*.

"Hello! Anyone home!" he yelled just before knuckling the screen door.

"Hey! Lisa! Adin! You here?" He pounded again, louder and harder. Nothing stirred from inside. A sense of panic flung through his fists, swinging down on the thin metal frame. He pounded so hard he left a dent beside the screen. "Shit," he mumbled, rubbing the concave aluminum. *Everything was shit. What's a little dent going to matter? Their whole world was all fucked up.*

He tried the handle, but it was locked. Stepping back, he cupped his hands around his mouth and yelled up toward the windows. "Hey! It's JP! Let me in! We gotta go!" The noise made him cringe, and he wondered if he'd attract any unwanted attention. It all felt so wrong, like making noise at a funeral.

Just then the door swung open violently, and he was greeted by the rusty barrel of an old wooden shotgun, pointed at his nose.

"Whoa! Whoa! Whoa!" He stepped back with one hand up and one on his pistol. "It's me!"

The shotgun instantly lowered. An awkward man in his late-forties with thin glasses and dark combed-over hair *and a total geek vibe* stepped out of the shadows and into the damp outside light. It was Tommy, his brother-in-law.

"JP! Good God, I about blew your head off!"

"Yeah, no shit," JP said, a little shaky after failing to be prepared for something so deadly.

"What are you doing here?" His graying beard and glasses sparkled in the cracking sky. "Come in, come in. Hurry, before they see you."

"Who?" JP drew his pistol as he pushed through the threshold and glanced over his shoulder at the dark windows across the street.

Tommy shut the door, locked it, and peeked outside the top arching glass to make sure no one was behind him.

"Who? Whose head are you trying to blow off with that old thing?" JP stared at Tommy's single-shot 12-gauge, which had to be an old hand-me-down acquired from his father or something. Its wooden stock was nicked and gashed, scratched, and tarnished with rust glinting from the barrel like an old penny. "What is that, like from the Revolution or something? Is it even loaded?" he asked nonchalantly, bending the blinds in the living room to take a look outside himself.

Tommy looked uncomfortable with the shotgun in his hand. He was a tech geek, sort of dorky, with a graduate degree and twenty years of experience as a security software engineer. Tommy reminded JP more of his brown hens jerking their heads above the window frame of the chicken coop than he did a defensive threat or shooter, as he peeped out the window. But even the awkward and incompetent can pull a trigger if they have to.

JP snapped the blinds shut and holstered his gun. "Here, let me see that thing."

Tommy leaned the barrel his way, still peering down the street.

"Whoa, man! Watch where you're pointing the muzzle. That's twice, now, it's been in my face."

"Shh. My bad. I'm looking," Tommy replied without much effort or care.

JP took the gun from Tommy's loose hand. He pushed the lever on top, and the break-barrel hinged open, revealing a corroded brass shotgun shell that seemed just as old as the gun itself.

"Jesus man. Does this thing even fire?" He pulled out the shell and inspected it.

Tommy flung the curtain shut and glared at JP, narrow-eyed and annoyed with all the questions. "I don't know, man. It was my father's. He left it when he died. You know I don't know anything about guns. I barely remember him teaching me how to shoot it on my fifteenth birthday. Damn thing cracked my shoulder so hard, I never wanted to shoot it again."

He motioned for JP to follow him past the set dining room table and stainless-steel kitchen to the basement door in the hallway.

"Come on. Everyone's downstairs. I'll fill you in down there."

Chapter Twenty-Six

specks

How pathetic is it
for those who are no more
than dust in the wind?

The ones who go
as others go,
blank and uniform,
being tumbled along
by no more than
a breath.

Cowardice. Weak. Useless.

Fear not.

Be as stubborn as a boulder,
as fierce as the waves
as deep as white oak roots grow
and stand your ground.

Fight the flow.
Fight the wind.
Feel the freedom.

Two hours after CME

Lisa, Adin, and Kristen huddled around a Monopoly board on the floor. A battery-powered lantern lit the finished basement like dusk in the summer when lightning bugs would just start to flare. Each had a flashlight beside them, with a bag of BBQ chips laid open between Lisa and Adin. Still in their pajamas, it seemed more like a snow day than the End of Days. No one lifted their head when Tommy led JP down the dark steps with a dim pocket flashlight.

"Was it them again?" Kristen asked, tucking her dark curly hair behind her ear and moving her silver shoe game piece past Go on the board. "We already gave them all we have. What more could they want?"

She glanced toward Tommy, then jumped up. "Who's that!?" she screeched, and Lisa scrambled in front of Adin as they shot to their feet.

"Calm down. It's okay." Tommy shined the light on JP. "It's just—"

"Dad!" Adin squealed from behind his mother's waist and trucked toward him. His gaze landed on the pistol on his father's right thigh, and he stopped dead in his tracks. Adin's glare shifted from the pistol to his father's desert fatigues and up the ebony staircase. "What'd you bring your gun for?" Adin pointed to the pistol, scrunching his nose in disgust.

JP looked down at the Glock in his holster. He hadn't even thought about what his son might feel seeing the gun that nearly took his life. *Crap,* he thought as he shifted the holster a bit behind his leg. Squatting down to his son's eye-level, he foraged for the right words to say while everyone in the room held their breath. "To protect you, buddy. I brought it to keep the bad guys away from you."

Adin was hesitant, analyzing his father's features. "You're gonna get the bad guys?"

"Yeah. If I have to. I'll do whatever it takes to keep you safe."

Adin looked at his mother's nervous smile.

Lisa had played out this scenario in her head many times before, though under very different circumstances. She had always hoped her son would be able to forgive his father and that her husband would be able to show their son his love. Now, holding her breath, she waited for Adin's next move while she nodded her approval.

"You promise?" Adin was as serious as an eight-year-old could be.

JP stiffened his chest and put his right hand over his heart. "I promise."

Adin studied his father, scrutinizing his every twitch and twinkle, a skeptical scrunch still on his face. "Pinky promise?"

JP snorted and gazed up at his grinning wife. "Pinky promise." His pinky lingered in the air, and Adin examined it.

Lisa was unraveling the emotional bundle she had packed on her back for quite a while. JP smiled and winked at her, then gave his son the warmest, brightest smile of all. Adin returned it with a toothy grin that lit up his face and then plowed, headfirst and arms out, into his father's chest. "I missed you, Dad. Where ya been?"

The collision nearly knocked JP to his backside. When he regained his balance, he stared down at the fuzzy brown head and body wrapped tightly against his. Affection—it scared him, and he scanned the room until he found his wife's misty gaze holding his own. Her soft smile held him in place, as she wiped her tears and nodded for her husband to embrace him.

Slowly, he entwined his arms around his son's bony body. "I've been…uh," he shifted his gaze again to his wife for answers, but she was a hot mess, "uh, working…on…*everything.*"

"Oh. Well, why didn't you ask for some help? I'm old enough now, you know?"

JP melted into an oozing puddle of reprieve and redemption. "Aw, Buddy." His breath shook as he sucked in his son's marvelous muddy scent. "Next time, okay?"

"Deal. I'm glad you came."

"Me too. Me too." They cradled and clung to each other.

"I love you, Dad," Adin whispered just loud enough for them all to hear.

Those short words stretched to the bloody streets of Iraq and back. They soared with the F-16s above the bronze plains and plateaus of a war-ravaged nation. Supersonic and stealthy, until they dropped their payload down into the heart of Sgt. Grimm. He blew into a million pieces, but like a magnetic liquid flowing back together, he was reborn, renewed, and rediscovered. "I…I love you, too…so much," he choked on his tears.

A room full of sniffles brightened the lantern-lit shadows of the basement.

When they unlocked arms, Adin burst into a mile-a-minute speech about how the lights went out, the bright storms, and the games in the basement before Lisa cut him off to kiss and embrace her husband.

All three stood there, wrapped in a group hug in the warm glow of light. JP kissed his wife's forehead and rubbed his son's messy hair. He squeezed them against his body, as if to make sure he wasn't dead or dreaming. But they were real. Just as real as he remembered them before he allowed his disorder, drinking, and destruction to take them from him.

Lisa snuggled her head under his scruffy chin, thrilled not to smell a drop of alcohol on his breath. She sank into the moment, hoping that this was it—that this was the moment their family would be back together.

Finally, she leaned back, still in his grasp, to see his face better. "Wait, what are you…why are you…*how did you get here?*" she asked.

"Well, I came to rescue you." JP shrugged like it should be obvious. "On Grandpa's old John Deere." His grin beamed in the light.

Stunned, she just stared at him. Despite all that he had become, the drinking, the anger, the distance, and the *disintegrating*, none of it could quell the love she felt for that man. Her heart fluttered at the thought of his quest to save them.

"Daddy's gonna rescue us! Daddy's gonna rescue us! Daddy's gonna rescue us!" Adin broke out into a song and dance, chanting in excitement.

"Whoa. Easy, killer. You're gonna wake the neighbors," his father joked.

Fear smacked Adin in the face as he froze. "Sorry," he whispered. "I forgot we had to be quiet."

JP shot a look at Lisa and then at Tommy. "You do?"

"Well, uh…" Tommy spoke first. "Just a little game we've been playing the last few days. Nothing serious." He forced a smile. A smile that even in the low light JP saw right through.

Cocking his head and raising his brow, JP glared back and forth at each of them. "Any of you want to tell me what's going on? Kristen? Don't lie to me."

He knew his sister-in-law was a horrible liar. A big heart, good conscience, and moral upbringing wouldn't allow her. Even at the hospital, she refused to lie to the dying patients she cared for. And up until now, she'd done her best to hold her tongue.

Kristen glanced at Tommy, who shrugged. Then she held out her hands at Lisa as if to say, *well, someone's gotta fill him in, so it might as well be me.*

Lisa nodded, giving her permission.

"Well, let's sit down on the couch. You thirsty? We have bottled water. Tommy had a few cases stored in the garage for work."

"Sure. Thanks."

Sgt. Grimm took inventory of the basement as he moved to the couch. The wood shelves along the far wall stood empty, except for some water and games. The TV and entertainment center sat dark and quiet. A half kitchen and bar area in the corner had plenty of alcohol, and JP's gaze devoured it before they sat down. There were no windows to the outside world, but a few corner lamps, a small billiards table, a gas fireplace, and a half bath under the stairs made for a nice retreat from the upstairs stress. But now, it was nothing more than a blank shelter on gray carpet, sharp shadowed walls, and a few thin blankets and pillows sprawled out on the floor for sleeping.

They sat down on the couch, and Kristen told JP about what happened after the power went out. She told him about the lack of information, at first. The lackadaisical approach some of her neighbors took. How they went to work even when they didn't have to because they didn't know what else to do.

"No one seemed too bothered by it all until after the second day. That's when the news spread that the power wouldn't be back on for longer than they first told us." Kristen and Tommy locked hands on her lap, and Tommy rubbed the top of her hand.

"That was the first real day of panic," he said, and then looked at his wife to continue.

"We had cleared the fridge and freezer on day four. That's when Tommy went out to find somewhere open to get more. Well, the shelves were mostly bare. He brought home a sack of canned vegetables, soups, and dry noodles. That's when I knew things were going to get bad. We didn't have enough food stashed. Sure, we had some in the cupboards. But we've been eating out so much lately, that we just stopped storing food. What was the point? It would usually go to waste, anyway."

Her shoulders slouched as she sighed.

"I wish we would've been more prepared," Tommy interjected.

"Yeah," Lisa said, "I think everyone does. I mean, how did we not see the signs? They were all over the place, looking back. How were we not better prepared?" Her hands were out and open as she shrugged and shook her head.

"Why weren't we ready?" She squeezed them and her jaw together when she finished.

"Why did we choose to look the other way?" JP added on.

They reflected in the pause until Kristen cleared her throat and carried on with her story.

"Well, anyway," she continued, "it just got worse from there. Looting and vandalism. Fires. Chaos. Panic. Even the police started disappearing. I guess they were too worried about their own families to come to work. Information was hard to come by, but one of our neighbors had a friend up north who told him to expect weeks or months before the power came back on. That's when everyone went mad. And well, that's when *they* started running things; they kind of just took over and forced some kind of order on the town."

"All right, so who's *they?*" JP asked as if it were a foreign word while he glared at Lisa. "And why didn't you tell me?"

Her gaze ducked his, and she shrugged. He knew the answer and was thankful she didn't say it.

"The Mavericks," Kristen answered, rescuing Lisa.

"The Mavericks?"

"Yeah," Tommy replied. "A real bunch of heroes who make up their own rules and laws.

"The *Mavericks?*"

"Yup."

"Shut up," JP chuckled. "No one calls themselves *The Mavericks*. What is this, a movie?" He laughed at his own joke. But looking around, no one else thought it was funny.

"Well, it's the leader's last name. Bill Maverick. He's a sheriff deputy, or uh, was. I really don't know how that works anymore." Tommy looked up to the ceiling when thunder rattled the walls. "But either way, him and a few other law enforcement officers," he made air quotes, "formed some sort of gang. I guess that's what you'd call it. Him, some of his family—The Mavericks—and a few gung-ho hillbillies with camo pants and rifles swooped down to save the day. Hell, they stopped the looting, redistributed caches of food and water…even fuel, at first. The first few days, they were a blessing. But, then…well, things got complicated."

"Complicated?"

"Yeah. Well, you know what power can do to a guy with a gun."

JP shrugged and nodded. "You gotta point there."

"They wanted to help. I feel like that part of this might be overlooked at this point. But they really did. Bill, I knew Bill from school. He's a good guy. But…I don't know…these aren't normal times, right?"

"Okay, but?"

"People who had extra didn't want to share. Bill and his group wanted them to. You see the conflict, right?"

"Makes sense."

"Well, a few gunshots later, and rumors of murder and self-defense blurred what they were trying to do. So, they got carried away. Started taking instead of asking. They started using force and intimidation to get what they wanted."

"Yeah, no shit. One of them shot at me on the way in."

"Really?"

"Yup. I think your friend Bill lit into him, though. He didn't seem too pleased."

"Friend? Not quite. But he did seem to have his heart in the right place, at first. The void the police left filled quickly with chaos. For a few days, The Mavericks helped stamp that out."

Tommy smoothed his hair across his forehead. "But now, they come and go as they please, taking what they want for themselves and *their* people, leaving the rest of us to fend for ourselves or try to run. Our neighbors tried to take off with all their supplies. But Bill stopped them, took their bicycles and food, and sent them walking down the road with nothing more than the packs on their backs and a little water. They even roughed up Dan a bit when he put up a fight. I don't know, I guess after Bill's nephew was shot, he just viewed everyone as the enemy."

Kristen shook her head in disgust. "Desperate times…desperate people." She sighed like she was remembering some distant memory of her teens. "Many left the city. They headed for the hills or whatever. And we talked about it too. Actually, we were just packing up what was left of our rations—food, water, fuel. Lisa convinced us the farm was better. Which, honestly, it was something we should've done a few days earlier. But…." Kristen looked at her husband and his shoulders dropped.

"I know. I know. I'm sorry. I'll say it a thousand times if you want me to. I was wrong. We should've left."

She kissed him lightly on the cheek and rested her head on his shoulder

"They came and took it all," Lisa said bluntly.

"Who? The looters?"

"No. The Mavericks."

"No shit? Just like that? They just…*took it?*"

"Yup," Tommy grunted. "I argued and tried to fight it. But look, I'm just a computer guy. Besides, they had guns, and I…" His eyes shifted to the floor, the wall, the steps, and his wife. "I had already seen them use 'em. They shot a guy down the street. Jenkins's son. He pulled a pistol when they came to gather up his supplies too. They said they were going to keep it safe in one place and pass it out as needed." He rolled his eyes.

"What that really meant was, they were taking it and dividing it up among themselves, their families, and the people they were close to. They shot that young man dead and just left him there in the street. No one really fought back after that."

"Wow. Unbelievable. Just like that? That quick?"

Everyone nodded their heads.

"And I had to play the quiet game!" Adin smirked and then frowned. "The quiet game *sucks butt!*"

"Adin!" Lisa scolded him. "Watch your mouth."

"Well, it does!"

"It most certainly does, Buddy." JP chuckled. He took a few moments to process everything. Chewed it up. Digested it. But it still left him nauseous. "I can see them being a problem on the way out. They already took a shot at me because I wouldn't stop. And well, I shot back, sending one little bastard tumbling from the tractor." He smirked proudly.

"How's it even running? Nothing else is. It's all dead. Even the car in the garage."

"No computer." Tommy blurted out.

"Yeah, that CME wiped out anything with a computer. I mean, nowadays, that's all these cars and trucks are—moving computers." JP shook his head. "But not Grandpa's old John Deere!"

JP stood up, exhaled, and looked around the room at their little *safe space.* "I mean, I figured the city would get bad but…I didn't think *this.* Hell, doesn't everybody know everybody in this town? And they all just turned on each other like that?"

Tommy joined him and pat his shoulder.

"It's crazy what people will do when they're scared and desperate."

"Yeah, no shit," JP muttered.

"Heyyy!" Adin protested. "How come he gets to say *shit,* and I can't even say *sucks butt?*"

Laughter bounced into the shadowed corners. Lisa covered her mouth to hide it, but there was no use. They needed to laugh. More than ever, they needed something to smile about.

Two hours and thirty minutes after CME

After a quick change of clothes and scavenging for food, water, medical supplies, and gear, they were all packed and ready to go. They huddled by the door while JP and Tommy peered through the blinds to make sure it was safe to leave. The sky had filled with gurgling black clouds blazing with vivid hues, like tumbling and flashing rainbows on fire. A terrible buzzing and crackling zipped in the background of booming thunder and lightning bolts.

The Hellish display had bought out the neighbors. They stood in shock on their porches and hillside yards, pointing and gawking at the sky.

JP's face filled with concern.

"What is it?" Lisa asked.

He grunted. "We have company…and possibly the apocalypse. But nothing to worry about. You ready?"

She smacked the sarcasm from his shoulder and bent the blinds to look for herself. She covered her gaping mouth. "Jesus, it *is* the apocalypse."

JP shrugged. "Told ya."

"If we're going, we gotta go now," Tommy said, hand on the doorknob.

"All right." JP moved to the door and drew his pistol. "It'll be a tight fit, but we can make it work. Tommy, you might have to ride on the back with that scattergun, *if it actually works*, and keep anything or *anyone* from jumping the bus. As much as I would love to take anyone with us, we just don't have the room or the time, and as far as I'm concerned, family first." He evaluated each solemn face. "So, we may have to make some drastic decisions, but no matter what, it's *us* first. Got it?"

Tommy scanned the top of his New Balance sneakers, stained green from mowing the grass, and nodded. Beside him, Kristen's breath was fast and loud. Lisa bit her lip, grasping Adin's hand as she searched her husband's combat stare. She didn't quite get it, until then: the type of mind it takes to prepare for death. She didn't know what might happen when they stepped across that threshold, from comfort to chaos, but her husband's blood-thirsty disposition was a consolation she felt protected standing behind.

"Lisa and Kristen, there's enough room on the wheel wells. Just hold on tight to the cage. Adin, I want you in the cabin with me where you can help keep an eye out for trouble. Got it?"

Sgt. Grimm barked orders like he was born for that moment. He felt alive, inspired to save his family. He stood gallant in the shimmer of Hell outside the window.

And they all nodded, thankful for the warrior leading the way.

"All right. Good. We're making it to the farm." He peered intensely at the group. "And *nothing, or no one,* is going to stop us. Let's go!"

He dipped his chin, and Tommy ripped open the door, letting JP and his pistol lead the rush to start the tractor. Lisa pulled Adin behind her, Tommy covered them with the shotgun from the left flank, and Kristen threw the bags into the cabin.

Just before he climbed aboard, JP glanced at the shattered sky. It appeared to be ripping wide open. The greens and reds encircled the glowing orange streaks and rippling bursts of super-heated plasma sliced into Earth's weakened magnetic field. Static was in the air, its hiss like the shake of a rattlesnake.

"Oh my God!" Lisa whispered aloud.

"What the hell is happening?!" Kristen yelled, following everyone's gaze.

"It's the magnetic field! It's being bombarded with electrified plasma! Holy shit!" Tommy's mouth gaped as the sky opened up and dazzled like food coloring dripped into a glass of water.

A bright, lingering bolt of lightning beamed up through the tip of the courthouse tower. Its fingers branched out as far as the eye could see. Its sun-like strobes reached like tentacles into the clouds. They all stopped in amazement, shielding their eyes but unable to look away.

The onlookers screamed as if the world were ending. And maybe it was. But JP wasn't going to let it end with them dying in the driveway on some cluttered city street.

"Just stay focused! There's nothing we can do about that! Come on! We gotta go!" Sgt. Grimm ordered them all in as he twisted the key and the tractor came to life.

Every face in the street or littering the lawns was bent to the fizzing sky. And if they noticed the tractor at all, it wasn't nearly as captivating as the Heavens crashing down on their city, as JP and his crew puffed on down the road.

Two hours and forty minutes after CME

With the heart of the city hot on their backs, they bumped up Stewart Avenue with guns at the ready. They would soon pass by The Mavericks—a hard choice to make—but it was the quickest way out of the city, and JP had outrun them once before.

"Be ready for anything!" he shouted, with his pistol in his lap.

Tommy slapped his flannel pocket, feeling the handful of shotgun shells he owned. They would be easy to grab from there, he thought, feeling queasy. His hands quivered as he squeezed the tarnished stock. He seemed unnatural, leaning against the back of the tractor, bracing himself with his foot against the hitch and mower hookup.

Lisa grasped a crowbar she had acquired from Tommy's garage. It was better than nothing, even if she hoped she didn't need it. She scanned the dark houses and car-packed alleys as they bounced along the center yellow lines.

Kristen clung tight to the shoulder bag she brought. Although she didn't know what to grab in their hasty exit, she refused to leave behind her heirloom silverware set. After all, it had been her mother's. And it brought her comfort as she hugged the sharp bag against her chest.

The diesel engine made harmony with the grumble above them. JP had hoped the noise would mask their escape, but he wasn't naïve. Beside him, Adin clung to his Nerf gun, scanning ahead for danger. His copilot. His wingman. He was his battle buddy, and he warmed with the thought of how much Adin was like him. Then JP wondered what type of father his son would turn out to be. It was more motivation to plow ahead.

Lightning cracked above them, splitting the sky into fragments. It's dazzling display of edges and angles seduced JP. He wasn't afraid anymore. The blades of the storm were upon him, in him; they *were* him. But he had his family by his side. He had the love of his son and wife. And he had a purpose. It was all he needed to fight the rage. It was a mighty arsenal against the monsters in his mind, and he grinned at the beauty of it all—the light show, his family, his grandfather's damn John Deere tractor. It was beautiful. It was a magnificent mess of what makes humanity worth saving. Love. Sacrifice. Salvation. And knowledge. He had come to face his demons, to save them all—but found that in doing so, in fighting for what he loved, he was saving himself.

Suddenly, up ahead, a shot rang out. JP swerved as it skipped off the pavement in front of him. *Warning shot? Or kill shot? Does it matter? They're fucking shooting at us!*

"Hold on!"

He whipped back and forth, trying to make a hard target. It nearly threw Tommy from the back. But he latched on with one hand and pulled himself back into a braced position.

Three men rounded the back of a brick house. All in camo, all with rifles, all bent on stopping their escape.

Why? Because scared men seek comfort in power, and desperate men will do the Devil's work to get it.

But Sgt. Grimm wasn't stopping for shit, as one skirted out in front of him with a pointy rifle, frightful eyes, and a hand up, yelling for them to stop. The burly youth dove out of the way a moment too late, and his sickening screams echoed as they bumped overtop of his legs.

Adin covered his ears and squeezed his eyes shut.

"Get down, Buddy! Cover your head! It's about to get rough!"

Another foot-soldier in the Apocalypse Brigade rushed down the grassy hill toward Lisa. He was a wiry man with thick shoulders and tattooed forearms. But his rifle made him unbalanced as he ran, so he slung it across his body just before he darted out between two dead cars and lunged for a foothold on the fender.

But Lisa would have none of it. Holding onto the rusting corner beam attached to the roof, she swung the crowbar as he reached out for her foot. His *Oh, shit!* eyes saw the crowbar too late before she cracked his skull with a mighty farm girl swing. His body went limp, knocked out cold, and he fell to the pavement, where he stayed, soaking it with his blood.

The third man, who had managed to angle himself to the front by sprinting along the parallel hilltop, shouldered his rifle as he leaned against someone's back porch. Seeing the fate of his comrades and huffing to catch his breath, he took no chances, firing a shot that struck the radiator. A jet of steam poured from the hole, hissing with the sky.

But JP never let off the throttle when he drew his pistol and downed the man in three quick shots. He scanned quickly for the others but didn't see them. *They have to be out there somewhere!* He pierced the windows and corners with diligent, shifty eyes. *Nothing!* "There's more somewhere! Be ready!"

The tractor turned up the hill on 22, leading out of town. It groaned and sputtered as he passed the last stop sign and rounded the turn to freedom.

"Come on! Come on! Just a little farther!"

If we can just make it past the interstate! They could walk the rest of the way if they had to. But he needed to escape the city, to escape the chaos of crazy people. He rubbed and slapped the dash. "Come on, girl! I know you got it in ya! Keep going. Keep going!"

Three quick rifle shots blasted the road in front of them. JP swerved hard to his left, tossing his wife from the fender to the hood of a station wagon. He slammed the brakes and came to a grinding halt.

"You okay!" he hollered, standing and leaning over to where she was just sitting.

Bruised, she nodded and scrambled, limping, to get back to the tractor.

Hoping to give her some extra time, JP fired his pistol at the first sight of a rifle barrel sticking out of the second-story window up ahead. The hot brass casings fell and plinked onto the cabin floor, landing near Adin's feet. JP reached down and pulled Lisa up to the fender. She shifted and latched onto the frame.

Then Tommy's shotgun blast snapped their heads to the rear.

A man in camo wallowed beside his rifle on the pavement. Red specks dotted his face, arms, and chest. Tommy's steel birdshot had the man feeling the sting of his evil intentions.

The few people who were around to see it all unfold scurried like wild animals to the cover of their homes, leaving JP and his family all alone against the remaining men of The Mavericks. No one came to help. No one offered a hand. They all just hid and hoped it would all be over with soon. A pathetic display of humanity, watching them cower to the men who abused and tormented the weak and helpless. JP caught the sad glance of an older gentleman as he flung his curtain shut.

JP's teeth were showing as an empty magazine smacked the metal floor, and he shoved a fresh one into his pistol. He realized now, more than ever, their fate was up to them. Nothing and no one was going to save them. Nobody cared for their struggles because they all had their own. They were the Gods of their own lives. They were their own saviors. And JP was set on salvation and redemption.

He thrust the throttle forward. The tractor bounced and hissed. Steam poured from the engine. It shuttered and bubbled as it idled down and shut off. "No. No. No. No. Not now! Come on!" JP jumped down from the tractor, used his camo blouse to lift the scalding hood, and stood back as a cloud billowed from beneath. The radiator had a hole in it. The fluid had leaked out. And the tractor had over-heated half a mile from the Interstate 77 overpass.

It was a crushing blow that rattled him to the core.

Two hours and fifty-five minutes after CME

Thunder rocked the city with a godly boom that shook their souls and rattled the frames around them. The blast vibrated the ground and reverberated from hill to hill. It pounded in their chests.

And for JP, it was the rockets and mortars of his past coming back to take him away from his family. Even the flares overhead, the electric whips and tracer rounds through the clouds, wrecked his stressful mind. A war was upon them.

And he was standing in the spotlight, in the kill zone, beside his gasping tank and turret. They were stranded in the fire and smoke, dazed by the violence that wedged itself into their murky existence. Hell was coming to collect for his sins, and JP's ghost floated from its grave, finding itself a new home on his face. The blow to the tractor was a kill shot to JP's hopes and spirit.

Three men jogged toward them with two with pistols drawn and one with a rifle, all raised and ready to fire. They were surrounded on three sides—*Broken Arrow*—the enemy was inside the wire. Sporadic gunshots ricocheted and plinked around them. *Gunshots in the city.* Confusing for its people, normal in Sgt. Grimm's mind. That's why he stayed away. That's why he loved the farm. Because Death hangs out on city streets and sleeps in dark, narrow alleys. It cuddles up with the hate and hostility that burns in angry men—damned men that come to places of congregation to feed on the souls of the charitable and kind-hearted. The city was a monster, alive and hungry. Even the houses, with sad and broken window eyes, looked down on him, judging his faults and weaknesses.

JP and his family huddled behind the tires of the steaming tractor. JP's eyes were wide and hollow, far off and afraid. The downing of their chariot deflated his ego and settled his vigor. They were stuck. Motionless. The world crashing down around him had brought him back down to Earth. He gurgled and gasped inside his head. *I couldn't save them. I was so close, but I couldn't. They trusted me. They believed in me. I had purpose and importance. But…I wasn't enough. I'm so fucking worthless. I don't deserve to live. They're all going to die in this war because of me. I'm pathetic. Useless. Just like in Iraq. I fucked up. I failed. You're a failure, JP! You're a goddamned failure! And, now…everyone's going to be blown to pieces because of you. You couldn't save them, just like you couldn't save Joey.*

Snaps and cracks splattered the pavement to the front and rear of the tractor. Bullets. Hot lead. A hazy smoke lingered like a thick fog. The approaching men were bent on destruction, testing their fate one shot at a time. They were cocky in their approach, unshielded as they jogged from car to car. The bearded man with a rifle ran dry on bullets and raised his gun like a club, sneaking closer in the smoke. The others took careful shots behind the peppered hoods of cars where Tommy had pointed at flashes in the gray haze.

"Last mag!" One shouted to the other.

His comrade fired three more shots before his Glock went empty. His panic spread as his other hand searched his body for another magazine. "Damn it, John! I'm out!" He holstered his pistol and unsheathed a knife from his belt.

In the eerie lag of booms and snaps, Lisa looked to her husband for direction. But he had his back pressed firm against the front tire, eyes closed, and pistol hanging in his hand like a dead cellphone. His cracked shell was shedding its pieces. His warrior had wandered away with the smoke and wind.

"JP! JP!"

And when he opened his lost eyes, Lisa met the shell-shocked stare in her husband's pale face. Every snap and pop jerked his body; every flinch, every cringe, every whimper from the explosions around him, within him, she could feel. She had lost him again in the torments of war. He wore a familiar face she had met on those bed-soaked nights. And now, it was staring right back at her, *through* her. The shattered man before her was the same beaten husband she had seen when he came home. His light had left him. His fight had turned inward. Slices of his being floated away with the flashes in the steam. And she held his trembling hand while he held his gun.

Here they come. Here come the mortars. The rockets. I can hear them walking in. Any second now, it'll all be over.

The men crept closer, bounding from car to car. Their guns all dry but one, their blades drawn, they dashed from cover to cover with eyes as intense as the storm. They were fifty yards away, coming up the road like stalking wolves. Tommy's last blast peppered the car door in front of the closest man. A fierce volley of returned fire had them all balled up tight, Kristen and Adin in tears, behind the tractor.

Distortion and turbulence surrounded JP. Gunshots and ricochets, blasts and exploding skies; he was sinking fast and hard to the bottom of a red pool where he intended to die in the blood of his sins. Sucking air, he withered in the noise.

So, Lisa took charge. With Adin cradled to her chest and her husband's limp hand in hers, she saw her husband drowning. All else faded into white noise and static—a humming fog and echo of existence as their love lingered in the shelter and shadow of a John Deere tractor.

He was fading out of existence, shallow breaths and blue. Lisa knew it was up to her to save him. She had to be his buoy—his life preserver. If they were going to survive the storm, she had to be the one to paddle, to steer, to point their sinking ship toward the sun and give it one last thrust on the throttle.

She grabbed JP by the shirt collar and jerked him close to her face. He was like a rag doll, loose and flimsy. "JP! Jacob Paul! We need you! Come back to us!"

He blinked in her hot breath. She slapped him across the cheek. He flinched. She whacked him again, and he scowled.

"Snap out of it, damn it! You gotta fight! Fight back! Fight for *us*!"

Her blue eyes were full of waves and a soothing breeze. They calmed him. A tropical paradise, her face an island in the rough seas. He took refuge there for a moment, letting her beauty break his spell. An angel to a dying man, he saw light in her eyes. *She* was his light, his life, his liberation. *She* saved him, time and time again, day after day after day—*she* was the purpose, *she* was the point, *she* was the reason for his existence. And his blur was becoming clearer.

She pulled him into her embrace. Cradled him. Enveloped him. Covered him. His heart thudded like a war drum against his chest. He *was* at war. And for the first time, she could see it like a movie playing in his wounded eyes. She felt it. She understood it. She was living it right there with him. In the *booms* and *bangs* and *blinding lights*, she felt the breath of Death on her neck. She felt the Devil pulling at her limbs. She felt the insanity and frustration of being pushed to the brink of delirium, of being torn between helpless and hopeless, action and inaction. She connected with him on a level like she never had before. And for the first time, she understood him and his demons.

All was silent. Only the two of them existed in that moment. No war, no death, no destruction or violence. Just them in the calm of their bonded spirits, basking in the rays of love illuminating from inside of them. She leaned forward and rubbed her cheek on his, a gentle nudge that calmed the raging seas inside him. Her grace touched him, moved him, and made him whole again.

She calmly kissed his cheek and whispered in his ear. "Babe. You're my love, my life, my breath, and soul. You are *my* storm, *my* chaos, *my* hurricane. And I will *not* let you weaken without a show. You. Are. The storm. Now, stand up, be the mighty force that you are, and blow these motherfuckers away. It's time to go home."

She squeezed his cheeks and kissed him with the power of the bolts above. She kissed him with all the rage and fury of a woman who loves her man. She kissed him, and he exploded into life.

The footsteps of the walking dead were near them when he raised his pistol, eye level and true.

"This…is…MY FAMILY!" he hollered to the fiery Gods above.

And as a family, they fought together. Lisa with her crowbar, Tommy with the cracked buttstock of his shotgun, Kristen with her silver kitchen knife, Adin with his Nerf gun, and JP with the power of his family's love. Together, like a storm front, a derecho, a squall line ripping south, like a tornado outbreak in Death Valley—they sent those feeble men to Hell.

And then, hand in hand, they headed home to the farm.

Read on for the first chapter of book two in the series.

Available July/Aug. 2022

NO BLADE
CUTS THE SAME

Jacob Paul Patchen

Chapter One

"Thanks for coming along. I needed someone to watch my six." JP spoke just above a whisper, blending in with the woods in his camo fatigues while holding a branch back for Tommy to pass by him on the trail.

They set out on foot fifteen minutes earlier, heading down the back pasture and into the woods toward The Warner Farm. *More tactical.* Sgt. Grimm decided when he planned to check in on his old friends and neighbors. Though the black plume of smoke he saw that morning rising in their direction wasn't a welcoming sign, he tried to stay hopeful. After all, the Warners were from Grandpa's generation, just as hardheaded and as tough as leather. A different breed of men lived back then, and JP had no problem admitting it. He respected the scarred-knuckled generation—the ones who didn't need seatbelts or smartphones to survive. And before they stepped off the back porch of Grandpa's farmhouse, he wondered how he'd measure up to that caliber of man in this new world void of modern comforts such as electricity, computers, and cold beer.

Though still nursing a healing wound, Tommy tagged along with Lisa's Ruger 10/22 rifle in hand and Grandpa's buck knife on his belt. He looked small in JP's Mossy Oak hunting clothes, but at least he wouldn't ruin his jeans or his Polo shirt if things got too messy.

"Happy you asked." Tommy ducked under a limb, stepping carefully while keeping his eyes ahead of him. "Honestly, I needed to get outta there for a bit. Kristen was driving me nuts with all her yacking." He paused behind a tree to let JP back in front of him again.

JP snickered. "I bet. Well, let me know if you need to take a break or rest—with the shoulder and all." He took a knee and scanned the next wooded hillside for movement.

Tommy followed his lead. After all, JP gave him explicit directions to do so *if he wanted to make it back in one piece*. Dramatic? Maybe. But it got the point across as Tommy crouched low and motionless, waiting for JP's signal to move.

With his AR-15 still in his shoulder, JP scoped out the fluttering bushes and behind the mossy trunks of trees for any sign of danger or desperation. None was present. He waved his hand and started moving again.

"I'll be fine," Tommy whispered. "It's just a scratch."

"That's what I told Lisa! She was worried," JP said over his shoulder, moving down the hill toward the small creek trickling at the bottom.

"They're always worried, aren't they?" Tommy kept up as his point man zigzagged between trees, picking up his pace when they approached the creek and the next hillside.

"That's just what they do." JP's eyes were on the crest of the next hill.

"And God bless 'em for that! The world needs more caring hearts like theirs."

"Especially now."

"Exactly."

The air was thick in the woods, earthy and hot. It cooled a bit as they walked the creek the rest of the way to Mr. Wamer's back field. With sweat pouring down their backs, they rested on the creekbank, where they planned to trace the fence line along the edge of the field, up to the barn, and then to the back of the house. Sitting on a rock that stuck out of the hillside, they sucked down water from their camelbacks and shared a few pieces of jerky.

No more death. Not today. Not after what we just went through, he had asked of the rippling sun and indigo sky before they left. Slow and steady. Cautious and alert. It had taken them all of an hour to get there. Sgt. Grimm didn't want to take any chances of stirring up the wrong type of people: territorial hunters, hard-nosed scavengers, or maybe a group of gunners out looking for thrills and kills along the way.

"What do you think he'll say?" Tommy chewed jerky and wiped the fog from his glasses on his shirt.

JP raised his brows. "*Thanks for checking on me.* I hope."

"And what if…" Tommy looked at his black rifle leaning on a tree beside him.

"Then we'll do whatever it takes to make it back alive." JP exhaled loudly as he scanned the trees and leaves around him. "Is that something you can handle?"

Tommy scoffed. "I'll do what we have to."

"Good." JP grinned and stood up. "I guess getting shot does make you a bit of a badass. C'mon. Let's go see what's up."

As soon as they crest the bank and made it to the edge of the woods, they knew that something wasn't right. Buzzards circled the field like leaves in a swirl of wind. Their giant shadows swatted at JP's face. A pungent smell crinkled Tommy's nose and put the taste of the death on Sgt. Grimm's tongue. It was the smell of rotting flesh. The same smell Sgt. Grimm became familiar with when his squad would often be tasked with returning to friendly villages for more intel on ISIS movements and supply lines. But all too often, he would be rudely greeted with the sour scent of the dead and dying as he wrapped the villagers' wounds with his own med-kit.

Kneeling at the edge of trees and tall grass, Sgt. Grimm put his finger to his lips and motioned for Tommy to get on his belly. In the silence and stillness, he could hear them. The flies buzzing to flesh, eating and laying eggs in the soft tissue of the dead. With piercing eyes, Sgt. Grimm gestured for Tommy to stay put and watch his back. Sinking to his belly, JP felt the blades of grass poking into him like a hundred fingertips trying to hold him back as he low-crawled toward the sound. But he kept going, head low, rifle in his hands, elbows lurching him forward, again and again. Closer and closer. Like his grandfather's stories of a sniper in the jungle, like Hathcock crawling up to a company of Viet Cong. He knew he was heading toward death, but that didn't stop him from going further.

The smell intensified. He could taste it. He chewed on it like jerky, spitting it out like a tendon. It stuck to the blood on the grass and burned his eyes until he was sure he could reach out and touch whatever it was. In his mind, the buzzing hummed and throbbed, stirring images of flies on eyeballs, skirting chapped and bloodied lips, going in and out of dead men's mouths. He remembered how unphased he thought he was when those black, buzzing bastards would pop out of bullet holes in the chests of damned men and fly off one after another. *Now* it made his stomach turn. Death was a damn disgusting thing. And he wished he could turn around and crawl away. But he couldn't. Sgt. Grimm had to know what was just beyond the bloody blades of grass up ahead.

His hands parted the blades until he saw them. Two mutilated cows. Their throats were slit, hindquarters hacked off, and the rest was left to rot.

Dave would never do this. He wouldn't waste all this meat. This wasn't him. This was someone else. Someone in a hurry. Someone desperate. Someone without skill.

"C'mon! We gotta hurry!" JP motioned for Tommy to follow him as he scurried along the fence and woods toward the house.

"What's wrong? What was it?"

"I think they're in trouble. Be ready for anything."

The black smoke still lingered from the charred barn, burned to the ground with only a few black, stubborn timbers pointing to the sky.

Was it the CME, or someone who came for destruction? The thought of something more sinister quickened Sgt. Grimm's tactical pace. His rifle was gripped in front of his chest. His eyes were like spears piercing the space between them and the brick house. His muzzle swept from left to right, from crevice to shade, from farm equipment to bales of hay. His finger straight and thumb on the safety.

Nothing would ambush them with him on point. They were only a hundred yards to the back door when JP noticed it was wide open.

Tommy did as his brother-in-law did: they bound from tree to tree, from defilade to defilade, from cover to cover with their rifles at the ready, until they were at the back of the house. There, the same rotten smell battered their senses. It flowed out of the farmhouse door on the stale air like poison gas. Tommy gagged as he sucked in his breath.

Sgt. Grimm crouched next to the doorway, rifle up, and angry eyes behind it. Behind him, Tommy watched the corner of the house. Smoke lingered in the air. Between that and the smell from inside the house, their eyes, throats, and hearts burned.

It was time to break the threshold. Sgt. Grimm motioned for Tommy to stay at the door and watch his back. On the count of three, he'd go in. With his rifle aimed at the shady entrance, he held up one finger. Two. Three. Then, like a snake slithering into a hole, he disappeared into the black rectangle before them.

The smell was overpowering as Sgt. Grimm crossed the threshold, muzzle up, eyes down the barrel, knees bent for balance—heel, toe, heel, toe. In the dim light of the mudroom, he crunched across broken glass, cringing at the sound under his boots. A sound so familiar, so cruel—like glass shards on the hardball road leading into the city of Hit. Shattered windshields and bullet holes, a family dead before their time. Iraq was on his mind, and he scolded his lack of focus.

His foot nudged an empty tin can that rolled across the floor. Painful and deafening, it froze him mid-step.

Goddamnit, JP! Pay attention!

His focus was on the two doors down the hallway, one on each side, where danger could emerge with bright flashes from gun barrels. Or maybe the monsters carried blades—blades that cut jagged and deep. JP wanted no part of steel ripping his flesh. His grip whitened his knuckles. The buttstock squeezed into his cheek. His knees bent, his jaw flexed, and with shifty eyes he pushed forward, each step crunching glass.

Then came movement up ahead. From the living room, at the end of the hall to the left, he thought. He clicked the gun off safe with his thumb, lingering his gentle finger on the cold trigger. He'd shoot at the first sight of a weapon. There'd be no hesitation if the danger was real. He'd kill like he'd done before. There was no doubt in his mind about the power in his hands, the strength in his will to survive, or in his faith of family. That was his motivation—his family. He'd kill for *them*. He'd kill mercilessly, without care or caution. Empathy had burned down with the wires. Nothing was left to connect humanity—nothing, but the shared fate of death.

More debris in the hall: fallen picture frames, scattered family possessions, books, wrappers, blankets and pillow stuffing. The house was a mess of littered life. If he didn't know any better, he'd had thought a tornado whipped through the Warner's farm, leaving pieces of shattered hope in its wake. A smiling elderly couple, clad in Sunday clothes and glasses, each with an arm around each other's waist, posed beside a purple lilac bush in the front yard and stared up at him from the floor. He stepped over them as he inched closer, careful not to make any other noise besides the soft sole of his boot rolling forward to his toes on the hardwood floor.

A rustling sputtered ahead. The sound of something heavy dragging, something ripping.

Fabric? Is someone stealing the damn couch? What the hell?

An image of a monstrous man in a cutoff flannel, with muscles bulging, missing teeth, and a fat lip full of dip manifested in JP's mind.

Damn rednecks. Hillbillies. What the fuck you gonna do with their couch?

It didn't matter. It wasn't theirs. None of this was for them—the intruders, the scavengers, the killers. And Sgt. Grimm was bent on stopping them all.

He swung wide at each door along the corridor, pivoting his muzzle until the corners of the bedrooms were clear of danger. Silent like a ghost. A spirit. The spirit of all the warriors before him, all the hard men who had to do the hard things in life, like kill and love. He floated toward the end of the hall. Ahead, the living room was to his left and the kitchen to his right. He favored the left half of the hallway, careful not to knock over any of the remaining pictures, crooked and loose on the wall. Slowly, he let his muzzle see the kitchen first: the wooden table with four chairs, the open cupboards with bare shelves and contents thrown about, the sink, the fridge, the checked linoleum floor, the busted and cracked sliding porch door. Inch by inch, he pointed his muzzle at them all until he was convinced it was clear. His focus shifted to the left. He prepared with a deep breath. His mind and muzzle were ready to spin around the corner and into the living room.

Two more steps. Easy now. Quiet. You got this. You're better than them. You're quicker. You're deadlier. You're a fucking warrior.

But the floorboards betrayed him. They let out a sad, shameful moan that ended the rustling a few yards away from him.

Fuck! Fuck! Fuck!

He pulled the rifle tighter into his shoulder, squeezing his body into itself, smaller, set, ready, spring-loaded, and cocked. He gritted his teeth, waiting for a flinch of movement to flutter around the corner in front of his face, so he could end it before it ended him. Like a statue of King Leonidas, he stood firm and still, his rifle a spear, his love for his family a shield. He waited. Five seconds felt like days. Ten was a lifetime. Twenty, thirty…one minute. An eternity passed by, time enough for the universe to be born, for galaxies to burst into existence, all life, all beings, all rocks, and water, and earth—he stood there in the dust while the universe formed and sparked around him. He was like a god, the creator of his own destiny. In his hands, he held his fate. In his eyes, he held the future. He saw it float by ember after ember. At the corner of the hallway, he stood firm,

frozen in a death stare with the edge of time—a bright white end of the drywall—
—where his breath pulsed, and whatever was on the other side merely existed.

It's me or them. Here we go.

His weight shifted slightly to his toes for more spring in his step. In a fraction of time, he imagined himself turning the corner and squeezing the trigger until they all fell like timbers in the forest. His mind saw them in front of him, bulky men, one at the end of the couch and the other by the door. In his imagination, he blew fire from his barrel and brought those bastards to the ground. With one deep, shaking breath, he pushed forward and pivoted the corner, ready to squeeze the life from dark, dirty souls.

But there were no men when he entered the living room. Only furniture and more chaos greeted him. A yelp drew his attention to the floor by the TV. In the dank air and curtain darkness, it took a moment to see the long shapes on the floor and the furry beasts beside them. It was Buck and Lilly, the Wamers' German Shepherd dogs. They were pulling and ripping at the forms on the floor.

"Hey! Get away from there! Buck! Lilly! No!"

They pulled away with red mouths and sticky fur. Lilly limped over to him, whining. His left hand dangled for her to nuzzle. But where it brushed, her chin was wet. Where she licked, his hand was crimson. He could smell it—blood. He could taste it—death. Before him on the floor, he realized the sickening scene was real. Mr. and Mrs. Wamers' throats were slit, and their dogs were feasting upon their dead bodies.

"Jesus Christ!"

JP stepped closer, the smell gagging him. The scene making him ill. The desert death land flashed before him: the dead hanging from streetlamps in Iraq, the throats of Iraqi children, women, and men sliced by an ISIS blade, their bullet holes trickling blood, the frothy pink at their mouths, the cold, dead stare of death looking back at him. *The flies. Those fucking flies.*

The bodies were the same. The death was the same. The war was the same. It was all for survival, for beliefs and values, ideology and life. For nothing. For *everything*. It was a war on humanity, and JP wasn't prepared for its barbarity. It was finally all too much for his gut to handle. He scurried to the front door, flung it open, and vomited all over the WELCOME mat.

Veteran Suicide and PTSD Help

<u>Phone Numbers</u>:

Veteran's Crisis Line:
800-273-8255 (press 1)   or   Text: 838255

A Vet-to-Vet crisis hotline, the Lifeline for Vets:
888-777-4443

VA Coach for Helping Veterans Adjust:
888-823-7458

<u>Suicide Prevention Links</u>:
https://afsp.org/military-and-veteran-suicide-prevention
https://suicidepreventionlifeline.org/help-yourself/veterans/
https://www.veteranscrisisline.net/
https://theactionalliance.org/veteran-and-military-suicide-prevention-resources

<u>PTSD Awareness Links</u>:
https://www.ptsd.va.gov/
https://www.helpguide.org/articles/ptsd-trauma/ptsd-symptoms-self-help-treatment.htm
https://www.maketheconnection.net/
https://www.psychiatry.org/patients-families/ptsd

Author Info

Jacob Paul Patchen is an award-winning author and poet of inciting fiction and provocative poetry.

Jacob earns his inspiration through experience and believes every book has a purpose. He writes powerful, emotional, and thrilling stories about mental health, war, social stigmas, and other taboo subjects in order to bring awareness, change, and hope to those who need it.

Raised in Southeast Ohio, he's a sucker for fast workouts, long laughter, and power naps. Snacks are his love language, and he thinks he's a Pisces. Check him out and join his newsletter at Jacobpaulpatchen.com.

*Jacob truly appreciates your support and interest. If this book moved you in any way, please leave a review on Amazon, Goodreads, and social media. You can sign up for Jacob's newsletter at JacobPaulPatchen.com or follow him on Facebook (author.jacobpaulpatchen), Instagram (@jacobpaulpatchen), TikTok (author.jacobpaulpatchen), and Twitter (@jacobpaulpatchn). Jacob also started a group on Facebook called "Let's Talk About Mental Health and Books."

**Jacob is seeking ARC readers to join his team. If interested, message him on his social media and sign-up for his newsletter.

***All poems are from Patchen's poetry books, OF LOVE AND WAR and WE FIGHT. WE LOVE. WE DEVOUR.

Books by Jacob Paul Patchen

Award-Winning Fiction

At Daddy's Hands: Courage Knows No Age

Sheltered: When a Boy Becomes a Legend

Poetry

Of Love and War

We Fight. We Love. We Devour.

Creative Nonfiction

Life Lessons from Grandpa and his Chicken Coop

Talking S.H.I.T.
(Social, Humorous, and Inspirational Thoughts)

Children's

Words that Matter
(series)

Booboo Dino-Sore
(series - coming soon)